REAPER

DRONE STRIKE

ALSO BY NICHOLAS IRVING

ALSO BY A. J. TATA

*For my father, Bob Tata, my mentor and
role model in life.*
—A. J. TATA

*For my son, Kayden—you've widened the view
of the world and expanded its universe.
Forever dream big, son.*
—NICHOLAS IRVING

CHAPTER 1

Sassi Cavezza

Alessandra Cavezza knelt in the dirt road that smelled of burnt tires and urine as she brushed away the grime from the young girl's bleeding face. Big doe eyes stared back at her, unblinking.

Who could do this?

On only her third month in Syria with the United Nations, Sassi, as her friends called her, had resettled hundreds of families that had fled to Europe and were now returning home. These were peasant kids, cannon fodder in the riptides of war that crisscrossed this country. Ten miles north of Damascus in al-Ghouta, a shantytown filled with tin roofs and adobe huts, Sassi had methodically worked her way through the village with her interpreter, Hakim. Now she was bandaging the shrapnel wound on Fatima's forehead.

Standing above her, Hakim said, "Sassi, we must go."

She looked over her shoulder at him. Hakim's outstretched hand pointed at a dust plume in the distance, coming from the east, out of the hills. Two T-72 Russian tanks were rolling toward them from about a quarter mile away. The lead tank commander stood tall in the hatch like a conquering hero parading his recent victory.

Russians? Syrians? Turks? Americans? Hezbollah? She knew the differences between the forces, but they were all singularly unhelpful to the olive-skinned girl in the potato sack dress with matted black hair standing in front of her. Several of them used the Russian T-72, which made the equipment less of a clue than she might hope.

"Help me," the girl whispered, looking over Sassi's shoulder. "I can't find Aamina."

The tanks *were* returning, it seemed. Today she was operating in the Russian sector, but the lines were always changing. She did her best to keep abreast of the political and military shifting winds in this once vibrant country. Fights raged back and forth. Peace treaties came and went. UN resolutions and orders were issued from on high quicker than they could be printed and disseminated. What was the current status? Well, for today, Russia maintained this sector, but it wouldn't be long before even that changed.

What Sassi cared most about was human dignity and serving the oppressed, such as the young girl standing before her with her face full of mud, dried mucus, and salty tears.

"What's your name?" Sassi asked.

"Fatima is her name," Hakim said impatiently. Then, "Sassi, this is not good."

"Fatima, what happened? Who is Aamina?"

Fatima pointed over Sassi's shoulder at the tanks. Tears bubbled from her eyes.

The UNHCR had assigned Sassi and Hakim this sector as part of the resettlement plan, placing families back into the abandoned dilapidated neighborhood. Three months ago, it was a ghost town, fresh off the heels of the UN chemical cleanup after Syrian president Bashar al-Assad's troops dropped sarin gas in the neighborhood. Sassi had been here in a hazmat suit two years ago, men, women, and children dead in the streets, dried blood and mucus running from their noses; sarin gas didn't discriminate. It was the single most lethal tactical weapon of mass destruction.

Now thirty-two families were hiding in their homes with intermittent electricity and only communal potable water that Sassi had established with water trailers dotted throughout the neighborhood. She had contracted with a company to haul in fresh, clean water from Damascus daily. Fatima had been drinking from the faucet when a mortar round exploded twenty meters away. Shrapnel had sliced her forehead. In one sense, she was lucky. In another, of course, not. Fatima's misfortune ultimately was that she lived here.

Sassi had served in Iraq, Afghanistan, and the Balkans over the last fifteen years. She understood the hardship that came from being born in the wrong place at the wrong time. As a fresh college graduate from the Università Cattolica del Sacro Cuore in Milan, her idealism had propelled her to Iraq, thinking she could make a difference in the wasteland of Anbar Province. Sunni warlords had detained Sassi and thrown her into a dank basement for days with just bottled water, until American forces rolled through and claimed the land in what eventually became a vacant Hollywood set. Fallujah was unlivable for the most part. But she had dusted herself off and then began executing her mission during the Sunni Awakening, moving families back into the city of rubble. Day by day, she had helped restore services, coordinate with American forces, and especially secure clothes and books for the children, to help them read and learn about something beyond the war-torn walls of the city. Today she was a weathered and rough-hewn veteran of military action. Sassi knew firsthand war's human toll, and she had stood up to larger forces than two tanks.

Fatima shook as the tanks squealed to a stop behind them. Hakim's hand was on Sassi's shoulder, but Sassi's eyes remained fixed with Fatima's.

When she glanced up, two fixed-wing drones flew circular routes in opposite directions. Sassi didn't know her drones, but she tried to memorize all the new technology she saw when entering a location so that she could report it to headquarters upon return. These unmanned aircraft had about fifteen-foot wingspans and looked like stealth B-2 bombers. Some type of munitions hung below each wing, perhaps miniature rockets.

"Take me home," Fatima begged.

"In just a minute," she whispered. Sassi pulled the

girl close, pressing Fatima's frail chest against her shoulder, and then stood and turned toward the leering tank commander, blocking Fatima's small body with her own.

"What is it today?" the commander shouted in broken English. "More *al-kalb*?"

Sassi knew enough Arabic to know the Russian-inflected voice had just called Fatima a dog, a high-order insult to Arabs of any stripe. Sassi could tell that Fatima had heard and understood the word by the way her small hands clutched Sassi's cargo pants and how her frail body pressed into Sassi's hamstring.

"This is a *child*, not a dog, Commander. And what it is today is to make sure she has enough water and food to survive."

"Survive? No one survived this village after Assad's attacks. Everyone left. And now you bring back. Better to leave them where they were in Turkish refugee camp."

Their one common language was English. Sassi was mildly surprised at this low-level tank commander's English proficiency but was glad to pursue communication.

"What is it you need today, Commander?" Sassi asked.

The commander leered at her from his hatch. His smile showed a couple of chipped teeth. He removed his tank crewman's helmet and set it on the turret holding the long tank bore. She wasn't sure of the size of the tube or the ammo it shot. It could spit flame and destroy buildings, and that was all that mattered to her.

"You, gorgeous," the commander said.

A spider of fear crawled down her spine. Hakim was not a fighter. The families she had helped resettle couldn't afford a public squabble with the Russians. These eight men might have been weeks or months without a woman, and she had witnessed the horrors and excesses of combat visited upon women, though she had never been violated in that manner herself.

"You're barking up the wrong tree," she said.

The tank commander cocked his head and laughed. "Now you're calling me the dog?"

"Interpret that however you wish," she said.

A harsh breeze was blowing from the north. Along with the smell of diesel, the wind carried the rancid body odor of the tank crew.

The commander pushed himself up onto the hatch and sat on the top of the turret, then swung his legs onto the deck of the chassis and stood.

"If we are all dogs, then we shall be in heat. No?"

"Sassi," Hakim said.

"You smell worse than a dog, Commander." Sassi laughed and retrieved a knife from her cargo pocket, flicked open the blade. "And you'll have to fight like a dog for it, too."

"Tough woman. I like it." The commander began walking down the chassis, his hand along the smooth tank tube, a phallic gesture if she'd ever seen one.

The radio inside the tank squawked with something unintelligible to her, but obviously not to him. He stopped, looked over his shoulder, and then turned to stare at Sassi. He had a worried look on his face, and Sassi could only imagine it was some higher-level commander complaining about something. Nonetheless, she sensed for the moment she was spared.

"Saved by bell," he said. "But I'll return to kiss that beautiful face."

"You can kiss my ass," she said.

"That, too."

He scurried into his hatch and the tanks quickly Y-turned, their tracks chewing up the road, spitting gravel at them, as they departed to the north. The drones circled high and lingered, as if covering their retreat. One of them swooped low along the middle of the street, buzzing just above them. Both then lifted into the sky and darted ahead of the tanks, leading the way back to their base camp.

"That was too close," Hakim said.

"Another day, another tax-free euro, right, Hakim?" Sassi joked. Their pay as UN members was not taxed when working in hazardous duty zones, such as Syria.

"Not funny, Sassi. These Russians are serious. And those drones. I've never seen those before."

"It's all part of the show. Intimidation." Sassi shrugged and looked at Fatima. "Show me what you wanted me to see, Fatima."

The girl grabbed Sassi's hand and walked her through a series of narrow alleys between adobe huts with tin roofs. Entering one maybe four blocks off the main road where they had been, Fatima let go of Sassi's hand and pointed.

It took a moment for Sassi's eyes to adjust from sunlight to the dim interior, but eventually her pupils dilated enough to let her see again.

"Aamina," Fatima said, pointing.

Tilted against the back wall of the home was a hinged wooden trapdoor. Sassi walked carefully toward the hole in the floor and shined a light into the darkness below. The beam skidded across the face of a doll, and Sassi smiled.

Aamina was Fatima's security blanket, comforting her amid all the chaos and confusion. She swung her legs over the hole and searched with her feet for a ladder, found a sturdy wooden rung, eased her weight onto it—fully clothed and soaking wet, she was barely pushing 120 pounds—then lowered herself into the basement. It smelled of urine and grease, which she found unusual. Kneeling, she lifted the doll and began to stand up.

A light flickered to her right. It was a brief flash like a strobe. Aiming her flashlight, she saw the beam disappear into a long tunnel. With the doll in one hand and the flashlight in the other, she began crawling through the low tunnel, which was maybe three feet high and across. After traveling about twenty meters, she reemerged into another basement, probably that of a neighboring house.

"Sassi?" Hakim's distant voice floated into the tunnel.

Poking her head into the room, she saw a naked light bulb shining from the ceiling of a cavern similar to the one she had left behind. This room was different, though. Maps and diagrams were tacked to the walls.

A dozen chairs in a circle were facing inward toward what looked like a child's sandbox.

Her curiosity propelled her forward. She crawled from the tunnel and stood in the room, the ceiling nearly touching her head. When she took a step, her shoe rolled over a pebble, causing a slight scraping noise.

After a moment, a footfall shuffled above her. Someone was in the house. There was a ladder to her right leading up to the floor above. The layout was similar to the house Fatima had led her into. She looked at Fatima's doll in her hand, remembering her mission to get Fatima back to her home.

The map on the wall, though, was intriguing. It was a picture of the entire world with several stickpins in Syria, Lebanon, and around the world. There was a single string from the Beqaa Valley in Lebanon strung to Lebanon's Port of Tripoli. Another string was taut between Tripoli and Cyprus. Even more strings spiderwebbed out from Cyprus to multiple locations along the East Coast and in the Midwest of the United States and Canada. The map alone was inert. There was nothing untoward about it. It could be a kid's geography lesson. The Port of Tripoli was Lebanon's second-largest port. Cyprus was a well-known transshipment and logistics hub. The rest were shipping routes or ports. Maybe this was homework. Or better yet, perhaps the people who once lived here were merchants and endeavored in the shipping industry. Maybe they sold carpets, cotton, or grains, which Syria was renowned for producing, and these were the trade routes. Perhaps they were targeting American markets. This could be a business plan on the wall. Though Syrians would most likely use the port of Latakia. Why Tripoli? she wondered. Lebanon's biggest port was Beirut.

Pinned to the map was a ragged sheet of white paper with a list of words written in Arabic characters. Most she did not understand, others she could decipher if she had some time to think about it, which she didn't. The word *Sieg!* was written in large print with the alphanumeric designation: Hunter 5X. Sobirat 2X. Then the word *Tankian*. Maybe that was a business? She'd heard it before but couldn't place it. Below that was an oval, like an American football, which they played in Italy. Inside the oval, someone had drawn stick figures. Sassi turned her head, trying to comprehend. It almost looked like pictures of the slave ships used centuries ago. The stick bodies and arms lay head to toe.

Curious, she removed her smartphone and took a few quick pictures and uploaded them to the cloud, or at least tried to. Underground, she had no signal. She blacked out the phone, hoping they would upload when she got a signal, and turned toward the tunnel.

The hatch in the ceiling opened without warning. The hinges squawked, metal against metal. Her heart leaped. She reached for her knife and flicked it open. The muzzle of an AK-47 appeared in the opening and began spraying randomly, bullets raining everywhere, ricocheting around like pinballs. The noise was deafening. A constant metallic *clang, clang, clang* like a hammer on an old-time trash can lid.

Fire spat from the flash suppressor, and the noxious

fumes of spent gunpowder permeated the small room. Miraculously, Sassi had not been struck by a bullet yet. She scrambled into the tunnel, low crawling and scraping the twenty meters back to her original point of entry.

"Sassi!" Hakim was still calling her name. She'd been gone less than five minutes, but in Syria, those moments could be a lifetime, literally.

Scrambling up the ladder, she pocketed her knife and popped into the daylight. She looked at Fatima, who saw the doll and threw her hands up, shouting, "Aamina!"

"Let's move," she said. Clasping Fatima's hand, she jogged through the streets to their white UN vehicle. The sound of men running echoed through the alleys. She was fast and decided to carry Fatima as she ran. Hakim's skinny legs pumped as hard as they could.

Their white SUV with the blue UNHCR letters painted on the side was parked where they'd left it. She opened the back door, dumped Fatima in the SUV, and jumped in the driver's seat. The vehicle was moving as Hakim jumped in the other side, yelling, "Wait! Wait!"

Three men with AK-47s tumbled into the street two blocks ahead. She turned the car around and spat gravel at them as she raced toward the UNHCR base camp in Turkey.

She would return Fatima to her home tomorrow, though Sassi was never one to retreat. While she never wanted anyone to mistake her good intentions for a lack of skill, with the child's safety at risk, she chose to fight another day.

Sassi carried compassion in her heart and a .22-caliber Beretta Bobcat in her cargo pocket. This combination was a metaphor for Sassi's life—caring and tough.

Her family was close with Italian gun mogul Franco Beretta, perhaps the only man to give her any advice when she'd decided to join the United Nations.

After she had made this "regrettable decision" as her father labeled it, Beretta had been kind, in a fatherly way—a manner her father could never duplicate. For Luigi Cavezza, appearances were everything. His ties with the upper echelons of Italian society were more important than his ties with his children. Accordingly, they had socialized with the Berettas and Machiavellis of Italy. Beretta's headquarters being in Milan, it was a short two-hour drive from the Cavezza estate on the outskirts of Florence to the Beretta compound. When Franco Beretta learned that she was embarking on her UNHCR mission, he flew in his helicopter to Florence, picked up Sassi, and took her to the private Beretta firing range outside Milan. For two days, she fired everything that Beretta made, including shotguns and rifles.

"Which do you want?" he had asked her.

"None, Franco," she had said. "My job is to help families. There's too much of this in the world already." She had waved her arm across the firing range, where men and women tested different weapons. The *pop, pop, pop* was as constant as the ticking of a clock.

"My family has been providing weapons to every

war in Europe for five hundred years, Sassi. Man causes the war, not the weapons."

"Still. My purpose is the complete opposite of war."

Beretta had paused and retrieved a small box. "Your father is a bit of a social climber. I think you know that. He has his banks and serves his purpose in society. I'm sure he's a good man and a good father to you."

"You have more confidence than I, Franco."

He had raised a hairy gray eyebrow. "I've always liked you for your pluck. Without people like you in the world, it would be a much worse place. Take this gift from me and promise me one thing."

"What is that?"

"That you will bring it back to me when you have completed your UN mission. I will take this from you in exchange for making you an executive in my company."

Sassi had laughed. "From UN missionary to arms dealer? I don't think so, Franco. Your generosity is appreciated, but my mission is pure, and I hope to keep it that way."

"Then take the gift," he had insisted. "Keep it, but you still must return."

She had accepted the box, opened it, and seen the Bobcat lying in soft velvet with a magazine filled with .22 bullets. She imagined this was his equivalent to giving a woman a Cartier watch or bracelet.

"Use it wisely," Beretta had said. Oddly, it had been her favorite weapon of the two days of shooting. Lightweight and agile, the pistol wouldn't stop much, but it was at least more than a mosquito bite.

Today, though, the Beretta was no match for wild-eyed

terrorists with AK-47s. Sassi held Fatima's hand and watched al-Ghouta disappear in the rearview mirror, knowing that she would have to return the poor girl to this black hole of a village tomorrow.

CHAPTER 2

Maximillian Wolff

Maximillian Wolff switched monitors from the Russian drones over the small town of al-Ghouta to the video feed piped by satellite Wi-Fi from the container ship *Sieg* passing from Lake Huron to Lake Michigan using MasterEye software that gave him an omnipresent view.

When planning this mission, Wolff had taken into account the harsh winters and ice formations that dictated the shipping season through the North American Great Lakes. Open from April to November, the waterway provided for the transit of large container vessels to service the ports of Québec, Toronto, Montreal, Detroit, Chicago, Marquette, and Milwaukee, among others.

Still smarting from a €5 billion missed opportunity in Iran and a sharp rebuke of no confidence from the

Daimler board of directors, Wolff had spent $25 million of his $30 million annual compensation on upfitting the *Sieg*, a container vessel originally intended to service the Persian market. As the beleaguered CEO of the luxury automobile manufacturer, Wolff had led the company to new heights, only to ride it into near bankruptcy after placing most of his chips on the Iran deal and a faltering bid at a U.S. defense contract.

With the evaporation of the Iran market, he was now furiously trying to save that U.S. Department of Defense deal that he'd thought was in the bag. The U.S. government had provided a notice of intent to award letter to Wolff regarding a billion-dollar contract to build the U.S. military's new truck fleet. Now his fate hinged on whether or not he could reclaim it.

He was a big man with a big ego. He had a barrel chest from working the Mercedes-Benz assembly line as a kid. Eventually, he'd quit that and attended university, where he'd breezed through his finance degrees, both a bachelor's and master's, and entered management at Daimler AG. It had always been his path, but he wanted a currency that few if any of his eventual competitors might have. When it came time to hire a new chairman, there was only one leader in contention who had the bona fides of an actual line worker in the pit. As a rule, the employees loved him because he was one of them, which of course had been his plan all along.

Always angling to grow new business and please the stockholders, four years ago, Wolff had invested $500 million on preparing Daimler for the southwest

Asian markets, especially Iran. He had authorized the build of a new factory licensed under the Iran Khodro Diesel Company license. Under his direction, Daimler had purchased two million square feet of new space in Mannheim to ramp up production both for the Persian market and for the lucrative U.S. defense contract. He had outsourced all the small things, such as the Persian characters printed inside the vehicles, the owner's manuals, advertising, and navigation systems translations. And he had made dozens of trips to Tehran to sell to the government and its dealers. It was a significant investment.

The nuclear status of Iran was of little import to him. What mattered to Wolff was that the previous U.S. administration planned to open the economic opportunity to Europe and America, a brilliant move in his view. The Persian markets would fuel global growth with an additional fifty million consumers that otherwise had been shut out of the marketplace. Conservatively, Iran would add five billion euros to Daimler's bottom line. The $500 million was a solid investment by anyone's standards.

Two years ago, however, the new American president had canceled the nuclear deal and imposed sanctions on Iran, which included forbidding any nation from trading with the Persian government or the country's consumers or companies. Wolff had met with the Iranian president, the former U.S. administration officials, leaders of the European Union, and anyone with the power to prevent the loss of five billion in opportunity, all to no avail.

Now he was trying to save his company . . . and his own ass in the process.

On the monitor in front of him, the map display showed the *Sieg* approaching the northernmost point of Michigan, where it would traverse south of Mackinac Island and turn farther south toward Chicago at the very end.

The MasterEye software also provided video feeds in each of the main compartments of the ship. In the bridge, Wolff's hired gun, Sam Kinnett, stood admiring the passage from Lake Huron to Lake Michigan. Mackinac Island was to the north, its bluffs and towering forests etched against the morning sky. He guided the massive ship beneath I-75, which connected Michigan's Upper and Lower Peninsulas. Soon he would guide the ship to the south and aim it toward Chicago, where he would make his first port of call since boarding as a river pilot in the Saint Lawrence River.

Because of the locks and narrow passageways throughout the world's largest connected water route, professional river pilots were required to navigate the Great Lakes Waterway. Wolff had a complete dossier on Kinnett, who had been steering large container ships through all the Great Lakes and Saint Lawrence River for thirty-six years, since he dropped out of Syracuse University and moved back to his hometown of Watertown, New York, home of the army's Tenth Mountain Division.

Instead of joining the army, though, he pursued what he told Wolff was a childhood passion that he had developed from years of sailing on Lake Ontario. Wolff figured the river pilot could most likely navigate the entire route from memory, but no two voyages were the same. The weather and currents always mixed to create a new experience, and his cargo was most definitely precious.

In the shadows of the bridge, two guards stood watch over Kinnett. They were large men, scarred and weatherworn, wearing nearly identical black cargo pants and fitted black shirts with olive field jackets like the American soldiers near Mannheim, where Wolff had grown up. Eighteen of their peers were scattered about the ship.

Wolff had conveyed to Kinnett that the shipment was equipment for a new automobile factory "somewhere in the Midwest." Indeed, it had been exactly that. Scheduled to deliver the first of the new factory equipment for the primary production facility of trucks in Illinois before that deal was disputed by General Motors and its conniving CEO, Andrea Comstock. It was all very top secret, and Wolff had been burned before by economic development bureaucrats eager to leak to the media that they had secured the next big deal from the automaker from which thousands of jobs would flow.

Thus, the secrecy. The *Sieg* was one of the first vessels picking its way through the waterway in late May. Wolff's handpicked crew of twenty-two men were fine, skilled workers who managed the ship well, even if their previous duties required better marksmanship than sea navigation. The plan so far was running smoothly. The ship had departed Hamburg on schedule and now just needed Kinnett to complete the port calls in Chicago and Milwaukee before returning to Québec. There were two containers to pick up in Chicago, and then it was on to Milwaukee, where their instructions were to off-load the entire shipment and then onload over one thousand new containers.

The map in front of Wolff showed the path of the *Sieg* as it traversed the Great Lakes. A few days ago, it had sailed from Lake Erie to Lake Saint Clair and into Lake Huron. As it did so, the cameras showed the Detroit skyline.

In Detroit sat the headquarters of General Motors.

In the General Motors headquarters sat its CEO, Andrea Comstock, whose actions had threatened Wolff's existence.

As he vowed to save his career, he thought about Comstock and Detroit—as he had obsessively done ever since Comstock's power play with the U.S. Congress to steal his $1 billion DoD truck contract—and conjured a Sun Tzu maxim.

The greatest victory is that which requires no battle.

CHAPTER 3

Vick Harwood

Approximately eighty miles south of the Syrian town of al-Ghouta, Vick Harwood sighted through his Leupold scope, searching for Syrian tanks and logistics vehicles.

Harwood and his new spotter, Corporal Ian Nolte, known as Clutch for hitting a game-winning shot for Notre Dame in the final seconds of a March Madness Elite Eight game, had been in position for two days in the foothills of Mount Hermon, just across the border from the northernmost part of Israel. Their mission was to collect intelligence on logistics convoys between Lebanon and Syria while also covertly assisting Israeli Defense Forces in undermining an Iranian-backed plot that had Syria and Hezbollah attacking Israel's Golan Heights.

U.S. Army Ranger Regimental Command Sergeant

Major Murdoch, as usual, had delivered Harwood and Clutch their mission papers. They were part of a five-man element, including another sniper team and a squad leader. From that point a week ago, his squad leader, Staff Sergeant Frank Stoddard, and his three other teammates had traveled from Fort Benning, Georgia, to Hohenfels, Germany, where they spent two days firing their SR-25s and SIG P320s, both with and without silencers.

From there, the two teams were taken into separate mission planning rooms where Sergeant Stoddard gave them assignments. The other two-man team consisted of Ranger teammates, Corporal Anthony Patalino, a stocky lacrosse player from Long Island, and Sergeant Walt Ruben, a lanky Texan from San Antonio, both of whom had been in the Rangers for a few years. Their last night in Germany had been the last time Harwood had seen Patalino or Ruben. They had been talking with Stoddard when Harwood retired to his bunk and never saw them after.

The morning of their insertion, Harwood and Clutch received an intelligence update from Ron, a man in civilian clothes, whom Harwood pegged as CIA. Ron wore khaki cargo pants, a long-sleeved navy cotton shirt, and a black outer tactical vest. He had a thin beard across his tanned, wizened face. Stoddard and Ron reiterated that Harwood's instructions were to get to a high point on the east side of Mount Hermon and within range of two suspected Syrian and Hezbollah attack routes. The squad's presence was deniable, which meant that they were on a black operation to support a U.S. ally where neither the United States leadership nor the Israeli Defense Forces wanted to acknowledge their existence.

"We are primarily interested in a logistics operation led by a merchant in the Beqaa Valley. Our ability to operate in Lebanon and Syria is limited. We're putting you where you can overwatch the resupply points. There's a new theory that the chemical weapons are coming out of Lebanon, not Damascus. We need intel on who is resupplying Hezbollah and the Syrians. It could be Russians. Could be private business. Could be a little bit of both," Ron had said.

"What about Patalino and Ruben? Where will they be?" Harwood had asked, knowing Ron couldn't answer the question.

Ron smiled at Harwood's attempt to extract more information. "This is compartmented. They'll be in the AO. Stoddard will be command and control over both teams." Harwood was accustomed to sparse information on black operations.

"What do we do if we find the supply guy?"

"We don't necessarily expect you to, but any information you can provide on the convoys would be helpful. If you see any hazmat suits, decon equipment, extra-careful handling of artillery shells, report it. In the meantime, report on the enemy advancement. Before you engage anything, clear it with Sergeant Stoddard."

The next night, Harwood and Clutch found themselves rigged in high-altitude parachutes aboard an MC-130 Combat Talon that took off from the Hohenfels airfield. Flying in international airspace and entering

Israeli airspace under terminal guidance of the Israeli Air Force, the MC-130 released them at ten thousand feet above sea level just south of the border near Galilee. They gained canopy quickly after exiting and flew the prevailing winds into their designated landing area east of Mount Hermon. They climbed and walked all night until they found a suitable sniper hide site as the sun was rising.

They had moved twice since that first night two days ago to improve their position. By Harwood's map recon and calculation, they were in one of the two best locations possible relative to the chosen Syrian route of attack and their likely resupply points.

Now, as the sun squeezed below the ridge to the west and painted the sky purple, they were to report any sightings of logistical operations and, if approved, kill any Syrian or Hezbollah logisticians they could while sending encrypted text messages to Stoddard, who was positioned on a ship in the Mediterranean Sea behind them some forty miles.

"Anything you saw or heard in Germany inspire you with confidence, Clutch?" Harwood said.

"Not especially," Clutch replied. Then, after a minute of silence, he said, "Speaking of which, some of the guys have said, you know, that after losing LaBeouf and Samuelson, *your confidence* is a bit shaky."

"Why bring that up, bruh?" Harwood growled.

"I mean, I'm your third spotter in a couple of years. You keep living and they keep dying. What's up with that?"

Harwood bristled at the comments, but this was what

happened when you spent hours, even days, lying in a hide site with your spotter. You discussed fears, hopes, and sometimes even the most intimate details of your life, made plans for the future, passed the monotony with wild dreams of what you would do if you won the lottery, or even left the service and entered private life. And now Clutch had broached the most intimate of topics with Harwood, the deaths of his two previous spotters.

Harwood thought about Corporal Joe LaBeouf, who had been killed by Harwood's dead nemesis, a Chechen sniper named Basayev. Then Sammie Samuelson, who had been forced to commit suicide on a Facebook live feed by terrorists attacking the family members of the president's cabinet while framing Samuelson.

"Keep talking and you'll be number three, Clutch," Harwood joked.

Clutch shook his head. "Damn, Reaper, you've been bitching about my bad breath for the last twenty-four hours. How about I just breathe on you a bit."

"That'll definitely make you number three, bruh."

"Let's just make sure we get out of here in one piece," Clutch said.

"I know, I know, Clutch," Harwood replied. "Your daddy's a rich-guy senator, and you're going to follow in his footsteps."

"That's the plan."

Harwood respected Clutch for joining the army when his father was the senior senator from Indiana and chairman of the Senate Intelligence Committee. The kid could be either playing professional basketball or cruising on easy street pursuing a political career, a modern-day Pat Tillman. Instead, Ian "Clutch" Nolte chose to go through the toughest training the military has to offer and be on the front lines doing special operations around the world. If there were ever a doubt about today's all-volunteer force, all anyone had to do was look at this two-man sniper team, Harwood thought. The white son of one of the wealthiest politicians in the country was paired with a black orphan foster kid who didn't know who his parents were. They both slept, fought, and ate in the same exact places. There was no privilege in the Rangers, nor were there any exceptions for rich kids. Every Ranger wore the standard high and tight, had to do the intense physical training, and had to carry their weight on missions. No exceptions.

"Total respect, but why even go into politics, man?" Harwood asked.

After a brief pause, Clutch said, "You ever read Deleuze?"

"Doo-who?" Harwood joked.

"Gilles Deleuze."

"He invented the ghillie suit?"

"Shut up, Reaper. He's a French philosopher, like Hegel, but more modern."

"Just yanking your chain. I read about him but can't remember much," Harwood said.

"Deleuze says that the past actualizes the present. Who we were leads us to who we will be, and that desire drives production and becomes reality."

"Fancy way of saying, 'Stay motivated.'"

Clutch stifled a laugh. "You're a modern-day philosopher, Reaper."

"I saw you reading all that shit on your Kindle in the airplane. Searching for meaning in life?"

"Always, brother. Without meaning, what's the point?"

"Good thought. Plus, keep your dad happy, right?"

"Always. Here's a real philosophical dilemma, Reaper. If you had to choose between saving a fellow soldier and completing the mission, what's your choice?"

"Still on that, are we? You know the mission comes first, but why not do both?"

"Huh, think it's possible?"

"I think you and me can do anything we set out to do, Clutch. Now, focus," Harwood said. Despite his admonition for Clutch to stay focused, Harwood's mind reeled with previous failures regarding his teammates. Sure, he'd been successful at killing bad guys, but Clutch was right. He couldn't seem to keep anyone close, except maybe Monisha, his adoptive daughter, whom he had saved from certain death a couple of years ago. She was a thriving teenager preparing for medical school now.

A new column of tanks poked through the gorge and spilled onto the valley floor beneath them.

Clutch patted his arm and said, "Look at that. Tiger Forces leading the advance."

"Okay. Call Stoddard and tell him," Harwood said.

The Syrian Tiger Forces were the most elite and well

equipped in the Syrian military. A combined arms task force, the Tiger Forces had been ruthlessly dispatching the Syrian rebels who were attempting to overthrow the Assad regime. In a nighttime pivot that was not overtly telegraphed, the Tiger Forces vacated their defenses, assembled, and began an unrehearsed attack on the Golan.

"Roger that," Clutch said. He fumbled with the radio handset and whispered, "Zodiac base, this is Zodiac one."

Stoddard came back immediately, "Roger. Send it." His voice was crisp and clear.

"Tiger Forces advancing within range in approximately forty T-90 tanks," Clutch said.

"Any sign of a logistics column?"

"Negative at this time."

"Roger. Continue to monitor. Engage if you have a clean shot. Might activate medical personnel."

"Wilco."

"Heard that," Harwood said. To their left, the towering ridges of Mount Hermon climbed into the sky until they were shrouded in clouds that appeared snagged by the peak. Harwood had accounted for the slight breeze from the northeast. The valley below was lush with fields and groves of olives, barley, and chickpeas. A highway threaded the farmland and then climbed into the Golan Heights.

The ambient light of dusk provided him a perfect sight picture. He squeezed the trigger and watched the bullet work its magic on the tank commander's head. The rest of the crew searched frantically for where the shot might have originated, but Harwood and Nolte looked like rocks over a half mile away. There was no way that the Syrians or Hezbollah would find them. The tank continued forward, the driver wanting to get out of the kill zone. The tank was a Russian T-90, recognizable by its 125 mm smooth-bore main gun, the 12.7 mm Kord machine gun, its distinctive shallow, angular turret, multiple plates of reactive armor, and even spacing between its tracked wheels.

"Good shot," Nolte said. "Still moving."

"No shot on the driver, but the gunner is doable," Harwood said. He aligned the sight and pulled the trigger. Two shots, two kills. The silencer on the barrel of his SR-25 muffled the sound of the shot so that only someone in proximity could hear the metallic ratcheting of the weapon and its muted *pop*.

"Another column heading up the road," Clutch said. He was using the M-151 sniper spotting scope with an AN-PVS-14 night-vision device attached to the scope's eyepiece. His job was to identify the target and observe the sniper's shot. Harwood, the sniper, who had earned his nickname *the Reaper* by killing thirty-three Taliban commanders in Helmand Province, Afghanistan, had a clear mission—to kill the target. The Third Ranger Battalion had been on its counterterrorism rotation in the Kandahar and Helmand areas, and Harwood had seen more combat in those ninety days than in the rest of his entire career. He had been executing daily missions as the Taliban came crawling out of the Kandahar Mountains like cockroaches. He'd done his duty and served the Rangers well, as he continued to do. The reputation, though, had landed him on the classified mission list, and he found himself training and executing more top secret missions than he had ever imagined.

"There it is. Resupply convoy," Clutch said. "Ten o'clock. They're stopped."

"Call it in," Harwood said.

"Zodiac base, Zodiac one, over."

"Send it."

"Logistics convoy of multiple snub-nosed Mercedes-Benz trucks moving from north to south at projected resupply point number four."

Harwood shifted his weapon, lifted his head, got his bearing, and then sighted in on the trucks that were stacked up. A large man was walking along the convoy, shouting like Patton at the crossroads. One of the logisticians stepped down from his truck and was at least a foot shorter than the big man, who pointed at the lead truck and was saying something emphatically. Harwood couldn't see it, but he imagined spit flying into the shorter man's face. He appeared to show the man a piece of paper or a tablet, pointed at what was in his hand, and kept shouting.

He drew a bead on the center mass of the big man, dialed in his sight, and put his finger on the trigger. He was about six hundred meters away, which was a midrange shot for him. Should be no problem at all.

"Big guy or little guy?"

"Big guy looks like he's in charge," Harwood said.

As he was pulling back on the trigger, the big guy

eyed his tablet, then looked up in Harwood's direction as if he were staring right at him through the scope.

"What's that noise?" Nolte asked.

"I'm focused," Harwood said. "Figure it out."

The big guy was moving his hands as he walked quickly and then darted to the opposite side of the trucks. Harwood squeezed off a rare wild shot—like the baseball pitcher with his 100 mph fastball who lost control of a high-and-inside pitch into the netting behind home plate.

"Damn. Someone's shooting at us!" Nolte said.

Bullets pocked the rocks that hid their location, which was providing both cover and concealment.

"We should be okay," Harwood said calmly. "We've got good cover, but find whoever is shooting at us." He was still scanning for the big man but coming up empty. Instead he focused on the fuel tank of the truck the man had fled behind. Harwood pumped three rounds into the tank but got no immediate explosion. The bullets continued to rain down on their position. The only thing he was concerned about was their lower legs, which were exposed beyond the granite overhead cover that protected them.

"Watch your legs," Harwood said.

"Roger."

"Got it. UAV at two o'clock. Maybe a hundred meters. Taking the shot."

Harwood rotated his weapon so that he could aim at the UAV. It was weaponized with some type of small machine gun, which was spitting lead at them. The aircraft swooped high and banked like a racing jet, which provided Harwood with a good view of the drone as it flew toward them for another gun run. The device looked like a B-2 stealth bomber with its swept wings. He memorized the dimensions. About twelve-to-fifteen-foot wingspan, one machine gun under the nose like a fighter jet, and small rockets on the rails under the wings. Both rockets released and smoked at them with a *whoosh*.

"Rockets!" Harwood said through clenched teeth. He kept tracking the UAV, though, knowing that it was nearly impossible to hit an object this small and flying so fast. He waited for the drone to begin lining up for another run at them. It turned on a dime, exposing its flat broadside to him. Leading the nose, he fired five rounds in quick succession. At first, it appeared he missed, but then the aircraft wobbled, broke its orbit, and began to recover toward the convoy. Harwood continued to track it until the rockets exploded into their redoubt. Shrapnel and rocks spat into their faces through the firing port they had created.

"Shit," Nolte coughed.

"You okay?" Harwood asked.

"Roger. Face just got sandblasted."

The dirt and rocks sprayed into his face but bounced off his ballistic eye protection. The big guy had to be controlling the aircraft with the tablet he was holding, so Harwood shifted back to the truck. Saw nothing. Scanned the sky. Saw nothing there.

Another swept-wing UAV lifted into the sky and locked on to their position. Harwood and Clutch unloaded two magazines on the aircraft strafing their position. The drone pinwheeled and slammed into the ground.

They continued to scan the convoy, which had deposited the supplies and turned around. Stacks of wooden ammunition crates and ration cartons lined the road.

"Anything?" Clutch asked.

"Nothing but ammo and chow."

The convoy dipped over the horizon to the north, then took a left-hand turn to the west, toward the Beqaa Valley.

CHAPTER 4

"We need resupply. Stat," Clutch said.

It had been an hour since the drone shootdown, and they needed to move. Their position was burned. Harwood contemplated the tipping point between moving too soon and too late. Too soon, and you could miss opportunities or step into an ambush. Too late, and you could allow the enemy to maneuver on you.

One issue that Harwood had with black missions was that they were lean on details and leaner on resupply. They had jumped with enough food, water, and ammunition for up to seventy-two hours. This being the third day, they were low on all classes of supply. The arid climate increased water intake, and the constant movement burned calories that needed to be replaced with the delicious Meals, Ready to Eat. The truth was that Harwood never complained about MREs. They were better than 90 percent of the chow he had eaten as a young orphan and foster kid in Maryland. When he joined the army, the food had been one of the perks. And while food and water were important, ammunition was *essential*.

Nonetheless, Harwood continued to plink away at the Syrian Tiger Force tanks and infantry that were wandering amid the battlefield littered with the decimated remnants of an entire tank brigade, nearly a hundred tanks. The combined arms effects of Israeli tanks, attack helicopters, artillery, jets, and Harwood's invisible sniping had stalled the attack. The sun was setting behind Mount Hermon's massive peak. Shades of gray began to blend with the terrain until darkness enveloped them.

"Switching to thermal," Harwood said.

"Roger."

To Harwood's right was his depleted rucksack. He had two magazines of 7.62 ammunition remaining. Each night, they had repositioned slightly despite having secured what they considered the best terrain from which to fight. With each move, they risked detection. However, if they remained stationary, they risked the Syrians or Hezbollah doing the forensics on how their tank commanders were getting shot in the back of the head with NATO ammunition. From there, the remaining Tiger light infantry would about-face and climb the hills in search of them.

"That was close," Clutch said. "Still not sure why the Israelis can't do this instead of us."

Harwood continued scanning the battlefield. "Israeli soldiers can't be found anywhere inside Lebanon or

Syria. They're trying to play fair and square to show the international community that they are on the defense. Israel has to be squeaky clean on this."

"Roger that."

Harwood sighted again.

"Jets," Clutch said. "Two o'clock."

Two jets buzzed low overhead, lifted into the sky, and released bombs on the Israeli troops dug into a trench about two miles away, just across the border in Israel. Air Defense missiles smoked into the sky, their white contrails parallel exclamation points punctuating the night as the two airplanes exploded in bright fireballs.

"Let's move," Harwood said.

"This was a good spot—but, yes, it's burned," Clutch said.

"Roger that."

"Probably take them an hour to get up here if they're coming."

"Unless they have helicopters."

"If I'm a pilot, I'm not liking flying after two jets just got smoked," Harwood said.

"Roger that."

"Okay, look at position number five and call for resupply. We'll get the resupply here and then move."

"Good plan."

Harwood's left forearm buzzed. He and Clutch maintained small tactical satellite radios—called TacSleeves—on their forearms, like the play sheets NFL quarterbacks wore during football games. The

TacSleeve had all the power of a smartphone, was encrypted, and allowed the chain of command to geolocate soldiers. Harwood had covered his with a thick chunk of burlap to deaden any noise—it hummed lightly with an incoming message—and block any light from the control panel. He had the light dimmed, but there was a switch that allowed him to modulate the brightness if needed. The burlap was more preventive than anything. If he accidentally turned on the light, then the cloth would still keep the device concealed.

Noise and light discipline was paramount when operating behind enemy lines. Harwood didn't care as much about the epic struggle between the Israelis and the Arabs as he did about keeping himself and Clutch alive so they could get back to their respective families.

Harwood said, "Poncho."

Clutch slowly slid a poncho over their heads as Harwood peeled back the burlap and stared at the message that had appeared on his TacSleeve.

Resupply ready. Send coordinates.

"Stoddard's reading our minds," Clutch said.

"He knows how much we've been shooting and killing and how long we've been out here. Not sure he knows about the drone."

Harwood typed in their position and sent the encrypted message to Stoddard.

A message pinged back to him quickly.

One hour max. If not received, exfil at own risk. If received, 5 min on station.

Harwood responded and muttered, "Roger."

"I can't handle all the love," Clutch said. He was shoulder to shoulder with Harwood under the tarp.

As they waited, men shouted for medics and ammunition cooked off inside the turrets of flaming tanks in the valley below. Israeli F-35 Adir jet fighters buzzed along the border, attacking obliquely into Syria. The tanks stacked along Route 7, the road running north to south from Damascus to the Israeli border in the Golan Heights. The jets' 20 mm guns did as much damage as the AIM-120 air-to-surface missiles. The sheer number of jets the Israelis had in the air was overwhelming the Syrian air and ground forces. Air-to-air Sidewinder missiles smoked through the night sky as Israeli F-35s dominated Syrian MiGs in dogfights.

A light hum resonated behind them, all but extinguished by the roaring jets and exploding rockets.

"What's that?" Clutch asked.

"Behind us," Harwood said.

The hum became a buzz loud enough for Harwood to determine it was within fifty meters of them. Half a football field away. He covered the tablet and withdrew his pistol from his holster. Moving imperceptibly, he lifted himself to his elbow and looked to the rear of their position. Clutch was doing the same thing in the other direction, always keeping 360-degree security.

"What the . . . ?"

Harwood held up his hand to quiet Clutch.

An aircraft the size of a small SUV, but sleek and modern, with at least a twenty-five-foot wingspan circled their position and then flipped its four Fenestron

blade-in-rotor engines upward so that it could land vertically on a level spot less than fifty meters to their
north. The pilot had found the one spot that was not
immediately detectable from the valley and landed.

"Okay, pack up and let's roll," Harwood said. He collapsed the bipod, and they spent two minutes sanitiz-
ing their position. With three minutes remaining to
offload their resupply, assuming that was what was
occurring, Harwood hustled over the ridge and toward
the gray vessel. It had four blades turning inside their
circular protective sleeves that were three feet in diam-
eter. He was impressed with the stealth of the aircraft,
the buzzing and humming of the blades and motors
significantly more muted than, say, a helicopter that
could be heard for miles in this valley.

By Harwood's count, they had maybe two minutes to
offload the aircraft or get into a firefight if this was an
enemy insertion. Breathing hard and feeling the lightness of the rucksack on his back, Harwood raced to the
open ramp of the aircraft, rifle at the ready. Inside the
dimly lit cargo bay was a small pallet of MREs, two
green ammunition containers, and two cases of water
bottles. Almost exactly what they needed for the next
three days, should the mission last that long. He gathered the supplies, noticing the Sabrewing logo for the
new autonomous resupply drones that could carry a
thousand pounds a thousand miles.

"Provide overwatch," Harwood said. He ran into
the bay, saw that there was no pilot in the cockpit,
loosened the cargo strap, and dragged the resupply
items onto the ground. Whoever had packed them

had conveniently placed the supplies on a burlap tarp, which Harwood tugged off the ramp. Clutch came toward Harwood, exposing himself barely above the ridge, and was hit by a bullet, spinning him sideways as he fell at Harwood's feet.

"Shit," Clutch moaned.

Harwood dropped his rucksack, laid his rifle atop it, and retrieved his Blackhawk knife before popping open the blade and cutting through Clutch's ghillie suit and uniform near his left shoulder.

"Bad?" Clutch asked.

"Be fine," Harwood said, though he wasn't sure. More gunfire pinged overhead. The resupply drone beckoned in the background.

"This should get me elected one day." Clutch grimaced.

Blood oozed from the wound like a weak water fountain. The burlap ghillie suit made applying the field dressing more challenging than if he were just dealing with a uniform, but then again, they weren't wearing body armor and perhaps there'd be no wound at all if they had been.

The resupply Sabrewing aircraft buzzed ten meters behind them. According to Stoddard's timeline, Harwood had maybe a minute to stop the bleeding, stabilize Clutch, get him in the back of the aircraft, and continue with his Ranger mission, whatever that may be. He poured a half bottle of rubbing alcohol on the wound, flushing it, as he ripped open the first of two field dressings. Applying the gauze directly on the wound, Clutch muttered, "Fuck, that hurts, Reaper."

"I'll pop you some morphine in a few seconds, brother," Harwood said as he wrapped the pad, pushing as much as he could into the entry wound. As he was rotating Clutch's body, he saw the slightly larger exit wound, opened the second field dressing from its sealed pouch, and repeated the process of alcohol and tight packing on the rear wound.

"Damn," Clutch said.

"Through and through. You're going to be okay, brother. I've got to drag your ass and your shit onto that Star Wars thing," Harwood said.

"Not leaving you, man. I can hang," Clutch said.

"Real doctor needs to work on that, like ASAP," Harwood said. "I'll go with you. We're in this together."

He stood, lifted Clutch into a fireman's carry, and placed him on the ramp of the Sabrewing. As he bolted back to grab Clutch's rifle, scope, and rucksack, the ramp began to rise. It was obvious that the timing of the flight mission was precise and automated. He scratched against the shale and rocks in the small depression behind their sniper hide where the Sabrewing had landed.

He stepped onto the slowly rising ramp, dragged Clutch inside, and was able to find the ramp control toggle in the rear of the aircraft. He pushed Stop as the ramp was at a 45-degree angle to the ground. The momentary pause allowed him to situate Clutch comfortably in the aircraft and secure him using the two cargo straps, cinching one directly on the wound to stanch the blood flow. The cargo bay would be big enough to hold both of them. There was a small box with flashing lights near the front of the aircraft. To his surprise, there was no cockpit where someone might be able to take over and fly the aircraft—not that he was qualified to do so—though he supposed that might be possible from the rectangular box, which had a small screen display.

The ingress and egress routes were on the screen. A flashing red dot was where they were presently located. He presumed it was red because they were behind schedule or there was a threat, or both. The egress route was indicated by a dashed line to the west, whereas the ingress route was a yellow line, most likely indicating that portion of the route was completed. Other numbers flashed next to the map. Hours, minutes, latitudes, longitudes.

"This thing's like a flying coffin, Vick," Clutch said. His face was dimly lit by the blue and red lights inside the cargo bay.

"Zodiac base, Reaper, over," Harwood said.

Stoddard's reply was quick. "Send it."

"One wounded. Casevac coming your way."

"Roger. Station time critical. Send patient, stay on location, sanitize area, relocate, and send grid once in position."

"No. I'm coming back with him."

"Negative. Orders are to continue mission," Stoddard said.

An explosion rocked the earth, and shrapnel whizzed like ninja stars in every direction, pinging off the aircraft. The display showed EMERGENCY OVERRIDE, and Harwood realized their equipment was on the ground

next to the aircraft. He bolted out of the ramp door, saying, "Got to grab our shit."

He grabbed Clutch's gear and his rifle, some ammo
and water, and flipped it all into the diminishing gap
between the ramp and the cargo bay. He turned and retrieved his rifle and rucksack before climbing up the
ramp and attempting to slide between the narrow gap.
The enemy gunfire intensified, causing him to let go of
the ramp twice before braving a third attempt to climb
in. Bullets pinged off the rocks around him, spraying
dust in his face.

As Harwood was wedged between the ramp door
and the frame of the aircraft, the drone began lifting
vertically. Stoddard was most likely monitoring the
situation and needed to get the aircraft out of there
before they were overcome by the enemy. Harwood's
foot was caught between two rocks, twisting his ankle
while the upward force of the drone wrenched his
shoulder. It didn't help that he had his rucksack and rifle
in one hand and his other arm in the ramp, trying to
open it.

"Stop this thing!" Harwood shouted.

"Vick!" Clutch replied.

Harwood fell to the ground, ankle twisted, as the
door sealed shut with a snap and the four rotor blades
spat sand and rocks everywhere, powering the vessel
into the sky. The blades then tilted forward slightly, and
the vertical lift became horizontal, as well. The Sabrewing quickly sped around the backside of the crest
and began flying an automated map of the earth route,
maybe twenty meters above ground level, to the west.

Harwood lay on the ground for a moment, cursing. The heavy machine gun fire reminded him he was in enemy territory. He quickly grabbed his equipment and pried open the ammunition box that had come with the resupply. He loaded two belts of 7.62 ammunition into his rucksack and scurried out of the compromised impact area. He jogged up and down goat trails, staying on or below the military crest of every ridgeline, never silhouetting himself to the enemy tanks stacking up to the east. Artillery fell a couple of hundred meters behind him, shaking the ground beneath his boots. Random rifle fire pinged near him occasionally, and he was convinced that the aircraft had been the target.

After fifteen minutes, he found a rock outcropping at the end of a trail that afforded him a view to the east. He settled into a hasty sniper hide, which was perhaps a half mile from his previous position. He had been moving due north, away from the artillery and burned hide site, but deeper into Syria or Lebanon. He wasn't sure and needed to check.

A sniper's first task is always to put his weapon into operation. He popped the bipod on his SR-25 and aimed toward the column of tanks now a farther half mile away. He noticed that there was a road below him to the north. The bright lights of what he assumed was Damascus shone off the nighttime cloud layer, providing him some light for his night-vision goggles and Leupold scope. He used both to assess his surroundings.

The location wasn't ideal, but he could continue with the mission and feel relatively secure. He was far enough removed from the compromised location that he could survive until sunrise. There was no way to scale the cliff to his front that he could see. The minor trail he had taken to the location was the main enemy axis of approach. The ridgeline running north and south was jagged and severe.

He dug through his rucksack and found some fishing line and a flash-bang grenade. He low crawled down the trail and set in an early-warning indicator by securing the fishing line to the pin of the grenade and creating a trip wire across the path at its narrowest point. It was far enough away so that the grenade shrapnel would not injure him while also giving him sufficient time to spin and fire his sidearm at whoever might make it past the grenade.

He plucked at the trip wire. It was taut.

He returned to his new hide site and settled in, promising himself to improve his camouflage when he could see better. As it was, it was decent. Of course, the ammunition and water he'd left behind would be damaging clues that might lead Hezbollah or the Syrian Army in his direction. Countersniper operations were relatively simple. Intelligence analysts studied the target and then used simple mathematics to calculate the distance the average sniper—not that there was anything average about the Reaper—would use for a hide site. A quick map analysis would lead any experienced analyst to the ridgeline that Harwood and Clutch had been using. There was a finite number of locations that would be within the range of the sniper weapons and provide the cover and elevation a sniper required to do his business.

Harwood had maybe twenty-four hours in this location before he would have to move. Good counter-sniper teams would work the ridgeline methodically from north to south with one element and from south to north with another, squeezing him. As he moved north tomorrow night, there was a very real chance that he would bump into enemy infantry searching for him. Once they discovered the left-behind equipment, the Syrians would escalate the search.

As Harwood slowed his breathing and thought through his problem set, his thoughts returned to Clutch.

Another spotter wounded. As Clutch had pointed out, he was Harwood's third spotter in as many years. Harwood had dismissed survivor's guilt primarily because the sniper business was dangerous and to be behind enemy lines shooting at them carried a certain amount of risk that other professions might not. Either the sniper or spotter surviving a mission was always, to him, a fifty-fifty proposition. There was no point in feeling guilty about something that both men had agreed was an insane but necessary mission. Like every soldier, Harwood knew that death was also a leering Peeping Tom just waiting for the right moment to crawl inside your window and harvest. The key was to tightly lock down all the windows and doors, keeping death at the doorstep. And when the time came, Harwood would answer the door, open it, and confront the killer man.

An old army physical training cadence popped into his mind:

I am a man of death / killing commies right and left /
I'm not the killer man / I'm the killer man's son / But
I'll do the killing / until the killer man comes . . .

Eventually, the killer man would come for him, Harwood knew. It was only a matter of time. His narrow escapes in Afghanistan, Iraq, Iran, Crimea, Azerbaijan, Syria, and even in the United States were all lucky breaks as far as he was concerned. There was skill involved, but he believed a person made their own breaks.

But still, three spotters. Clutch's fate gnawed at him.

Harwood looked at his TacSleeve, which was monitoring Clutch's trek around Mount Hermon. The soldier-monitoring chip painted a blue line that was his route through valleys and over ridges toward the Mediterranean Sea, where Harwood presumed Stoddard would recover the drone and Clutch.

An explosion thundered in the distance behind him. He pulled away from his sniper scope and saw a fire on a far ridge, miles to the west.

His TacSleeve buzzed. A red *X* appeared on the blue line, indicating that the route had stopped.

Clutch's chip was no longer broadcasting.

CHAPTER 5

Sassi Cavezza

Sassi held the phone to her ear as she looked at Fatima.

It was almost midnight. They were standing in the UNHCR forward operating base near the Turkish border. The UN had built a small encampment around the refugee area, locating the tent in the middle and painting UNHCR letters in blue on the top. Fatima's parents had called the resettlement center via their satellite phone and asked why their daughter had not returned.

"We were being chased by some terrorists, Mr. Abel. I'll return Fatima tomorrow," she said.

Normally, she didn't disclose operational details about when and where she would be going. In this case, however, she sympathized with the Abels' concerns. Their daughter had left her home for water and never returned.

"Why didn't you just bring her back to our home?" Fatima's father, Ahmed Abel, asked.

"Because your house was several blocks away, and we were in danger. My priority is to protect all of you. It is your first night back in the house, and between the Russian tanks and the ISIS terrorists, we had to flee. I'm sorry." And she was. She was sorry about the entire situation. She didn't know whether any of them would survive the resettlement, and questioned the higher command's decision to begin this early. With ISIS "defeated," the UN leadership made a decision to unburden its refugee camps and begin returning the refugees to the neighborhoods and homes. Some areas were still off-limits because of sarin gas residue.

"How do I know you have not kidnapped her?" Abel pressed.

Sassi tugged at her curly light brown hair and shook her head. No matter all the positive things she did, there was always suspicion and gamesmanship. She understood that the father was worried about his daughter, but this was the same man who was a constant rabble-rouser in this very same refugee camp before Sassi had resettled the family. Either the conditions weren't good enough, the water and food weren't plentiful enough, or the high command wasn't sending them back soon enough. Fatima's mother was submissive, allowing the father to dominate the conversation not only for the family but for the entire neighborhood, too.

"I'm here to protect you and your family, Mr. Abel. I haven't kidnapped her. She's in my protective custody."

Fatima was sitting on a low stack of water bottle cases, playing with her doll. The one success of the day had been recovering Aamina. Sassi's experience had been that the children impacted by this war survived best when they had a tangible reminder of home. A picture, a shirt, a soccer ball, and, yes, a doll. Anything to transport their young minds from the horrors they confronted to whatever imaginary world they crafted with the memorabilia.

"I want her back tomorrow. It's too dangerous to travel at night, but first thing in the morning. Do you understand?"

"Yes. Would you like to speak with her?"

"No," Abel said, and then hung up. The phone clicked in her ear.

"Another satisfied customer?"

Sassi looked up to see Hans Schmidt, the UNHCR regional director. In other words, her boss. He was in his midfifties, a native German, built like a weight lifter, and had a mop of gray hair he kept disheveled to add to a somewhat natural rough-hewn look. He wore khaki cargo pants, dark brown hiking boots, and three layers of outerwear—a black stretch T-shirt, an untucked button-down dress shirt made of heavy cotton, and an UNHCR zip-up windbreaker. All of it was stylishly put together. While it wasn't rare that Schmidt made the rounds of the refugee camps, he did so only with armed security. For the last several months, the German had been hitting on Sassi in an obvious way.

The advances had been most frequent in the last month, but the undertone had been there since they first met. He had shipped in from UN headquarters in New York City for a rare field assignment in his career. Like many Europeans, he spoke multiple languages, including some broken Italian. At first, Sassi found his attempts to communicate with her in Italian mildly humorous, if not obviously contrived.

"I speak fluent English. Let's stick with that," she had told him. And so they had.

Today she didn't have the patience for his nonsense. Sassi was still concerned about what she had seen on the walls of the basement. Was it something that had been forgotten? Or was the plan she had briefly studied an actual viable operation that someone intended to implement?

"Heard you departed your sector rather quickly today," Schmidt said. As usual, he invaded her space and put his hand on her shoulder. She flinched and stepped back toward Fatima. Hakim looked up from the wooden crate he was sitting on as he peeled an apple with a small pocketknife.

"Sometimes that's required when the situation doesn't look so well," she replied.

"Really? What happened? The UN intelligence report is quite clear that your sector is free for return of refugees. By the way, you look lovely this evening."

That, she knew, was not true unless he liked the disheveled, stinky, grimy look on a woman. No makeup, which she hardly ever wore anyway; no bath in two days; stale breath; totally sexy. With that thought, she inched closer to him and spoke directly into his face.

"That's inappropriate, don't you think, Mr. Schmidt?"

This time, Schmidt was the one who stepped back.

"Of course, no offense taken, I hope." Schmidt spoke with a thick German accent that Sassi understood well. She had traveled throughout Germany, skiing the Bavarian Alps near Garmisch and vacationing at Lake Chiemsee. Nothing could compare to her Tuscan home overlooking the Mediterranean Sea, but she so enjoyed the cultures of other countries that she made it a point to travel on her limited budget to neighboring countries in Europe and Africa.

"First I was approached by two Russian tanks, and then we were chased out of town by what appeared to be ISIS thugs. Remnants, most likely."

"Might they have been local hooligans?"

"Hooligans? I don't think hooligans carry rocket launchers and AK-47s, but you're welcome to come inspect the area with me tomorrow."

"The last thing I want to do is be a miniature manager," Schmidt said.

Sassi suppressed a laugh. Perhaps he'd made a self-effacing faux pas intentionally, to be charming, or more likely it was a language issue. Fatima stared up at them with wide eyes. She clutched her tattered doll as if it were a life raft, which perhaps it was.

"You mean *micromanager,* and you're the furthest thing from that," Sassi said. Schmidt puffed his chest, taking Sassi's subtle shade as a compliment. "But it might be helpful to you to actually see the areas we are returning families and children to."

"My schedule is packed this week, but maybe next," Schmidt said. "An American military commander would like to meet with you."

The change of topic caught her off guard.

"American military commander?"

"Yes. He flew into İzmir today. He wants to know about your progress."

"I don't have time for commanders, American or otherwise," Sassi said. "My responsibility is in the field. You talk to him."

"I already have. He requested you by name," Schmidt said.

Sassi deflated, shrugged. "And what do you want me to do with her? Them?" She swept her hand across Fatima and the tent behind them filled with hundreds of children and parents with weary eyes and threadbare clothes. Ripped jeans and dirty T-shirts for the men and filthy hijabs for some of the women, while others dressed more progressively, wearing only scarves around their heads. It was an eclectic group Sassi was charged with managing. Early in her career, she had made the mistake of becoming too familiar with the refugees. After watching Sunni warlords slaughter a family she had befriended, Sassi had taken a year off from the United Nations and escaped to the Seychelles to reflect on her life.

Her purpose. Did it really matter how many people she helped? Was her compassion just fuel spent into the ether, or did it make a difference? There on the beach at Anse Source d'Argent, she had decided to return, but only after building a protective wall inside her mind that allowed her to compartmentalize her work.

Several of her friends from school had gone on to be bankers, lawyers, or entrepreneurs making loads of money and living on the Tuscan bluffs overlooking the Mediterranean Sea. Here, she was unbathed, surrounded by swarms of people with no home, no hope, as the German playboy made his moves. She had allowed Fatima inside her protective wall, though, and taken unnecessary risks.

She thought about the pictures and diagrams she had seen on the wall of the basement, mulled them over in her mind, and said to Schmidt, "Okay, where is he?"

"Across the compound. I'll walk you."

Fatima tightened her grip on Sassi's hand and said, "I want to go home."

She knelt in front of Fatima and said, "It's dark now. We can't get back into your neighborhood. It's four hours away. I'll take you back tomorrow. Okay, Fatima?"

The eyes killed her. Fatima looked at her with the most pained gaze. This was why she could not let anyone inside. She had slipped with Fatima, but once she returned the girl to her parents, no more. Sassi steeled herself, led Fatima to a guardian in the tent, and said, "Watch her until I get back."

She would get Fatima and let her sleep on a cot in her room on the base camp, which was really nothing more than a Sealand container modified into sleeping quarters. Fatima squeezed her hand tightly, forcing

Sassi to use her free hand to remove Fatima's surprisingly strong grip.

Sassi turned before her will broke, and walked toward Schmidt, who was staring at her approvingly. The Germans, she had learned, in general were better at being hard and dispassionate than certainly herself and some of the few friends she had made along the way. Prior to the Iraq and Afghanistan wars, she had been told, the UN was easy. Kosovo, Macedonia, Bosnia, and other former resort countries were plentiful times for the UN. While there was still suffering, it was mild compared with what she had witnessed in Iraq and Afghanistan. The Macedonian army had caused tens of thousands of civilians to flee into Kosovo, but most of them were quickly absorbed into the Kosovar Albanian society.

No, these kinetic wars had an entirely different texture to them. The human suffering was deep. The loss was painful, like that captured in Fatima's hollow gaze. Would there ever be a future for her? For any of them?

Sassi shook off the negativity when she felt Schmidt's hand on the small of her back. She swatted it away and said, "I'm fine to walk by myself. I know where the building is."

Schmidt was undeterred and pressed ahead, though he did remove his hand. The night air was cool as they walked up a gravel road past several modular buildings that were tantamount to a modern trailer park. The light hum of the generators constantly buzzed in the background. Sassi was certain she would experience hearing loss before her tour here was done. They approached the equivalent of a double-wide trailer and ascended the wide, wooden steps.

She kicked her hiking boots against the doorjamb before entering—a habit—to shake the dirt and mud off the soles. Inside, a black man nodded and rose from his chair. General Cartwright towered above the desk. Like Charles Barkley or Zion Williamson, the man was big, wide, and powerful. The army uniform strained the seams around his biceps and chest. The three stars stuck with Velcro to the front of his uniform enhanced the gravitas of this man with the gleaming shaved head, looking like a black Mr. Clean.

"Hi. I'm General James Cartwright." He held out a catcher's mitt of a hand, which Sassi shook.

"Sassi Cavezza."

"Please, Ms. Cavezza, have a seat. Mr. Schmidt, thank you, but I'll just be talking to Ms. Cavezza."

Sassi liked this American already.

"As her supervisor, I prefer to stay," Schmidt said. He sat in one of the two well-worn chairs facing the general's battleship-gray desk.

Cartwright turned his head in Schmidt's direction and glowered, a predator sizing up prey.

Schmidt pushed his chair back and for a moment seemed to want to challenge the imposing general but evidently thought better of it. "I understand," he said as he departed the room.

Sassi smirked. "That may work on him, but not on me."

"I got the impression you rather enjoyed that," Cartwright said. He lowered his frame back into the chair.

"Oh, I did," she said. "He's a total PITA."

"PITA?"

"*Pain in the ass,* as you Americans say. The Italian version sounds much harsher. But enough with the pleasantries. Why am I here and not with my people planning for tomorrow's resettlement operations?"

The list in her mind was endless, filled with logistical and organizational requirements. As it stood, she was going to get precious little sleep anyway. Now a time-suck meeting was distracting her from her primary mission.

"I like it. Straight to the point," he said. His voice was a deep baritone, which worked well with his physique. She imagined he was a force of nature. His uniform had several subdued badges on it. Airborne, Ranger, Special Forces, and other insignia that were equally impressive.

"None of us have time to waste, General."

He nodded. "True. So, I'll get right to it. My people tell me that you took some pictures today. In a basement in al-Ghouta?"

Sassi remained expressionless. How in the hell could this general know that she had taken a few pictures in a basement? She had been underground, negating any possibility that drones had captured her movements. Even if there were a drone in the air, the most they could have seen was the Russian tanks, her entering and exiting the same house, and then her, Hakim, and

Fatima racing away under gunfire. He might have deduced something from that, but nothing as specific as *taking pictures.*

"Ms. Cavezza?"

"General, what are you talking about?"

"I thought you didn't like to waste time? Play games?"

Touché.

"Okay. I took two pictures," she said.

"Walk me through it," he directed.

She told him about the doll and the light at the end of the tunnel, realizing how stupid she sounded.

"Very compassionate of you to help Fatima Abel. Her father is upset, by the way."

"I know. He called me."

"As he did me, Ms. Cavezza, but back to the point. The pictures?"

"They shot into the basement. Weapons. Automatic rifles."

"AK-47s?" the general prompted.

"I don't know and don't care. I was nearly killed."

"Why do you think that is the case?"

"Because I saw something that they didn't want me seeing."

The general aimed his thumb and forefinger at her, cocked like a pistol, and let the hammer fall. "Who is 'they'?"

"Terrorists? Book club? Cartographers? How am I supposed to know?"

"You've been there every day for the last couple of weeks. I'm sure you've established relationships."

"Minimal. It's a tough area."

"Roger that. Can I see the pictures?"

"First, let me ask you how you know I have the pictures."

Cartwright stared at her for a moment, his leaden eyes unblinking.

"We have intelligence methods here that help us operate in the region. There's a Turkish base just up the road that has American air force jets and nuclear weapons. In the opposite direction are Lebanon, Syria, and the Palestinians, all dominated by Russia and Iran. We have Israel, our ally, surrounded by Hezbollah and Hamas. The Syrians and Hezbollah are attacking our ally in the Golan Heights. I didn't agree with the Iraq War back in 2003, but I didn't get a vote. I was just a major doing my duty in Mosul. But I'm not sure the replacement is any better than Hussein. Iran now has a land bridge into Jordan and Syria. That's not good for our geopolitical advantage. We work with the UN and other NGOs to try to bring stability here and elsewhere. All of that is to say that we have intelligence assets invested here that you can't imagine. And one of those assets noticed that you had two pictures upload into a secure cloud. Now, we could go in there and take them, see them, or you could just give them to us. We're not in the habit of stealing property of the UN or its people. We will if we have to, but I thought I'd ask first."

"That's kind of you, sir. Tell me, have you and your minions already been roaming around my personal stuff in my cloud storage? Looking for nude pictures to get your jollies?"

"I understand you're angry. I am being completely honest with you. We could just go in there and get them. I have no idea what is in those pictures, but I'm extending the courtesy to you."

"That's a whole lot of talking for just saying you aren't going to tell me how you got the pictures," Sassi remarked.

"I thought some context would be helpful."

She retrieved her phone from her small black rucksack. Thumbing in the password, she said, "What is it that you think is on the pictures?"

"We have no idea. I understand that you were in a former ISIS stronghold that has changed hands many times. ISIS, Syria, Russians, and so forth. We have indicators of a terrorist attack—"

She cut him off. "Yes, you left out one group, General."

"Who is that?"

"The people who live there. Remember? It's my job to return them to their homes. Would you like to return to America and see your neighborhood ravaged?"

"Of course not. I get your point. Well made. Still, it's bad-guy country big-time there."

"We don't go in blindly, General. Our intelligence folks noticed a considerable drop in ISIS activity a couple of months ago."

Cartwright's eyes remained fixed on hers. "I'm interested," he said.

"Nothing more to say. There were about twenty-five

ISIS leftovers there. Now there are about five. We figured we could begin to resettle."

"Twenty ISIS operatives missing?"

"Well, maybe not missing, but certainly no longer in the area."

"Any idea where they went?"

"Not our job."

Cartwright nodded and after a moment said, "Okay. The pictures, please?"

She was swiping through her pictures and not finding the photos she had taken just hours ago. "*Mannaggia!*"

"Pardon me?"

"That's Italian for many things. In this case, it appears your troops have already invaded my space."

"What do you mean?"

"The pictures aren't on my phone anymore," she said.

Cartwright picked up his cell phone and dialed a pre-loaded number.

"Flanigan, get your ass in here now."

A moment later, a young sergeant scrambled through the door to the office. He was wearing the same style camouflage uniform as Cartwright but was opposite in every other way. He was skinny, white, and wore black-rimmed glasses propped on a large nose. He was carrying what appeared to be a ruggedized iPad. Computer nerd, Sassi guessed.

"Talk to me," Cartwright said to the young man standing at attention in front of the desk. "Have you been inside Ms. Cavezza's computer or cloud?"

"No, sir. I was waiting on the word from you."

"Stand by."

Cartwright looked at Sassi. "Can you open your cloud and tell me if it's in there?"

Sassi nodded, punched the cloud app, and waited as it spooled up. She thumbed on some folders inside the application and opened her picture albums. She normally organized her photos at the end of each day, spending a few minutes to capture her history. She had folders for Iraq, Afghanistan, Syria, several African countries. She divided the folders into travel, UNCHR, and family. She checked them all. There were a few loose pictures that she hadn't placed in folders from this morning's drive into Ghouta. They had taken the coastal route, and Sassi had reflected on the harsh reality of the beauty of the sea smashing into the cliffs to her west and the barren combat zones to her east. She felt as if she had been on a thin dividing line between life and death. Often the line was no wider than a strip of asphalt.

"Either you guys are excellent liars, and this is all some kind of a hoax, or someone took those two pictures from my cloud and my phone."

"Well, technically, if they take it from your cloud, it removes it from your phone," Flanigan said.

"Be quiet, Flanigan. We don't need explanations. What we need are solutions. Can you find those pictures?"

"I can try, but if we're dealing with pros here, and I suspect we are, then it might be impossible."

He opened his tablet and began punching some icons.

"Username and password?" he said without looking up.

Sassi told him, though she felt violated. She used the same password for just about everything, and now she was going to have to change all her bank, email, and app logins. After a few minutes of Flanigan rooting around in what she suspected to be her storage, the sergeant said, "There was access to the cloud at 19:23 hours local. It's 21:14 right now. So, basically, two hours ago, someone jailbroke your phone and took your pictures and probably stole your password. Do you have it saved in your phone?"

Sassi nodded. She did. "But it is encrypted and in code."

"These guys knew what they were doing. Sorry, boss. Everything's gone. The memory card on her phone doesn't have a trace. Real pros. I've got nothing," Flanigan said.

Cartwright sighed heavily. "I should have authorized you to grab them when we got the alert."

"No. No. That's not the lesson to be learned here," Sassi said, shaking her finger. She stood and leaned forward on the general's desk. "The lesson is you stay out of my shit."

Cartwright looked at Flanigan and said, "That will be all, then." Flanigan raised his eyebrows, tucked his tablet under his arm, and conducted a proper about-face as he exited the room.

"Roger that," Cartwright finally said to Sassi once the door had clicked shut. "I can handle you breathing down my neck. That rolls off me like water off a duck's back. What I can't handle now is the threat that you may be under. We're going to have to lock you down."

"Lock me down?" Sassi spat the words as if she'd just eaten bad sushi.

"Think about it. If someone penetrated your cloud and phone just to get two photographs, what do you think they'll do to your brain to erase the memory, the details?"

"They'll penetrate it with a bullet before I let you lock me down," Sassi said. "I'm happy to tell you what I saw in there if you can convince me that you didn't take it. I don't know who to trust here."

"We didn't take it. We could have, but we didn't. U.S. policy is to go through the Five Eyes intelligence experts—you know, our allies—first before we do anything like this. We do monitor external activity. For example, we knew you had uploaded something to your cloud in the area of operations. Our policy, however, prevents us from looking at precisely what you uploaded. Two pictures. That's all we know. Then our satellite picked up the fighters that chased you out of town. We did facial recognition on them, and they are three well-known ISIS fighters, meaning they are bandits who will fight for the highest dollar, usually more. They could be on the Russian, Syrian, or Iranian payrolls. It changes too quickly for us to know for certain."

"But they're not on your payroll?" Sassi quipped.

Cartwright nodded. "Touché. No, they're not and never have been. At least not these particular mercenaries. I won't lie. We've had our share of alliances here in the area that I'm not proud of, but these guys aren't one of them."

Sassi sat down in the chair and leaned back. "There were maps with pins and strings. The main pin was in the Port of Tripoli, Lebanon. That string led to Cyprus. And then there were multiple strings from Cyprus to North America."

"That's helpful. What do you think it meant?"

"You're the army general. You tell me," Sassi said.

"Well, it could be that the people who live there are opening a business and they see Tripoli to Cyprus as their best trade route to go to market in the eastern United States. Lots of black market in Cyprus and lots of disguising point of origin. Might be Syrians trying to evade the sanctions."

Sassi stared at the general, whose eyes remained fixed on her. It was obvious that he didn't believe a word he was saying. She gave him credit for having an active imagination. There were no merchants in sight at that location or neighborhood, and he knew it.

"You seem unconvinced," Cartwright said.

"I was about to say the same thing about you," Sassi replied.

The general chuckled. "Fencing with you is no easy task."

"Nor should it be. I have an inherent distrust of the military. Not just the United States but all militaries. I'm no pacifist or kooky believer in utopia, but neither am I giving the benefit of the doubt to the military, regardless of the country. I've seen the horrors you people inflict. You drop your bombs from miles up in the sky or shoot your rifles from hundreds of yards away. Your artillery comes out of the sky from nowhere. And innocent men, women, and children suffer. I understand that there is evil in this world. I've seen it when I was chained to a wall in a basement in Fallujah. I'd made my peace. Soldiers didn't save me that day. The village elder did. Eventually, the soldiers came, and the ensuing fight destroyed the town. Whose fault was it? Who knows? It was war. After the Sunni uprising, I moved hundreds of families back into Anbar Province only to find rubble. But they made do. You know why?"

She didn't give him a chance to answer.

"Because it was home. It was what they knew and where they and their ancestors had lived all their lives. It was easier to rebuild on familiar ground than restart on unfamiliar ground. I don't trust the military. I do trust the heart's desire to be home. Those are the principles by which I operate."

Cartwright looked over each shoulder, as if there were an audience behind him listening to Sassi's speech.

"Words to live by. I don't trust that my own government knows what the hell they're doing. The intelligence community is too busy spying on each other to be any good to us over here. All I know are my capabilities and mostly those of my men. Flanigan there? He may be the biggest nerd in the world, but there's nothing he can't do inside the wires."

"Except get my pictures back . . . if he doesn't already have them."

Cartwright shook his head with a rueful smile. He raised his arms in mock surrender. "I capitulate."

"I figured you for a tougher fighter than that, General. No wonder you guys are losing." Sassi smiled.

"Wasn't aware we were losing," Cartwright said.

"Part of the problem, isn't it?"

"Let's try this. You're obviously very smart and, it seems, creative. You've seen plenty of plots and schemes. Give me your wildest scenario that you think could stem from what was being planned on that map."

Sassi paused, held back a quip, and said, "Assuming it wasn't a child's homework assignment, my immediate impression was that al-Ghouta has been the site of so many chemical attacks. There have been rumors that the Syrians dropped the chemicals from helicopters and airplanes, and there have been rumors that the rebels gassed the civilians to blame Assad. I don't really care, because the net effect is the same. Civilians were gassed with sarin, a deadly nerve agent, and as I've made clear, everyone is culpable, regardless of army or affiliation. My point being that it is possible that someone has a stash of chemical weapons and is planning to transport them to Tripoli, load them on a ship that docks in Cyprus, and then something happens there that perhaps weaponizes the chemicals for some type of attack in Europe or the United States."

She held out her hands and said, "The best I can do."

"Pretty damn good," Cartwright said.

"Close?"

"We have no idea. I'm sure there are other markings on the pictures that could help us. Maybe I can send a team in with you tomorrow morning. Patalino and Ruben are two of my best."

"I won't even consider that. No," Sassi said.

"You're packing right now, so don't give me that. But, yes, that actually is an option. I'll have a small team go in with you tomorrow to try to get in the basement. We have an asset over that area right now studying patterns of life. I'm not authorized to send troops into that area—"

"I know you're not, but that doesn't stop anyone else from doing it. Russians were there today. I see Syrians all the time. It's a shit show. The last thing we need is to add Americans to the mix."

"You have to return the girl—"

"Her name is Fatima Abel."

"Yes. You have to return Fatima. So, we will send a small security team with you. You show them the house next door, and they'll go in and get pictures while you're returning Fatima to her family."

Sassi thought about the balance between her and Fatima's personal safety and the second-order effects the footprint of U.S. military personnel might create. If it weren't for Fatima, she would stay wedded to her consistent position that she does not conduct joint operations with military personnel or allow them in her sector. But she had taken Fatima from her neighborhood under the pressure of ISIS rebels looking for a place to reconstitute.

"No uniforms," Sassi said. "Civilian clothes. And none of that macho American cowboy bullshit. I'll lose all creditability if I'm seen with these guys. I go in separately with Fatima and Hakim, my interpreter, and your guys come in either before or after. I'll park my SUV four houses away and, assuming your guys can count, they enter the fourth house and they'll have access to the tunnel I was in."

Cartwright nodded. "Okay. Deal."

"I don't want to know your guys or meet them. I help in this fashion only. You Americans are famous for destroying something and then leaving it. I'm trying to rebuild a community here. I don't need your cowboys coming in and shooting it up."

"Should be a clean operation," Cartwright said.

"Famous last words of every military guy with whom I've ever spoken."

Sassi stood and shouldered her small rucksack. "I'm leaving at zero four hundred hours with Fatima and maybe another family. I haven't decided yet. I'll be there about eight a.m., give or take. My UN vehicle has the number twenty-seven on top."

"I know this."

"Of course you do. I'm telling you so that you don't shoot my vehicle. Or at least if you do, I'll be able to curse you with my dying breaths."

"I'm feeling all sorts of love here, Ms. Cavezza."

"You want love? Go find a Turkish hooker. You

want my help? Stay out of my way and don't look a gift horse in the mouth. I'm doing more for you than I have anyone else. And it's only because I believe fifty-one percent to forty-nine percent that you are being honest with me."

"Tight margin right there."

"That's as wide as it gets when I'm dealing with the military."

"You need me, call me," Cartwright said, handing her a card.

Sassi took the card, nodded, and walked outside, brushed past Schmidt, and bounced down the steps. When she returned to her room, Fatima was under a blanket, sleeping on a cot next to Sassi's bed, clutching Aamina tightly to her chest as she sucked her thumb.

Sassi didn't want to imagine what dreams might be coursing through Fatima's mind, so she focused on Cartwright.

Decent guy, she thought. But time would tell. It always did. She had an uneasy feeling about tomorrow and knew that she needed rest if she was to be on her A game. She brushed her teeth, stripped, wiped all the appropriate areas with a wet cloth and soap, pulled on fresh cargo pants, polypro T-shirt, and socks. She placed her boots at the bottom of the bed and hung her outer tactical vest and pistol on the metal bed frame next to her head, crawled into bed, rehearsed in her mind reaching for the pistol—one, reach; two, grab; three, aim; four, shoot—and began the process of shutting down her mind.

Something Cartwright had said had made her uneasy.

She couldn't remember it. The words floated in the outer reaches of her memory like a soaring hawk.

Should be a clean operation.

And peace would also fall upon the Middle East by the morning.

CHAPTER 6

Jasar Tankian

Jasar Tankian unhappily stood on a ridge that on the map looked like a bony finger reaching into the Beqaa Valley. The moon hung brightly above the Anti-Lebanon Mountains in the east, reminding him that the long night of combat was still at hand. In the last six hours, one of his drones had been shot down and a sniper had nearly killed him. He'd had better nights.

Despite his lack of sleep, he ensured the Mercedes-Benz trucks were properly parked in the motor pool at the far end of the compound and then instructed his drone operations team to scout for any following enemy forces. Three fixed-wing drones flew below him in a synchronous pattern in the wide canyon, the northernmost section of the Great Rift Valley, a series of volcanic peaks and fissures running from Lebanon through the Red Sea all the way to Tanzania's Mount Kilimanjaro and Olduvai Gorge.

These Russian Sobirat drones had twelve-foot wing-spans, could fly at altitudes up to two miles, and could reach distances two hundred miles away. *Sobirat* was the Russian term for "gather," and the reconnaissance drone was a complementing aircraft to the new Russian Hunter S-70 Okhotnik attack drone.

Hunter-gather.

The Sobirat drones were like synchronized swimmers in the air, dipping and diving all in concert with one another. Tankian nodded at his engineer, who cut the radio feed, and the drones continued apace to their target across the valley, swooping like graceful eagles eyeing a kill. A small bald man named Rafik Khoury was standing next to him with the remote operating viewer, commonly called a *ROVER*.

Khoury was Tankian's longtime business partner. Originally from Beirut, Khoury had been alongside Tankian for every major transaction and had partnered with him fourteen years ago. Khoury knew about Tankian's isolation and skepticism, while Tankian knew about Khoury's womanizing and alcohol binges. Khoury was the operations officer to Tankian's chief executive role.

Tankian lowered the night-vision goggles and said, "Okay, collect them when they return. Let me know if there are any problems. I want to see the results broken down by aircraft for the entire length of the flight. Don't hide flaws. Last night was a disaster. We should have killed whoever that was in the mountains shooting at us."

He spoke with a thick Arabic accent. Lebanese by birth, he was raised by a father who ran the largest bank in Lebanon before radical Islam had destroyed the financial center of the Middle East. His mother had been a businesswoman as well, running a commercial real estate enterprise in Beirut that was once the envy of most Mediterranean nations and was now nothing but a hollowed core of steel and jagged glass rising from the streets like zombies awaiting the call to action.

During Operation Peace for Galilee in 1982, the Israelis had killed his parents with an errant air strike. He had been wounded by a burning white-phosphorous marking munition. The bomb had exploded outside their summer home, which was situated on the western plateau overlooking the Beqaa Valley. A favorite terrorist hideout, Beqaa became the target of the Israeli air strikes, which everyone in Lebanon also believed were directed by the new American president, Ronald Reagan. A year later, terrorists had bombed the United States Marine barracks, and the entire country began circling the drain.

Tankian's face was scarred, his flat black eyes peering out from skin grafts that looked intentionally placed there by Hollywood horror makeup artists. His eyelids were folded tufts of skin, decreasing the range of how wide he could open his eyes. He was eternally half-lidded, a lizard caught in mid-blink. His lips were malformed, peeled back against his teeth in a perpetual sneer. When he smiled, which was infrequent, Tankian's only tell was the slight, nearly audible crinkling of the skin on his left cheek.

The left side of his body had been badly burned. The explosion was nearly a hundred meters away, but he had turned too slowly, and the burning phosphorous had whizzed through the air, smothering his left side like a blanket as he turned away. Rolling down the hill into a stream, all unintentional on his part, had been the only way for him to survive. While underwater, dousing the flames that seemed stuck like jelly to his skin, he had heard the muffled thuds, like mattresses dropping on a floor, along the ridge above him.

He had crawled back up the ridge to his home where he found his childhood in smoldering ruins. The marking round had done its job. The subsequent bombing run had killed his parents and brother. To this day, he had no idea why Israeli jets had indiscriminately bombed his family and the other homes along the ridge. It was true that the Beqaa Valley was home to Hezbollah and Al Qaeda terror training camps. There, they traded tactics, techniques, and procedures in the 1980s and 1990s before Al Qaeda had become the dominant gene among the terrorist organizations. But to his knowledge, his parents were the successful businesspeople they claimed to be, and his older brother was simply a teenager who liked a girl. As a kid, Tankian liked to run along the ridge where he now stood, chased by his brother in a silly game of tag. Tankian had been fast, but his brother was quicker. They darted underneath the electric fence lines designed to keep the cattle in their pasture while also holding would-be thieves at bay.

Tankian had been just ten years old at the time of the bombing in 1982. In an instant, his entire family was obliterated. Oddly, he didn't harbor any resentment toward the Israelis or Americans. The one thing he had learned at the knee of his business-oriented parents was that everything was indeed about business. Money was the ultimate motivator. Ideology was for the pawns, the true believers who could be mobilized in the name of some cause that served a higher purpose—which, it turned out, was typically a monetary one for those ultimately in charge.

Tankian knew that groups such as ISIS were, at their core, businesses. ISIS raided a village or town, controlled its assets, kidnapped dignitary children, charged ransom, and moved to the next village to repeat the process. The leaders were millionaires, the ideologues were dead or wounded. Over the last four decades, he'd observed the comings and goings of terrorist leaders through the Beqaa Valley and Beirut. They were all capitalist heathens who violated every principle of the Koran in private, while extolling its virtues in public and during information operations. The Koran meant nothing to Tankian. The only god he worshipped was currency, and on that he was even agnostic, preferring dollars and pounds but willing to accept euros and a few other types of exchange that held their value: gold, silver, and diamonds. It was rare that he bartered in anything else.

Tankian had met both Osama and Hamza bin Laden,

Zarqawi, Baghdadi, Maliki, Kuwaiti, Soleimani, and others who used the land in the Beqaa Valley as training and transshipment grounds. Unbeknownst to Tankian as a child, his parents had purchased a large portion of the valley and the ridge above, allowing them to control its ingress and egress points. Tankian had parlayed this thousand-acre asset, which included tunnels and mock villages, into a massive commercial real estate enterprise: a training ground for terrorists. His bona fides as a war orphan at the hands of the Zionists provided him the authenticity required to do business with every unsavory actor in the Middle East. They all assumed he hated America and Israel, and he did nothing to dissuade them from believing this notion. The very fact that he leased land to terrorist organizations that attacked Israel and America was good enough to make him valid in the eyes of the ever-suspicious Bin Ladens of the world.

"Yes, sir," Khoury said. He was a sharp businessman himself and expert engineer. He had replicated the aircraft, their engines, weapons systems, and the cameras. In the light manufacturing area next to the stables in Tankian's compound, Khoury had assembled and tested the aircraft that were now flying over the valley. He had built twenty fixed-wing unmanned aerial vehicles that could fly connected to radio, satellite, or by way of GPS guidance. In addition to spying on copycat logistics competitors, Tankian intended to also spy on the terrorist training camps to potentially blackmail his clients. He could sell this information to the highest bidder, typically Max Wolff, his German benefactor, but he didn't discount opportunities with the Americans, Israelis, Syrians, and Russians. Money was money.

Khoury held the ROVER up so Tankian could see the thermal image on the display. A Russian cargo truck was bouncing up the severe terrain, negotiating the switchbacks, and cresting the plateau. He handed the ROVER back to Khoury, who frowned and said, "What could he want?"

"Something important if he's driving here," Tankian said. In the floodlights of Tankian's compound, the Russian truck stopped, coughed, and spat black diesel from its charred smokestack poking above the cab. Captain Igor Padarski stepped out and walked toward him. The Russian had black hair, a sharp-edged nose, and beady black eyes. His olive uniform was unkempt and dirty, and he smelled of diesel fuel and onions.

"Commander," Padarski said in greeting.

"Captain," Tankian replied. "Tell me about the woman we saw on the video." Two of Tankian's drones had also accompanied Padarski's tanks into al-Ghouta, part training, part operational.

Padarski held his crewman's helmet under his armpit as he spoke through chipped teeth to Tankian.

"I'll tell you about the woman, and then you tell me what intelligence you collected with these aircraft." He nodded at the ROVER and then pointed at the sky.

"Perhaps we can trade information," Tankian said. The captain was his liaison with the Russian government for the last six months. Tankian had higher connections, but he preferred to deal with the individual who could spend the money.

"She was in the village with a little girl and her interpreter."

"She's coming back, no?"

For the past six months, Padarski and his Russian tank company had been using his land for a logistics base. They were the quick-reaction force for Syria should the Israelis invade. Russia needed to protect its port in Tartus. If the Israelis stormed up the valley, the tank company could hold them off until Russian jets scrambled and evened out the playing field.

As with everything he did, Tankian developed a personal relationship with the Russian tank commander. In addition to running resupply convoys to Syrian combat units, he sold the Russian peacekeeping units fuel, food, water, and medical supplies. Tankian's enterprise was about forty personnel strong, which included a security team of twenty hardened fighters whose collective strength was appearing to be ordinary mechanics or day laborers, yet they were armed with pistols, knives, and rifles.

Listening to the tank commander talk about the UNHCR woman, ideas pinged in his brain. It was almost always a bad idea to kidnap a relief worker for a nongovernmental organization. It drew international attention and unwanted visitors. But he listened, because he was always angling for the financial upside. He had no moral issues with kidnapping anyone or housing people others had kidnapped. There was a price for everything.

"Yes, she's coming back. She comes back every day with more families."

"What has happened that makes this an emergency?" Tankian asked.

"Some rogue elements, either ISIS or Syrian rebels, came out of the neighborhood chasing her. I think she saw something," Padarski said.

"What might she have seen?" This was Tankian's real concern. He had equities in al-Ghouta that promised a larger payday.

"I'm not sure. But she ran out of one of the houses, and next door, three men ran out at the same time, chasing her. She got in her UN vehicle and sped away with the child and her interpreter."

Part of the barter Tankian had with the tank company was that they would provide him information on the resettlements in the villages around Damascus in exchange for smuggled cigarettes and vodka. There was no shortage of useful goods in one of Tankian's supply warehouses. Initially, he wasn't sure about the financial opportunities in the resettlement operation, the UN being cash rich but stingy when it came to doling out contracts. At the very least, he saw opportunities to sell supplies and perhaps even construction services.

Tankian Logistics Group *had* won a small UN contract to build or reconstruct ten homes in the village of Ghouta. The contract called for purifying the area, cleansing the chemicals Assad's Syrian air force and army had dropped there. Tankian's bulldozers had scraped three feet deep and hauled away the contaminated soil, which he'd dumped along the Turkish border at night.

"So, if there's something she believed to be valuable, she would have reported it to UN headquarters, correct?" Tankian said.

"Yes, most likely."

"We have contacts there, right?"

"We do," Padarski said. Then, as if the thought were a hammer to the head, he slapped his forehead and said, "I will discreetly inquire."

"Discreetly," Tankian said. "But also, go see what she saw. I'll make it worth your while."

Tankian thought he knew what she might have seen, and it would not be good for his German investor, Max Wolff, who was providing Tankian Logistics Group with its largest payday yet.

"I may have already taken a look."

"Even better," Tankian said.

"There's a basement with maps. Something to do with ports. Maybe blocking them," Padarski said.

This was a problem. Someone had gotten sloppy with preparations and rehearsals. The question for Tankian was whether to kill the Russian now or later. He decided he had enough on his plate at the moment and would wait.

"Thank you. You've been very helpful," Tankian said.

"What do I get for giving you this information?"

"I will include steak and lobster in your next rations delivery."

"We're due for that anyway."

"Then I will make sure it doesn't go away."

Padarski glared at him as Tankian stood silhouetted against the mountains and the moon, and then turned and walked toward his truck. Once the truck departed, Tankian left Khoury in the parking area and walked about a quarter mile up a small ridge, where he stared at the crater that was once his childhood summer home. He felt nothing. No hatred. No remorse.

When he looked in that crater, he saw opportunity, not loss.

His phone buzzed with an encrypted text from Khoury: *Aircraft down vic Lake Qaraoun.*

Lake Qaraoun was twenty miles south of his location. The Sobirat had served its purpose again.

He called Khoury. "What do we know?"

"Just the imagery. I'm looking at it now on the ROVER. Small aircraft. Looks like a cargo plane."

"Okay, I want a four-man team to Lake Qaraoun. Tell them that an airplane has crashed and to bring back everything and everyone they can. Immediately."

"Yes, boss."

He lifted his night-vision goggles to his eyes and watched his men jog to the warehouse where they kept the Suburban SUVs. Two of them pulled out and raced to the south.

He looked back in the crater, now overgrown with grass and weeds and nothing more than a useless piece of land. Turning back to the east, he saw the Russian truck lights navigating the switchbacks and chided himself for being harsh with the captain. The Russian resupply contract was his mainstay at the moment—at least until the operation planned in al-Ghouta came to fruition.

The resettlement of refugees to the city of al-Ghouta had been a windfall, but the UN contract—if they ever paid—was minor compared with the opportunities that had spun off from that contract. Like the men who had provided the picks, axes, dungarees, and pans to gold miners, Tankian understood that being a supplier and facilitator generally carried less risk than the bounty hunters pursuing the prize or bounty, whatever it may be. One month, it could be the utopian notion of peaceful resettlement of all civilians in the Damascus suburbs. The next month, it could be the Syrian drive to reclaim the Golan Heights or Galilee. And the next, Turkey could pursue eradicating ISIS from its borders. Ideas and movements came and went, as did the true believers subscribing to the latest scriptures. The one thing they had in common, Tankian had figured out early, was that they needed safe houses, training ranges, supplies, and transportation.

The beauty of having the lines of supply inside the Beqaa Valley was that Tankian's business enterprises could cater to all these activities in a legitimate way.

Now a plane crash? What bounty could that bring?

Tankian punched the code to enter the back gate to his compound. Ascending the steps to his pool, he turned and looked into the valley. Lights twinkled along the north-south artery road that provided for the life functions of war: training, personnel replacement, and resupply.

His phone buzzed again: *Eyes on plane crash. On foot. More to follow.*

His curiosity was piqued. He hoped his men were first at the location. If it was a Syrian jet, he could secure the crash site and claim that he had tried to rescue the pilots. If it was an Israeli jet, he could call the Syrians or Hezbollah and sell access to the location. His mind clicked into overdrive, considering the possibilities.

However, unlikely, if this was somehow an American plane, then the possibilities were endless. His first obligation would be to Wolff, of course. If he deferred, then he would go to the Russians, Iranians, and Syrians, in that order.

But Wolff would come first. Tankian had an interesting relationship with Wolff. They had met in Beirut as Tankian was picking up a delivery of new trucks. Wolff had combined business with pleasure, as he was known to do, by visiting the port, observing the off-loading, meeting some of his customers, and then heading off to an exclusive beachside retreat near the Israeli border.

Tankian and Wolff had connected initially because they were about the same size. Both were large men at six and a half feet tall and over 250 pounds. Where Tankian was dark and had black hair, Wolff was fair, though ruddy, with thick gray hair. They towered over everyone else, and when they were watching the stevedores off-load the ships three years ago, Wolff had approached him, saying, "They could use a couple of guys our size to help break those blocks and chains, huh?"

Tankian had replied, "I'm ready if you are."

Lighthearted chatter led to a more serious conversation, which led to a substantial overture from Wolff. If Tankian would be his eyes and ears on the ground in Syria and Lebanon, then Wolff would make it worth his while. Hesitant to accept Wolff's sincerity on blind faith, Tankian had told him he'd consider the offer. But before leaving the port that day, Tankian's convoy of purchased new trucks included an additional brand-new Zetros 6×6 truck valued at two hundred thousand euros.

In exchange, Tankian had provided Wolff one kilogram of hashish and one kilogram of opium for his vacation. He would have provided more, but the stevedores had already loaded his shipment to Greece, and what he gave Wolff was what was left over after rewarding the guards, customs officials, and dockmaster. A month later, the next shipment of trucks included another Zetros 6×6 truck, this one with an extended cab.

The trucks weren't no strings attached, however. Wolff had called soon after delivery of the second Zetros and said, "Check the container," and hung up.

Tankian had checked. Inside was a false floor filled with sealable containers. The message was clear. Tankian was to ship Wolff premium heroin and hashish, for which he would be rewarded. The relationship had proved fruitful. The typical shipping route was from Tripoli, Lebanon, to Cyprus, where the containers were triaged and laundered to new destinations every time.

Tankian lifted his head to the wind. He could feel

the breeze only on the right side of his face. It was cool and calming. The left side of his face was hard and unfeeling—like his psyche. All business, no emotions. A theater mask.

"Bring me some good news," he whispered to the wind.

Angling behind his home, he walked near the pool with the white paint and lights reflecting the water upward into the sky. His phone buzzed one final time for the evening. It was Khoury about the plane crash.

Americans.

CHAPTER 7

Vick Harwood

Harwood slapped his wrist a couple of times, hoping the TacSleeve was experiencing a connection issue, but everything else seemed to be in working order. His own latitude and longitude were correctly displayed.

After securing his position by emplacing an early-warning trip wire, he had done the triangulation using an old-school compass by calculating reverse azimuths from the peak of Mount Hermon, a well-marked radio tower toward Damascus, and the smoldering tanks on the valley floor, a location he already had memorized. Drawing the lines backward from those three points created an intersection and validation of his position.

He was exactly where the TacSleeve said he was located.

Just as he made a decision to pick up and move to the crash site to find Clutch, the flash-bang grenade exploded behind him. The report was thunderous, heat washing over his position like a tsunami. He spun, SIG Sauer at the ready in one hand and knife popped open in the other. The ghillie suit was restricting, but he had no time to remove it.

Through his night-vision goggles, he saw two men at the base of the trail. They had tripped his early-warning device. Seeing the wounded or dead men reinforced in his mind the usefulness of this position, which was now burned. He would have to move again anyway. Before he could think about any of that, though, he needed to clear the surrounding area and then conduct sensitive site exploitation of the men who had breached his position.

He started by low crawling to the lip of the outcropping and scanning for good overwatch positions. Any sensible mission included an assault force and a support force. On his third pass of the ridge to the northeast, his infrared goggles detected a faint shimmer, which to Harwood looked like a rifle scope.

The bullet washing over him confirmed this belief.

Scrambling back to his hide position, Harwood retrieved his SR-25 and repositioned. He figured the play was to try to flush him out and have the sniper pick him off.

Behind Harwood was a quarter-mile drop to the jagged rocks lining the base of the ridge. To move north or south would expose him to the enemy sniper on the higher ground to the northwest. His only avenue was the small gorge through which he had entered and where two dead attackers currently lay.

The question Harwood entertained as he gathered his gear and slowly tightened everything into one tight ball was, how big was the assault force? Two people? Four? The typical team included four to eight personnel. Two or four on assault, two or four to support. Some personnel on the assault and support teams would be securing the operation from outside infiltrators. Just as he was a doing mental calculation about how many people he was confronting, so were they. In fact, his pursuers most likely found it difficult to understand that he was a singleton out here all alone. Their belief was most likely that he was part of a larger team. Perhaps they saw the Sabrewing resupply drone enter and exit the area. That, too, would confuse them. Did it drop off more personnel, supplies, or what?

Exploiting that confusion was his best play. How to reinforce his enemy's belief that there *had* to be more soldiers would be difficult, but psychologically, they would be protecting in all directions, which would give him a small window of opportunity.

Harwood low crawled through well-protected terrain to the two dead bodies. They wore olive uniforms with insignia that were difficult to discern in the dark. Their weapons had been thrown during the blast. He collected two AK-47s and set them aside. He had a covered area in which to prepare, as long as the remainder of the assault force didn't come barreling through the opening about ten meters to his front.

The sniper would by now be zeroing in on the one spot that allowed for egress. Assuming the sniper had a spotter, Harwood opened the three-point sling of one of the AK-47s. He then lifted the body of the first dead man, who actually wasn't dead.

"Whaaa," the man muttered. Harwood doubted that anyone heard him, but he couldn't be sure. He quickly looped the sling around the man's neck, seated the magazine, and ensured there was a round the chamber of the AK-47. With the man's arm around him as if they were two drunk buddies walking home from a bar, Harwood nudged the man forward toward the gap. He slid his hand down and placed the man's finger in the trigger housing. As they arrived at the edge of the opening to the trail, Harwood let go of the man, who stumbled forward.

Harwood heard the wet smack of the bullet into the man's chest. Reflexively, the man's finger squeezed the trigger and popped off about three rounds spraying the hillside. Harwood quickly lifted the second man, who was dead, and pushed him through the gap as best he could. This time, the sniper fired a double tap.

Two down, they had to be thinking. The typical makeup of a sniper team was two men.

Harwood retrieved his rucksack and prepared to engage the remainder of the assault force. Two different voices were most likely uttering commands over radios. He braced against the rocks nearest the trail with his rifle hanging from a snap link hooked into his outer tactical vest. He took deep, silent breaths, thought about the moves he had performed a thousand times that would duplicate what he was about to face. A well-trained team would enter with one man clearing to the right and the next clearing to the left. He would have to be fast.

Boots scuffed against the shale directly on the opposite side of the rocks from Harwood. One man whispered something. They were probably checking the dead men. He couldn't give them time to call in that they had just shot their own men who were already dead or close to it.

One man barked a word in Arabic. Boots shuffled. Weapons charged and pinged off the rocks as they clumsily entered the defile. The first man went obliquely left. Bad form, poorly trained.

Harwood shot him in the back of the head with his pistol.

The second man was close behind the first and was better. He turned toward Harwood, raising his rifle, but Harwood was too close, as he had planned. Harwood blocked the upward lift of the man's rifle with his left hand and shot the man in the face with the pistol in his right hand.

He wasted no time and darted through the gap, running north toward the sniper position. The sooner he could get into the dead space beneath the hide site, the better. He sucked in quick breaths, feeling the burn in his lungs. A bullet pinged off the rock wall to his right and spat chips in his face. He powered through with the single purpose of surviving, and survival was about fifty meters away. The rucksack was heavy on his back. His SR-25 slapped against his legs as he did his best to pull it away while still holding his pistol and knife in either hand. His night-vision goggles tilted away, giving him a half view of the dangerous trail ahead. He stumbled and fell forward, his rifle clattering against the rocks.

Speed overrode the need for silence. His legs churned forward like a football player pushing a training sled. He powered up and rounded a bend, rocks falling away to his right. He had come upon a sheer drop-off, barely missing speeding over the ledge and plummeting to certain death. All of it was noisy. His rifle chattered against the snap hook secured to the sling, and his rucksack swished against the rocky walls.

The geography of his immediate vicinity now resembled something like Yosemite's El Capitan. He was on a narrow trail that fell away sharply to his right and was the base of a massive concave wall above. The enemy sniper was located at the top of the concave wall, affording Harwood protection from direct fire from just about any location.

Except helicopters.

He took a minute to adjust his equipment and drink some water from his hydration system. The water found its way through his system and reappeared on his skin as perspiration. The sleeves of his polypro shirt made his arms tingle when wicking away the moisture. Deep breaths in and out. Heart beating against his chest like a bass drum in a rock band. Maybe five feet between his position on the ledge and a mortal fall over the cliff.

As he gathered himself, he thought about Clutch. His TacSleeve was still not showing any ping from

Clutch's locator chip. There was no communication from Stoddard, despite repeated attempts. He tried again, to no avail.

His new mission, whether Stoddard liked it or not, was to move to the last known location of Clutch's tracker. Whether Clutch and the chip were in the same location was a different story, but Harwood believed in the Ranger creed to never leave a fallen comrade behind. The Rangers had taught him as a young soldier the discipline required to prioritize his missions. Whatever his purpose here in the Israel-Syria-Lebanon nexus that was Mount Hermon, he automatically had a new mission: find Clutch. He had maybe six hours of darkness remaining that would cover his movement.

He shaded his TacSleeve with one hand to block the light from shining upward, swiped his thumb across the screen, and studied the map display. He pinched and spread his fingers until he had the location of Clutch's last pin on the display. When he pressed a route function tab, a dotted yellow line chose the most expeditious route to the location that was nearly fourteen miles over the Mount Hermon ridgeline and across the Beqaa Valley to the west.

Not too bad.

He popped the magazine on his pistol and clicked in a new one. He used the kerchief around his neck to wipe his forehead and clean his knife. He tightened his night-vision harness, memorized the route, and darkened the TacSleeve screen. Moving north on the trail, he knew there would be only one spot where the sniper could range him, and that was when he hit the valley floor west of Mount Hermon.

The going was slow at first, Harwood picking his way along the rocky trails. He traversed an area that appeared to be a ski slope, replete with lifts and broad, grassy swaths of land falling away steeply to his right. These runs were danger areas. He moved quickly through the slopes and angled toward the Beqaa Valley and his ultimate destination.

His TacSleeve vibrated, indicating he had a message. He dashed another fifty meters, found a large Syrian juniper with a faded, pale trunk and branches that reached outward in a low semicircular arc. Harwood tucked inside the protective cover and knelt. He lifted the burlap Velcro cover from the TacSleeve and studied the message:

Tracking your movement. Continue mission. Report when on location.

He thought, *Finally!*

Harwood closed his eyes. He assumed that Stoddard was communicating with headquarters. Everything was cryptic and compartmented. He understood classified missions, having conducted several during his short but storied career. He believed in minimizing the people who knew what he was doing and where he was located, and in this age of cyber communications and operations, he was okay with having the tenuous link of encrypted text messages. He was glad that Stoddard remained his lifeline, connecting him to possible medical evacuation or resupply.

But a concern nibbled at the back of his mind. Who

else could track his location and predict where he might be headed? In this heavy cyber-offensive environment, Harwood wasn't sure he wanted to think about all the players. The Russians? The Syrians? The Israelis? The Iranians? Any number of terrorist groups that might have been outfitted with cyber capabilities from any of the other countries? Perhaps all of them were tracking him, or maybe none of them gave a shit about who he was or where he was headed?

Roger. Keep eyes on my route/inform if any bogies. Roger. Out.

With Stoddard back in comms, Harwood pulled the burlap cover over the TacSleeve and began maneuvering through the forest of junipers. The low branches brushed at him, sweeping across his face. The nightvision goggles helped him find the trails through the rocky terrain. Boulders the size of cars poked through the earth, making his descent more problematic than he had anticipated. But he made progress.

It took him five hours to traverse the fourteen miles. When he reached to within a quarter mile of the location where Clutch's beacon had gone off the system, he stopped on a small hillock in the valley and observed. The Sabrewing aircraft was crumpled on the ground.

By now, the sun was edging over the horizon to his back. Everything looked different in the daytime. He knew the saying that everything would be better the next day, but that was not his experience.

Two Suburban SUVs were parked with their lights shining on the Sabrewing drone. Four men milled about the location, searching. The men were carrying AK-47s and appeared military. They weren't wearing any uniforms that he could determine. They were most likely from a terrorist organization, probably Hezbollah. He could hear the men talking but couldn't discern the words. The Sabrewing appeared to have been navigating a gap in the ridge that formed the western side of the Beqaa Valley when it was either shot down or had a malfunction.

Was Clutch alive? Captive?

It occurred to Harwood that the men might have thought there were two people and were looking for a second, having already secured Clutch in one of the SUVs.

He did what any good sniper would do and slowly set up his SR-25, adjusting his scope and lifting his goggles to shoot with the naked eye. Chambering a round, he took a deep breath and placed the crosshairs on the man nearest the Suburban and fired. The silenced weapon was loud in the tranquil valley. The other men lifted their heads in his direction.

They were quick. Harwood snapped off a second round at a man who had already begun moving. The man fell to one knee, and Harwood used that momentary stop to drill a bullet through his head.

The other two had maneuvered behind the Sabrewing, but Harwood still had a shot on one of the men, which he took. The man's head snapped back.

Three down, one to go.

The remaining man must have low crawled to the second Suburban, because the vehicle started, backed away, and began turning onto the road.

Harwood put two bullets into the front driver's-side window, but the glass didn't shatter. It spiderwebbed. Bulletproof.

Harwood stood and ran the remaining quarter mile as the Suburban tore up a dirt trail and onto the asphalt road that led west and north through the gap. It took him a few minutes to run the distance to the other Suburban, and a three-minute head start might as well have been an hour advance lead.

Breathing heavily, he quickly scanned the Sabrewing, saw that it had endured the wreck in survivable fashion. There were bullet holes in one of the tilt-rotor blade housings.

Clutch was shot down? Even if so, the interior was not collapsed, and there was no evidence of blood. The aircraft must have auto-rotated safely to the ground. Someone had cut the cargo straps. Had Clutch done this or these men? Backing out, he checked the three men he'd shot, all dead, and retrieved their weapons and cell phones.

Tossing the gear—including his rucksack—into the passenger's seat of the Suburban, he punched up the Home function on the dashboard display and saw that he had to navigate north along the base of the ridge that overlooked the valley to the east. Curiously, there was a blue icon on the navigation display that was moving along the same route, only it was about three miles ahead of him. It had to be the first vehicle with the one survivor of his ambush . . . and possibly Clutch.

The tracking function was the equivalent of "find

my friends" for vehicles, like the military's blue force tracker. Of course, if he could see them, they could see him unless this was some kind of master vehicle, but he doubted that was likely.

Harwood navigated the pothole-ridden road at 140 kilometers an hour according to the speedometer, passing fields of wheat with the occasional cluster of single-story brick homes. The Beqaa Valley was not unlike the Shenandoah Valley in Virginia. It served as a farming breadbasket for much of Lebanon, Syria, and Turkey. Centuries-old trade routes funneled north and south, with smaller arteries branching off to the ports and cities in the west and Damascus in the east.

The major difference between the Beqaa and Shenandoah Valleys, in Harwood's mind, was that the Beqaa was notorious for being a terrorist haven. If Clutch had been spirited away in the other SUV, there was a strong possibility that he was headed to a terrorist camp. The brief inspection of the men he had killed indicated they were armed and dangerous and had done *something* with Clutch. There was an off chance that Clutch had been thrown from the aircraft during the crash, but that seemed unlikely given the structural integrity of the aircraft. It had landed almost as if it were a glider coming into a French landing zone during the Normandy Invasion. The explosion he heard had to have been something else.

Harwood slowed the SUV as the map display automatically zoomed in, indicating he was close to his destination. He steered the vehicle to a small depression on the reverse slope of whatever lay a half mile ahead.

He threw the SUV gearshift into Park and grabbed his rucksack, the three cell phones, and one of the AK-47s. Sliding out of the front driver's-side door, Harwood ducked low and slid around the back of the Suburban. He found a ditch that was at least five feet deep and paralleled the road. He moved forward in the ditch and found a perpendicular offshoot that climbed up the hill, most likely a water-drainage ditch. He used this funnel as cover and concealment until he had climbed a significant ridge.

The valley below him was in full daylight now, glistening with the morning dew atop the wheat fields dipping slightly with the breeze. The temperature was in the midfifties, perfect for Harwood's trek. Fresh-cut hay and horse manure filled his nostrils. He climbed the steep ridge, pulling against rocks, slipping around boulders, and skirting past a refuse area. Piles of empty water and Coke bottles, assorted food packaging, and similar detritus clogged the narrow gulley he had been climbing.

He low crawled to the top of the southern spine of the gulley and followed that fifty meters up to the ridge. The road he would have taken through the gap was a short fifty meters to his right, beyond the ditch he had traversed. Twenty-five meters to his front was a tan stucco wall with a gate, most likely the path for disposing of trash.

Voices floated over the wall, the words muffled

by the barrier, but barely audible. The men spoke in Arabic, giving Harwood no chance of interpreting the conversation. Both he and Clutch were sanitized. There wasn't an identifying piece of information on them other than their bodily DNA, teeth, and fingerprints, which would require the captors to have access to U.S. military databases.

The unfortunate part of his situation was that he had arrived at daybreak, putting him in potential enemy territory under full daylight for an entire day. He considered his options. He could either use the element of surprise and attack now, or he could hole up somewhere and hide until nightfall. The pros of attacking now were that he would continue his forward momentum and maintain the initiative. The biggest con, of course, was that he had little intel on the compound, no idea of the enemy situation.

Waiting to conduct a raid had its merits. He could recon the location and develop a plan. Of course, waiting also meant that he would lose all element of surprise. The men in the compound would figure out quickly—if they hadn't already—that they had three dead comrades and one live opposing sniper, most likely the partner of the man they had captive.

It would be foolhardy to rush the compound with no information on what he was up against. Against all his baser instincts, he began to slowly shift so that he could move downhill and seek out a decent hide site. He would prefer to be on higher ground, but for the moment, this compound dominated the plateau above the Beqaa Valley. To his right was the road and flat, wind-swept land. To his left was fenced-in farmland with horses and cattle.

As he began easing down from his low perch, Harwood heard a word float over the fence.

"American."

It was sandwiched in the middle of a sentence, a single English word framed by Arabic.

He froze, making sure that no one was talking to him. He'd not seen any movement from any direction, but with the vehicle parked a few hundred meters behind him on the valley floor, it wouldn't take an Interpol agent to know that he was somewhere within however far a person could walk in thirty minutes. A mile in this rugged terrain, maybe two in the flatter valley.

He was lying flat on his stomach with just a sliver of the compound in his view.

The gate opened, and two men came running directly at him.

CHAPTER 8

Sassi Cavezza

Sassi held Fatima's hand as they bumped along the road. Fatima clutched Aamina tightly to her chest in her slumber. They had departed at 4:00 this morning, a full two hours before there was enough sunlight to see the treacherous roads. They were in the back seat with Fatima's head resting on Sassi's lap.

Hakim drove because there were multiple checkpoints where his Turkish, Arabic, English, and maybe even Hebrew skills might be required. Fluent in all four languages, Hakim had worked for five years as an interpreter for the highest bidder, which was usually the cash-flush United Nations, filled with its bureaucrats making fat six-figure salaries. Hakim had told Sassi he was making nearly seventy thousand euros a year, which, in his world, was close to millionaire status. He deserved it, she figured. The job was dangerous, and he was constantly having to negotiate and haggle his way through difficult situations.

On one occasion, they had been stopped at a checkpoint with four men in ski masks and AK-47s, which were aimed directly at her. They emphatically requested "the woman," but Hakim had stepped out of the car, negotiated with them, paid them some amount of cash, and then they moved along.

They followed the winding road from the higher ground to the coast. The trail vehicle's headlights flickered in the rearview mirror every few minutes. The plan was for the Americans to stay a quarter mile behind. She reluctantly had allowed General Cartwright to convince her to allow a two-man team of his soldiers to accompany her so that they could gather the intelligence that had been stolen from her phone. If not for the fact that someone or some entity had violated her electronically, she would not have made the concession. It was heresy to allow military combat personnel on UN missions. Commingling the sacred functions of UN peacekeeping activities with clandestine military missions often backfired on the UN and destroyed its image of neutrality. Today was different, though. She had an uneasy feeling about reentering Ghouta after being chased away yesterday. Fatima's father had called her no less than a dozen times between last night and this morning, yet she let the calls go through to voice mail. She understood mission security better than most, and she held this morning's information close. Except for the Americans in the trail vehicle, only Hakim and General Cartwright knew the arrival time in al-Ghouta.

She hoped. She hadn't even told Schmidt, hoping that by the time he awoke with whichever UN worker he'd been able to coerce into his quarters, he would be so far behind the information flow it would be too late for him to do anything that could negatively impact the mission.

They made decent time until the port town of Latakia, which was already bustling with merchants and smugglers ferrying goods along the streets. Old Peugeot cars and flat-nosed Mercedes-Benz trucks zipped along in both directions. Their white UN SUV was conspicuous by its markings on the two front doors and the roof. In one sense, it said, "Nothing to see here but a couple of global public servants." In another, it said, "Huge target. Harass or kidnap us now."

Next, they approached the port town of Tartus, and the sun was beginning to peek above the mountains to the east. Yellow beams poked through jagged sawtooth peaks like ever-expanding triangles. The Mediterranean Sea was a brilliant blue, the sun skidding off its surface in yellow ribbons. Seagulls hung in the air, gliding against the wind, appearing stationary and defying the laws of aerodynamics. Small waves lapped at the T-shaped jetties that punctuated the coastline. They followed the coast road past low-slung commercial buildings and souks with merchants lifting cages and setting up their catch from the morning or fresh fruit and vegetables picked from the fields the day before.

Traffic was light but building. The gate to the Russian navy base was secured with two soldiers in olive uniforms standing guard at port arms with the AK-47s. The spring morning was cool, and they wore their standard-issue Russian soft cap. Sassi's throat tightened as they passed the Russians, thinking of yesterday's interaction and showdown. After another thirty minutes, they hooked due east and wound their way through the mountains, skirting the northern edge of the Beqaa Valley. The sun now was above the mountains, shining spectacularly through a thin layer of clouds. Springtime in Syria and Lebanon was actually quite beautiful when the clouds were simple moisture in the air as opposed to the wafting smoke of bombs and dirt blown into the sky or the acrid fires started by tracer ammunition.

As they wound along the road on the final thirty minutes, she clutched Fatima's hand tighter, waking the young girl.

"What's the matter, Sassi?" Fatima asked in a tired, soft voice.

"Nothing, Fatima. We're almost there."

"Have you talked to my father?"

"I'm about to call him. We wanted to get close to Ghouta before we did."

"Why? Because of the bad people?"

"No, Fatima, it's just because we don't have reception until we get close."

"Okay," Fatima said. She laid her head down on Sassi's leg again and snuggled close.

Sassi didn't like lying to Fatima, but she couldn't tell

her the truth. Their movement was off schedule intentionally, and they had not publicized their new arrival time. While in many cases it was standard operating procedure to vary travel times and routes, today was unique.

The trail vehicle was about a quarter mile away, a metallic speck in the rearview mirror. As they approached the town, two Russian army tanks were just outside the first neighborhood.

"Tanks," Hakim said.

"I see them. The crew are probably asleep. Keep driving."

Hakim swallowed and nodded.

They slowly passed the tanks without incident. As they cleared the first hurdle, Sassi said, "See. Told you."

"There's that saying about counting chickens," Hakim said.

"Trust me, I know," Sassi said. "Those guys behind us still need to get through."

"You've been pretty quiet about those two."

"Nothing to say. The general said they needed to come into the village to see some things, and I told him we could use the escort. It's borderline, but after yesterday, do you disagree?" she said.

"No. I'm glad they are there, but I would have preferred to at least talk to them up front, before the mission."

"Things are moving fast. Turn here," she said.

"I know the way."

They made a left and then a right and paralleled the main road.

"Stop at the fourth house from where Fatima's doll was yesterday."

"Okay," he said. There was a hint of confusion in his voice.

Hakim slowed and stopped, counted with his lips moving, and then pulled up to one house.

"Here?"

"Looks right," she said.

The homes were small, rectangular, single-story wood-and-brick structures, about one thousand square feet max, maybe a shade deeper than they were wide. Dull gray and brown paint was peeling uniformly across all the houses. Fatima's house was two blocks away, farther into the neighborhood. It was just past 8:00 a.m., the drive having taken them a bit over four hours. Another advantage to leaving early was that they had missed all the significant traffic in the cities that dotted the road. The Lebanese police and military had barely noticed them. Just another UN milk run.

She nudged Fatima. "Okay, honey, let's go."

"Are we home?"

"Almost. We walk from here."

Sassi helped Fatima out of the SUV, and Hakim stood from the driver's seat also. Fatima rubbed her sleepy face with the back of one hand as she carried Aamina like a football with the other.

"I need to pee," Hakim said. "I'll join you in a second." He disappeared behind the first house as Sassi walked along the road to the east holding Fatima's hand. They walked past a few chickens pecking next to the road as a rooster crowed somewhere close by.

The town smelled of burnt coal, spent from a night of warming homes. Even in May, the temperatures hovered in the fifties at night, even cooler at higher altitudes.

She retrieved her phone from her cargo pocket and lifted it, using her thumb to find Fatima's father's number. The trail vehicle pulled to a stop somewhere behind her, its brakes whining. She shook her head at the amateur mistake. If they really were on a mission, they just woke everyone in the neighborhood.

Her phone buzzing with the soft dial tone of the Syrian network provider, she lifted it to her ear.

"When are you coming?" Ahmed Abel asked. "I want Fatima back now."

His voice was laced with anger, as if the man had been pacing all night long. Sassi felt a pang of guilt course through her, despite knowing she had made the right decision. As they rounded the corner two blocks away from where they had parked, she made another mental note to expedite placement of a water trailer on this block. The logistics plan called for one trailer per block, but rebel fighters had hijacked one of the flatbed trucks carrying two trailers. Fatima's block had yet to receive theirs.

Fatima's father was standing in front of their house. He was pacing quickly, holding the phone to his ear and running a hand through his hair. His back was to her as he walked toward the house next door.

"We are close," Sassi said.

He stopped walking and said, "What do you mean?"

"I have Fatima here in the village. We are twenty meters from your home."

Abel turned around. "What do you mean!?"

She punched off the phone as they approached Fatima's father. She confirmed that it was him and that the house was the one she had moved them into a couple of days ago.

"Here we are," Sassi said. She spread her arms, with one hand holding the phone and one hand still clasping Fatima's hand. The effect was Sassi raising Fatima's arm as if she were declaring her champion. Though perhaps there was no victory in reuniting her with this angry man, who was conversely more upset at the timing of their arrival than happy with the fact that she had actually delivered his daughter back to him.

"Why did you surprise me? No warning?" Abel accused. He looked over his shoulder with a twitchy motion and then jerked his head back toward Sassi.

Sassi focused on her peripheral vision, noticing movement a few houses up the road. It occurred to her that the two or three people who were scurrying around were near a house that was two blocks directly behind the home where she had retrieved Fatima's doll.

"The reception was bad most of the way. You were so upset last night, we wanted to return Fatima to you as soon as possible. As you can see, she's happy and healthy. She ate a big meal last night and slept well on the trip this morning. I'm not sure I see the issue," Sassi said.

For the first time, Abel looked down at his daughter.

There was a moment of empathy, love reflected in his eyes. The nervousness shifted for a flash to a soulful, wounded look. He had missed his daughter, Sassi registered, even worried about her. So, why the agitated behavior? If she had been in his shoes, she would be on two knees hugging Fatima, glad to have her back, promising never to let her out of her sight again.

"Fatima. Come. Let's go," Abel said. His demeanor shifted quickly back to agitation. The activity in her periphery increased.

She knelt and kissed Fatima's forehead, then hugged her. Running her hands down Fatima's shoulders, Sassi whispered, "You've been a good girl. So brave and strong. I will come back to see you."

"Every day? Please?"

"Every day. Yes. Of course," Sassi said.

"Let's go, Fatima. Come into the house now," Abel barked.

Something was happening up the road, but Sassi maintained eye contact with Fatima.

"Be brave, Fatima. I'll check on you every day that I can."

"But that's not every day," Fatima said.

"It will be every day possible."

After a second, Fatima seemed to register that the balance between Sassi's promises and her father's demands had shifted toward her father. She hugged Sassi's neck one final time and stepped away.

"Thank you for getting Aamina back for me," Fatima said.

"You're welcome, Fatima. Now, go with your father."

Fatima walked to her father, who didn't hug her but simply guided her into the house while looking over his shoulder intermittently at Sassi and the house up the road. He urged Fatima into their newly resettled home. Fatima looked over her shoulder with large, seemingly reluctant brown eyes. She waited until the wood frame door slapped against the jamb and the clicking of the dead bolt rang like a pistol shot before turning to head back to the car.

Sassi had been so absorbed in the moment that she just now realized Hakim was not with her, nor was he anywhere in sight. She strode quickly back to the street she had followed to reach Fatima's house and then made her way toward the main artery they had taken into town. To her left, there was movement, as if someone was tracking or following her. From Fallujah, Iraq, to Herat, Afghanistan, Sassi had been in difficult combat situations. Those circumstances had helped her develop a sixth sense when operating in different locations. While she was certainly concerned about being chased from the village yesterday, Sassi had chalked that up to poking her nose where it didn't belong. If the armed men had been serious about coming after her, they would have pursued. It was just another near miss, like so many others she had encountered and survived.

But being followed in a nearly vacant war-stricken town was never a positive development unless children were the ones following in pursuit of relief or safety.

After all, that was Sassi's life mission: taking care of the displaced families of the world, especially the children, who deserved so much better.

She spotted their UN vehicle, but still no sign of Hakim. She saw the men who had been in the trail car dash across the street, running from her right to left in the direction of the house from which she had retrieved Aamina. They were carrying M4 rifles with silencers and wearing outer tactical vests over their black shirts and olive cargo pants. Their desert-tan hiking boots kicked up dust as they sprinted. One was tall and lanky; the other was short and stocky. They both had short hair, not completely shaved, but as if they had been trying their best to grow it out.

Two men charged at her from her right, a direction that she had not anticipated. All the activity had been to her left. Before they could reach her, she dashed ahead of them toward the UN SUV. Heart racing and lungs burning, she dug deep. Always a good athlete, Sassi was able to outrun these two men. She doubted they would shoot her in the back, even though she hated to even think about such an eventuality. Her motive was pure. Her mission was universally respected and accepted. It would be senseless to harm her in any way. The foundation of her belief system was that she had survived so many tough situations because of the purity of her motive and mission. Even the evilest, vilest people could see through their hatred and understand that children required protection.

Nothing could happen to her because, well, it simply wasn't allowed. Not by international law. Not by the lowest standards of human dignity. Not for any reason. The children came first, always.

Three things were happening all at once, as best she could determine. First, she was being chased by two armed gunmen who were ten meters behind her. Second, two American military members were stacked against the wall of the house with the maps in its basement. Third, a motionless figure was lying in the side street to her left. It was the same street that Hakim had veered onto in order to relieve himself.

As Sassi reached the UN vehicle, she remembered that Hakim had driven and had the keys. She hoped it was unlocked. She leaped across the hood of the car, sliding to the other side, where she adroitly landed like a gymnast doing a dismount. Instead of raising both arms to the sky, she retrieved her pistol and sighted on the two men closing on her.

An explosion rocked the map house, and the muffled *pop, pop, pop* of gunfire echoed from below. Her immediate concern was that her pursuers stopped running and leveled their AK-47s on her. She hadn't had to fire her weapon in defense in the ten years since Iraq, but she did so now without reservation.

She fired at the man who already had his AK-47 leveled at her. The shot caught him in the arm, spinning him away from her and causing him to reflexively squeeze the trigger. Wild shots zipped over her head, but she didn't flinch. The second man had just completed raising his rifle, having fumbled with it for a brief moment, giving her time to squeeze a second shot, which was far more accurate than the first.

The man fell like a shot quail, dropping straight to the ground with a bullet wound to his chest. She was up quickly, running around the front of the SUV and kicking away the weapon of the wounded man. Both men wore gray shirts and black pants with red bandannas. As Sassi recalled, they were members of an ISIS offshoot, but she couldn't remember its name, which was unimportant at the moment anyway.

Her immediate questions were, how many more of them were there, and why were they coming after her?

What was happening in those two houses with the maps and the doll?

Was Hakim okay?

Her mind tumbled with all those thoughts as she put away her pistol and searched both men for weapons and cell phones. She had learned to do this in Anbar Province. Tough times had sharpened her combat edge, even though she was loath to use the skills. First gathering two knives and two cell phones, she stuffed them in her cargo pocket as she jogged in the direction she had seen the body lying in the street—*Please don't let it be Hakim!*

Rounding the corner, she nearly collapsed. Hakim was lying motionless in a pool of blood, his throat slit, most likely by one of the knives she had just collected from the men she shot.

More gunfire erupted from the map house and its neighbor. Two men dressed the same as the two she had just shot came barreling from the back door as two Americans popped out close behind them, giving chase. As soon as the two ISIS splinter cell gunmen disappeared behind a house, a barrage of gunfire opened from the windows of a house just kitty-corner from where Sassi was kneeling above Hakim's body.

Ambush.

The gunmen were the rabbits, and the Americans raced directly into a baited ambush. They dove for cover quickly, but she had no time to process the rapidly deteriorating situation. A presence behind her was preceded by foul body odor. The arm of a man reached around her neck with the other hand lifting her hair, as if he was preparing to slice her neck open, perhaps as he had done to Hakim.

She took a deep breath, caught off guard that this could really be the moment she died. She would die because she had returned a little girl to her family and home. A war-torn, shithole of a home, but the only home Fatima had known, nonetheless. It was home, and that was where she had committed to returning Fatima and thousands of other children and families.

It was years since Sassi had been home to Tuscany, and now there would be no one to mourn her. She thought of her secondary school and university friends, all fleeting relationships once they saw she was an international justice vagabond, marching to the sound not of the cannon but to the shrieks of young children. Perhaps the children would be her angels? Her family certainly would barely notice that she was gone. Maybe a quick funeral to pay respects and not lose status in the community, followed by a larger party to celebrate the fact that she'd died for a noble cause despite repeated admonishments about her career path. It would be a highbrow soirée with the Tuscan elite, including the mayors and governors of several towns and provinces. They would celebrate one another and their feigned support for the dignified pursuit of human justice in the grittiest of circumstances.

She saw the blade glint in the morning sun. The man poured stale breath on her. His prickly black beard scratched her face as he leaned in close and said, "Pray to Allah."

Sassi closed her eyes, trembling against the cool steel of the blade.

CHAPTER 9

Vick Harwood

Harwood made himself small, as Command Sergeant Major Murdoch had always instructed him to do. He crawled inside a deep cut in the wadi so that his body, weapon, and rucksack were fully beneath the level of the slope.

He was inside a ragged gash that had been hollowed out by repeated rain. Back in Georgia where he lived, torrential downpours created these man-sized ravines. The only climate he had experienced here in the Lebanon-Syria border area was arid, but he imagined that when it rained, the water sliced through the clay and shale like a sharp knife. Up close, his nose was pressed into the dirt. Rocks and pebbles poked from the wall of the gully, one storm away from being washed downhill. Dirt smelled pretty much the same wherever he was—musty, fresh, and oddly comforting. Burlap from the ghillie suit mixed with the aroma as well, helping conceal his position. Harwood had spent what seemed like a lifetime boring into the dirt. The ground had saved his life on several occasions, and he hoped this would be another one for the record books.

Boots trundled past him downhill. The two men shouted at each other in Arabic. He imagined they were discussing who might have driven the SUV and where that person might be. They probably received a GPS ping on the Suburban. The man who had escaped knew it was unlikely that any of his three comrades had survived. It wasn't a stretch to assume that the man who had ambushed them—the Reaper—had also commandeered the vehicle. That suspicion would have the entire compound, if not the entire valley, on high alert.

Harwood considered his options again. Attack in broad daylight with the initiative, if not the element of surprise, or wait until nightfall and conduct a full reconnaissance. The enemy always had a vote in his plans also. His experience had taught him that even the best-developed plans included envisioning all the enemy options and possibilities. He could be discovered in this prone position and shot dead, for example. The likelihood of someone tripping over him increased with every hour of daylight, with every minute that the team at the compound realized what had taken place.

Harwood didn't discount the idea that there might be a connection between whatever was happening in the compound and what was happening along the Israeli border with Syria. Without much warning, Syria had attacked Israel in the oft-contested Golan Heights in an attempt to reclaim what the Syrian president saw as historically Syrian land. Whoever owned the Golan Heights had the strategic and tactical advantage, particularly from a defensive point of view with respect to Israel. Hezbollah and the Syrian Army worked side by side with the assistance of Iran to fight the United States via proxy in Israel.

All those entities were invested in some fashion in the Beqaa Valley. Training, logistics, recruiting, and other crucial military functions took place here. Harwood had done his homework regarding the region prior to deployment. There were any number of terrorist groups and very few lifelines to be found in the Beqaa.

After a few minutes of contemplation, he had reached his decision.

He rotated his body so that he was on his back, looking skyward. A few wisps of high-layer clouds floated like jet contrails in the sky. His rucksack poked into his back, straightening his spine a bit. A flood of exhaustion swept over him, but he couldn't succumb to it. To do so would be certain death. He listened, taking in the distant sounds of the two men running. They continued downhill. He had kept the key to the Suburban but suspected they had a spare.

A few minutes later, the SUV engine rumbled and whined as it climbed the hill. Two doors slammed, accounting for both men. The gate squeaked as it opened and then banged shut. Men spoke loudly in the backyard. The agitated tones said more than the words he couldn't understand. Their men were dead. Someone had stolen the truck. They needed to find this person.

A baritone voice of a presumably big man silenced the four or five men talking. He barked out instructions. Harwood visualized the alpha among the group pointing at one man and then another as he issued concise directives. The voice was commanding and authoritative. He conjured an image of the big man in the logistics convoy in Syria who had been controlling the drones. His final directives were peppered with the word *American*.

Either they had Clutch and he was issuing instructions on what to do with him, or he suspected an American was behind the kills at the Sabrewing drone crash site and was detailing a plan of how to pursue the killer.

Or both.

CHAPTER 10

Sassi Cavezza

The problem for the man was that he flinched.

Sassi sensed that the soldier who held a knife to her throat had looked away. It was nothing obvious, just a simple turn of the shoulders, a slight distraction that caused the blade of the knife to fall a millimeter away from her neck. The lessening of pressure communicated to her that the man was momentarily distracted. This, coupled with the cessation of breath on her neck, prompted her to act. It was a calculated risk, but better than any alternative she could envision. Like a high-speed microprocessor, her mind had been processing the options, which primarily centered on dying quickly or dying slowly when the knife was biting into her skin.

The warm trickle of blood reaching her collarbone was the only reminder she needed to move swiftly.

The first order of business was to get the knife away from her neck, even if only fractionally, to prevent any errant movement from cutting her carotid artery. That was a game ender. Her muscled arms shot straight up toward the powerful forearm of the man holding the knife. She made her hands into bladelike wedges, stiffening her fingers as she had been taught in her UN-sponsored self-defense classes. Palms facing outward, she jabbed her fingers between the man's forearm and her neck. Her first target was the arm holding the knife, which was his right arm extended across his left arm that was bracing her.

Her logic was that his dominant hand was the one holding the knife. Getting control of that would force him to use his weaker side to control her body. She was powerful in her own right. Constantly lifting and running, Sassi had prepared herself for moments like these by focusing on her physical and mental condition. Her quick reflexes and initiative paid off. She was able to grasp his forearm and wrist, controlling the knife hand, and push it away enough to slide her left shoulder into him while ducking.

Her rapid spinning motion created a centrifugal force with the arm holding the knife, which was reflexively flexing inward, toward where she once was located. His left arm was powerful, but his left hand was not positioned well enough for him to prevent Sassi from rolling away. As soon as she was free of his grasp, she assisted the knife's forward movement into the man's abdomen. She wanted the penetration to be higher, but there were too many bones at the rib cage and sternum. At least she would get shock effect with the knife embedded deep in his belly.

The man let out a loud, "Aahhh."

She stepped away, retrieving her pistol from her cargo pocket and holding it steady in the man's face. Blood was running from the corner of his mouth, the crimson rivulets streaming down his long black beard. His trembling hands tugged at the knife, slipping on his own blood, unable to remove the blade from his stomach.

An artery was bleeding. The blood poured over his lips. His eyes turned milky and rolled upward toward his skull. He slumped to the ground, Sassi's pistol following him the entire way. She stepped toward him and put her foot on the knife and shoved the hilt beneath the skin, embedding the knife into his abdomen.

"Fuck with me," she spat.

She turned and jogged toward Hakim's motionless body. Kneeling next to him, she looked into his wide, dead eyes staring at the sky. His throat was slit much as she'd anticipated hers might have been. She ran a hand over his eyes, closing them, vowed revenge, and ran toward the house where she had originally retrieved Aamina for Fatima.

This time she was on the back side of the home instead of coming in from the front. She inched her way around the corner and saw one of the terrorists dead on the ground in the gap between the two homes with the connecting underground tunnel.

Sassi approached the soldier, knelt, felt for a pulse, got none, and realized why when she saw the marksman's bullet in his forehead. The entry wound was neat and clean, having entered his forehead, but the exit wound was ugly. The back of his skull was a mangled mess of brains, bone, and blood.

She removed the man's HK P320 pistol, popped the magazine, checked it—full—then ratcheted the charging handle. She caught the ejected bullet in the air, popped it in the magazine, and reseated the box into the grip of the pistol. She charged the weapon, seating a bullet, now confident that the weapon was loaded.

Now she tucked the Bobcat in her cargo pocket and lifted the P320 as she slid her back against the wall of the second house, the one with the intelligence trove sought out by General Cartwright and his men. The alley between the homes was her friend now. She had protection on both sides. There were no windows on the sides of the homes. She stepped carefully on the gravel in the alley, which made a soft crunching sound. She rolled her feet from the heel, along the outside, to the toe, diluting her weight distribution.

The wooden door slapped against the front of the target house. Two men stumbled outside. The general's men. It appeared one man was holding the other up. Both seemed wounded. They fell forward off the small porch onto the dirt road. The vehicles were five houses to the east along the same road. One of the soldiers gazed with a faraway look in his eyes as he dragged his partner along the road when two things happened at once.

A bearded man ran from the house to her left and lifted an AK-47. To her right, the Russian tanks turned onto the road, their high-pitched squeak signaling their arrival.

Sassi spun to her left and fired two rounds at the bearded man. The pistol bucked twice in her hand, its power more like the Beretta 9 mm than her peashooter. The man tumbled, surprised and wounded. She pumped two more rounds into him until he was motionless. The American dragging the body nodded at her and kept moving, picking up his pace.

The Russian tanks sped up the road toward them, firing machine guns at their cars until they caught fire. There was no escape from this hell for Sassi, it seemed.

The Americans crawled behind one of the burning cars as Sassi hid behind the house to her right. A tank round whizzed past her, cutting through the home's wood and bricks like Mike Tyson's fist through thin drywall. The second round bored through the house to her left, causing an explosion that catapulted her into the street.

She crawled forward slowly, listening as the tanks stopped less than five meters from her head. The tank's machine gun chattered endlessly, chewing at the ground near the two American soldiers. She'd done what she could to save them, but their bodies jerked as large-caliber ammunition smacked into them.

Her ears were ringing as the muffled commands of the tank commander penetrated the chaos.

"Take her," he said in Russian.

This command she understood all too well.

CHAPTER 11

Jasar Tankian

Tankian stood at the bay window looking into the Beqaa Valley with an expansive view from north to south as he considered the last twenty-four hours. His convoy had been attacked in Syria. An airplane had crashed in the southern end of the valley. Someone had killed three of his men as they recovered a wounded American.

The inevitable turning tide tugged at the back of his mind, a full moon ascending and accelerating the tidal retreat.

Tankian normally kept twenty security personnel at his compound. Once one of his team leaders, Shakir, returned from the wreckage site with the wounded soldier, Tankian went to full alert.

There were four teams of two posted at the four corners of his compound, where he'd constructed firing parapets of sorts. One observer and one shooter. He had three men as his personal security and another two-man team guarding the American in the basement, where he'd constructed holding cells. He'd used these cells previously for random kidnappings and ransom operations, but only sparingly. At his disposal also were Shakir, Khoury, and another two-man roving patrol. Having lost three men at the aircraft location, he was still comfortable with seventeen men on hand.

Below his compound was a tunnel complex with two exits into the valley. The exits were practically indiscernible to someone walking the terrain, but a professional could possibly find them using thermal scopes at night. He considered putting one man at each tunnel entrance but decided his spotter/shooter arrangement at the four corners was best for daylight. Then perhaps he would reposition the security.

"Tell me exactly what you saw," Tankian said to Shakir.

Shakir had black hair, a thin beard, and narrow eyes. He was wearing baggy pants, a long-sleeved pullover, and an outer tactical vest filled with ammunition magazines.

"We recovered the soldier from the drone and put him in the Suburban. I was checking him for weapons and identification. He had the P390 pistol, a spotter's scope, and a KA-BAR knife used by U.S. Marines."

"You think he's a Marine?"

"Either that or Army Ranger or maybe Navy SEAL. But definitely American."

"What makes you say this?"

"On the inside of the lens cover of his spotter's scope was a picture of a young woman and a baby. On the back of it were the English words, 'Love you, baby.' It appeared to be the flowery handwriting of a woman. In the background of the picture was an American flag."

"Where are these items now?"

"In the locker in our team room," Shakir said.

"And then what happened after you inspected the man?"

"I heard a metallic sound from across the valley. It wasn't the loud bang of a rifle but the sound of a silencer. I've heard it too many times not to realize what it was."

"Let me see your pistol," Tankian said. He trusted Shakir, but he was sending a message by inspecting his equipment.

"Of course." Shakir retrieved his Ruger from its holster and handed it to Tankian. Tankian ejected the magazine, pushing his thumb against the stack of brass-jacketed rounds in the well. None budged, meaning it was full. He held out his other hand, and Shakir placed two additional cartridges in Tankian's palm. Tankian repeated the process, pressing on each stack while eyeing Shakir.

"Did you have any issues with any of the other men?"

"No! They were my brothers," Shakir said.

"You left your brothers to rot on the hillside, Shakir. You did so to save your own ass," Tankian said.

"I did so to return the prisoner, whom I considered

a high-value target, to you. The others were dead. Head shots. Whoever was shooting was very good."

"Yes. The only reason you're still above the earth, Shakir, is that you brought home a great bargaining chip. But you may have also invited something into our premises that we don't want. At this moment, the spotter's partner is evidently looking for him. Our GPS tells us the vehicle is a half mile from here. How do you think it got so close?"

Shakir's narrow face began to visibly sweat. He wiped at his forehead.

"I did not mean to do anything but honor you with the captive, Commander."

"The butterfly's wings have beaten," Tankian said. "Their wind has caused a movement. The series of events that are visiting us at this moment are a result of this incident. Poor security at the location allowed this to happen. You were in charge. Instead of deploying two guards and two to inspect, you went into the aircraft with all four of you. A sniper-spotter team would have perhaps prevented the beating of these butterfly wings. The gentle breeze I feel against my face is not a friendly one. It portends something nefarious, something that I do not welcome."

Shakir ran a trembling hand through his black hair. It was oily and matted to his forehead. His eyes were wide with fear, uncertain of his fate. The dressing-down was punishment enough, but would Tankian stop there?

Tankian might have killed him had he not needed

the people on hand. He was sure of Shakir's loyalty and had no worries there, but there was always the issue of making an example out of someone. Perhaps there would be some justice for Shakir's teammates in their team leader's coming face-to-face with whoever this phantom sniper might be. If Tankian could capture the presumptive American sniper, he could then put them both in a cell armed with knives, promising that the victor of a fight to the death would be given the chance to live. That would be good sport.

His business acumen took over. He had a valuable prisoner, a multimillion-euro deal to move drones to Tripoli, and a thriving potpourri of logistics work streams. Not only had he worked hard to leach ideology out of his business practices, but Tankian had also cast a net far and wide. If the Americans were to pay him to do some unsavory deed, he most certainly would entertain the offer. His rationale was that his parents would prefer that he be successful. They were businesspeople first and foremost. There was no god that he believed in. He'd seen enough death and depravity to realize that everyone was rendered to the maggots in the end.

"Shakir, you failed your men. You were lazy, but I will let you live to fight another day."

Shakir nodded.

"You will deploy two Sobirat drones to scan the valley for this sniper that killed your team. Once you find him, he's yours to kill."

"Thank you, Commander."

Tankian stepped outside with his Iridium satellite phone, popped the antenna, and waited for the connection. When the light flashed green, he pressed a speed dial number.

"Yes," a voice with thick Germanic accents said.

"I have a commodity you might be interested in," Tankian said. He was calling his powerful and Machiavellian business acquaintance, Max Wolff. In addition to making German luxury automobiles, Wolff dabbled in the black markets for sport, particularly since the Iran market never opened to the West.

"Let's go secure."

They each pressed a button on their phones that would put them in an encrypted conversation, blocking the prying Israeli, German, American, and Chinese satellites.

"We recovered an American soldier from a plane crash. Before I did anything, I wanted to give you the first option."

"Danke. Do we know who the soldier is?"

"I have Khoury chasing that information now."

As if on cue, Khoury ran outside and handed him a picture. Shown were an American senator named Ian Nolte Sr.; his son, Clutch; Clutch's wife, Melissa; and their child, Amber. Before Wolff could say anything, Tankian continued.

"Khoury has run face recognition on a picture we found in the soldier's gear. It appears he is the son of a very powerful man in the United States."

"Do tell."

"His name is Ian Nolte. They call him Clutch."

He could hear Wolff sucking in a deep breath. "You're sure he's the son of Senator Ian Nolte?"

Tankian texted the picture of Nolte sitting in his cell and then the picture of him playing basketball at Notre Dame.

"You have two pictures. This is a first report, but I'd say yes, or at least give me some time to confirm. Meanwhile, you can see for yourself," Tankian said. Wolff's phone chimed with a *ding* as his texts were delivered.

"Confirm, and either way, don't give anyone else the option."

Tankian smiled. "What are we talking?"

"If it's the son of Senator Nolte, we're talking seven figures."

Tankian smiled again. "Okay. He's yours."

"*If* he's the son, I'll want you to take special precautions. There has to be at least one more out there. He wasn't alone. Be careful. Let's put him with the drones tomorrow."

"For seven figures, I follow directions well."

"I'll be standing by." Wolff hung up.

Tankian turned and looked at Khoury, who smiled as well.

"That sounded good."

"Treat the prisoner well," Tankian said.

Thinking about Wolff's warning, Tankian left Khoury to plan, came in through the front door of the compound, and found Shakir in his study off the living room. He put his finger in the man's chest. "You have full resources to do what you need to do to find the prisoner's partner. Hold nothing back. Find him."

"Yes, Commander."

"Execute."

He turned and walked past the leather sofa and chairs to the back patio. The sun was high over the mountains now. He wanted to catch the prisoner's teammate before the inverse happened. If he were the sniper, he would be close, maybe a mile or so. It was a mistake to leave the Suburban at the base of the mountain. He could think of no reason for doing so. It made no tactical sense to give away a proximate location. No one but the sniper would have driven it so quickly after the killing at the crash site. His network of eyes and ears along the valley would have eventually returned it, but not so quickly. The sniper probably followed the home function on the vehicle and decided to either come up the hill to recon or head across the valley while the sun was still nosing over the mountains. It had been a few hours since the ambush, and Tankian's assessment was that the sniper was on the other side of the valley using his obviously considerable skills. The man was probably an American, trained to follow the rules of war. Here Tankian was standing in the open when a sniper was out there somewhere, perhaps even with the crosshairs on him. It wasn't a big, brave move. It was a giant *fuck you* to the sniper.

Tankian had the spotter.

The sniper would come to him.

His first option was always to give Wolff right of first refusal, while he considered the Russians, Syrians, and Hezbollah as fallback positions. However, if they caught wind that he had an American prisoner, any of them could make his life difficult. He had originally thought the prisoner would be a low-ranking pawn in the war with no familial connections worth noting and nothing of value to trade, but a *senator's son*? This could even be the sniper team that had shot down his drone.

In his study was a compact command center with live streaming videos of the drones circling the valley like hawks. One of the monitors showed another Russian military truck traveling from south to north in the valley. It turned up the hill toward his compound, a dust plume billowing in the air like a speedboat rooster tail. The canvas tarp covering the ribs of the truck billowed like sails as the driver accelerated up the hill.

Why so soon after the last visit?

Tankian walked outside and along the trail atop the ridge, looking down at the crags in the land. Good hiding places. The sniper could be in a million places down there. The cliff was nearly vertical, but it had enough slope that a soldier with skill could climb and blend. He reminded himself to ensure that Shakir tilted the camera enough to get accurate oblique imagery. He wanted Shakir to flood the zone and kick over every rock. However, he also knew that to attack everywhere was to attack nowhere.

The truck's brakes squealed to a halt. Captain Padarski climbed out of the passenger's seat and jogged over to him.

"Long time no see, as the Americans say," Tankian said.

"Yes, but I have something valuable in the truck," Padarski said.

"And everyone knows," Tankian said. He swept his hand across the valley below them and the plains upon which they stood. "Perhaps you could have put a loud-speaker on your truck and advertised what it is you're about to tell me. Two visits in twenty-four hours? This is not good business."

"Commander Tankian, I make almost daily runs to your compound for logistics. Sometimes we do it in trucks and sometimes in our tanks. Sometimes you send your convoys forward. No one thinks anything but perhaps I need more fuel or food for my men," Padarski said, some edge in his voice.

Tankian snarled, his face crinkling audibly. "Your confidence tells me you have information, maybe more?"

"There were Americans in the village. Delta Force. Undercover. Terrorists killed both Americans."

"That's useful information," Tankian said. Delta Force? Sniper team? Could the two be connected? What were the Americans doing in Syria? It made no sense. There was no good reason for them to be there. He knew about the American general across the border in Turkey. A man named Cartwright. Two of his operatives who ran the laundry service for the refugee camp were using their phones to snap secret photos of the man. He was large, Tankian's size, with a shaved head. Tankian imagined the general looked after his troops and his mission the way Tankian looked after his businesses. The general would not be happy to have a Delta team winged in a clandestine mission. The potential for international embarrassment was huge, which of course was where Tankian made his money. If he could solve Cartwright's problem, there could be another sizable payday in the near term.

"I came to you first, Commander," Padarski said.

"I appreciate that. I would know if you hadn't. What is it that you want to show me?"

Padarski motioned him to the back of the truck, where one of Padarski's men, a medic judging by the black cross on his sleeve, was kneeling next to a woman and two bodies covered by a tarp. The woman had a sandbag on her head and was cuffed with flex ties.

"Two dead American soldiers and one Italian United Nations worker," Padarski said. "The woman you asked about yesterday, that you saw from your bird." Padarski pointed skyward.

Tankian held up his hand to silence Padarski. He certainly didn't want the United Nations individual hearing his voice. He retrieved his phone and texted his interior team. Three men bolted from the compound and sprinted through the side gate, running over the dusty terrain to his location. Tankian walked to meet them twenty meters from the truck.

"Two dead American soldiers and one live UN worker. Place the woman in a cell and the dead men in the freezer."

The men nodded and jogged to the back of the truck, nudging Padarski out of the way. They ferried the dead soldiers first and then came back for the woman. As they carted her away, Tankian sighed and said to Padarski, "For me to take these people off your hands, tell your general I'll need one hundred thousand euros."

"But, Commander—" Padarski began.

Tankian held up his hand. "I know, it's a friends-and-family rate. You can thank me later."

"I was thinking that you would pay me," Padarski said.

Tankian shook his head. "And what would you do with them had you kept them? Start World War III?"

"You should pay," Padarski said. "There was risk in getting them to you."

"There is also risk to you if I show your commander and wife the pictures of you with some of the whores."

Padarski's face flushed red. Prostitutes were another service Tankian provided—with hidden cameras, of course. To lessen the blow, Tankian said, "Your secrets are safe with me if you do not cross me."

Padarski didn't budge. Tankian lifted his hand and put it on Padarski's shoulder.

"There's an American sniper somewhere in the valley. He could be close enough to hear this conversation or he could be five miles away. If you and your men find him, I'll pay you one hundred thousand euros."

Padarski's face brightened. "Where can I get the details?"

"My man Shakir is inside. He has all the information you'll need. Maps. GPS coordinates of where he parked the Suburban he stole. The pictures of the three men he killed. The crash site of the airplane. Everything.

Instead of just protecting UN supply convoys, perhaps you can have your men also search for this very dangerous man. But be careful. He's already killed three of my best men."

"I'll bring my tanks in. We have night-vision and thermal sights. When the night comes, we will easily capture your sniper."

Tankian was doubtful but shook Padarski's hand. It was soft, and he could tell that the man did not do the fieldwork; rather, his soldiers did. He was a perfumed prince, attempting to rack up points and get promoted. Nonetheless, he could give orders and his men could perform the heavy lifting. Tankian didn't care. He just wanted the sniper captured.

"We have a deal," Tankian said.

He dismissed the captain and made a second call to Germany.

"Go secure," Wolff said.

"Secure," Tankian said.

"Why the sudden call?"

"In Lebanon, we have a saying, 'When the star Suhail shines, expect rain.' Suhail must be shining, because it is raining good luck."

"Explain."

"Americans say, 'When it rains, it pours.'"

"Ah. Better news, then?"

"We have a second prisoner. And two dead American soldiers."

A deep sigh over the phone, then, "Details?"

"A UN worker. Female. Alessandra Cavezza."

"Cavezza?"

"Yes. We will have more information for you shortly."

"I still want the live American first, but don't deal away the Italian. And keep the dead Americans handy. They'll be useful."

"Understood. Compensation?"

"I'll move a half million to your account now, and upon successful delivery, a full million euros for a total of one point five million euros."

"I usually don't quibble, but I'd like a million up front and a million on the back end," Tankian said.

"There's a saying about not looking gift horses in the mouth also," Wolff said. "But I'll accommodate your request based upon our prior strong relationship if, and only if, the soldier is confirmed as Ian Nolte. And in the meantime, I'll do a little research on my end." Wolff hung up.

Tankian whispered to himself, "Two million euros." He summoned Khoury, who appeared dutifully from the kitchen.

"Commander?"

"The two dead Americans. Take them to Tripoli and keep them in the morgue. It's near the airport. We may have a buyer."

Khoury nodded, retrieved his personal mobile radio, and barked out instructions.

Tankian climbed to the deck of his home and stared into the valley. Tanks roared north and south. Drones buzzed the skies like circling hawks looking for a rabbit. His guards manned the firing parapets in each cardinal direction.

Shakir had wisely put his men on secure footing. Defend the compound while conducting reconnaissance.

Feeling good, Tankian walked down the steps, into the back of the house, through the kitchen where his staff worked preparing this evening's meal, and into the basement where the prisoners were being held in two of eight available cells. There were four on each side of a narrow hallway. The cells had heavy steel doors with sliding rectangular portholes that opened just enough for a guard to see in or pass food through.

The basement was dark, wet, and cool, smelling of fresh concrete. He opened the slider on the woman's cell door. She was standing in the middle, arms hanging by her side, fists balled, wrists bleeding from the flex-cuffs Khoury had removed.

"Why am I here?" she said. Her voice was calm, devoid of fear.

Tankian was impressed. He figured the metal manacles on the wall might scare her, but evidently not.

Tankian just nodded and closed the slider.

He walked to the soldier's cell and opened the slider. The soldier was sleeping on the metal bed that protruded from the left wall. Tankian closed that slider. He walked past the two dead soldiers and inspected their wounds and gear. They'd been stripped of anything valuable, but he noticed the uniforms were the same as the captive's.

Walking to the stairs, he felt a text buzz on his phone.

Confirmed. Prisoner is son of U.S. Senator Ian Nolte.

Another text followed.

Army Ranger. 24 years old. Partner is deadliest sniper in Special Forces history. They call him the Reaper.

He texted Wolff: *Confirmed.*

CHAPTER 12

Max Wolff

Max Wolff set down the phone after texting Jasar Tankian and made a temple with his fingers under his chin as he stared at the video feed. The ship was doing just fine, but now he had an entirely new dimension to add to the mix.

Leaning back in his chair, he sighed and ran a hand along his silk black-and-blue-checked sport coat. Wolff stared at the gold-plated Daimler logo on the wall next to the display screen in the conference room. Floor-to-ceiling windows provided him a panoramic view of the German Alps. From the Daimler retreat near Garmisch, Germany, the jagged, whitecapped teeth of the Alps crawled south through Austria and into Italy.

The big takeaway from the phone call? Ian Nolte Jr. was in the basement of his Lebanese logistician's compound. The opportunities were limitless. With Andrea

Comstock, the CEO of General Motors and presidential candidate walking up the steps to the mountain retreat, he had little time to process all the ways he could use the information.

What he did, though, was arrange Tankian's pictures of Nolte into a quick presentation. He spent a minute reading about Nolte online. Notre Dame. Basketball. Famous senator father.

His security at the front door welcomed Comstock into the retreat, and he met her in the lobby.

"Andrea, welcome."

"Max. I don't have much time, but thank you for the invite."

She was dressed in an open-collar blouse with the sleeves rolled up on her forearms. Her brunette hair was clipped just below her collar and parted on the left side. Her blazer hung over her shoulders perfectly; its dual Comstock–American flag pin stuck to the left-side lapel.

"Please, have a seat." They walked into the conference room and chose facing leather chairs separated by a wide oak conference table.

Her toned calves showed as she crossed her legs. Her silk navy-blue skirt made a whishing sound as she shifted in her seat and gave Wolff her signature campaign smile. Wolff thought about her résumé and his play here.

Comstock had played basketball at Dartmouth and attended Harvard Business School. After that, she had joined a private equity firm in Manhattan that led to a series of opportunities in management. Thin and wiry, she was nearly a half a foot shorter than Wolff's six-and-a-half-foot frame. She was polling well through the primary season and had a slight advantage over her nearest competitor. There seemed to be some appetite for a businesswoman with progressive values to challenge the businessman in the White House. She had taken a short break from the campaign trail to meet with major donors in Europe and attend her first-ever Bilderberg conference, which she described as a NATO fact-finding mission. Wolff had lured her to the Garmisch ski resort with the tantalizing whiff of dirt on her primary opponent. A full dossier, Wolff had told her. So, here she was.

A beautiful view and all he could think was, *Just kill the bitch now.* But that wouldn't win back his $1 billion DoD deal. His board could understand that the Persian failure was beyond his control, but the DoD deal they attributed directly to him.

Now that he had Ian Nolte as a hole card, however, he had the perfect play.

"I'm concerned," Wolff said. His voice was guttural and deep, sounding like it passed over gravel every time he spoke.

"Can you be more specific, Max? I understand you're on the ropes with your board. Is that what this is about?" Comstock asked.

"I think I've got that about worked out. As I was saying, your president's withdrawal from the Iran deal hurt us."

Comstock nodded and pursed her lips.

"If I'm elected, I'm going to turn that around. Not for you, per se, but for our country."

"I've been following your platform. I want to support you. If you win, I'm back in favor with my board. We will have five billion in deals lined up for Daimler alone. Probably the same for GM. There's maybe fifty billion to be had in trucks, cars, maintenance, and service in Iran. It will be life changing. We've tried everything under the sun to have the United States change. Open dialogue. Closed dialogue. Bilateral meetings. Multilateral meetings. Opinion pieces in the world's major newspapers. And nothing. You think I'm going to sit here while China and North Korea work that market?"

Comstock shrugged. "Support me, then, and you have a chance. This isn't about the defense deal we beat you out on, is it?"

Everything was about that deal. He was losing his job because of that and Iran!

Wolff tried to hide his fury and thought his passive expression provided no tell of the thoughts raging in his mind. His team had lost a $1 billion contract with the United States government to General Motors for the construction and delivery of new cargo trucks. GM's version was a complete rip-off of Wolff's new truck line. Comstock had led the charge to Congress, proclaiming that America could not turn over its defense needs to a German company. These were trucks, not rockets, yet the U.S. Congress quickly added a line to the National Defense Authorization Act, which prevented the foreign acquisition of products for defense purposes that could be replicated in the United States. Comstock had snatched the already awarded contract from the hands of Wolff and Mercedes-Benz.

"That, my friend, is water under the bridge. You know I've been passionate about this Iran market for a long time."

"Okay, then, you invited me here, Max. Said you had something urgent. Maybe about my opponent in the presidential race. I understand you may want something from me first, but eventually, I want to get to that. I have a campaign to run. Let's get to it."

"In due time, Andrea. Hear me out."

"I'm open to conversations about how to move forward, but there will be no change until I'm elected president."

Wolff smirked. While Comstock actually had a chance, he didn't think she would be around to accept the nomination. If it weren't for Comstock's maneuvering after the U.S. DoD had awarded the contract to Daimler to get that award held in contractual quarantine, he would actually support her for president. After all, she had leaped to the forefront over the career politicians by being the most electable candidate. Her business acumen garnered the support of the moderates happy with a strong economy and faithful that she would be a good steward. The simple fact that she was a woman CEO in a tough business won her props with undecided voters. She was consistent on all the standard party platform planks, such as being pro-choice, having a plan for the environment, and common-sense gun control, whatever that meant. She steered away from far-left kindling, such as the Green New Deal, Medicare for All, and sanctuary cities. She was a moderate in a field of panderers outracing one another to the far end of the spectrum. Comstock positioned herself as the winning alternative. And while she despised the current commander in chief, Comstock chose to focus on her policies and agendas as opposed to joining the incessant Pickett's charges on the man's every move. She played her game, not his, Wolff noticed.

"Well, your president and his administration have destroyed this opportunity for the time being, and they've lost sight of what's important."

"No argument there, Max."

"I've always struck back if someone has gotten in my way. That's why I convinced Rouhani and Assad to attack Israel. Not that they needed much urging. A few new up-armored cars and a couple of million in cash and, presto, we have a new incursion in the Golan. There is no ideology in the world today. Even groups like ISIS only pretend to be concerned about ideology. They're just one big gang on the biggest, most badass street corner in the world—the Middle East. Syria needed to stoke those embers anyway. Had been too long since Israel annexed the Golan and no response from Syria? Now we turn that screw and get the Americans looking at Israel to sharpen the divisions in your country. It helps you, correct?"

"Perhaps, but I'm not sure where you're going with this."

"I'm thinking like Machiavelli. 'The safest course is to destroy. Otherwise, if you only harm a man, he will seek revenge.' Or words to that effect. Conversely, this president of yours. He has harmed me. You. Many others. He did not kill us. Are we to lie down and accept it? Or seek our revenge?"

"My revenge is destroying him at the polls. That's how we do it in America," Comstock said.

"Don't be naive, Andrea. A few very powerful people run this world. We both just came back from Bilderberg. Welcome to the club. Not sure I can do another of those, by the way. I only go for the distraction and business development. You really think the American people choose their own president? Or is it people like us? Without Google, Facebook, Amazon, YouTube, Instagram, and Twitter all pulling for you, writing algorithms that favor you, do you really think you'd be where you are?"

Comstock shifted in her chair. Wolff imagined that the prospect of becoming president was like the proverbial rabbit in front of the greyhound at the racetrack for her. Always teasing and always a few steps away. He could see that Comstock's mind was considering the question. Where would she be without the influence of a very few people?

Wolff's experience had taught him that a man or woman properly incentivized would rarely turn down an opportunity to either get rich or seize power, preferably both. An animal sports enthusiast, Wolff recalled his recent visit to Nîmes, France, where he had spent the day watching the French version of bullfighting. Purportedly, the bull had an option not to fight, but rarely took it. It was an instinct in both animal and man to fight. Comstock was a fighter. He was in the political ring scratching his hooves and aiming at the matador. Wolff imagined himself waving a muleta in front of Comstock, the red cape fluttering with a flick of his wrist.

"I like to think the people are responding to me based upon my vision for America. My business approach. My values. My background."

"Of course. All of that is the baseline. The bare minimum. Anyone who can walk and chew bubble gum could contend against your current president. But what is it that makes you different? It's your access to people like me."

"Yes, and I appreciate that, Max." Comstock looked at her watch, impatient.

"Just stay with me for a moment, Andrea. You're polling dead even with your challenger, but both of you are polling ahead of your president. Living in Michigan, a battleground state, your worst case is that you could be the vice president."

"Or best case is president."

"Yes, that, too. Either works for me, actually. While you are ahead in the polls, nothing is a sure thing. And you and your party need a sure thing, right?"

"I'm sure they—we—would like one, Max, but again, that will be solved at the ballot box, not by way of whatever manner you're suggesting."

"Are you so sure?"

"Last time was a fluke. The entire country is polarized. He'll be gone."

"And last time he had a two percent chance and won?"

Comstock paused. No response, just a shrug. The actual number was less than 2 percent.

"In America, we have a process."

"Andrea, please don't play coy with me. You are in a tight primary race. You've been on the debate stage shouting that you want to personally oust this president. You've spent twenty million dollars of your own money. I watch you on television every day. Your anger is tangible. Your passion pure. I say to myself, 'Is that my friend Andrea Comstock of General Motors, or has a demon possessed her body?' And you know what? I'm just as angry as you are!" Wolff slammed his open palm on the lacquered conference room table.

Comstock rubbed her chin. "I gotta tell you, Max, I'm uncomfortable with this conversation."

"Your comfort is not my concern. Your victory is my concern. Why? My five billion euros, that's why. Your additional five billion euros. The Iran market. Undoing that deal is a huge lost opportunity that you never mention on television. Me? It's all I really think about. That market is right there," Wolff said. He pointed south out of the window in the general direction of Iran as if he could see it, which perhaps in his mind, he could. His obsession had consumed him. His wife, Gretchen, was so done with his theatrics that she had moved to their house on Lake Chiemsee in Bavaria, and he wasn't sure if she was coming back. Regardless, the five billion was significantly more important than his trophy wife of five years. She had dragged their two-year-old son, Heinrich, with her. That was problematic to the point he had told his security team to prepare to go snatch the kid and bring him back to their home in Stuttgart.

"I think I'm done here," Comstock said.

When Comstock stood to leave, Wolff smiled and said, "You're not going anywhere."

"Watch me. Unless you've got some oppo research or something of value instead of some obtuse conversation of how important it is to beat this president, I'm out of here. You don't think I know how important it is, Max? I'm giving up my job. My life. I'm getting attacked every day so that I can save my country. So, I'm done here." Comstock collected her bags and began to retrieve her cell phone to call her staff, who were being entertained by Wolff's security team outside.

"How about if I can guarantee your win?"

Wolff picked up the remote and pushed a button. A high-definition image appeared on the display monitor mounted on the wall at the end of the conference table.

Comstock stopped and stared.

Wolff flipped to another image and then another. All pictures of U.S. Army Ranger Corporal Ian Nolte Jr., the son of Senator Ian Nolte Sr.

"What is this?"

"Army Corporal Ian Nolte Jr.," Wolff said. He let the name sink in for a moment. Her face registered it a few seconds later.

"Any relation to Ian Nolte, the senator from Indiana?"

"Of course. Father and son. Junior, or Clutch, as they call him, is evidently collecting his bona fides so he can run after his father retires. He's been taken prisoner in Lebanon."

"Lebanon? Ian is one of the senior conservatives in the Senate. He's the chairman of the Intelligence Committee. Does he know about this?"

"I'm aware of Senator Nolte. I know him. However, I thought this might be more valuable to you than him at the moment."

"That's his *son,* Max," Comstock said.

"I'm aware. I've just come upon this information and thought you might be interested."

Comstock turned and looked at the Alps. Her shoulders heaved, something that Wolff imagined she did to release stress.

"What are you trying to do, Max?" Comstock asked, but it was clear she saw the play.

"Whatever you imagine I'm doing is only to help you. Nothing illegal is happening."

"I want no part in this."

"I think you're aware of what I'm offering. I have no recording devices turned on. This is not an effort to scam you. On the contrary, it is an effort to help you and rid the world of the scourge that is your president. I'm offering you the chance to be a hero. Missing Army Ranger. We work some back-end diplomatic channels. Keep the world in suspense for a few days. Paint the president as someone who can't negotiate the release. Then you offer to negotiate. I put you in touch with the right people. We make it look bleak, get the world on the edge of their seats. Everyone leaning into this."

Comstock had turned around and leaned forward over the table. Her collarbones poked from the open neckline of her blouse.

Wolff continued, "Then you come in as the leader of your party and secure his release not in competition with the president but in concert with him. Parallel. Not together, but not in conflict. I'll leave that up to you to decide."

Comstock's eyes narrowed. Wolff could see that she was flipping scenarios over in her mind. Maybe this was an opportunity after all. Her hands fidgeted, fingers spinning her wedding band and engagement ring, something he'd noticed she did when she was thinking. He'd watched her during the debates. Even Twitter had a hashtag #spinthering that made lighthearted fun of her nervous tic.

Nodding, Comstock said, "How do you have this information?"

"I sell many vehicles in Lebanon. One of my merchants there also has logistics connections throughout the region. One of his teams rescued the American." More like kidnapped, but it was a minor distinction. "At the time, they didn't know who he was. Because of my working relationship with them, they asked for my discreet help."

"What if I don't like it?"

"What's not to like?"

"What if I go straight to the administration and tell them where he is and that you've got him?"

"I don't think you're that stupid, first of all. Secondly,

none of what you said is true. You don't know where he is, and I don't have him. Lastly, if you try to beat me to the punch, something worse could happen to this young man."

"Are you threatening an American soldier?"

"No, but it sounds like you're uninterested in his release."

"I never said that!"

"See how quickly this can turn?"

Comstock sat down again and opened her hands as if to say, "Proceed." She leaned back in the chair, attempting to act uninterested.

Wolff tossed his hands in the air. "I'm handing you a massive victory here. We release him to you or your emissaries and you can ride this wave into Election Day."

"The media and internet trolls will smell a rat right away. They'll think that a meeting just like this took place and that instead of releasing the soldier immediately, we used him for political purposes."

"Of course. And you can be assured that all your friends in Silicon Valley will make sure that all the right hashtags are trending, information is front page on the searches, and so on. They'll highlight this president's inability to close the deal."

"What is the soldier's status right now?"

"My NATO intelligence sources tell me Corporal Nolte was on a classified mission in the Middle East. He was wounded, and now he's missing. His partner abandoned him in the mountains of Lebanon."

"Lebanon?"

Comstock's voice lowered an octave. Her eyes narrowed. Maybe she had no idea that Americans were supporting Israel on a classified mission. Foreign policy was not her strongest policy area, but she was no neophyte, either.

When Wolff had quietly protested the American president's withdrawal from the Iran nuclear deal, the man had taken to Twitter to embarrass him around the world. While the lost face had only motivated him to work harder and be more successful, his desire to strike back had never faded.

"Using a soldier to get what you want is ultimately a losing tactic for you, Max."

"Not rescuing an American in captivity would ensure your loss, Andrea. You should quit questioning me and focus on what's important."

Comstock leaned forward, interested. "Okay. Tell me what it is that you supposedly know."

"Your soldier is safe right now. He was wounded but has received expert medical care. He was shot while on a mission in Lebanon or Syria. My people are still checking. We can make a plan for the announcement of his capture. Allow enough time for the information to gestate, then you can simultaneously admonish the president for involving U.S. troops in a covert war to help Israel while also offering to help with the negotiations for his release. He'll decline, of course, and probably even call you names on Twitter, all of which will strengthen your public persona."

"I'm still not comfortable with extending this for any length of time."

"You've heard of Ross Perot sneaking people out of Iran during your country's crisis there, correct?"

"*On Wings of Eagles*. Sure," Comstock said.

"Ross Perot was a billionaire executive like you. Like me. We can do this as well. My information is solid. I have the means by which to return him to you, but you have to trust me to do so."

"I'm not sure I've ever trusted you, Max, but if what you say about Corporal Nolte is true, then I'm willing to work with you."

"I speak the truth." And at that point, he had her on his team. "Would you like some water? We have some work to do."

"Sure."

Wolff stood, walked through a side door into the kitchen, and grabbed two bottles of water and some pretzels. He kept walking into another room until he was staring north through a large bay window at the jagged peaks and ravines lowering into the valley floor in Germany. He took a deep breath. Sometimes when you worked hard enough and did most things right, the chips fell your way.

His plan had been missing some panache, the flair that was Max Wolff's usual style. He made big entrances, big statements, big profits, and, yes, two big losses. But he was on the brink of snatching victory from the proverbial jaws of defeat. His plan now included everything he needed to get Comstock to succumb.

He pulled out his phone and texted Tankian.

Protect the soldier at all costs.

Then he went into the conference room, gave Comstock her water, and began planning how to make her a hero.

CHAPTER 13

Vick Harwood

Two men stood above Harwood and spoke in harsh Arabic. Tanks rumbled in the distance. Helicopters flew overhead. They were searching for him, no doubt.

He clutched his pistol in one hand and his knife in the other. He had no intentions of being found, but if so, he was going to fight his way out and find Clutch. Only his nostrils were above the ground.

The men walked next to him and stopped, but of course it was impossible to tell what they were talking about. Perhaps they knew where he was located, and they were discussing how to kill or capture him.

Or perhaps he had done such a good job disguising his position that they were discussing their children. Who knew?

Harwood had slowly covered himself such that he looked like a piece of the terrain, the ghillie suit helping to break up the patterns of his body. A twig here, a leaf there, some grass, some dirt, and over the course of two hours, his sniper training had helped him make his position next to invisible.

After some debate, the men moved on, one stepping on Harwood's left thigh. The man stopped, said something else, and then continued.

Harwood let out a long breath that he had been holding, for fear that even the slightest exhale would be heard or detected. He sipped some water, having positioned his drinking tube in his mouth earlier in order to stay hydrated. He realized his mistake when he was finally able to think more clearly. He had been two nights with no sleep and had been in hot pursuit. His initial hope had been to catch the escaping SUV and have a mano a mano fight with the lone survivor of the ambush before he could retreat to a location where the numbers would not initially make sense for Harwood to continue.

If the man had secured Clutch prior to his arriving on the scene of the accident, then he was confident that by nightfall he could extricate himself from his predicament and find a more suitable position to conduct reconnaissance. As it was, he had listened intently. Drones had buzzed up and down the valley in gridlike fashion. The whining engine would be distant and then close and then distant again. That pattern repeated itself over and over. They were definitely searching for him.

Tanks rumbled near and far, as well. The growl of their diesel jet engines roared loudly. He was close enough to smell the exhaust. Because he had selected a deep cut in which to hide, he wasn't that concerned that a tank would, or could, run over him. The squeaky tread diminished and grew loud at intervals.

Voices carried over the lip of the plateau throughout the day. Some sounded Arabic and some sounded Russian. A truck had climbed the hill and then departed. Footsteps pattered along the ridgeline, especially during the time that the truck had been there.

It was a delivery of some sort, he decided.

Maybe the compound he had briefly glanced over was a supply depot of some sort. It looked like a normal habitat for a wealthy Arab. Stucco walls, Spanish tile roof, sprawling two-story layout, metal grates, maybe vents in the ground that indicated a basement system of some sort.

Harwood's study of the Beqaa Valley had indicated that there were just such places dotted along the valley floor or the ridgeline. Redoubts for the wealthy. Some preferred the beach, others preferred the mountains, while still others preferred the magnificent views into the breadbasket of the Middle East.

He had left himself enough of a visual gap that he could see that night was falling. The sun was beaming upon the mountains in the east and then was replaced by a pleasant shade of gray and then, thankfully, darkness. Still, he waited. The guards would be on full alert for the first hour or two after nightfall. Drones with thermal cameras were working their patterns, no doubt frustrating their operators.

He had situated himself in between two boulders

that would retain the heat almost as much as his body. Painstakingly, he had scattered pebbles all over his body in a random pattern, moving his hand an inch every few seconds so as to avoid detection. His ghillie suit had thermal and radar scatter properties that helped diffuse the penetration capabilities of modern sensors. By his guess, it was nearly midnight. The guards might be more interested in their smartphones, if he was lucky, than some phantom intruder. The longer he waited, to a point, the more their belief in his presence would wane. He had no doubt that someone in the compound was absolutely convinced he was out there, which explained the persistence of the drones and the constant footfalls, until about an hour ago.

His pursuit of Clutch came with a risk and a price. If Harwood was able to retrieve him and get him back to safety, Clutch would still be affected. Who knew what kind of injuries he had already suffered other than the gunshot wound that Harwood had treated in less than one minute as the Sabrewing aircraft was taking off? Was he ambulatory? Head injury? Conscious? These questions brought to mind Clutch's philosophical discussion earlier about having a purpose in life. While Clutch had graduated from Notre Dame already, Harwood had yet to attend college. Here he was, though, mentoring and now searching for his missing spotter. Clutch had a point. Harwood was now on his third spotter in as many years. He missed LaBeouf and Samuelson and blamed himself for their loss. He should have killed Basayev in Afghanistan before the Chechen had an opportunity to kill

LaBeouf. Likewise, with Samuelson, Harwood should never have let him resign and move back to Maryland only to work as a military contractor. "The money's better," Samuelson had said. It didn't matter once he was dead.

Survivor's guilt was a real thing. Sometimes when he looked at Clutch, he saw LaBeouf or Sammie. He had even called Clutch "Sammie" or "Joe" a couple of times. Sniping was a solitary business, and he bonded with his spotter. Besides Murdoch, Harwood had no close friends in the Rangers. Sure, he was buddies with everyone, but only on a surface level.

And given all of this, there was still an odds-on chance that Clutch wasn't in the compound. That he was splattered on a hillside somewhere or that he had been only slightly injured and was able to walk away and hide. But that didn't make sense to Harwood. The search party had seemed focused on the inside of the Sabrewing aircraft and its immediate surrounding area, as if they had already found what they were looking for. No, his gut told him he was in the right place.

And it was time to move.

Almost as slowly as he had covered himself and his equipment, he began to remove the camouflage. It was a calculated risk, but one he had to take. He had his night-vision goggles and his thermal scopes. If he could set up in a decent hide site, he could conduct the reconnaissance necessary to penetrate the site. After thirty minutes of removing his concealment, he slowly turned and lifted himself from his position. Even though he was accustomed to lying in wait in sniper hide sites, his muscles ached from his unusual position on his back.

Soon, he was kneeling and surveying his position. His head was still below the level of the gulley lip. Like a puma, he was climbing the steep gulley up to the lip of the ridge. He secured his SR-25 across his chest, tightening the three-point sling so that there was no rattle to the weapon and his gear. The night-vision device was snug on his head, the harness biting into his scalp.

There were two guards at the northeast corner watching the road. At least that was what Harwood imagined they were supposed to be doing. Instead, they were leaning against the firing port with their backs to Harwood. His immediate decision was whether to kill them or use the blind spot to move to the wall.

He chose moving to the wall. While killing the guards might have been a good option, he would have had to take a few seconds to unleash his sniper rifle, and that was time he didn't want to lose and noise he didn't want to make. And he had time to kill them now that he was snug against the seven-foot-high wall. The two men were directly above him, and he was glad that he had screwed the silencer on his pistol.

At the base of the turret, a gate swung outward to the path that the servants used to toss the trash into the gulley in which Harwood had been hiding. The turret had two outward protruding chunks of concrete and two open gaps where men could observe and shoot, if necessary. It was very much like a medieval castle where the guards could observe, roll back behind the protected area, nock their arrow into the bowstring, and then spin back out and fire at the previously acquired target.

Harwood tossed a pebble outward toward the road where he had earlier heard the truck. It was the oldest trick in the book, but perhaps that was because it typically worked. In his goggles, he could see tire marks where a large wheeled vehicle had stopped and Y-turned. Most likely, that was the truck that had moaned up the ridge and idled for a bit. A delivery or a pickup. The vehicle had emitted the gurgling rattle of a diesel engine, a noise that Harwood was intensely familiar with from having sat in the back of military two-and-a-half-ton trucks. This truck had been here long enough to complete a transaction, but not long enough to be a part of the operations of the compound. It had come and gone, like the mailman or FedEx guy, but maybe a little longer. Something heavier than the average package that maybe took more than one person to lift and move. The guy in charge might have had to summon extra people or even lend a hand himself. Or the driver had to get out and help—but not for too long because the engine continued to idle.

Harwood didn't think it was a reinforcing action. Men would have jumped out of the back of the truck and boots would have thundered on the ground. Instead, there was maybe one person who jumped from the truck, a dialogue had ensued, and then maybe another set of boots hit the ground. Something was off loaded or loaded onto the truck.

The two men above him gathered in the opening and spoke in Arabic. Harwood threw a rock into the driveway, then tucked tightly into the dead space beneath them. The first head that presented itself from the small opening was turned in the direction of the noise. He was wearing night-vision goggles, maybe an earlier version, because they seemed bulkier on the man's face than what Harwood was accustomed to. With a heightened sense of alarm given the night-vision capability, Harwood wasted no time in firing two shots into the man's temple. A second head briefly appeared as Harwood was backing away from the wall to improve his angle.

The head backed away and was replaced with a rifle that was awkwardly attempting to depress into the dead space. Harwood snatched the rifle with his left hand and stood up fully as he pulled the man forward in an acrobatic three-point move. Pull, step, and shoot. He pumped two rounds through the man's left eye as he wrenched the rifle away. The pull resulted in forward momentum that caused the man to tumble through the parapet.

Harwood stepped back as the man thudded at his feet. He checked for a pulse, found none, stared into the open eyes of the dead man, chose to see evil, and convinced himself that he was on the right path, that Clutch was in this compound against his will. Otherwise, why have armed guards?

The dead man before him had a pair of night-vision goggles hanging around his neck. Little good they did there. The man was heavy, not thin and wiry as Harwood would have expected, but large and soft. The guy in charge definitely did not get reinforcements from the truck. Otherwise, why put a chubby, unconditioned man on the front line of defense? It smacked of unpreparedness or desperation. Or maybe he had killed three of the tough guys and there were no replacements yet. If there were two men at each corner of the seven-foot wall, that meant the man in charge had originally placed eight on perimeter defense. Naturally, he would keep the fitter guards in tight with him. Two, maybe three, depending on what kind of operation he was running and what personal defense skills he might possess.

Making good use of the large, dead man, Harwood rolled him against the wall and stepped on his fat ass, affording him a grip on the back side of the parapet. He hoisted himself up, like doing a pull-up and then a dip and then an L-seat on the rings, but less graceful. It was more difficult because of the rucksack on his back, but he managed.

He landed softly on the elevated platform that was specifically designed to provide guards or observers long lines of sight into the northeast section of the Beqaa Valley and the plain upon which the compound sat. He knelt next to the first man he had killed and repositioned the body along the ten-foot-by-ten-foot platform so that it was perpendicular to the wall, which ran about a hundred meters to the north and a hundred meters to the southeast corner. The man had a Motorola radio secured to his belt. Harwood removed this, turned the volume down, and stuffed it in his pocket.

The rising sliver of moon highlighted at the northwest corner the faint outline of two men in the same general disposition as the two he had just killed. Looking to the south, he saw that the two men were scanning using night-vision goggles.

Harwood unsnapped his SR-25's sling from his outer tactical vest and lay prone on the platform, first aiming to the south. He adjusted his scope, switched it to infrared, and pushed the button of his PAQ-4C infrared aiming light. Through the scope's magnification, it was obvious the two men at the southeast corner were scanning and poised to defend. It was also clear that Harwood had been quiet enough that he hadn't been discovered yet. Both men were kneeling and scanning their sectors, looking east into the valley and south along the plain. One man held night-vision goggles to his face, like holding binoculars, as he searched. The other turned toward the main house in the compound, as if he'd heard a noise or someone was talking to him. Harwood waited a moment to see if someone was approaching. The scope didn't afford him the peripheral vision necessary to see anything other than that contained in the circular retina. He had two good shots. Take the one looking inward first, then the one focused outward. One, two.

The inward-looking man's lips weren't moving. He wasn't talking. Maybe listening or observing something. Could be a hand-and-arm signal from the house. Might be an animal wandering through the property.

His head turned toward Harwood's position, fixed on the location, and then tapped his partner without turning to look at him, which was when Harwood fired.

The alignment was slightly off. While Harwood was going for a center forehead shot, the bullet appeared to graze his head, spinning him around. He was already moving to the second man, who was lifting and turning toward his partner.

Harwood squeezed the trigger twice with the crosshairs on the man's midsection, then moved swiftly to the wounded man, who was on one knee and lifting a radio to his mouth. It was a perfect profile shot to the skull. Harwood added a second for good measure and then came back to the second man, studied him for a couple of seconds, thought he saw a breath, the slightest exhale, so he put a bullet in the man's head.

Harwood pulled away from his rifle and lifted his head, looking toward the compound as he switched from his PVS-16 night-vision goggles to the Integrated Visual Augmentation System, or IVAS, which would provide him a more enhanced site picture as he transitioned inside the compound.

The IVAS monitored his heart rate as well as provided him night, thermal, and infrared capabilities. Made by Microsoft, whose employees had petitioned the CEO not to deploy the system because it could aid soldiers in killing people. Well, no shit. That was the point. Eventually, the enemy would have that capability, and it was better that the U.S. Army had it first. A few of the employees quit, but most carried on. Thankfully, the CEO had told his employees to pound sand and enjoy the liberties that the military provided them.

Regardless, Harwood was thankful to have a

technological advantage when he faced such an over-whelming disadvantage in simple numbers.

He raised the IVAS to his eyes. Nothing. No move-ment. He might have been more satisfied to see whatever the man on the southeast platform had seen, but the lights were off and all that was visible was a sprawling stucco two-story home with Spanish tiles overlapping on the roof.

He rolled and spun around so that he was facing northwest. The situation had changed. Had the grazed guard been able to transmit a radio message? Were they going to high alert? The two men from the northwest platform were climbing down. They were jogging down the path to the house. It was a harder shot, but he'd done it a thousand times before. He focused on the lead man, placed the scope on his midsection, and squeezed. The second man bumped into the stumbling lead guard and stopped to look at his fallen comrade. Harwood took the head shot on the stationary man and felled him.

Moving the scope back onto the lead man, he put two more bullets into his midsection since he didn't have a head shot.

Six down, how many to go?

Correction. Nine down, at least two more to go. Probably at least five more. He liked those odds a lot better than whatever they were previously.

Because the house was two stories, he couldn't see the southwest-facing platform, but he assumed there was one and that it had two guards who were perhaps repositioning. A common tactic for a seasoned commander was to collapse his security force in tighter if he had taken losses on his outer perimeter. Harwood recalled a mission in Afghanistan when his Ranger unit was attacking a senior Taliban leader redoubt. He had killed several of the outer perimeter security in similar fashion as he had done tonight. The Taliban commander pulled the remaining guards from the outer defenses to the inside of the house, forcing the Rangers to make several decisions without great intelligence on the home's interior. Were there women and children inside? Other noncombatants? Could they cover the open space without being shot? What kind of weapons were inside the compound? Machine guns? Could they use an AC-130 aerial gunship to simply flatten the home and all the terrorists?

Of course, tonight, Harwood didn't have aerial support. He had absolutely no support. Thankfully, he had been able to top off his ammo and water resupply from the Sabrewing drone that had either been shot down or crashed of its own accord. Maybe even Clutch had crawled up to the controls and tried to fly the thing, if that were possible. He didn't know.

Wasting no time, Harwood clambered down the sloping steps and dashed directly at the house. He felt the adrenaline and momentum of being inside the enemy's decision cycle. As he ran, he carried his SR-25 at port arms. He let his IVAS flop around his neck as he bolted as swiftly as possible to the house. He passed a pool surrounded by palm trees and a patio that led to a sliding glass door. A switchback stairwell cut north and then south, leading to most likely the master bedroom on the second floor.

Harwood took the stairway, thinking it would be better to fight his way from top to bottom, clearing the enemy as he went. Kneeling next to the sliding door, he took a breath and placed his IVAS to his eyes. The augmented reality brought the entire inside of the bedroom to high-definition relief like a video game.

The slider was unlocked, and he stepped into the massive master bedroom. The large bed was unmade. His reflection in the giant mirror above the bed momentarily startled him. Two doors to his left were open. One led to a large bathroom with a tub, shower, vanity, and toilet while the other was a walk-in closet the size of Harwood's bedroom in Georgia.

Clear in the bedroom and adjacent areas.

His IVAS was connected through a local network to a fiber-optic camera inside his aiming light, which meant that he could see wherever he aimed the muzzle of his rifle. He poked it around the corner, the IVAS now truly looking like a video game. The curved stairwell led down from the landing on two sides. A giant chandelier hung above the foyer, which had a heavy wooden door. The windows were small and boxy. The light was minimal, and Harwood wondered if everyone had congregated in a basement. The heart rate monitor showed a steady sixty-four beats per minute, up from his resting rate of fifty-two.

In either direction, there were doors that opened to the second-floor landing. The door to his left opened slowly. Harwood kept the muzzle trained in that direction while he was still on one knee leaning against the open door in the master bedroom. A man carrying a weapon walked slowly along the landing bypassing the first stairwell and headed toward Harwood. The floor was wood but carpeted with Persian rugs. Harwood laid his rifle on the floor in the doorway, easing it down soundlessly as he retrieved his knife. While he had the shot, the silencer would be loud in the confines of the house, and there would be no mistaking his location.

He assumed that by now everyone in the compound understood that they were under siege by at least one, if not two or three commandos.

The man approaching was not wearing night-vision goggles, and the entire upstairs was dark. The floorboards creaked under the man's weight. Harwood stayed low and waited until the attacker presented himself in the doorway and took a tentative step across the doorjamb, spinning into the room in moderately trained fashion, clearing right and then left with his AK-47.

It wasn't his most graceful move ever, but Harwood lunged upward as the man almost tripped over him. His Blackhawk knife bit into the man's abdomen as Harwood raked it upward until it caught on his sternum. The man gave out a loud gasp, aspirating blood as he coughed. Louder than Harwood wanted but quieter than a silenced pistol shot. Fifty-fifty whether someone heard it downstairs. Blood gushed over his hand as he heard the front door open down below.

Two men tumbled inside. Maybe they were the

southwest guards that he couldn't see from his original point of attack outside.

"Fawq!" a voice called out from below.

The two men looked up. One held night-vision goggles to his face and most likely saw Harwood. He pointed up the opposite steps, and each man ran up opposing staircases, attempting to envelop his position. One guard stopped midway and took up a supporting-fire position. These guards appeared to know their tactics.

Harwood spun his weapon to maintain observation of the man coming up the opposing steps and then switched to split screen on his IVAS, giving him a dual display where he could see where his rifle was aimed and the direction his face was aligned. The man who was still moving came up the opposite stairwell and quickly put his back to the wall, preventing Harwood from getting a clear shot.

The man in the supporting position moved up the stairwell and put his back to the wall on the opposite side of the door. He was enveloped, exactly as they had planned.

In his split-screen display, both men inched toward the opposite sides of the door. He stayed low, leaving his rifle on the floor as he retrieved his SIG pistol. The two sentries halted their advance, maybe confused about the rifle in the hallway. Harwood could see them using the "around the corner" function of the IVAS's Bluetooth connection to his rifle scope. They were motioning toward each other, as in, "You go first, then I'll follow. You go right, then I'll go left."

The first man spun into the room. Harwood fired two rounds center mass, stopping him upright with the 9 mm hollow points. The silencer made a ratcheting *pfft* sound. The second man stumbled into the lead, firing wildly everywhere but where Harwood was lying in the middle of the floor. He waited patiently until the lead man fell to his knees, dead, and exposed the trail.

Another double tap to the chest had the second attacker falling across his partner, landing with a thud. Harwood moved forward, scooped up his rifle, and stood on the landing overlooking the foyer and living area below.

CHAPTER 14

Jasar Tankian

Tankian stood in the kitchen holding a Luger pistol and a Gurkha knife he had stolen off a dead British soldier that he had sold to famed terrorist Abu Musab al-Zarqawi during the Iraq War.

"Fawq!" he shouted when the men from guard tower four had entered the front doors. He numbered his towers starting from the northwest corner in clockwise fashion.

Between the two captives, Tankian now had maybe €3 million worth of commodities in his basement. The transactions were never clean, though, and were fraught with double cross opportunities, which was one of the reasons he preferred to stay out of the kidnapping business. He did it better than most, but it was his least favorite business line.

While the financial prospects were good, Tankian

had an ironclad survival instinct about himself and his business. After inspecting his prisoners, he had gone upstairs and lain in bed for a bit, his mind spinning from the potential payday to the fact that someone had killed three of his men earlier this morning. Whoever had done so was still out there, perhaps lying in wait for him. He tossed and twisted the sheets as his men stood in the hallway and on the balcony guarding him.

Then he had either heard something or dreamed it. A sound like thunder had come from outside. It took a moment for him to register it, but he awoke to the guards coming inside and conducting their protection plan. Their mission was to keep him alive, not pursue the attacker. They had gone downstairs into the kitchen and then outside, where he had watched his two men get shot at tower 3 in the southeast. Then came the noise from the deck, and he abandoned protocol, ordering his men up to eliminate the threat. The two men ran upstairs, one awaking the third personal security guard as they approached.

Now he was alone in the kitchen, feeding men into the fray with no idea who this man might be who was slaying his employees. If six were dead outside—he'd had no response on his radio calls to tower 1, 2, and 3—and five inside, with the three at the plane crash location, that left him with six men, two downstairs with the prisoners, Shakir who was outside with the drones, Khouri who was in Tripoli, and two from guard tower number 4. He had some ranch hands above the stables a quarter mile away on the property but they weren't fighters.

The guard post 4 men were up the stairs, their tactics providing him hope. A double envelopment with one man watching over the other, negating the attacker's angle of fire. As soon as he felt the slightest whiff of momentum, it was quickly snuffed. The gunfire he'd heard did not portend well for him and his compound. Two more dead. Four left.

By his calculation, he had maybe a minute before the soldier on the top floor realized there were no more men coming upstairs. This was not a man, Tankian presumed, who would allow momentum to ebb. Rather, he was an unstoppable force hell-bent on rescuing his fellow soldier.

This was the curse of the kidnap.

The American soldier was not a prize but an albatross. Like a stock market crash, Tankian's fortunes had gone from soaring to diving. Twenty men to, now, six. In business terms, that was a 70 percent loss.

In human terms, the loss was incalculable. He had trained these men, and they had been a team for five, ten, or fifteen years. But they had failed him now. Even Shakir, one of his most trusted advisors, had failed him twice in less than twenty-four hours—first at the plane crash site and then by haplessly leading the man here to the headquarters as he fled with the prisoner, not thinking of the second-order impact of doing so. And then he had given him the drones to find the man who had killed his comrades, but Shakir had failed even there.

How had his team failed him so spectacularly? They were not trained commandos, but neither were they neophytes in the business of war and combat. Some even had combat time on their résumés. But mostly they were businessmen running supplies and maintaining contact with his vast network. Sure, they had seen the brutal violence of terrorists, but it wasn't their trade.

Yes, in some ways, he registered the loss of his business colleagues even more than he did the loss of his family as a child. If his life was all about business, the transaction, then this deal was a catastrophic loss for him. The financial ruin that might follow would be swift if he didn't take extraordinary measures to prevent it. His network of Russians, Iranians, Hezbollah, and assorted terrorist groups would see the lack of preparedness as a major flaw in his operation. They would no longer trust him unless he stemmed the losses.

Tankian heard a noise from above. In one hand he gripped his Luger pistol and in the other hand, the Gurkha knife, its large curved blade prominent. From his position in the kitchen, he could see the shadow of a man descending the stairway. Was it an illusion? He couldn't see the man, but the image was there. Faint moonlight skidded through the small windows, making it difficult to distinguish shapes. There was movement. The creak of a board. The soft placement of a foot.

There. The man came into view. He was holding a long rifle to his eyes, as if he were shooting. The attacker was wearing what looked like a small swim mask, but Tankian knew these were state-of-the-art night-vision goggles.

Could Tankian get a shot? He considered the odds. This man had presumably killed half his company by continuing to press forward like a shark, always swimming. Tankian had forever seen himself as the shark, the apex predator, not in a murderous way but in a cunning business acumen manner.

The man was moving slowly. Tankian lifted his pistol with one hand—believing that he could do what his other men had failed to do—and waited for the compact body of the attacker to step into full view.

He had three of the fingers of his left hand on the door to the spiral staircase, one of two ways into the basement, and the thumb and forefinger holding the knife. His right hand firmly held the pistol, but he couldn't deny the slight quiver in his hand. Nerves. Fear. Both were manifesting right now, but he did his best to shut down those unhelpful emotions.

His hand steadied.

The man stepped into full view . . . and quickly spun toward Tankian, the Luger bucking in Tankian's hand at the same time the man's rifle fired.

CHAPTER 15

Sassi Cavezza

Pacing back and forth in the cold, damp cell, Sassi relentlessly muttered to herself, "You dumb bitch, you dumb bitch, you dumb bitch."

Once she had been situated in this place, they removed the sandbag from her head, but her nose had sucked in so much burlap, that musty straw odor was all she could smell. She'd had a bad feeling about this mission and knew that she should never have let the Americans in on the deal. Returning Fatima to her home had been paramount and consistent with her mission. Maybe the pressure she had felt from Fatima's father pushed her to act on his timeline instead of hers, but still, UN workers were *off-limits* to terrorists and armies.

She blamed the Americans for whatever had occurred in al-Ghouta. Hakim was dead. She couldn't escape the image of her friend and interpreter lying dead on the ground, his throat slit from ear to ear by the same man who assuredly intended to do the same to her.

"Oh my God," she whispered. Tears flowed. She covered her eyes, her wrists bleeding from the flex-cuffs. She took in a deep breath, sighing, half of it coming out as a plaintive moan, interrupted by sobs. "Get your shit together," she muttered.

She'd lost count of how many hours she had been in captivity. Something more than twelve and less than twenty-four. She'd bounced in the back of the tank for a short period of time and then the truck for hours, sucking in diesel and burlap. Russian voices had seeped through the burlap and the ear protection her captors had placed on her.

Hakim had been right. The Russian captain was bad news. Of course, she'd known that, but never would she have predicted that the Russian government would underwrite the kidnapping of a UN employee. *They were on the Security Council, for Christ's sake.*

First on the assessment agenda was the status of her confines. Cement on four sides. No windows. Steel door. A naked bulb, probably 40 watts, that shone from directly above. A metallic tube snaked along the plaster ceiling from the top-left corner of the cell. A slight draft pushed upward from the thin space between the edge of the door and the concrete floor. She tested the handle, which was a lever, not a knob. It didn't budge. Running her hands along the seam of the doorjamb, she checked for any imperfections, but could find none. She used her palms to press and feel for any anomaly. It was just her luck that the cell to which she had been delivered was constructed by a master craftsman. There were no seams or loose blocks. On the back wall, though, she snatched her hands away when she saw she was traversing a darkened splotch.

Blood?

It was difficult to tell in the dim light, but her imagination reeled with the possible scenarios. *Don't go there,* she kept telling herself. *Stay in control.*

Next on the list, after determining there was no easy way out, was a physical assessment of her condition. She still had her hiking boots on, and her feet felt fine. Her legs were sore from the extreme exertion this morning, but they otherwise felt okay. Running her elbows along her ribs, she winced when she lifted her right shoulder.

Dislocated? Maybe, but doubtful. As her mind focused on the shoulder and the adrenaline ebbed, it was obvious that she would have trouble with the right shoulder if she were presented with an opportunity to fight her way out. Rotating her neck, she felt only the twinge in her right shoulder again, but it was manageable.

She ran the backs of her hands along her pockets, which were empty. No more knife or pistol, not that she'd expected them to be there. When she lifted her hands to touch her face, the right shoulder bit back at her with pain, but she moved through it. Tears flowed from her eyes as she inspected her face and neck. A few minor cuts, damp with clotting, nothing major.

Her growling stomach led her to the next item on her list. All she'd had to eat was a stupid Clif Bar washed down with Gatorade. The guards had given her two water bottles, which she'd yet to open, and a bucket to pee in, which she'd not yet used.

Final assessment? She needed food and painkillers.

Then she needed to escape. She'd killed today and would kill again for her freedom. She was not a victim; rather, she was a champion of the downtrodden, and there was nothing that could stop her. This affirmation had led her away from her privileged Tuscan life to the ragged existence on the edge of human depravity. While she struggled to understand for what reason that might be at this moment, Sassi let go of any concerns she had and placed them in God's hands, where they belonged.

Another sigh.

Another feeling of peace washed over her . . . when she realized that she still had on her hiking boots where her small Beretta Bascula knife with its two-and-a-half-inch blade lay hidden.

Then she heard muffled shouts and gunshots followed by a man shouting.

"My name is Nolte! Corporal Ian A. Nolte! They call me *Clutch*! I'm from South Bend, Indiana!"

CHAPTER 16

Vick Harwood

Once he confirmed that the two men who had tried to envelop him were dead, Harwood used his stalking method to traverse the landing and the steps.

Better to maintain the momentum before another quick reaction force could storm the stairs. He had to leverage his element of surprise and the advantage it had gained him into meaningful success. He could kill bad guys all day long, but he couldn't lose a third spotter. He had to find to Clutch!

And Clutch had to be here. Why else would these guys be fighting so hard? Maybe he'd even kicked over a major terrorist hornet's nest. These guys weren't super skilled in the application of the tools of war, but they were quick and knew how to shoot. They most likely had just not rehearsed an Army Ranger raiding their compound. They should have thought about that before kidnapping Clutch. Harwood's experience was that the enemy always reached a tipping point when fighting back was no longer worth the cost. Harwood's plan was to make the commander of these troops determine that his losses were no longer worth the pain he was inflicting.

As he stepped silently, bodies lay askew on the landing, all dead by his hand. Rolling from heel to outer foot to the ball with each step, he held his rifle in firing position, trigger slack reduced until all he had to do was twitch his finger. The IVAS gave him a clear picture, allowing him to quickly determine that there were no more live threats on the landing, steps, or in the front of the foyer.

Beneath the opposing stairway was an open space. He suspected a similar one was below this stairwell. A giant mirror hung above him on the right and above the stairwell on the opposite side. They faced each other, and Harwood wondered about their purpose. Were they windows instead of mirrors? The mirror's reflected image of him was large, a ghostly apparition on the wall. Upon realizing this reflection could alert someone lying in wait, he quickly spun and aimed at the only distinguishing break in the darkness, a doorway that led to the rear of the house, perhaps a kitchen or dining room.

Harwood saw movement. The IVAS gave him an augmented, high-definition view of a man holding a pistol.

Quick to squeeze the remaining tension out of the trigger, Harwood realized the man was shooting at him. He intuitively dove to his right, knowing that pistol shooters often allowed the buck of the weapon to cause them to drift high in the direction of their shooting hand.

The bullet washed past Harwood and smacked into the mirror above him, which shattered into a million daggers raining down like flechettes. He slid down the stairwell headfirst and canted on his right side, the ammunition pouches on his outer tactical vest making the descent bumpy. At the bottom of the stairwell, Harwood popped up to one knee, shook off the shards of glass like a dog out of water, and used the thick banister and newel as cover. His heart beat loudly against his chest. Two deep, silent breaths did little to slow the heart rate, but he was still in control. No ensuing shots boomed through the living room.

Only the high-pitched octaves of a squeaky door opening and closing pierced the silence. Harwood maintained his momentum by spinning off the bullnose step and sliding across the marble flooring near the front door.

No shots. Complete silence.

He followed the view on his IVAS, which threaded him between two facing leather sofas divided by a low coffee table. Through the doorway was a kitchen island, and behind that a kitchen counter with a small square window above. He moved through the open doorway and cleared to his right, the direction of the door noise, and then to his left.

Nothing.

He pushed into the kitchen, noticed an open knife

drawer with knives scattered, and then checked a small pantry and utility room. Boxes of pasta and sauce were stacked high, most likely by servants. Harwood was still trying to get the feel of his designated enemy. Despite having killed over ten men so far, he didn't get a distinct military vibe from this dwelling. Heavily armed, yes, but there were no stacks of ammo cans or explosives that he would expect to find. It was a comfortable home, not a secret redoubt.

Pushing his way back to the center of the kitchen, Harwood checked the back door, saw the pool and the fence he had scaled in the distance. The southeast guard tower was visible—his second target and the one with the man looking back at the house—and Harwood determined that someone had come to this door about the time he'd engaged the two men in the tower. Beyond the kitchen was a large dining room, which Harwood cleared, finding nothing more than two large hutches filled with plates, bowls, and glasses and a long table with ten chairs surrounding it.

He came back to the door that had been closed.

Running his fingertips along the seams, he checked for any type of improvised explosive device. While finding none, he learned the door was metal and thick. Not a normal door. Possibly a safe room or some kind of fire wall off the kitchen.

Most likely a safe room.

He tried the lever. No free play at all. Locked tightly. He tugged against the door—no give. Backing away and reentering the pantry and storage area, he faced the open door and laid his rifle on a shelf to his right. The smell of burnt gunpowder was replaced by the pungent odor of spices. Clove, cumin, pepper, and rosemary all competed with the lingering aroma of combat . . . and brought horrifying memories ricocheting back from his foster childhood.

Harwood had one foster family that had been borderline acceptable until they weren't. The foster parents— Sid and Raynel Filser—didn't pimp out the girls and didn't totally use the kids as child labor. Sid was a mechanic in a Frederick, Maryland, auto shop and mostly gone seven days a week. Raynel was a decent cook and a strict disciplinarian. Every time a child made a mistake, she would grab a wide leather belt from the pantry in the kitchen. She was a broad woman, always wearing a grease-stained white apron over some floral-patterned dress. When she reared back to gather force for the descending blow, her entire body turned like a cleanup batter in the lineup. Young Vick had reached his limit. He couldn't stand to see a favorite target of hers, eight-year-old Maggie Chitworth with her freckled face and buckteeth, get hammered anymore. With the mother dragging a screaming and crying Maggie across the cracked linoleum toward the pantry by her natty brown hair, Harwood ran and blocked her. He grabbed the belt. Raynel kept hold of Maggie with one fleshy fist and swatted at Vick with the other. He had been maybe eleven years old and was little more than half her height with less than half her mass. Harwood pulled hard as Raynel stared at him with feral eyes and a leering grin.

"Little Vickie Harwood, my weird little boy." She

heaved her massive arm and snatched the belt from his small hands. He tumbled backward into the rows of spices, which all crashed down on him. As he was digging himself out, a cayenne bottle had opened, pouring the powder all over his face and in his eyes. The main ingredient of pepper spray was in his eyes, blinding him as he tumbled forward toward the *smack, smack, smack* of the belt and Maggie's howling screams.

"Little Vickie is crying," she howled with laughter. Suddenly, she had him in her grasp. Maggie's feet slapped the tile as she ran into the next room. He blacked out when the belt whacked his bottom and back for the twentieth time.

He was breathing hard now, the memory only flitting through his mind. Ever since that day outside Frederick, he vowed to get stronger and be the best. To rescue those that needed help. Here he was in a pantry with spices perhaps standing above the level where his Ranger buddy was being held captive.

He reached into his rucksack and removed a block of C-4 explosive, some detonation cord, and a blasting cap. He rigged the breaching charge, grabbed two stun grenades from his ruck, shouldered his pack, inserted some earplugs into his ear canals, grabbed his rifle, and moved forward to the steel door. He put the grenades in his right-side cargo pocket. After securing the sticky C-4 to the door handle, he pulled the ten-second time fuse and hustled back to the pantry, closing that door behind him.

The explosion cracked in the air, shards of metal hitting the pantry door like ninja stars. He gave it five seconds and bolted from the pantry, eyed the damaged door, and saw it was buckled but not completely off the jamb. He snagged a small spring-loaded grappling hook from his outer ruck pocket and fed it through the baseball-sized hole where the handle had been. He popped the prongs so that they extended once they were through the door like a fishing hook barb.

Stepping away, he threw his weight into the coiled rope secured to the hook and popped the door loose. It spun off the hinges and landed on the marble kitchen floor with a loud smack. His IVAS penetrated through the smoke as he began walking slowly down the steps.

This staircase angled to his left with a solid wall to his right. It opened quickly to a cavernous basement below and then appeared to funnel into a single hallway about twenty meters from the bottom step. The hallway ran away from him between two concrete block walls that appeared eight to ten feet high with the same width. A door was visible on the left side of the hallway, perhaps leading to a small room. There was no movement near the stairs, though someone may have quickly peered around the corner of the hallway. If he didn't need to remain in the moment in pursuit of the remaining gunmen in the compound, he could rewind his IVAS and play it back to get a more accurate picture of what exactly was there.

But there was no time to review the footage. He pressed forward, doing what had been working for him: momentum and violence of action. Before rushing headlong into the potential kill zone of an ambush, he held his rifle in his left hand and slowly retrieved a grenade from his cargo pocket. He used his teeth to pull the pin, swallowing its metallic taste with what little spit he had in his mouth. With his fingers firmly on the spoon, he leaned over and flipped it beneath the stairwell and then darted back up the steps behind the protective cover of wall near the kitchen.

Two shots followed him up, pocking into the cement behind him.

He quickly shut down his IVAS and turned away, burrowing his body into the wall, smelling the musty odor of concrete and mortar. The light and the bang came all at once. The building shook. Heat spread along the concrete stairway. The smell of gunpowder permeated the air.

As far as explosions went, this was one of the louder ones Harwood had experienced despite the earplugs. The tight acoustics and his presence in the same room were perfect for a concussion grenade, but the entire premise was that the grenade was meant to be deployed without the thrower in the same room.

He pressed his advantage by powering up the IVAS quickly and securing it to his face, then removed his earplugs. He bolted down the steps again and spun to his left, looking beneath the stairway. A covered and concealed position beneath the steps had been built into the original construction, a hollowed-out storage area where a man had been lying in wait but was now on the floor moaning and writhing. The aroma of burned flesh singed Harwood's nostrils. A pistol was lying next to the man's hand. Harwood kicked it to the side and covered the twenty meters to the far wall in record speed.

Gunfire erupted from the opposite end of the long hallway. The bullets chipped at the block in front of his face. He pressed his back into the wall and breathed deeply. If he had cleared everything from the top of the compound to this point in the basement, the only enemy that remained was whatever might be at the end of the hallway that began a foot to his right.

If was the operational word. He was confident he had killed everyone *he* had seen. What else remained upstairs, he didn't know. But he did believe that he was in the right place. His experience had always been that the closer he got to an objective, whether it be military or personal, the intenser the enemy fire. It was pushing through that fire that won the day.

Bullets continued to chip away at the block. Harwood watched the steps. No action. The wounded man on the floor had been hit by at least three shots. No worries there. Harwood knelt and laid his SR-25 on the concrete floor as he switched to the around-the-corner sight function again. In his IVAS, the weapon's crosshairs moved wherever the muzzle was aiming. Thanks to the enhanced sensors and technology that Harwood thought existed only in Hollywood, the IVAS brought the dark hallway into reasonable viewing relief.

Along the opposite wall, there were five doors that looked exactly like the detention facility in Kandahar where he had delivered too many detainees to count. While the near wall was more difficult to discern, what little he could see made him believe that it was a facsimile of the other.

Two men were prone at the end of the hallway, weapons aimed at his position. A third man disappeared out of sight behind the prone shooter at the near wall. He appeared to be carrying something large over his shoulder.

Three men left to kill, maybe more, but three he knew of and could engage. The sight of the cells reinforced Harwood's belief that Clutch was being held captive here. The crash. The Suburban. The heavily armed guards. The prison cells. What else could it mean?

More confident than ever that he was in the right spot, Harwood assessed the distance to the end of the hallway. Maybe thirty meters, max. The IVAS gave him a better view of the situation than his opponents had of him.

He could use the IVAS around-the-corner function or he could toss another flash-bang grenade into the hall, but the light and burst emitted by the grenade were only temporary. Once the men recovered from the initial shock, even poorly aimed fire would funnel along the narrow hallway, ricocheting off the concrete block and inevitably finding anything moving in the funnel.

The concrete was cool to his touch when he lay down and put his finger through the trigger. He had practiced these shots several times at the range but had never fired using the IVAS connection in combat. His line of sight was perpendicular to the direction of the muzzle, which was aimed in the general vicinity of the gunmen at the end of the hallway.

The crosshairs were on the chin of the man on his left. The trigger gave twice with Harwood skipping two shots just above the floor. The man bucked and dropped his weapon. Return fire was immediate and fierce, causing him to retract his weapon as bullets sparked off the walls and along the floor. While grateful for the technology, Harwood knew that from a normal firing position, he would have shot both men in less than a second.

He reached into his pocket, grabbed the flash-bang grenade, yanked the pin, and risked his left arm as he flipped the canister maybe fifteen meters down the hallway. He repeated the same maneuver as before, where he'd powered down his IVAS and turned away. However, this time he also secured his weapon and prepared for detonation.

The concussive blast shook the walls with a thunderous boom. Harwood powered up the IVAS, spun into the hallway, weapon raised, and fired rapidly, squeezing off single shots as he gained clarity through the smoke.

Backing away and standing, the gunman turned his back to Harwood, who fired three more times, striking him. Harwood dashed along the hallway, making a mental note of the doors, some of which had locking bars over U-bolts and others that were open. He didn't discount the fact that someone could be hiding inside the cells with open doors, but he had a legit, known target hobbling away from him in the same direction the third man had been moving seconds ago.

The limping man was fumbling with a door similar to the one Harwood had breached. It was evidently locked as Harwood barreled into him and then backed away and used his rifle to butt-stroke the man, knocking him out.

He stepped over the man and tried the door. Just like the one above, the handle didn't budge. He would deal with that shortly, but for right now, he had two missions: save Clutch and interrogate this gunman, in that order.

The gunman was heavyset, making him a challenge to move. Harwood finally decided on dragging him by his outer tactical vest. He tugged the man into the first room he reached. It was a standard torture cell. Manacles hung from the walls. The two latrine buckets in the corner were probably the source of the urine smell that permeated the cell. A metal bed with a neatly folded wool blanket was up against the wall. A Beretta pistol and knife sat on the empty bunk, out of place.

Harwood dropped his unconscious prisoner on the floor, thought about how he had happened upon the downed Sabrewing aircraft and followed the intelligence wherever it led him. He had been on the outside looking in at multiple defenders, and he had worked his way through the outer perimeter into the house and now into the basement, where he was dropping another defender. *How many more were there?*

The chain scraped against its hold as he locked the man's hands in the steel cuffs. He briefly frisked him for other weapons and came away with a cell phone, pistol, and a small knife, all of which he pocketed. Snapped onto the man's belt was a cord that led to a tablet that was pocketed in a Velcro pouch on his outer tactical vest. The tablet showed images of terrain, a highway, and some buildings. Drones. They had been looking for him. Was this the same drone operator that had fired on him and Clutch?

He turned and looked to the bunk, where he saw the small Beretta pistol and knife, which he pocketed as well.

Exiting the cell, he closed the door and lowered the locking bar in place. It was secure.

Now to find Clutch.

First, he cleared each of the open cells, just now realizing that all but one were empty. Each cell was a replica of the others. Bed, piss buckets, manacles, and blankets. It registered with Harwood that there was an unfolded blanket in one of the cells, as if one of the guards had been resting. Perhaps this was where they did shift change and stored their weapons? The middle cell on the right had its locking bar firmly in place.

Clutch was banging on the door. It had to be Clutch. His entire purpose for being here was to find and rescue his spotter.

He moved to the door where he had confined his captive and checked the handle again. Nothing doing. That was only coming open with some C-4.

Next, he went back to the stairwell. All quiet on that front.

Now he approached the door, carrying his rifle with

his rucksack on his back. He was ready to snatch Clutch and exit the house. He would take Clutch back up the steps and find one of the Suburban SUVs, provided everything remained quiet.

The locking bar had a Master lock securing it in place. Harwood removed his rucksack, fished around for his bolt cutters, and made quick work of the lock.

The fist continued to pound on the door.

"Quiet, Clutch," he whispered.

He lifted the locking bar from the U-joints, then set it down and noticed there was an interior door that opened inward. This had another set of U-brackets with a two-by-four piece of wood holding it snugly in place. He retrieved his weapon, which had been leaning against the wall, and then lifted the two-by-four, freeing the door.

He shouted, "Reaper coming in, Clutch!"

In case Clutch had fashioned a shiv out of a toothbrush or something else, he didn't want him surprised as he entered the cell. The last thing he wanted was to have come all this way to save his spotter and have lack of communication cause an unnecessary struggle.

Harwood threw his shoulder into the door. It scraped against the floor with a loud screech. A dim light bulb cast a pale glow in the dank cell. The bed to the left had a rumpled blanket on it. The door opened inward and to the right, making him clear to the left first. Nothing there.

He spun around the door and came face-to-face with a screaming banshee who leaped at him.

CHAPTER 17

Sassi Cavezza

Sassi shuddered, covered her ears, and bolted into the corner as men were running in the corridor and yelling in Arabic.

"Quick, get the soldier," one had said. A door had opened. A chain had rattled. Mumbling and heavy groans followed.

Sassi removed from her boot the small Beretta Bascula knife that her captors had overlooked. They'd retrieved from her Beretta's personally delivered pistol that she carried for self-preservation and which had preserved her this morning, and her Beretta dagger. At least she was still alive.

After the second explosion, Sassi figured they were coming for her. Everything was happening so fast, she figured that rival gangs or even the Russians were here to take whatever they wanted, including her.

There was a faint sliver of hope that the UN had dispatched a rescue operation, but she wouldn't let her mind go there only to get her hopes dashed. The UN couldn't make decisions quickly enough to have a force on the ground and executing within twenty-four days, much less twenty-four hours. The leadership would debate which nations would contribute forces, who would be in command, what risks were acceptable, and so on, until she was dead or wished she were. The violence happening outside her door reminded her of a basement she'd been locked in when Zarqawi had been executing so many civilians and nongovernmental organization employees.

She remembered in Fallujah she had huddled in the corner, waiting for Zarqawi to barge in and film her beheading. Just as she was now, she had been holding this very same knife, prepared to fight to the death. Then, U.S. Marines had come storming in, led by the village elder, and she was almost insulted that they had come instead of Zarqawi. Sassi had of course been ultimately thankful that the Marines had saved her. It was a completely irrational thought that she could have defended herself against Zarqawi and his thugs, but nonetheless, she was a proud woman and believed in her abilities.

Sassi also believed that lightning would never strike twice. There was no way that this was some rescue attempt meant to save her from the clutches of this band of pirates. While she had no idea where she was, the voices she had been listening to possessed the Lebanese dialect of Arabic, rich with its Mediterranean influences.

Softer words and hushed tones, almost sounding apologetic. Bartering tones, where give-and-take is expected, as opposed to the harsher inflections of Iraq and Saudi Arabia, where demands ruled the day.

Convinced that she was about to duel with someone meaning her harm, Sassi backed into the corner to the right of the door. She had studied the hinges, welded in place, and noticed the door opened inward. When the intruder came in, she would have a brief advantage. She knew where he was entering, and he had no clue where in the room she would be. It was her best shot. After that, the odds were that he would be heavily armed and able to quickly subdue her.

"Reaper coming in, Clutch!" a voice called out. It was muffled but sounded distinctly American.

Now was not the time for indecision. She could either fully commit or back away and bet on the best possible course of action. She had never been a big believer in blind luck, though she was sure that sometimes it happened. But this did not appear to be her lucky day. Kidnapped at daybreak and in combat before midnight.

The door screeched open, wrestling against the tight hinges and concrete floor. The muzzle of a rifle poked to the left as Sassi lunged against the door and swiped down at the arm that followed the rifle into the cell. The knife blade sliced through the uniform and bit into muscle.

Her attacker darted to the far corner of the room, placing his back into the 90-degree angle. He was wearing a rucksack and some type of night-vision device she had never seen before. It looked more like a virtual reality headset, only smaller. He aimed the weapon at her as she charged him.

"I am friendly! Not foe! American soldier!" the man shouted.

She stopped directly in front of the muzzle of the weapon. The man's arm was bleeding. Was he trying to trick her into stopping her momentum? Once you lost momentum, it was so hard to regain, if not impossible.

Nonetheless, she stopped when she realized that no one was coming in after him. He was just one soldier. When it had been the Marines, an entire platoon of them came into the corridor, several into her cell, and some even started taking pictures for the inevitable, "Hey, look at me; I saved this woman" photo. None of that ensued here. Even though there had been maybe five seconds of action, it appeared to be just this one soldier.

"Where's Clutch? And who are you?"

She eyed the door. Could she escape? What if she didn't have what this guy wanted? She edged to her left.

"Don't even think about it," he said. He wasn't a terribly big man, maybe five foot ten, she thought. She was nearly as tall as he was, but he looked monstrous in his gear. A modern-day warrior kitted out to create all the conditions that would eventually require her services.

As if he could read her mind, he started moving toward the door, his foot kicking the manacle chains on the floor. She was still holding the knife up in a protective posture.

"Tell me," the soldier said.

Her throat was dry. She was dehydrated and struggled to speak but finally said, "I'm a United Nations employee."

"How long have you been in here?"

"Just today," she said.

The standoff was filled with tension. She was continuing to edge to the left, toward the door. Could freedom be just five feet away? She'd escaped from tougher spots in the past. The man's arm continued to bleed where she'd cut it. She inched another step toward the door.

A loud bang resonated from above. Voices followed. Short commands in Arabic. "Move. Downstairs. Now!"

"Follow me."

The man clasped the top of her biceps with his left hand. It was covered in a glove cut off at the middle knuckles so that his fingertips were exposed. He had a firm grip and was moving through the door. She had no clue what was happening, much less who Clutch might be, but she determined that this devil she had tugging on her arm just might well be better than the ones above her, heading toward the stairwell.

They ran into the hallway to their left. Footsteps thundered down the stairs, with men screaming *"Tankian!"*

Her rapid breaths and pounding heart gave away the anxiety she felt. She didn't like giving control to anyone else, but she relented. Her only weapon was a knife, leaving her nearly defenseless against the high-powered weapons in play here.

They ran past open doors on their left and right,

leaving her thankful there were no other captives—but hadn't she heard someone else during the day? The pounding on the door. A man screaming, though muffled and nearly unintelligible.

Then it hit her. *Clutch.*

My name is Nolte! Corporal Ian A. Nolte! They call me Clutch*! I'm from South Bend, Indiana!*

They made a right turn as she shook her arm loose yet still followed the soldier. He seemed to have one goal in mind, to exit this compound as quickly and safely as possible.

He turned toward her, baring his teeth, and said, "I need you to shoot this rifle. Can you?"

She nodded and said, "Yes."

"Here. The magazine is fresh, and you've got twenty shots. Use them wisely. I'm going to put some explosives on this door."

The man removed his rucksack as he handed Sassi the rifle. She studied it briefly with footsteps pounding on the concrete at the other end of the corridor. He reached into a medical pouch and tied a quick bandage around the cut she had inflicted.

"Lie down next to this guy and shoot in that direction," he said.

At her feet was a dead man with a rifle lying next to him on the concrete. The floor was slick with blood. She knelt and lay down in the blood, using the man as a shield as she peered above the weapon's sights.

The feet and lower legs of two men running down the steps were barely visible in the dim light that shone in an opening at the end of the corridor. They were moving too quickly for any kind of shot, and she was too unfamiliar with how this particular weapon functioned to be confident of any accuracy.

As if reading her mind, the soldier said, "If you see anything, just pull the trigger. Keep them at that end of the basement."

She stared along the iron sights. Nylon scraped against metal behind her. Hands made wet smacking sounds. Feet shuffled.

Two men turned around the corner simultaneously. She squeezed the trigger once. The weapon erupted. Squeezed again. Erupted again. The attackers were black forms moving through the darkness. They scurried to protective cover behind the wall and out of her sight. She continued to fire.

"Slow down. Only when you see them," the man said. It was as if he were visualizing what she was seeing. Perhaps he had experienced the ebb and flow of close-quarters combat many times before? He was a soldier, and that would make sense.

Sassi cradled the warm weapon using the shooting position that Beretta had taught her at the range that day. The buttstock was against her shoulder. Her right hand cradled the grip and trigger housing group. Her left hand grasped the stock beneath the barrel. Her elbows were sharp pointy edges poking into the hard concrete.

When she thought she saw movement, she pulled the trigger. Better to err on the side of caution.

"Waste some ammo now," the man said in a rushed voice.

She squeezed off five shots in a row. Thunderous booms from a pistol rocked her eardrums. He grabbed her arm and spun her around the corner directly into the field of fire from the attackers!

She resisted, but he was strong. As soon as he muscled her into the first room on the left, an explosion rocked the building, shaking it to its foundation. As quickly as they were in the room, they were out. Smoke and debris were still pulsing outward from the blast.

And they were moving toward it!

Back toward their original position. What the hell was happening?

The man shined a flashlight into the boiling smoke and debris. The noxious fumes were overpowering, and she thought she might be sick but realized she hadn't eaten anything. That didn't prevent the dry heaves from having their turn. She gulped a couple of times and followed the pull of the man. They were stepping through a jagged portal into a black tunnel. He was wearing the space-age device over his eyes, which had to be helping him because for the life of her, she couldn't see a damn thing.

For the first time in her life, Sassi entrusted her safety to another man, a soldier by all accounts, perhaps even an American soldier as he claimed to be.

Gunshots echoed as they raced into the bowels of hell.

CHAPTER 18

Jasar Tankian

Tankian hustled through the narrow escape tunnel he had built into the side of his compound.

He had made a split-second decision that the American commando would be of greater value than a random UN worker. His calculation included the estimate that the attacker was most likely coming to retrieve his friend and that the two of them would make an even more formidable pair than the lone gunman.

How had this one person decimated his carefully laid plans and defenses? News of this account would reverberate up and down the valley like a never-ending echo. The weight on his broad shoulders was heavy, but much less so than the grave that would assuredly be pressing down on him if he hadn't fled. His father had always taught him to live another day to make a deal. Survive and the deal survives also.

He arrived at the end of the tunnel after loping along the seven-foot-high passageway he'd had built into his compound for exactly this purpose. While he never could have imagined precisely this clusterfuck occurring, he was prescient enough to foresee the need for an undisclosed exit. Reaching the heavy steel door with the captain's wheel, he turned three dead bolts, all tight and rusty from lack of use.

The wheel squeaked as Tankian got leverage. The prisoner was on Tankian's back, cuffed and deadweight. The gag in his mouth was stained with oil, and Tankian hoped that he would survive. He was going to need a chit in the near future to barter his way back into business.

Finally, the door gave way at the same time he heard voices behind him.

Tankian stepped out of the tunnel, dragging the captive by both his arms over the lip of the door and depositing him on the sloped shale of the ridge that angled east into the Beqaa Valley from just beneath his compound. Tankian put his shoulder into the heavy door and closed it. Looking for something that could impede the madman who had attacked his compound, he found nothing, so he took a deep breath and lifted the man onto his shoulders as though he were carrying a bag of cement.

He climbed up the hill and flipped the soldier onto the plateau. Pushing himself up, he lifted the man again and strode to the garage off the main compound building. A black Suburban SUV was sitting idle on the concrete slab. Part of his emergency escape plan had included an evacuation route, a vehicle, and supplies. He flipped the bound soldier into the rear compartment, next to two cases of bottled water and two cases of MREs. He hustled around to the driver's seat and cranked the engine, then shot out of the garage and found the road to the west.

Harwood saw the door at the end of the corridor slam shut as he clasped the hand of the woman who had been in the cell where Clutch should have been. They moved quickly, chased by the shouts of the men who had entered the basement moments before.

The slamming door echoed like a gunshot. The voices approached closer behind them. It was only a matter of seconds before they would be in the funnel of fire and near inescapable death.

"Hurry," he said to the woman whose hand he held.

They approached the door, and he lowered his shoulder.

"Stay with me," he growled.

"I'm here," she said defiantly.

The voices behind them called out.

He threw his body into the door, and it burst open. An immediate difference between the stale air in the tunnel and the cool, fresh air outside was noticeable. Pulling the woman outside, he said, "Stay right here," as he put her in a protected position out of the line of fire. He lay down, propped his rifle on the lip of the door, flipped on his IVAS, and saw two men running toward them about twenty meters away.

He fired twice at each man and, satisfied with the

results, leaped up and said to the woman, "Follow me. Quick."

They ran up the hill to the plateau upon which the compound sat just as a black SUV was racing to the west. To his right was the adobe-walled compound he had invaded earlier. Up ahead was a complex of buildings he hadn't noticed before. Because of their positioning opposite of where he had made his point of entry, his view of this small cluster had been blocked by the main home he had just blown through.

By now, he trusted the woman to stay with him, and he released her hand so that he could run faster. When he did so, she actually began to outpace him, running toward the first safe harbor, which was a cavernous garage. They slammed into the side of the building.

"You first," the woman said. She had a slight accent that Harwood tried to place. Something European.

He nosed around the edge of the garage door opening, black as midnight. He turned on the flashlight under the rail of his SR-25 and swept the cavern. The flashlight assisted his IVAS in providing the ambient light needed to see more clearly. Another vehicle sat inert in the back of the garage.

"There's an SUV. We'll take that," Harwood said.

"Okay."

First, Harwood cleared each corner of the interior and then motioned to her to move to the SUV. "Clear!"

As Harwood jogged to the SUV, there was a flicker of light in his left-side periphery. He changed course and darted toward the light. The woman noticed and followed suit, not wanting to be too far from protection, he presumed. Her breath was on his neck as they had their backs against the adjoining wall. He reached into his cargo pocket and handed her one of the pistols he had secured from the compound's basement during his assault.

"Don't shoot me," he said.

She took the pistol without hesitation and whispered more to herself than to him, "My pistol."

Harwood sneaked a quick glance at her. There was more to this woman than had met his eye. She had substance to her, making decisions quickly and executing them without hesitation. Harwood nodded and reiterated, "Don't shoot me . . . with your pistol."

She nodded back, wavy hair dangling in oily tendrils across her face. Her eyes were wide, her breathing slow and steady, her face determined. She nudged him with her left shoulder and whispered, "Let's move."

Harwood spun into the room, lit up by his IVAS. Inside the expansive bay were several unmanned aerial vehicles in various states of disrepair and a fleet of Mercedes-Benz snub-nosed cargo trucks. Probably about ten trucks. Double that number of UAVs. One of the UAVs had a running light that was flashing weakly, which must have been the faint light he had seen moments before. He pressed a button on his IVAS several times, taking still photos of the room, which downloaded automatically to his TacSleeve and uploaded to his RangerSat cloud service.

"Let's go," Harwood said. He exited as quickly as they had entered. He tossed his rucksack into the back seat of the SUV, placed his SR-25 muzzle down into the passenger floor well with the buttstock lying across the console, and kept his pistol in his lap. The woman sat in the passenger's seat, quick eyes scanning the back of the SUV.

"Where are we going?" she asked.

Harwood found the keys above the visor, cranked the engine, and let the GPS power up. He pressed a few buttons and was happy to see that the same multiunit GPS tracking system was at work in this vehicle as well.

"There," he said, pointing a finger at the blue dot moving west along a winding road about five miles from them.

He punched in the route to follow the other vehicle, which he presumed was the last man standing who had escaped from the compound. The timing was right. Did he have Clutch?

As they wheeled out of the garage, the woman asked, "What was up with all those small airplanes?"

Harwood navigated the gravel driveway cut with washboard rivulets from high mountain rains, all sloping toward the Beqaa Valley to their east.

"Terrorist compound. Prisoners. Cargo trucks. Unmanned aerial vehicles. Not a good combination. I took pictures." He looked at the woman, who was staring straight ahead into the night.

All they could see was the headlights stabbing into the blackness. The only differentiation was the bleached gravel and dirt upon which they drove. His IVAS, however, provided him a high-definition view. Boulders framed either side of the road. Lights winked in the distance. Low mountain pines hung over the road like sinister spies.

"Sassi. My name is Sassi Cavezza. I'm a worker with the UN High Commission for Refugees."

Harwood nodded. "Nice to meet you, Sassi. I assume you were not voluntarily visiting that compound?"

"No," she said. "Thank you for helping me."

"Roger that."

After a long pause, she asked, "Do you have a name?"

He replied after a longer pause, "Vick Harwood. United States Army Ranger."

CHAPTER 19

The terrain was formidable with its high mountain buttes and deep ravines. Tankian switched back on the road that descended into the Adonis Valley. He had no time for mythology or gods, but he understood the allure of the region and why people might make up mythological stories about its beauty. Even in the darkness, the terrain felt overwhelming with its sheer cliffs looming overhead. The SUV lights poked into the black night as Tankian strained to stay on the narrow road.

After an hour of navigating the fierce terrain, he hit the coastline, bouncing north on Route 51 around coastal villages. Traffic slowed as he entered the town of Byblos at 4:00 a.m. Red brake lights flashed as fishermen moved toward their boats, preparing for a day on the sea. Tankian respected the drive and determination of the men who woke up early, prepared their vessels, and ventured onto the water to provide for their families. They were businessmen like him. He could relate.

He called Khoury using his Bluetooth headset.

"I'm inbound to your location. Need you to visit the morgue and prepare our friends for a trip."

"And do what with them?"

"Put them in the containers."

"Part of the exchange?"

"We are pooling all valuable commodities given what has transpired."

Khoury paused. "I understand."

Tankian would now spend more time at sea than he had planned. His best option was to oversee the execution of his big payday rather than put the pieces back together at his compound. The compound and its strategic position served a functional purpose, primarily that of being a logistics hub. He could easily rebuild it and resume his enterprise or—as the sun rose on the Mediterranean Sea to his left—he could buy a nice home with some servants and live a simple, luxurious life.

It might be nice not to have to hustle and work with the terrorists of the world, always believing he was one wrong move from having to kill or be killed. The constant exposure to daily threats of life and limb had reinforced his dispassionate disposition. Always calm and collected, Tankian had encountered very little that could fluster him.

About 6:00 a.m., he pulled up to the outside gate of the Port of Tripoli. He used this port for all his supplies, but a few times, merchants had accidentally shipped his goods to Tripoli, Libya, two thousand kilometers away. At the gate, the guard was dressed in a gray short-sleeved police officer's shirt and black pants. He had gray hair, a three-day beard, and smelled of alcohol. Seagulls squawked overhead in their perpetual cry as they rode the onshore breeze. The musty smell of the maritime shipping industry—oil, grease, diesel, salt water—wafted in when he buzzed down the window.

"Gabir," Tankian said, handing his identification to the guard.

Gabir leaned forward and stared into the SUV with a perplexed look on his face. "No driver today?"

"Thought I'd take a little spin in the countryside," Tankian said.

"Mr. Tankian, Khoury came here a few hours ago, then left, and he's back again. He's waiting for you in the container yard."

"Thank you, Gabir."

It was good news that Khoury had retrieved the two dead American soldiers without incident. He would have contacted Tankian otherwise.

The guard pushed a button, and a chain-link gate rolled backward, allowing Tankian to drive into the port. He navigated past stacks of rust-colored containers. The large blue container cranes hung in the distance like giant storks standing above the water. Tankian drove into the container yard, where he found Khoury standing next to the cargo truck.

"Everything go smoothly?" Tankian asked.

"Of course. Both are in the ammunition container. I wrapped them in a tarp. Won't keep the smell down, but they're frozen right now. In less than a day, they'll be ripe."

Tankian nodded.

Khoury looked inside through the window Tankian had buzzed down and raised his eyebrows.

"Everything okay, boss?"

"All good," Tankian said.

Khoury nodded and said, "Ship's at the berth. Cargo-handling equipment is on the way. They're ready for our two containers."

"Want to take a boat ride?"

"Whatever you say," Khoury replied.

"Leave the truck here and jump in."

Khoury entered the passenger side of the SUV, and Tankian drove to the ship.

"We have a prisoner that is very valuable to us."

"The American?"

Tankian chinned toward the back seat. Khoury turned and looked.

"What's the offer? Not sure anything is worth what we've just experienced."

"Two million euros. The catch is that we have to personally deliver him. So, we take him on the boat, stop in Cyprus, and make the trade there. Wolff has a plan."

Khoury nodded, then said, "I've received some calls from the valley."

"Yes?"

"The destruction sounds . . . total," Khoury said.

"That's why we're getting on the ship," Tankian said. "A business decision."

"Our motto *has* always been to live to do another deal."

Tankian nodded.

A top-pick container handler pulled up and lifted the first container, then drove to the berth and placed it on the ground. It returned and repeated the process. The ship was stacked to the sky with containers, and Tankian was curious where these might fit. The crane reached down and plucked the first from the yard and lowered it into a nook even with the ship's deck. Repeating the process, the crane placed the second container directly in front of the first.

"My instructions are to board the ship and ride it to Cyprus," Tankian said. "We can disembark there and stay at the beach a couple of days, relaxing." Tankian walked to the back of the Suburban and said, "Leave the SUVs here. They'll watch them until we get back. Meanwhile, help me with this guy." He popped the hatch. It rose slowly, revealing the bound and gagged American soldier from the airplane crash site.

Khoury looked at the soldier and then at Tankian. "You're sure about this?"

"Like I said, 'two million euros.'"

"Let's leave him here in the back of the truck." Khoury stepped away from the SUV. His bald head glistened in the morning sun. The seagulls continued squawking above their heads. Tankian was more worried about one of the gulls dropping a shit bomb on his head than he was about Khoury's protests. Khoury had been a loyal business associate, fully subordinated to Tankian's leadership and management. The businessman from

Beirut narrowed his eyes at Tankian and repeated, "He's a curse. Leave him, Jasar."

Jasar. When was the last time Khoury had called him by his first name?

"I'd prefer to have you come along. If you don't want to, I can't stop you from driving away."

Khoury said, "Think about what you're doing. It was one thing to hold the American for Wolff until he figured out what to do with him. It's an entirely different thing to drag him onto that boat and kidnap him. We will have the entire U.S. military looking for him!"

"And they'll be looking where? On a boat?"

"Once they find our cars, they will!" he said, pointing at the Suburban.

Tankian shrugged. "We will deal with that when and if we ever have to. Now, either get in the Suburban and drive away or grab one of those dock carts and help me stuff him in there."

Khoury shook his head but walked toward the terminal operations center about a hundred meters away. Tankian retrieved his prepacked go bag and checked the equipment. There were two 9 mm pistols, body armor, and several boxes of ammunition. The gravel crunched behind him. He turned around and saw Khoury pulling a large fishing cooler.

"I'll go on one condition," Khoury said.

"You know me better than this. Either you are in or you are out."

"I get half the total."

"You're a thirty percent partner. You get your thirty percent provided we execute."

"I'm taking half the risk here. I should get half the money."

Tankian ignored him as he shouldered his duffel. One pistol was still in his side holster plus two more in the duffel. He could kill Khoury and board the ship with the American, but that would bring unwanted attention. A better idea was to get him on board and then toss him off the ship at some point.

He sighed, as if relenting. "Khoury, you drive a hard bargain, but you've always been a loyal partner. Okay, fifty percent it is."

Khoury smiled. "Well, then, let me help you with that."

They loaded the barely conscious prisoner into the cooler, which was made for very large fish. As they were positioning the detainee into the six-foot-long container, Tankian stood upright. Something had alerted him. He suddenly had the distinct feeling of being watched. Across the hardpan of the port yard, an SUV pulled up to the gate. A man stuck his head out the window, followed by a hand holding something. Maybe a gun?

"Hurry," Tankian said.

He closed the lid, and they dragged the cooler to the gangplank where they entered the ship and stepped past the containers that had just been loaded. With Khoury behind him, Tankian walked through the first galley and into the bridge. They left the cooler in the corridor and stepped into the control room.

In the captain's seat was a Russian admiral, who

said, "Welcome, comrades. Have a seat, and we will discuss the plan."

Tankian looked past the admiral through the thick salt-stained Plexiglas. A man and a woman exited the SUV—one of his SUVs—near the vehicle they had used to drive here.

"We must go now," Tankian said.

The admiral chuckled. "Yes, of course. We were just waiting on you."

The ship began moving, a tugboat nudging it out to sea.

The man and woman turned toward the ship. The man pointed and said something, then they both began running toward the berth.

Tankian began thinking about things he had never really considered before, such as the thickness of the Plexiglas and the maximum speed of container ships. If this was the same man who had single-handedly destroyed his business—and it certainly appeared to be—then there was no telling what he could do to a defenseless ship.

"Admiral, do you have any scouts or snipers on this boat?"

"Of course. I've got both. Why do you ask?"

Tankian pointed.

The admiral turned and saw the two running toward his ship. He picked up a radio handset and said, "Red team. Threat at three o'clock."

"Roger. Tracking."

"Shoot to kill," the admiral said.

A few seconds later, two gunshots rang out as the

ship pushed away from the tug and gained momentum in the open sea.

Harwood grabbed Sassi and dove to his right behind a rust-orange forty-foot Sealand container. At the last second, the morning sunlight winked off the shooter's scope lens, giving away the position.

The vortex from the two shots created a wake of turbulence off his ear. Sassi stumbled into the gravel, and for a moment, Harwood thought she'd been hit.

"You okay?" Harwood said. He never took his eyes off the shooter. The ship appeared to be moving away from the berth. He took a deep breath and exhaled slowly.

"I'm fine," Sassi said. "I'd like to know what's going on. You hardly spoke on the ride here."

"I was focused, and you slept," Harwood said. "Just stick with me. I'll explain later."

"What if I want to leave now?"

Harwood didn't have the time or bandwidth for an argument. "And go where? You're in Lebanon, and I just released you from captivity. We're going to find my partner, Clutch, better known as Corporal Ian Nolte."

Sassi looked at him. Her hair was matted to her forehead, and her breath stank. Harwood winced and turned away.

"Sorry. Haven't brushed my teeth in a while. I was going to ask, though, this soldier isn't related to Senator Ian Nolte, is he?"

"Yes. That's his dad. Why?"

"Nothing," Sassi said, looking away. Then she turned

back toward him. "He was on a visit to Afghanistan when I was there. I briefed him. He seemed to have a real sense of compassion for our mission. Most politicians don't care. They're just there for the cool places they go to like Croatia and Italy before visiting the combat zone for a few hours. Me? I go to ten crazy shitholes for every one vacation I take."

"Sounds like my life," Harwood said. "Can't remember my last vacation."

Harwood managed another peek around the corner of the container providing them protective cover. The container ship had turned and was headed into the sea.

"Quick. Let's go. There's a marina this way." He shouldered his ruck and clasped her hand, guiding her across the hardpan to the dock. They remained covered most of the way to two piers poking from land into the blue-gray water. White fishing and sport boats were moored along two wooden piers that ran perpendicular to the bulkhead. They watched a man wearing shorts, sandals, and an orange T-shirt walk back and forth between the dock and his car in the parking lot fifty meters away.

"Hang tight. Don't move," Harwood said. "Bring this when you see me running to the pier."

Sassi didn't argue this time as Harwood left his rucksack with her and darted toward the parking lot, which was vacant this early in the morning. He closed on the pickup truck quickly with the man leaning into the passenger side of the truck. Harwood removed his pistol and landed a solid blow on the back of his head. It wasn't in his code to injure innocents, but he really had no choice. He doubted that debating with him would yield a ride to follow the container ship.

He snatched the keys from the man's hand, lifted him into his truck, checked his pulse—elevated but okay—and shut the door. He jogged back toward their covered position, motioned at Sassi with an upraised fist, pumping it down in the universal move for "let's haul ass." She lifted his rucksack, grimaced at the weight, and then darted toward him at a fast pace.

The man's boat was a Riva twenty-three-foot center-console boat not unlike one Harwood had stolen when chasing his prior nemesis, the Chechen.

"Untie the lines," Harwood said as they jumped into the vessel's deck. The man had carried four gas cans onto the boat, which might give them enough gas to either go wherever the ship's next stop was, provided it was just up the coast, or, less preferably, catch up with the ship and board it.

Sassi did as Harwood instructed, and soon they were heading into open seas with the container ship now fully under way. Harwood nudged the throttle forward, the Riva gaining speed until he had it full and open with a rooster tail spitting out the back like a fire hose.

CHAPTER 20

Valerie Hinojosa

Valerie Hinojosa walked along Juneau Avenue in Milwaukee, Wisconsin, huddled against a spring breeze snapping off Lake Michigan. She was completing a run along the lake and finished in Veterans Park, a tree-lined open space that jutted out from Milwaukee's Lower East Side into the seemingly never-ending lake. Might as well be an ocean.

She wiped some sweat from her face, adjusted her sports bra beneath her windbreaker, and checked her phone. Her ex-boyfriend, Army Ranger Sergeant Vick Harwood, had been gone a week on another undisclosed mission. He had done so before, and she should know. Valerie had been his handler during the Team Valid mission that had led to the killing of Virginia senator Sloane Brookes.

Valerie disliked politics, but here she was thrust into

the fray again on her first assignment back in the field after extensive rehab following the Valid mission. She walked along the lake edge, riprap poking upward like sawteeth. Gray-blue water went as far as her eye could see to the east. Less than a mile to the south was the Port of Milwaukee, and farther south by about fifty miles was Chicago. To the immediate west was downtown Milwaukee, flush with bars, restaurants, and hotels. To her north was more shoreline and the home the wealthy Milwaukee elite.

Walking along the asphalt path, Valerie stepped from the tunnel of trees into the sunshine and lifted her face to the sky. Anything to get warm as she cooled down from her run. She found a grassy spot and sat down so that she could stretch. She was still recovering from being roughed up by former Marine sniper Griffin Weathers, who had turned traitor. Processing their relationship in her mind, Valerie still couldn't quite fathom what she had seen in the man, and questioned her own abilities as an FBI special agent. She should have seen his murderous personality at some point during their six-month relationship.

Weathers was dead now, killed by Vick, the Reaper, her former beau. How odd was that? Transitioning from a man who betrayed his country to the man who had slain him. Harwood had done so at a critical moment, of course. Weathers was in the process of attempting to kill both of them. While she was certainly more than capable of defending herself, Valerie had suffered a beating at the hands of Weathers and barely survived. Bruised ribs, broken jaw, fractured forearm. It would have been much worse had Vick not intervened when he had.

When both she and Vick had been admitted to Walter Reed National Military Medical Center, they found the time to come together every night. It started with Vick visiting her room when she was still immobilized. He'd been injured himself. Weathers had sneaked in a few cuts of the knife on Harwood as they'd fought in the secret tunnel beneath Senator Brookes's compound on the Chesapeake Bay.

During that week of recovery, she had fallen for Vick. His smile, a slight upturn on the right side of his mouth, was the first thing she saw when she woke up that morning coming out of surgery on her jaw. His soulful brown eyes had made her heart clutch. She didn't know when it had clicked for Vick, but she had felt the connection from the outset, even during the mission. There was a chemistry between them that was hard for her to explain. She never mixed work and dating—she'd met Weathers on a dating app—and Harwood was a new foray for her. She let herself believe the relationship was safe, because Vick served in the army and she the FBI, two distinctly different organizations without much, if any, mission overlap. They both served their country, but that was about it. Still, though, it was too soon after Valid, and she was just getting her career back on track.

Valerie leaned forward and stretched her tight hamstrings and calves. Her shoulders and arms screamed at her with pain. Breath escaped from between her teeth, sounding like a hissing air hose. Her eyes welled with tears, but she continued to hold the tips of her shoes, leaning forward and ripping scar tissue.

"Damn it," she whispered to herself.

"Don't hurt yourself," a deep voice said from behind her.

She bounced up and spun around, only to find her boss, Special Agent Deke Bronson, standing there in the bronze, godlike flesh, wearing running shorts and a formfitting workout T-shirt. His leg muscles rippled like a Kentucky Thoroughbred on promenade.

"Shit, boss, you scared me," Valerie said.

"Down, kung fu. I know you can take me," Bronson said.

Valerie looked at her hands. She was crouched in a fighter's pose on the balls of her feet with fists ready to strike. Bronson jokingly flexed his muscles and acted as if he were prepared to defend himself.

"Sorry, Deke," Valerie said. "I'm just a tad jumpy."

"I know. That's why we're starting slow with something low profile like the national convention of a political party."

"Low profile. They're going to fill a basketball arena with a hundred thousand screaming maniacs supporting one tribe over another. If I'd wanted that, I could have joined the army and been in Afghanistan or Iraq."

Bronson was a former Marine who had served in Fallujah. He smiled. "Got that T-shirt. Let's take a walk."

Bronson turned, and Valerie followed.

"Heard from the Reaper?" he asked.

"I know you and Vick have a complicated history, Deke, but he'd probably want you to call him *Vick*."

"How about I just call him something that rhymes with *Vick*?"

Valerie rolled her eyes. "Oh my God. You're half a world away from each other and you still can't cut him any slack."

"Nope."

"Is it his charming good looks or the fact that you could never quite catch him?"

During a case involving Vick's sniper rifle from Afghanistan, Bronson had been searching for the most likely suspect—Vick Harwood the Reaper—and had come up empty-handed until Vick presented himself to authorities in an effort to find the actual culprit. He had assumed that Bronson would give him the benefit of the doubt for coming in voluntarily. Vick had been mostly wrong. Bronson didn't cut anyone any slack.

"I caught him," Bronson said. He visibly bristled at the memory, though. "I'll ask again, have you heard from your beau?"

"He's not my beau, but he's 'overseas,'" she said, making air quotes with her fingers. "I've got a clearance, but he still doesn't tell me anything."

"No need to know. And what do you mean he's not your beau?"

Valerie shrugged, not accepting his response as a meaningful answer and not wanting to dive into her personal life with her boss. "Topic changer. What's on your mind?" Valerie asked.

Bronson paused as if he wanted to stay on the topic of Harwood and then responded, "We've got intel coming in, and I need you to sift through it. I've got a SCIF set up in the hotel."

They were walking side by side along the path. The Milwaukee skyline loomed in front of them as they took the steps up to the street level. Bronson nudged them north and kept talking.

"Anything sticking out, or the usual crazies with rifles, snipers on the rooftops, and rental trucks filled with explosives?"

"All that and more. Nothing really making my Spidey senses go off, but you're the pro at this stuff, not me."

Hinojosa gave him the side-eye. Something was up. He was never this nice to her.

"Okay, level with me, Deke. What's going on?"

"I'm leveling with you, but I need to let you know that we've got word of one Army Ranger gone missing in Lebanon. Intel sources from the Beqaa Valley have circulated through Europe and Israel back to here. Did Vick say anything about being in Lebanon or Israel?"

Valerie stopped and spun at Bronson. "Why weren't these the first words out of your mouth? Why this song-and-dance bullshit?"

"I wasn't sure how to approach it."

"Whatever! What do you know?"

They passed a group of high school students walking toward the BMO Harris Pavilion as they continued toward Henry Maier Festival Park. The kids were chattering away, carrying their backpacks and smartphones, giggling and laughing as high school kids should be doing. Bronson remained silent until they had passed the teenagers.

"Our joint intelligence working group received a ping that there was a plane crash in the Beqaa Valley. We've got people moving to the scene, but our information is at least a day old, if not longer."

"Any word if this is Vick?"

"None. We know that four Army Rangers were on assignment in Turkey, Syria, and Lebanon. All close-hold stuff."

"I saw the news on another Syrian incursion on the Golan Heights. Could that be related?"

"I don't believe in coincidences, so yeah, I think there's something here that you need to know about. Honestly, I was hoping that the Reaper slipped up and fed you some intel."

"No. Never. He doesn't say a whole lot on a normal day. Less when he's got a classified mission. Plus, as I've mentioned, we're not a thing."

"Yeah, okay. I'll believe that when I see it. I guess I can try to find out some things," Bronson said.

If she weren't worried, she would have smiled at Bronson's concern for someone he supposedly didn't like. While she was sure there was some professional jealousy involved, most of Bronson's hostility was an act.

They finally reached the Marriott, where she followed Bronson into a suite on the top floor. It was a four-room layout with intelligence analysts sitting at three computer displays in the outer room. In the next room, the FBI had constructed a portable SCIF by erecting steel walls and latching them together. She stepped inside with Bronson, who closed the door, and they sat at the two terminals.

Pulling up a map of Milwaukee, Valerie studied the road networks, airports, seaport, and locations. She tried to focus on the potential threats, but she kept cycling back to concern about Vick. Was there something he had said to her about his mission before he left? They had briefly discussed Monisha and made the decision that she should stay at Command Sergeant Major Murdoch's parents' home in Columbus, Georgia. He had packed some cold-weather clothes, and she imagined that Lebanon in May in the mountains would be chilly. He had given no clue, though he did mention "having a beer" one night with his spotter, Ian Nolte, sending a picture before the mission started. They had texted on WhatsApp. She made a point to tell him that despite her strong feelings for him, she couldn't be involved in a relationship so soon after the death of her brother. He had understood, she thought. She had seen the pain in his eyes when he nodded and said, "Roger." They kept in contact, though, and now she thought about that photo. He could literally have a beer anywhere in the world, so it was no big clue. He had mentioned something about a hefeweizen, but wheat beer was sold all around the world as well.

Could be Germany, which would support the Lebanon theory, but she needed to focus on her job, instead of going through this useless spiral.

"Val?"

"Um, yeah. What I really need, Deke, is to have

those analysts out there comb through every airplane arriving, every rental car being leased or reserved, every ship coming into port here and in Chicago, every train coming up from Chicago and other places. All current and planned reservations. Run everything through NCIC, and look for any kind of connection, because I'm feeling nothing in my gut."

Bronson nodded. "That's either really good or really bad. Your gut is a combat multiplier, and if you're not feeling anything, that could be a sign that you think we're okay, or it could be a sign that you're preoccupied with the Reaper."

Valerie stared at him. "I'm *not* preoccupied with Vick. Get me the intel, and I'll figure it out."

CHAPTER 21

Vick Harwood

Harwood had changed the gas tanks three times, and they were on the fourth can. The Mercury 250 engines were guzzling the fuel. The headwinds and sea chop weren't helping the situation either. He navigated so that they stayed about a quarter mile off the stern of the ship, never losing sight.

"Why is Senator Nolte's son on that ship?" Sassi asked.

Harwood nodded. The salt spray from the swells colliding with the hull of the motorboat peppered the windscreen and Harwood's face. He had exchanged his IVAS for some Revision ballistic eye protection.

"I'm not sure why, but I can tell you that he's someone very important to me," Harwood said. "He was probably in that cooler they were dragging up the gangplank."

"But you don't know for certain he's on the boat, right? I mean, we could be on wild-duck chase," Sassi said.

"Goose."

"Excuse me?"

"The phrase is *wild-goose chase*."

Sassi stood next to him. Her chestnut hair whipped in the breeze. The boat was traveling at twenty-five knots.

"Whatever manner of fowl we might be chasing, the point is that we in fact might be wasting our time."

"Have you ever had something taken away from you to the point you would do anything to get it back?"

"Every day," Sassi said. "I work for the United Nations. My life is a never-ending cycle of disappointment, regret, and worry."

Harwood looked away from the sprawling sea and into Sassi's eyes. They reflected an honest accounting of her words. Kind eyes. Deep and compassionate. The adrenaline dump from having been kidnapped and freed from captivity most likely had her reflecting on life. The twenty-five-knot boat chase for the last few hours wasn't exactly high octane. Neither was it easy on the spine with the teeth-jarring swells.

"That's not good," Harwood said.

"Yes. Not good, but then again, very good. I get a lot of personal satisfaction from what I do."

"Same here," Harwood said.

"How so? You kill people for a living. You're a sniper."

"I help my country and our allies win wars to protect our freedoms."

"Do you really believe that? How could anything you were doing in Israel or Lebanon be helping your country?"

He looked at her.

"Oh God. Don't tell me you were in Syria?"

"I didn't tell you anything, and I won't. My missions are classified. I don't have to justify anything to you, and you can get off anytime you'd like, either now or when we dock."

"Seriously? You'd just have me jump off this boat?"

"It's a free world."

"There you have it wrong. It's far from free."

"I wasn't making a political statement. I was saying that I wouldn't stop you if you dove overboard."

Sassi laughed. "The hardened Army Ranger is living up to his billing. I think I'll wait until we hit land . . . if we hit land."

"Your choice. See? Free." He smiled.

"You're a piece of work," Sassi said. Her comment was lighthearted, not cross. The half smile turning up her lips reinforced the idea that she was at a minimum amused by him. He continued to navigate the sea and stay well off their target.

"Besides, you had your chance before we got in this boat," Harwood said.

"Not much of a chance, Sergeant. You practically kidnapped me," Sassi said.

"I'm not sure I could have, much less wanted to. You have skills, I believe."

"So, you think I'm here because I can help you." A statement, not a question.

Harwood nodded. He was conflicted.

After another hour of shadowing the container ship, Harwood saw an airplane flying low, as if landing or taking off. Landing, he decided. It was slowing down and losing altitude. On cue, the boat engine sputtered. Running out of fuel.

"There's an airplane," he said. "I think we're on our way to Cyprus. Regardless, we've lost our chance to board the ship unless we can find more gas." The fuel gauge read an eighth of a tank remaining. Maybe he imagined the sputtering. He eased off the throttle a bit, unsure about fuel-consumption rates on boats. Common sense told him that if he needed to conserve fuel, then he should put less strain on the engine.

Land appeared beyond the container ship.

"I've been there. Greek side is better," Sassi said. She was standing next to him, holding on to the windscreen with her hands as she flexed her knees and rode out the swells. After another mile, the wind seemed to shift direction, taming the swells and easing the ride.

"We're going to whatever side has gas," Harwood said. "If we can't catch up with that ship, we're screwed. They could take him anywhere once they dock."

"Yes, many airports and other seaports. Plus, lots of beach and shoreline where a boat like this could get in and out without being noticed. There's a lot of crime there, so it is easy to pay money to get something like this done."

"I'm all inspired now," Harwood said.

Sassi smirked. "We can't have that, now, can we?"

Whatever she was, Harwood thought, the woman had a lot of pluck. She'd just been captured and released, and now she was along for the ride with him acting as normal as a person could act.

The ship began to turn to the north on the south side of the island.

"Famagusta," Sassi whispered. "The ghost city."

Tankian stood in the bridge as the container ship steamed into port at Famagusta, Cyprus. The admiral sat quietly in the corner whittling with a knife and a block of wood. He appeared about sixty years old with a leathery face, wizened from years at sea. After they departed Tripoli, the admiral had said very little. He just sat there tilted back in an old lawn chair, chipping away at the wood, shavings falling onto the floor. It was clear his presence was mandatory either because of the ship or its cargo. A burly man had been at the helm from the start and also had said very little. They had been at sea for maybe six hours, having departed Tripoli the moment he and Khoury boarded.

The sun hung low on the horizon ahead of them, highlighting the sheer bluffs of Cyprus in gold-tinted shades of brown and black. The gray sky etched a backdrop worthy of a charcoal drawing. Tankian visualized the geography. Two hundred miles to the south, similar bluffs would mark Egypt's northern border. Turkey's coast was closer in the north, looming some seventy miles away like a suspicious parent. Seagulls squawked overhead, hoping for the slop buckets. A few perched on the edges of the containers stacked in front of him for the length of a football field.

The most noticeable landmarks were the scores of empty high-rise buildings in the distance. The skyline was peppered with dozens of buildings, all black from lack of power and empty of inhabitants. Tankian knew of the Turkish invasion here that had driven residents from what was today essentially a ghost town. The northern side of the city was still populated. The port divided the city in half and was a quick thirty-minute drive to Geçitkale Air Base, a Turkish fighter jet haven that doubled as a civilian airport.

Tankian had several clients that laundered and smuggled goods through Cyprus. Neither the Turks nor the Greeks had any particular standards that prevented illicit goods from transiting the Mediterranean Sea. Cyprus was the perfect pivot point for transshipment. Egypt, Israel, Syria, Greece, Italy, and Turkey were all within a day's movement by ship. Given the shifting geopolitics of the region, a shipper could hold goods there for a day or two and make the best call on how to proceed. Should he ship to Israel on an Israeli ship? American? A neutral nation such as Liberia? And likewise, to Syria. There were so many legal and illegal goods moving through this gateway that it was impossible to track anything.

He reflected on the two attackers that the ship's security team had shot in the container yard. The ship had been turning, and he lost sight of the engagement. He preferred to have verification that the madman and

UNHCR worker had been killed. He didn't need any more problems from them. Had never wanted them to begin with. The presence of the woman reinforced to Tankian that the attacker had entered his compound to secure the prisoner he kept in the hold below. The man evidently had released her, escaped his compound unscathed, and tracked him to the port. Where would it end?

"Where do we make the exchange?" Tankian asked the admiral.

The ship crawled alongside the berth and shut down.

"We wait until night. Then we move," the admiral said, ignoring his question. "We will offload your two containers and your prisoner and take you to the airport. My instructions are to make sure you arrive safely, board the aircraft, and depart."

Tankian was confused. "Where are we going?"

The admiral pushed off the wall and shrugged. "I only know this part of this mission."

"Is this even your ship?"

"Of course. And when I leave, it will be someone else's ship."

Tankian understood Max Wolff was managing him through this admiral. To date, he and Wolff had a trusting relationship devoid of any suspicion or duplicity, a rarity in this or any business. An entrepreneur all his life, Tankian had never technically worked for anyone, though he'd had plenty of customers he'd tried his best to supply with all their needs. Now, though, he wanted to prevent his control from slipping away. He had survived the attack on his compound. And while an attack was always technically a possibility, Tankian had never really considered it likely. Not at all. Just the opposite. He had been secure to the point that he had taken for granted much of what he wished he had on hand right now.

His satellite phone vibrated as they pulled into port. The tug nudged them closer to the berth as he held the phone to his ear.

"Yes."

"Status?" Wolff asked.

"Arriving."

"I know this. The cargo?"

Tankian had checked on the prisoner twice during the trip. He and Khoury had let him out of the cooler and tied him to anchor bolts in the floor of an empty hold using thick one-inch ropes. They'd given him water and some sea rations, which he refused.

"Cargo is in excellent condition."

"Make the transfer and then contact me."

"Yes."

Wolff hung up, and the admiral said, "Time to move."

Tankian took one last look out the bridge. He paused. A small boat sped away into a marina about a quarter mile away on the opposite side of the city.

"Commander Tankian. Time to move," the admiral emphasized. The man came up and grabbed his massive triceps, then released, thinking better of it, perhaps.

"Coming," Tankian said.

"Did you see a ghost?"

Maybe, he thought. Or maybe it was the Reaper.

CHAPTER 22

Harwood shouldered his ruck as he stepped from the stolen Riva, tied off the lines, and helped Sassi out by clasping her forearm and pulling her onto the pier.

They were moored at an abandoned marina that appeared to be connected to a vacant condominium complex. Harwood kept one eye on the setting sun, which was dipping below the horizon.

"This way," he said.

Sassi followed. She was carrying her Beretta pistol that Harwood had returned to her. Placing trust in Sassi was his only option. If he was to continue and secure Clutch from whoever his captors might be, he needed help. To the extent that she was willing to assist, he was happy to facilitate her. Harwood felt that he had gotten lucky at the compound. His element of surprise had provided him with a window of opportunity that had stayed open throughout his violent execution.

He couldn't count on that being the case in the future.

They were about four hundred meters from the port where the ship they were following had docked. He led her beyond a gate and found a path that wound between two blacked-out high-rises. The buildings looked like poorly carved jack-o'-lanterns with their shattered windows.

The ghost city was creepy and haunting. They passed through a building with no doors. It had been an office of some type. Desks were empty with no papers or equipment. Everything of value appeared to have been looted. Grime covered broken chairs and desks. There was nothing living in any of the buildings, not even rats. Rats needed food. With no grocery stores or leftovers in the trash cans, there was nothing to keep anything alive. This place was like Harwood imagined Chernobyl to be after the nuclear meltdown had subsided. Vacant. Desolate.

They popped out of the office building and were standing in a parking lot, looking across the pier at the ship they had been trailing. Harwood stepped back inside the office building and tugged Sassi to one knee next to a low window. From there, they could see the ship while still being protected from any direct fire.

Moments later, three men emerged from the ship's hull on the gangplank. Harwood donned his IVAS and focused the lens.

"That's them. They're pulling the same cooler. Clutch has got to be in that thing."

"Three of them. Two of us," Sassi said. "Seems like good odds, no?"

He liked this woman.

"Yeah, but the two SUVs that pulled up have four linebackers standing guard with long rifles."

What was the play? Shoot and the captors could easily flee with Clutch. There was no way to kill all of them in the thirty seconds it would take them to figure out what was happening and to evacuate the area. Worse, they could kill Clutch, making this pursuit moot.

To the north about another four hundred meters, Harwood noticed traffic flowing smoothly on a road. There was a stoplight that led to a freeway. Bright lights bounced off the thin layer of clouds about ten miles to the north also.

Major city? Airport?

Harwood had docked the boat in the closest spot he could for fear of running out of gas. He was quickly seeing the disadvantage to being in a desolate area. Great for hiding, but options were limited. Nothing worked. There were no transportation choices. Couldn't steal a car, a bike, or a skateboard. Nothing.

"I have an idea," Sassi said.

"Shoot."

"See those two Mercedes-Benz trucks driving up to the ship?"

"Roger."

"They came in with the SUVs and peeled off toward the crane."

"They're together."

"Yes, which means this team will wait for the other team."

Two snub-nosed Mercedes-Benz cargo trucks idled alongside the ship and beneath the overhead container crane. Their drivers exited and met midway between the trucks. One called out to someone across the asphalt yard.

"Maybe. Maybe not. But I think the best option is those guys. Let's go."

Harwood memorized the route he had studied. They could move behind the office building, across the railroad, and on the back side of the port main terminal building, which would allow them to avoid the bulky security guards by the SUVs and attempt to stow away on one or both of the trucks.

It was all he had.

They jogged through the empty office building onto a sidewalk covered with dirt from years of disuse. Stepping across the railroad tracks, Harwood saw movement near the gate where the vehicles had entered the port. Two guards dressed in olive-green uniforms were talking and smoking cigarettes. Both had blocky, wood-stock HK G3 rifles slung across their bodies with two-point slings. The tall guard laughed at something the chubby guard said. They both took a drag on their cigarettes and continued joking. While not a real threat, they could detect and report. He didn't want to risk shooting them, which would make noise and potentially alert the others. While there was minimal activity at the port—almost as if the people here were specifi-cally present because of this one ship—he didn't want to risk being detected when he was so close to securing Clutch.

"I've got this," Sassi said. She unsnapped one of the pockets on his rucksack and retrieved something; Harwood couldn't see what. He knew he had ammo, a knife, a phone, and flex-cuffs in the pocket she had opened.

Before he could say anything, Sassi was up and mov-ing from their prone position in the gravel on the port side of the railroad tracks. Sassi backed away and fol-lowed the tracks to the north, where she popped into the open near the gate and the guards.

Her voice floated through the air some fifty meters away. She walked up to the two men, holding her hands in the air, as if surrendering, and pointing back at the train tracks.

The two guards turned, startled, and drew their weapons.

"*Emergenza!*" she said. She spoke in Italian. These men could be Greek, Turkish, or some other national-ity altogether.

"*Poios eisai?*"

Sassi pointed at the tracks again and said, "*Corpo morto!*"

Harwood was unable to hear the conversation once the voices lowered. One guard stood back while the other seemed to be curious.

"*Pou?*"

Another question. Sassi waved her arms and ran back toward the tracks, turning to usher one of them forward.

The tall one walked quickly to the tracks where Harwood could no longer see Sassi or the tall guard. A couple of minutes passed before the short guard got curious and walked to where they had disappeared.

Someone shouted from across the yard. The crane whirred to life and moved with short robotic jerks. The long arm swung over the ship, its spreader opening its jaws wide to snatch the containers on the ship.

Realizing they were running out of time, Harwood became concerned. He knew very little about Sassi Cavezza, but so far, she had seemed both loyal and capable. Harwood didn't see her as a killer, but that could be due to his own prejudice. He knew women could kill as easily as men. All he needed to do was think of Valerie Hinojosa and add up her body count as an FBI special agent on the Team Valid mission last year.

After a few more minutes of lying in the gravel beneath the tall grass, Harwood pushed up, ready to move.

"This way," Sassi said. She was breathing hard, as if she'd just sprinted.

He followed her behind the tracks. They jogged past the two guards, both of whom were bound with the flex-cuffs that Sassi had retrieved from his rucksack and gagged with what looked like socks.

"My flex-cuffs?"

"I've been staring at those things when I've followed you. Glad I knew where they were."

Harwood's lips twitched as close to a smile as he was going to get under these circumstances.

"I'm guessing you're not the average United Nations employee . . . if you're one at all?" he commented.

"I am one, and for the record, you're not the only person with skills."

"Obviously. I'll move forward to the trucks. Stay here. Use your judgment on the tire shredders."

He took the lead as they knelt next to the open gate. The crane had one of the containers loaded into its maw as it swung around toward the waiting tractor. The two drivers watched intently.

Harwood crossed the gate and jogged to the terminal control building. It was a low-slung redbrick job with pillbox windows. A single glassed-in door provided access. Harwood slid beyond the door and crossed the asphalt before kneeling behind a generator. He turned and looked for Sassi, who had stopped at the guard-house and had activated the tire shredders that would slow the egress of the trucks.

The two SUVs started and quickly U-turned in the container yard about a hundred meters from the gate. Harwood was trapped, as was Sassi. She quickly ducked back into the guard shack, lowered the tire shredders, and slid out the other side, hiding behind concrete poles designed to prevent trucks from ramming into the shack.

Harwood had fifty meters of open yard between him and Sassi. If he moved, he would be seen. He slowly lay flat on the asphalt and extended the bipod on his SR-25 and tracked the two SUVs as they approached the gate.

Pulling away from the scope, he turned and saw the crane's boom swinging around with the second container.

The play had been to penetrate the more vulnerable trucks as opposed to confronting the heavily armed SUVs. He had about thirty meters to the trucks, over halfway there from the guard shack. One thing Harwood had learned in his combat tours was that a 50 percent plan violently executed was better than a perfect plan poorly executed.

The SUVs approached the gate. Harwood turned and looked at the tractor lifting the first container. The crane lowered the second container. He had maybe five minutes. The plan, such as it was, was all predicated on the notion that the trucks were going to the same location as the SUVs. It made sense, though. The containers had been loaded at the port. The big man had come from the compound Harwood had attacked. There had to be a connection.

After he placed the second container on the tarmac, the crane operator swiveled the boom back into place and turned the engine off. They were off-loading only the two containers, not the hundreds of others.

The driver of the tractor with the giant crab claw that would pick up the containers and place them on the trucks had summoned the two truck drivers and was pointing at the ship, maybe asking if he had the right containers. Harwood knew this was his opportunity.

He looked over his shoulder at Sassi. The SUVs

slowed as they rolled through the gate. He could see her crouched low. Given the angle of the SUVs, the drivers wouldn't be able to see her unless she moved.

Harwood quietly retracted his bipod and slung his weapon in the snap hook on his outer tactical vest. He knelt as if he were a runner in the starting blocks. The rucksack was heavy on his back, but this was his window, like a batter ripping a solid single to the outfield and then taking second base when the outfielder bobbled the ball. It was a perceived opening. The outcome was unknown. Did the outfielder have a rifle arm? Was his jump good enough?

To avoid lateral movement that the human eye more easily detected, Harwood ran directly at the men's backs as they conversed. The huddle was breaking up, and the tractor driver was loading the container on the back of the truck Harwood was now pressed against. It was an extended cab, an interesting choice for an island. It appeared either new or well maintained.

Without hesitation, Harwood moved to the passenger-side door and opened it. The latch clicked louder than he'd hoped, but there was nothing he could do about it. He crawled into the cab and removed his rucksack, pushing it into the sleeping compartment. The door was heavy as he pulled it toward him. He tugged open the handle to try to deaden the noise and prevent the latch from clicking again.

The tractor roared as it hefted the container onto the rig. The truck cab shook as the weight settled on the trailer, and Harwood used that moment to slam the door shut. He crawled into the sleeping compartment, pushed his rucksack to the side, and readied his knife.

Next to him were wadded-up sheets and some magazines written in Greek or Turkish. A half-full bottle of Diet Coke leaned in the corner next to some Little Debbie wrappers. The interior had the pristine odor of a new car. These trucks were in mint condition.

Like a good sniper, Harwood used the time available to improve his position. He moved to situate himself behind the driver's side, out of the driver's line of sight unless he looked in the compartment and turned in his direction.

The tractor roared again. Metal clanked on metal. The drivers shouted. Finally, the cab door opened. The driver climbed into his seat, slammed the door, buckled his seat belt, and cranked the engine, which hummed like the finely tuned machine it was. Before placing the truck in gear, the man reached back into the sleep compartment, searching for something. His hand was bouncing around, not finding what he was looking for. He muttered something Harwood guessed was an expletive and then leaned forward to unbuckle his seat beat. Harwood looked across the sleep compartment, saw the Coke bottle, and quickly placed it closer.

The seat belt came off, and the man twisted to look in the compartment when he saw the Coke bottle, grabbed it, muttered another expletive, and repositioned himself forward in the driver's seat.

The truck lurched forward and began rolling. Harwood could see across the passenger side and out the side mirror. He wasn't sure if they were leading or following. The trucks had been parked nose to tail, with this truck being behind the lead truck. They appeared to be following because they had not made a turn.

They looped around, passed the train tracks, and approached the gate before stopping.

Sassi had raised the tire shredders again. At least that was the plan; Harwood had no idea what was actually happening. After seeing the two guards bound and gagged on the railroad tracks, he figured she could be single-handedly taking down both drivers. Not the plan and not likely, but she had the skills.

After a minute, his driver buzzed down his window. Another man, most likely the driver from the lead truck, spoke to him, presumably in Greek. It was a quick conversation, most likely an update. Something like, *The shredders are up, and the guards are gone, but I fixed the problem.*

The trucks coughed again, and they were moving. He hoped that Sassi had executed her part of the plan and was with the two-truck convoy. Either way, he hoped she was safe.

His truck lurched and spun around winding turns, Harwood having to hold on so that he didn't spill forward or backward and make a noise. After thirty minutes, the trucks pulled through a different gate. An airfield loomed in the distance, and when the truck pulled around, a gigantic airplane was in plain sight with its cargo ramp leaning on the tarmac like a gaping jaw waiting to be fed. He searched for the SUVs and the cooler but didn't see them.

He had more decisions to make in an unknown

environment. Were they boarding Clutch on the aircraft? Had they already? Still, were the containers and Clutch connected? Was Sassi there, or had she missed the convoy? Where was the plane going? What was in the containers?

The driver stopped the truck. The brakes hissed. A similar tractor to the one at the port began moving to the trucks. This was a well-oiled operation.

Harwood waited for the driver to exit, but he didn't. He turned back toward the compartment, this time reaching with his whole body. It was impossible for Harwood to avoid detection. He gripped his knife in one hand and his pistol in the other. Ready.

He saw the arm. The back of the head. His right shoulder. All fluid momentum coming back, perhaps to change or to get another Little Debbie. It didn't matter. He would have to be violent and quick.

Someone pounded on the driver's door. The man snapped back around. More Greek, but Harwood was thankful for the interruption. The man opened the door, and the conversation began to float away, drowned out by the tractors and whining airplane engines. The truck shifted, unburdened from the weight of the container as the tractor snatched it away and drove toward the airplane, where a roller would slide it into the cargo hold. Harwood had been on many C-17 airborne jumps with heavy equipment. This was no different; only it was a civilian operation.

He could see out the passenger window. The drivers were near the tractor. Everyone was looking at the airplane. It was time to move.

Harwood placed his rucksack in the passenger's seat and then eased around the console. Sliding his legs beneath the steering wheel, he checked the dome light, switched it off, and then opened the driver's-side door. He clutched his rucksack and lowered himself backward from the truck. Once on the tarmac, he took a position behind the giant wheels. He scoped out his options.

There.

He saw the two SUVs near the private terminal maybe fifty yards away. Three big men were standing outside next to the vehicles, long guns held professionally at a 45-degree angle across their body armor–covered chests. He counted a total of six men, which probably included the drivers. Same as at the port. If they'd bothered to look in his direction, he would have been visible to them. The old army saying, "If you can be seen, you can be hit," popped into his mind. He slid beneath the truck, using the chassis for protective cover and an opportunity to conduct reconnaissance.

The SUVs were here, which meant that Clutch was probably here. The tractors were loading the containers on the airplane, which meant that they were going somewhere inaccessible by ship or they needed to be somewhere sooner than a ship could get them there, whatever their cargo might be. Sassi was nowhere to be seen, nor was there any commotion that might have indicated she had been compromised.

Again, he told himself, either way, she was better off than before. Free and tough, able to do whatever she needed to do to get back to Italy, her home country.

His rationalization didn't make him feel better. He still believed he had an obligation to her. He could have let her go in Lebanon. She could have headed north to the UN base camp in Turkey, but he had made a calculation that she could be useful in the hunt for Clutch, and she seemed to want to stay.

Two men came out of the operations building. One was the man from the compound. He was big. Six and a half feet tall and almost as wide, like a solid farmhand. He walked as if he owned everything in his path and that everything was his dominion. The man walking directly toward the trucks, toward Harwood, pushed outward with his feet. His legs were tree trunks that somehow managed to move. Harwood wondered how such a large man had been so quick in the basement and managed to escape. Carrying Clutch was most likely the easiest task, given the man's size. The registration of the vehicle they had taken from the compound had Tankian Logistics Group as the owner. The company's logo had crossed knives branching off from the stem of the *K*. Was this Tankian? He must be.

Harwood's mind cycled back to where all of this started. The man walking toward him had the same stride and presence as the man who had been controlling the drones attacking them in the sniper hide site.

The CIA wanted us to have eyes on this guy, so I'm in the right place!

The SUVs followed him as he walked. The bodyguards, save the drivers, walked on the outside like infantry guarding tanks. Tankian and the SUVs slid past his position and stopped at the ramp of the airplane. He slid behind the tires on that side of the truck, feeling secure in his makeshift hide site.

He counted the guards again. They had started with six. Two were driving. Two were visible. Where were the other two? Harwood spun around and checked the length of the undercarriage. Nothing.

He low crawled to the rear tires to recon from a different angle, hoping to see the two guards who were missing. Were they looking for him? Sassi?

He caught a hint of blue out of the corner of his eye. Two men had lifted the cooler from the SUV and were struggling with the weight. Both of them had to weigh 250 pounds apiece. Clutch probably checked in at 200 without his gear. More convinced than ever that Clutch was in the cooler, Harwood considered his options again.

He could attack now. Stow away on the plane. Call for reinforcements, though he knew neither whom he might call nor what they might do. Stoddard seemed of little use and was probably out of range to do anything.

No, saving Clutch was his fight. He didn't need to make the call and definitely didn't want to do it. He'd held the demons that haunted him every night at bay. LaBeouf and Samuelson were dead. Could he save Clutch? It didn't matter whether he was the son of a United States senator or a poor orphan; he was Harwood's spotter.

He steeled himself for what he was about to do.

With the first container loaded, Tankian, an older man in a white navy uniform, a short bald man with glasses, and two guards watched the tractor back away as two of the other guards pulled the cooler up the ramp, rolling it on its two black wheels.

Still two guards missing. Harwood looked over his shoulder in each direction. Nothing.

And still no sign of Sassi. Harwood blocked her out of his mind for the moment. He studied the aircraft. This was a Ukrainian-made An-124 airplane, one of the largest airplanes in the world. It swallowed the two containers as if they were appetizers. The two men and cooler looked like miniature toys as they climbed inside. The thing had to be four stories off the ground.

The men walked off the ramp. Tankian was talking to the navy man in an animated fashion. They were arguing about something. Despite his size and presence, Tankian did not appear to be winning the conversation.

Was the argument about a payment not made? Was he supposed to be rewarded for delivering Clutch to someone?

The tractor roared as it backed away from the cargo ramp. Harwood had one chance left to get on the airplane in a clandestine manner. He slid from beneath the trailer at the far end. Checked in every direction. Lifted his ruck and shouldered it. Found a handhold on the trailer and lifted himself onto the back. He was completely blocked by the container but could hear the tractor approaching. A perimeter fence was about a hundred meters from him. A thin forest lay beyond that. To his right was the gate they had entered through. To his left the runway. Behind him, the SUVs, the other truck, and the airplane.

He checked all the angles and thought it could work.

The container had two locking bars running vertically from top to bottom. He grasped one in each hand and used his feet to "walk" up the front of the container. He flipped over the top and lay faceup, ready to fight. After a few seconds, he leaned far enough over to see everyone following the tractor, which was headed in his direction.

He slid back to the middle of the container and lay flat, both hands holding his rucksack. His rifle bit into his chest. The jaws of the tractor clamped onto the container with a loud clang that rocked his eardrums. He narrowly avoided the center bar of the jaws that ran coincident with the length of the container. It slammed down with force directly in front of his face.

The upside was that the arm and bar would provide him cover and concealment should he need them. The container lifted from the truck and swung high over the tarmac. Harwood lifted one hand from his rucksack and used it to hold on to the center bar. Hydraulics hissed, and the movement felt like a carnival ride. The center bar had a logo in black letters against the yellow paint: SANY REACH STACKER.

The container hovered in the gaping maw of the cargo hold, and for a brief second, Harwood didn't believe he would fit in the gap. He pressed himself into the metal, made his body as thin as possible. The frame of the cargo hold scraped across his outer tactical vest as the container moved along the rollers on the ramp and into the belly of the aircraft. Once he was through the narrow gap, the ceiling of the airplane was a good six feet above him. This airplane was a cargo work-horse with rollers and tie-downs throughout. Looking up, he saw that the first container was in front of him. Beyond that, it appeared there were a couple of rows of seats, all facing forward as in a standard airliner. To the right just in front of the lead container was the blue cooler, possibly carrying Clutch. So close. He could move now, but there was activity at the back of the air-plane.

He looked at the container in front of him again, this time lifting his head a fraction more. Sassi Cavezza was not lying on top. Unless she had stowed away in one of the containers, she was on the ground and not making this trip.

The cargo ramp closed with a loud snap. Two men walked past the containers. It was Tankian and the short bald guy with glasses. His handler? His assistant? They buckled into the seats at the front. The engines whined. The airplane rolled and turned left, then right. The engines raced to high throttle, and then the pilots released the brakes. They shot forward and lifted into the sky, Harwood feeling the transition from bouncing along the runway to gliding smoothly into the air.

After a few minutes, as soon as the airplane leveled into a smooth ascent, Tankian unbuckled his seat belt, drew his knife, and walked to the back of the aircraft toward the containers.

Sassi willed the motorcycle to move faster. The trucks had moved too fast for her to snag a ride on the back of one, but she had rummaged the two guards and scored a set of keys for what turned out to be a red Ducati Monster 821.

Approaching the airport gate—because where else would they be going?—she saw the second container being loaded. The gentle slope down the hill toward the airport gave her enough of an elevated position to be able to see the top of the container as a strange-looking vehicle lifted it and slid it into the back of the airplane. She wasn't 100 percent sure, but she thought she saw a green figure on top of the container and maybe a backpack in front of it. Surely that couldn't be Harwood. But who else could it be?

She slowed as the ramp door closed and the airplane began taxiing soon thereafter. She admired the drive of the man who so desperately wanted to save his friend. Just as she had an intangible motivation to care for displaced families, this man had a palpable connection with his comrade. She respected that more than she'd expected. She had never seen a soldier exhibit this type of selfless sacrifice before. In her United Nations world, most of the military she had operated with were either trying to cheat on their wives with her or were somehow on the take.

She straddled the bike and clumsily walked it onto the side of the road. The trucks and SUVs would be exiting, and she didn't want to risk anything, even though she doubted anyone could place her at the port aside from the two guards who were no threat at the moment.

The pistol and knife in her cargo pockets reminded her of the ordeal she'd been through. The adrenaline rush was beginning to dump like a receding ocean tide, laying bare the memories as rocks in the sand.

From Turkey to Syria to Lebanon to Cyprus, she had been running on fumes. She and the Ranger had finished the combat rations he carried and sucked his hydration system dry. He had been generous with both his food and water. He had rescued her from perhaps an unspeakable fate. Certainly, she was in a better position today than she had been in yesterday in the cell of the basement at that compound.

Now Sassi felt she had to do something for Sergeant Harwood. She had no idea what that was, but knew where a good place to start might be.

She fired up the Ducati and took the road away from the airport, looped around to the north on the Turkish side of the island, and found a mobile phone store. She bartered with the manager to allow her to wire him the money from her online banking account. He refused to allow her to take the phone until she logged into her bank account, a decidedly dangerous move anywhere in Cyprus on an unsecure Wi-Fi, and wired €990 to the store, which included the iPhone and service provider.

Another hour was spent setting up the phone and pulling in her email and text messages from her previous phone. She didn't believe she was important enough to worry about anyone tracking her. As far as she knew, her kidnapping was opportunistic, not planned or intentional.

She sat on the curb and removed her hiking boot. The musty smell made her wince, but she'd smelled worse before. From her boot with the Beretta knife she removed the battered card General Cartwright had given her. She punched in the number he had written on the back of the card. The phone buzzed in soft muted European tones.

After the fifth ring, a voice answered. "This line is not secure."

"I need to talk to General Cartwright," she said.

"Who is calling?"

"Alessandra Cavezza from the United Nations."

"What is your business?"

"I saw two of his men shot in al-Ghouta yesterday."

"Stand by."

That had to be his communications guy, Franklin, or something like that, she remembered.

"Cartwright." His voice was commanding and authoritative. It was definitely Cartwright.

"This is Sassi Cavezza. I'm calling from Cyprus about two items. The first is two of your men were shot in al-Ghouta."

Cartwright said nothing.

"I was kidnapped by Russians or Hezbollah at the same time your men were shot by a Russian tank."

"Prove it."

She grimaced, understanding his reluctance at hearing such terrible news and years of battlefield skepticism.

"A U.S. Army Ranger, Sergeant Vick Harwood, is pursuing his teammate, Sergeant Ian Nolte, here on Cyprus."

Silence again. She imagined he was processing.

"Those are my men. What are they doing in Cyprus?" His voice didn't change inflection.

"Nolte has been taken prisoner by a man or company named Tankian. Nolte and I were both in captivity there."

"Where are Ranger Nolte and Ranger Harwood right now?"

"Sergeant Harwood is on an airplane that just took off from the airport here. It was a large airplane. Maybe the biggest I've ever seen."

"And Nolte?"

"We think he's on the airplane also, but I can't confirm that."

"We?"

"Yes, I was working with Sergeant Harwood."

After a long pause, General Cartwright said, "Sounds like I need to get to Cyprus. Tell me where you are."

She told him and noticed a car fishtail into the parking lot next to the Ducati. Two men jumped out. Sassi ran to her bike, raced the engine, and knocked one of the men down as she wobbled into traffic and sped away.

CHAPTER 23

Valerie Hinojosa

Valerie Hinojosa stared at a map of downtown Milwaukee. Next to her was Colonel Darryl Dawkins, affectionately known as "D-Squared" by his Wisconsin National Guard soldiers. He wore the army combat uniform with its camouflage olive-and-tan patterns. He stood at an even six feet, which put him at her height when she was wearing heels. He had thick brown hair fading to gray on the edges. He looked more like a businessman than a hardened army soldier.

"How many troops are you going to have on-site during the convention, Colonel?"

"Please, call me Darryl. And we will have five hundred soldiers working in three shifts of one hundred and fifty with a twenty-five-soldier quick-reaction force on hand at all times. We call it a *platoon*. They'll rotate as well. Every twelve hours, they'll switch. We will have static security at every entry point and every possible way into the arena. We will have plainclothes soldiers roaming the streets outside. They will be armed with pistols and nonlethal weapons. On the deep interior, we will have both fixed and roving teams. I'll be here in the command and control center with you."

"Okay. What threats are you contemplating right now?" she asked.

The colonel smiled. "I'm glad you asked. We have a list of fourteen white supremacist groups that we've identified from chat groups like 8chan. We've got Antifa, which we think is more supportive of this, and we don't really consider them a threat. There is some random chatter in the Islamist extremist chat rooms. Something about attacking the convention to make it look like the president is attempting to wipe out his competition. Plus, the usual tinfoil hat conspiracies."

Valerie was glad the colonel provided his analysis devoid of politics. Even though they were covering a political convention, her duty was decidedly apolitical. Her job was to protect the people in the arena from any criminal or terrorist activity. She had at her disposal an entire battalion of national guard soldiers.

"Other than around the arena, what kind of early warning do you have?" Valerie asked D-Squared.

"Good question. Everything starts tomorrow, right? We've been collecting for months. Establishing patterns on the highways and in the airports, transit, even seaports. The big hitters don't show up for a few days, but because this is still undecided, they're still campaigning in all these important states. So, we've got undercover CID agents in Chicago, Detroit, Des Moines, Moline, Minneapolis, and here in Milwaukee. They're checking all modes of transportation. Then we pull back in and look at the axes of advance into the arena. We've got roving patrols and Jersey barriers blocking anything moving. Immediately outside the arena, we've got more roving patrols and the same on the inside, like I said."

"I want to be plugged into any anomalies. Tell me more about this ISIS or Hezbollah plot."

"Not a whole lot to tell you. We picked up on some DoD intel from Syria. The timing of the fight over there is pretty suspicious to us. There was no real precursor event. It seems calculated to us, so we're looking at it. There are reports of a group of Hezbollah fighters missing, and there are reports of some fighting in the Beqaa Valley. None of that is particularly interesting in its own right, but it doesn't take a fiction novelist to put together different elements of the plot and see something real."

"Keep pulling that thread. It would be some pretty large muscle movements to have Syria attack Israel so that some Hezbollah fighters can infiltrate the U.S."

"Indeed."

"Iran and Russia are in Venezuela. Are we tracking that?"

"We are. Nothing right now. On the upside, there's no indicator or warning out there right now. Just random chatter like we've seen a million times."

As Hinojosa was scouring for clues of any threats to the political convention, the convention's most prominent attendee, Andrea Comstock, watched the monuments and memorials slide beneath the General Motors executive G5 as it made its final approach into Reagan National Airport.

She shook her head at the name. Reagan. Of all the presidents she most disliked, Reagan was at the top. Some had romanticized his legacy to the point that people forgot all the scandals such as Iran-Contra, the arms trade debacle that had made Ollie North famous. What a travesty. She guessed it wasn't so bad to have the hard edges of reality softened when someone passed, but *Reagan*?

She had vowed that when she was president, she would lead the country with purpose in a direction that was accommodating for all Americans. Reduced college tuition. Not free, because that was unsustainable. But if you made a half million dollars a year, you could pay a little more and help the less fortunate in society attend college or a trade school. Single-payer health care was the only way to get past the for-profit world of health care. She'd visited homeless shelters and was appalled by what she had seen. To be sure, she'd seen similar issues at the border with Mexico, but what made candidate Comstock stand out was the fact that she prioritized American citizens over those that were undocumented. When she'd made that clear, she nosed into first place in a field that was mostly promising the world to people who couldn't even vote . . . well, weren't supposed to, anyway. A woman could dream, couldn't she?

Still, her nearest competitor was closing in on her,

and the overnight trip from Munich had given her time to think about Max Wolff's offer. Wolff was a first-class hustler, but it was a reasonable gamble. On the upside, she could separate herself from the field going into the nominating convention, which was in two days. Polling showed the nomination was essentially up for grabs—41 percent for her, 40 percent for her competitor, and single digits for the rest of the field. If she were to "secure the release" of Corporal Nolte, son of the opposing party's senior senator, she could not only catapult herself to her party's nomination but also win over enough independent votes that she could upset the incumbent president.

The downside, of course, was someone finding out and exposing her plan with Wolff. There was no electronic or paper trail that she knew of, but that could be exactly what Wolff had in mind. She had snatched away a billion-dollar deal from him through some heavy-duty lobbying and negotiating with Congress, Senator Nolte included. While she didn't exactly owe him anything, it had been a rare moment of bipartisan support in the insanity of today's political environment.

He'd accepted her meeting today based upon the tenuous relationship they had developed and because she had received information about a classified mission in Lebanon. She had to be careful on many fronts. She didn't want to expose Wolff, for fear that he might turn on her, and she didn't want to give up the opportunity to attack the president on his lack of foreign policy in the Middle East. She needed to thread all the needles: safe return of a soldier, keep her contact with Wolff secret, and use this as a platform to score foreign policy points.

As a mother of two grown children and a wife to a rock-solid husband, Comstock tried not to think too hard about the fact that she ought to have reported her conversation with Wolff to the FBI, CIA, DoD, or all of the above, immediately. But she hadn't, and she knew well enough that she had to live with decisions and execute them as pristinely as possible.

Her driver delivered her to the Russell Senate Office Building, where one of the senator's aides—a young woman dressed in a white blouse and black slacks wearing low pumps—escorted her through a little-used door that led to an elevator, which opened into a service entrance.

The aide escorted her to the senator's office, where he waited in the rear chamber behind his desk. He stood and greeted her. He was a tall, white-haired man with kind eyes and an easy smile. Part of her wanted to dislike him because his affability made it harder to pigeonhole the rest of his party as white supremacists, racists, or warmongers, or whatever the outrage of the day might be. Dressed in a light gray suit, he gripped her hand and said, "I would give you an embrace as friends should do, but I don't want any of my staff to see my toxic masculinity up close."

She chuckled, shook her head, and said, "We're in a pickle nowadays, aren't we?"

"How's Bob? The kids?"

"All good, Senator."

He probably knew better than to discuss the primary

race with her. Even politicians knew that politics made for uncomfortable conversations.

He motioned her to a seat and said, "What is this about a mission in Lebanon? I've done as you asked and not inquired with SecDef or any of the usual suspects, just yet."

She looked over her shoulder at the senator's chief of staff, who was poised at the doorway and prepared to enter or exit, a play they had done thousands of time, she was certain. Nolte picked up the cue and nodded at the chief of staff, who promptly left and closed the door behind her.

"Better?"

"Yes. I've been traveling on a foreign policy fact-finding mission," Comstock said.

"Otherwise known as *Bilderberg*. Let's not play duck and cover here, Andrea. We're both too busy for any of that nonsense."

Well, damn.

"We both tend to speak in subtleties, but I'll be more direct. I did couple my trip with some foreign policy activities. NATO and such. I received a briefing that we have a Special Forces mission in Lebanon. Something about helping the Israelis in the current conflict in the Golan."

"I know we have supported Israel politically but was unaware of any boots on the ground. That would be highly unusual and irregular. Israel doesn't normally ask for our help."

"That's what I thought, but my source provided details that are compelling."

"Such as?"

"For the moment, that's unimportant. What is important is that your son, Corporal Ian Nolte Jr., has been captured."

"What!?"

His response was genuine surprise. Not even an Oscar-winning actor could have pulled that off with more authenticity. Part of her concern had been that he might already know what was happening with his son, but it was clear he did not.

His chief of staff stuck her head back in the door at her boss's outburst. "I'm fine, Claire," he said, "but stand by for when we're done here."

When the door clicked shut, Comstock continued, "My sources tell me that he was part of a two-man sniper team and his partner abandoned him. He's alive and, I'm told, in good condition. There's a market, it seems, and he's in the supply chain, so to speak."

"Supply chain? What are you talking about? I'm the chairman of the Intelligence Committee! I've not received any word of this!" Nolte leaned forward, hissing through his teeth. All pretense was gone. Concern for his son removed any camouflage that might have led to a more nuanced discussion.

"My sources don't want to deal with the official government, so we're treading on slippery ground here. Logan Act and all. I'm not violating it, because I'm coming to you so we can do something about it. Get your son back."

"We need to get the National Command Authority involved. Now."

"That's the quickest way to never see him again. We're being giving a onetime shot at a miracle here. One of my friends in Europe is on the periphery of this, and he has agreed to intervene."

The senator leaned back in his chair. "Under what conditions?"

"None. It's a favor to me. And it's a favor from me to you."

"I can't endorse you," he said sharply.

"Nor would I ask or expect you to. I'm a mother of two boys. I can't imagine how I would react if one of my children were in this situation. I'm frankly put off that you said that. I have come to you out of courtesy."

"Do you have any proof or evidence? Andrea, you seriously can't expect me to just leap right in here." He ran a hand across his face. His head lowered a bit, though. He understood.

"Yes. Of course. I have a picture here," she said. She lifted her iPhone and tapped the screen. The picture that Wolff had provided her was on the top of her album. Ian "Clutch" Nolte was standing in a dark cell, face bruised, uniform dingy, cinder blocks behind his head, staring into the camera with flat, expressionless eyes. She pressed that one and flipped the phone toward Nolte, who took it from her. He pinched and spread his fingers, enlarging the picture. His eyes moistened.

"That's him," he said. "How did he get there?"

"I don't have all the details," she said. "But what's important is that you know, and now you do. I'm going to work with my point of contact to secure his release.

Nothing is guaranteed, as he is being held by a hostile group."

She didn't imagine that he appreciated not being in control. One of the most powerful men in the Senate, Nolte was accustomed to being in charge and getting his way. Not this time.

"What do you need me to do?" he asked.

"Nothing. If and when we get him, I'll let you know. I can't promise this won't leak to the media. My role is unknown to anyone but my contact, so if it does leak, I'll know where it came from—here. And once I'm out there, I will no longer have access to my point of contact, which means you may never see your son again. Clear?"

"Crystal," he said.

She gathered her purse and phone and stood.

"If the media calls you, I'd suggest you claim ignorance. If you truly didn't know Ian was missing before I walked in here, then just think back to that time and wipe your memory clean. Say what's in your heart. That you're proud of your son and pray for his safe return. Whatever you feel. Anything but my involvement."

"Understood. When will you know?"

"Next twenty-four to forty-eight hours. If it doesn't happen by then, I'll let you know. If there's reason for me to call you, I'll call you."

"I wish there were something I could do," he said.

"There is. Answer the questions if the media comes at you. This thing could blow up on the other end, from Lebanon. That war still hasn't peaked yet. And if there's one soldier missing, you can bet there are others who are dead or missing."

"That's true. Here's my private cell number," he said, handing her a card.

"Thanks."

She shook his hand and turned on her heel. On the ride back to the airport, Comstock made two calls to her headquarters and then one to Wolff.

"Status?" he asked.

"All set," she responded.

"Okay. Your prisoner is on an airplane back to the United States as we speak. The plane will land in Chicago, where you'll meet a man named Tankian."

"Tankian. Got it."

CHAPTER 24

Sassi Cavezza

General Cartwright's airplane was a G3 with U.S. AIR FORCE painted on the side. It landed two hours after Sassi had called him. She knew that a lot of things had to happen right for that to occur—namely, the plane had to have been on standby, and the general had to have no more important business happening.

With the war continuing to rage in the Golan and Galilee, Sassi was surprised that the general actually had time for a couple of soldiers, but then again, Harwood's commitment to his fellow soldier had surprised her, so maybe there was a lot she didn't know or understand.

He called her once he descended from the steps in pretty much the same location that the giant airplane with Sergeant Harwood had taken off. He used one hand to guide himself down the rail and the other to hold a phone to his ear.

"Where are you?" he asked.

"Just outside the gate. I need someone to open it for me," she replied.

He looked to his left, found the gate, focused on her, and nodded. She returned the nod with a small wave as she straddled the idling motorcycle. Shortly, a golf cart buzzed her way with a man inside who quickly unlocked the gate by swiping a card across a reader. He allowed her to pass and then closed the gate.

She drove toward Cartwright, parked the bike near the operations building, and followed him inside. They walked past a small cordon of his security team and into a drab, windowless conference room with stained chairs and an old wooden table that was one meeting away from being discarded. He sat on the opposite side of the table from her. Two guards posted at the door.

"I need to know everything. I've got two dead soldiers and two missing soldiers, and you're the only one who has seen them all."

"To be fair, I never saw Corporal Nolte, but he was in a cell next to me, and I believe I heard him say his name. We believe Nolte was in a big fish cooler when he was loaded onto the ship and then the airplane, I presume."

"A fish cooler?"

"Yes. We didn't actually see him," she said.

"And you were with Sergeant Harwood when all of this happened?"

"He rescued me from the compound in Lebanon near the Beqaa Valley. I'm sure he was looking for Corporal Nolte. He blew through and found me when he was expecting to find Nolte. Tankian took Nolte."

"How do you know it was Tankian?"

"He's got a website. Looks like his picture. He owns Tankian Logistics Group."

"Yes, we know who Mr. Tankian is. His employees call him *Commander*."

"He's got muscle here and evidently some clout."

"He's got a global network. He's ninety-five percent legit and five percent this kind of stuff. I've got my comms guy working on getting the flight plan for the aircraft that you say has Harwood and Nolte on it."

"I know for a fact that Harwood is on it. And he's on it because he thinks that Nolte is there."

"Understand. You do know we have to verify your information. We've met exactly once, and you're confirmed to be in the location of two of my dead soldiers and two of my missing soldiers."

"I'm a suspect." Not a question. A statement of the obvious.

"I didn't say that, but you can understand my questions."

"Yes, I guess I can."

"Anything else you remember?"

"The two containers. Tankian boarded the airplane after the cooler with Nolte and the two containers were loaded."

"No idea what was in the containers?"

"None."

A text pinged on his phone, and he held up a finger the size of a hot dog and then somehow managed to reply to the text and perhaps get all the letters correct.

"Flanigan's got something," he said. "Because you're here and you have some knowledge of what's happening, I'm going to let you listen in, but I'm going to have to look at your phone now and hold it for a bit after."

She hesitated. This was why she didn't like the military. They called the shots. You either played by their rules or not at all.

"I called you," she reminded him.

"True. You could be setting me up. Setting up Harwood and Nolte. Set up my other two operators."

"I didn't and you know that."

"I believe you, and if you've got nothing to hide, then there's nothing to be concerned about."

"How about you show me your phone? I could make an assessment whether you're selling your soldiers out. Maybe you're on the take like most generals I've ever met."

Cartwright actually smiled, something she hadn't yet seen him do.

"You're a pistol," he said. "Here's my phone. Don't delete the pictures of my kids."

She scrolled through it, not really looking for anything, and handed it back to him.

"Here's mine," she said.

He did a more thorough job, but there wasn't much to look at.

"It's new."

"Yes. Tankian or the Russian took my original," she said.

"The Russian?"

"Yes. The Russian kidnapped me originally. Evidently dumped me at Tankian's compound."

Flanigan barreled into the room and said, "Sir, I've got it. They're headed to Chicago."

Cartwright scrunched his face up and said, "Chicago," as if that city were in another universe.

"It's an An-124 cargo airplane, like the second largest in the world. Holds shipping containers. I was able to hack into the transponder and get the metadata."

"Okay, I believe you," Cartwright said.

"You know those pictures from the basement that you wanted from me?" Sassi said.

Cartwright nodded.

"There were lines from Cyprus to the middle of the United States. Could be Chicago. I thought it was farther north, but it has been a while since I studied the geography of the States."

"Lines?" Cartwright asked.

"Yes. There was a single strand of thread from Tripoli to Cyprus and then another from Cyprus to the United States. I'm not sure why I'm just thinking of this now."

"Okay, that's something. Flanigan's been looking for those but still can't find them."

The general's comment caused Flanigan to lean forward in preparation for defending himself, but the general lifted one of those sausages again, and Flanigan retreated into the back of his chair.

"Anything else you can remember?"

Sassi leaned back and closed her eyes. She'd had other things to focus on in the last twenty-four hours. She remembered the yarn from Lebanon to Cyprus and then to the United States. Keeping her eyes closed, Sassi started talking.

"There was other yarn leading from the Middle East to other points, but I can't quite place them. Maybe Germany? Maybe Russia? And then a word I had seen as curious. It was written in English in the basement of an Islamic home. Or I presumed it was Islamic. There was a ninety-nine percent chance it was. There were also Arabic characters on the diagram or map."

She paused, took a deep breath, and exhaled, the only sound in the quiet room.

"The word *Hunter* was written in English."

"Hunter?" Cartwright asked.

"Yes. *Hunter.* I'm sure of it."

"Could be anything," Cartwright said.

Flanigan leaned forward and said, "Hunter is the new Russian UAV. Just FYI."

Cartwright looked up, pointed a sausage at him, and said, "Good comment."

Sassi thought about it. Why would Tankian have an enterprise in the basement of an ISIS household? She didn't know enough about the man either way.

"What was it that your two men were doing in al-Ghouta other than using me as a prop?"

"For the record, we weren't using you."

"Come on, General. I'm more offended that you don't tell me the truth than the fact that you actually used me as a soft entry into the area. As you know, it didn't work. Your men are gone, and I'm sorry for that."

"They were good men. The best. And I sent them to see the basement you had seen so that we could get in front of or disrupt any plot that might be coming from there."

"Plot to do what?" She was sincerely confused. The general was being vague, and she hated vague. Just get to the point and confront whatever realities lay ahead.

"There has been some chatter that we might have a few things to worry about in the United States. It's not uncommon for terrorists to plan attacks over here, like they did at Tarnak Farms in Afghanistan for the 9/11 attacks."

"I'm aware, General. You're being vague, though. I understand you have security protocols, but I've volunteered information and can help. I *want* to help. Something about Sergeant Harwood. Seeing his sense of duty and commitment. It actually gave me renewed hope. After everything I've been through, I thought I was losing my rudder. I've seen the basest behavior in humankind. I've moved families, children, into desolate locations knowing they would not thrive there, but it was what I had to do. And here I meet a man who not only rescued me but has relentless drive to rescue his teammate. He's an unstoppable force, and that's something I want to be associated with. So, read me on or do whatever you have to do, but I can be of value to you and your team, provided you're going to help Harwood in whatever capacity you can."

"That's some speech," Cartwright said, unimpressed. His face might as well have been etched in stone. Eyes unblinking, locked on to her.

"Wasn't a speech. Was just me telling you what I'm doing and what I hope you planned on doing."

"While this is not your business or your concern, I told you what little bit I did because I had you checked out. You have a NATO top secret clearance. You're authorized to see U.S. top secret if there is a need to know. I'm not sure I'm buying that you are a UN worker. Sure, that may be your cover, but you've got a few too many skills to be your average UNHCR resettlement queen."

"I'll take that as a compliment, and, I might add, those are hard-won credentials that help immensely with the performance of my job," she said.

"So, I'll make a mild correction to my line of attack here. Who do you work for, and what is your purpose sniffing around my men?"

One of the security men closed in on her to the point that even if she thought it might be helpful, she wouldn't have an opportunity to go for a weapon. She didn't need that, regardless, but she was outnumbered and wanted on the team. The truth was that she really did want to help find Sergeant Harwood.

"I work for the UN, and my purpose is to return families to their homeland or to provide them adequate opportunity for resettlement." That was the party line right out of the brochure.

"I can turn you over to Turkish authorities and tease

them with some intelligence that you were involved in the deaths or absence of four U.S. service members. How's that sound?"

"Untrue," Sassi said. But not entirely. She *was* the last friendly face to see all the soldiers, that much was true.

"That really doesn't matter anymore, does it? Especially when you're not being truthful with me, a representative of the United States, one of Italy's NATO allies."

"What does NATO have to do with this?"

"My suspicion is that you're Italian CIA—AISE, but you could be part of NATO intelligence also."

"I know what AISE is. They're all criminals just like your CIA. I'm a regional director for the UN High Commission for Refugees."

"Which is the perfect front for an intelligence operative looking to subvert American interests in the region."

"That may be, but that's not who I am."

She exchanged glares with Cartwright, who refused to break eye contact, as if he were reading the fine print in her mind, searching for any clue that she might be someone other than who she proclaimed to be.

"I can help you," she said, not really wanting to continue his game anymore.

"Okay. Let's say I want your help. Where do we start?"

"You believe what I saw is a crude map of a plan to attack the United States. I'm the only one who has been in that village every day for the last two weeks. I can tell you who all the players are."

"Okay, let's do that."

"Not so fast, John Wayne. Every negotiation includes two bargaining positions," she said.

"From my vantage, you've got none."

"Then you don't see very well."

Flanigan smiled and let out a short snicker. Perhaps he'd been wanting to make a verbal jab at his controlling boss for a long time. Cartwright turned his head slowly toward Flanigan, who retreated into the confines of the back of his chair, looking like he'd prefer to blend into the fabric.

"What is it that you could possibly seek from me, Ms. Cavezza?"

"I owe my life to Sergeant Harwood. I would like to repay that debt. He may be an Army Ranger, but I have a code of honor, as well."

Cartwright said nothing. He waited a few moments and finally nodded.

"Okay. As I've said, we've checked your clearances. They're solid. If you're going to be on my team, though, you need to cough up the phone. I want to control who you talk to and what you say."

"You're full of surprises," Sassi said.

"You'll actually come to believe that if you spend enough time with me and my team. We don't play. I want justice for my two missing Rangers—I'm not calling them dead until I see them—and I want my other two back safely."

His voice was like granite. There was no doubt he was serious. Her sparring jabs at him seemed childish in comparison. She had said what she needed to, but the gravity of the situation settled over her like a heavy blanket.

"Justice and safe return. I can help," she said.

CHAPTER 25

Vick Harwood

Harwood didn't move for the first hour.

Tankian was up and pacing back and forth directly toward him and back. Harwood had shipped enough containers as a soldier to know that his position was only two feet above the man's line of sight. Add in another foot for the roller platform and the fact that he was on the second container, the one nearest the rear of the aircraft, and he was just barely above Tankian's sight line.

He timed his head raises with the sounds of Tankian's feet slapping into the metal flooring. He took exactly twenty-two steps toward him and then another twenty-two away from him. Finally, Tankian stopped pacing and was joined by the two missing guards, who had evidently boarded the plane when Harwood was shifting positions beneath the truck.

The three men opened the cooler and retrieved a limp Clutch from its confines. He looked dead. White, pasty face. Limp arms. Buckling knees. Harwood sucked in a deep breath and exhaled slowly.

Tankian shouted at Baldy, but Harwood couldn't hear him above the din of the engines. Clutch was lying motionless on the floor of the airplane behind the last row of seats. Tankian knelt next to him with his fingers on Clutch's neck. One of the security guards jogged to the cockpit and returned with a small medical kit. Harwood didn't see any IVs. Clutch had to be dehydrated.

This was not good. Harwood had a medic's kit in his rucksack with two IV bags, which might be enough to hold him over. Yet the sticky issue of fighting against Tankian and his goons remained. He could do it, no doubt, yet where he'd used skill and brute force in the compound raid, he needed to apply a surgeon's touch here on the airplane. An errant shot could puncture the skin of the aircraft, destroying the structural integrity, and allow 500-knot winds to peel the rest away with ease. Even an accurate shot could pass through a man's body and have the same effect. His purpose here was to rescue Clutch, not kill everyone, including himself.

He began to back off the container, calculating his plan. Inch by inch. He would leave his rucksack at the base of the container and use his knife while they were all focused on Clutch. He used the locking bars to shimmy down the container, placing his feet quietly on the floor. He laid his ruck on the floor and removed his Blackhawk combat knife, opening the razor-sharp blade. Stepping to the side of the container, he saw them gathered around Clutch like a football huddle.

The lights glared near the front of the aircraft but were dimmer toward the rear, which helped with his concealment, though he felt exposed. Seeing Clutch confirmed every decision he'd made up to this point. He was right about the crash, about the compound, about the ship, and about the airplane. They were taking Clutch for some strategic reason. Perhaps selling him to the highest bidder. Countries like Russia or Iran would pay nicely to show a U.S. Army Ranger in captivity. Make up some story about finding him in Iran, maybe. Charge him with war crimes. Use Clutch as a weapon in an information war. When they were done with him, they'd kill him for sure.

He had to save his Ranger buddy. It wouldn't fully compensate for LaBeouf and Samuelson, but it was something. He needed this win or there might be no return from the abyss.

The short bald man with glasses ran to the cockpit and pounded on the door, which opened soon after. One of the pilots shook his head and then shouted back at Baldy, who promptly pulled a pistol from his waistband and stuck it in the pilot's face. He forced his way into the cockpit and shut the door.

Now it was three against one. If there were ever a time to exploit an enemy's weakness, now was the moment. Great force applied at a specific point was far more effective than that same force spread randomly. He stepped forward, gathering intelligence as he moved to the second container, paused, and let himself become part of the environment. He listened to the roar of the airplane. The slipstream whistled against the fuselage. The engines moaned. The wings flexed. All in harmony to keep one of the world's largest airplanes in the sky. He stepped forward to the leading edge of the container. He was practically in the open now.

Baldy opened the cockpit door. Looked in his direction, or was he looking at Tankian? Harwood froze.

The plane changed from cruising to a downward dive.

They were veering off course. Because of Clutch?

Baldy turned back toward the cockpit. Harwood backed away slowly, sliding between the two containers first and then all the way back to where his rucksack was.

When chaos hit, he wanted to be ready. If they were landing, Tankian and his team might only be using the regular passenger door. There was a chance they'd come off the back, but an equal chance they would be using the front.

His feet were on the rollers by the time the aircraft touched down on the runway. The airplane taxied fast until it stopped. When the front passenger door opened, Harwood breathed a sigh of relief. Blue-and-red lights bounced inside the aircraft. Sirens wailed.

Had the pilot reported a hijacking, or was it an ambulance and police escort? He could take action right now. No longer in the air. Everyone focused on the front passenger door and Clutch.

On the flip side, he was surrounded by about a million

gallons of gas, and there were cops at the door. Most important, Clutch had to be in bad shape. He was more convinced than ever that they were getting him medical attention. He might be able to rescue Clutch right here, right now, but he had no idea where they might be, nor did he have any assurance where the nearest hospital was. They'd been in the air maybe two hours, probably less. From Cyprus, they could be in Turkey, Egypt, Greece, Israel, and any number of cities within those countries. He ruled out Israel and Egypt but couldn't discount Greece and Turkey, two of the countries that shared Cyprus. Still, it was all spitballing. He needed to let the situation play out until a window of opportunity presented itself.

One did almost immediately.

Tankian and one of the two big men departed the aircraft and did not immediately return. Baldy and one guard remained behind. Baldy stayed focused on the pilots, most likely preventing their communication with anyone external. Harwood figured he had about an hour, maybe less. Depended on where they took Clutch. Tankian and the guard were there to make sure that Clutch returned with them. He had to have been in serious condition for them to stop the entire flight. Plus, they likely had a lot of money riding on Clutch living and being delivered to the right person.

Harwood leaned back around the corner and watched. The guard was standing like a bouncer next to the open door of the aircraft, his back turned to Harwood. No flight attendants, just the guard, probably doubling as the crew for the flight. Someone shouted at the guard from the tarmac. The guard leaned forward and rotated the passenger door, preparing to shut it.

Harwood moved quickly and placed his hand on the lever that opened the container door. As soon as the passenger door shut, sounding like a ratcheting weapon, he pushed up on the lever, creating a clang that stopped his heart. It was seriously loud.

He pressed his back into the left side door of the container. The right side swung open about a foot. The hinges squealed, but the whining jet engines masked the noise. Harwood braved another peek around the corner of the container, this time from a lower position. He was on his knees, knife in his hand.

The guard was gone from the door. Harwood quickly moved back and stood, preparing for the guard to come from the opposite direction. He steeled himself. Flipped his knife in his hand. Prepared to confront the guard.

Footsteps rang out like gunshots the closer they came. The window was opening. Harwood moved silently toward the opposite side of the container to reduce the guard's reaction time.

The footsteps stopped, perhaps calculating.

Harwood sensed the man was less than three feet from him, perhaps suspicious, perhaps distracted by something else. He wasn't in the mood for giving away the initiative. Harwood spun around the corner, knife held in his left hand, pistol in his right hand. The guard had decided at the same time to come around the corner toward him.

Harwood ducked low, using a wrestling move, and

raked the knife across the left man's interior thigh, hoping for the blade to sever the femoral artery. He would settle for a nick. If he had scored, the guard showed no sign of injury. He wheeled on Harwood, lifting his pistol as Harwood spun and kicked the weapon out of his hand. It clanked against the rollers and spun toward the aft of the aircraft.

A purple blossom began spreading on the man's inner thigh. For the first time, he stumbled and looked at Harwood with a distant stare, like a wounded buck that knew its seconds were numbered. Harwood didn't take chances and needed to move on to the next threat. He stabbed the man directly in the heart and felt no remorse. This cretin had helped lock Clutch in a fish cooler. Watching him crumple to the floor gave Harwood some small measure of satisfaction. He glanced toward the cockpit. Nothing moving. He could see Baldy's back, but that was it. They hadn't heard the commotion from the cockpit.

He returned to his original task, which was to recon the containers. They might hold some clue as to why they had kidnapped Clutch or where they might be headed.

Harwood used the flashlight function beneath his pistol to bathe the interior of the container in light.

The chrome Mercedes-Benz logo winked at him when his flashlight crossed the grille. A Mercedes GLS SUV was chained inside the container. He walked to the rear and what initially looked like the end of the container was a black screen. He pushed against the filmy mesh and it gave. Finding the seam where it met the perpendicular metal wall, he pulled at the material, which gave way. The flashlight shined on metallic canisters and ammunition crates, some new, some old. Stepping behind the screen, he saw computers, monitors, and other communications equipment secured on a pallet.

He backed out, checked to make sure no one was lying in wait to ambush him, managed to drag the dead guard into the container, and locked the door again. There wasn't much he could do about the blood, but a lot had seeped between the rollers and it wasn't as obvious as he'd expected it to be.

The airplane quit taxiing. He imagined they had been told to relocate and that Baldy stayed where he was to ensure the pilots didn't take off without Tankian and Clutch. He expected to see that the second container was the same as the first, but he was wrong. The odor was strongest directly outside the door of the container, which he was more careful opening this time, managing to deaden the noise as he pushed up on the lever.

Upon opening the second container, he was blasted in the face by the stench. There was something dead inside. The rotting smell of decay permeated the air.

Using his flashlight again, he saw a similar setup. The Mercedes SUV in the front. The black screen in the back. But this time behind the screen were two drones with wings collapsed upward the way jets on an aircraft carrier were stored to make enough room. These drones barely fit in the container with a collapsed wingspan of eight feet across. They looked like small B-2 bombers with their contiguous-fuselage-and-wing design. Like angry hornets ready to sting, they stared at him. He ducked under the wing and continued deeper into the container.

Beyond the second drone was a small command and control pod with chairs, monitors, and computers, all on an elevated platform. Surrounding that were stacks of ammunition crates. Machine-gun ammunition, rockets, artillery, and missiles. Some of the crates looked new, and some looked like they were being reused. Beyond the ammo were rows of silver canisters, like oxygen tanks, secured with ropes to the side of the container. He counted maybe twenty. Beneath the canisters was a tarp big enough for two people or one very large animal.

The thin walls of the containers echoed with footsteps coming toward him. He would have to inspect the tarp later. He made a mental inventory of everything else. It was obvious that someone intended for the containers to withstand a cursory visual inspection, nothing more. He slid out of the container, closing and locking it.

When he stepped out, the ramp began to lower. As he stood between the two containers, the light from the airport buildings and runway gradually seeped into the airplane. The footsteps grew louder. Someone was walking from the nose of the aircraft toward the rear. Had to be Baldy or one of the pilots.

His options were to hide in one of the containers and

risk being locked in, climb back up on top and risk being seen, or to exit the aircraft and risk not rescuing Clutch if he reentered. He considered other factors.

The pilots weren't in charge; Baldy was telling them what to do. Clutch was in serious condition, if he was even alive. He didn't let the thought enter his mind that Clutch might be dead. It was there, trying to shove its way in, but he was pushing back. He had to execute the mission and couldn't allow negative thoughts into his mind.

The ramp was all the way open. Light spilled in. The footsteps grew louder. One SUV pulled into view. Baldy appeared to his right. Harwood wasted no time.

He spun to his right and stabbed Baldy in the stomach, raking the knife up. The man's bespectacled eyes grew wide as he let out a soft, "Unnhh." Harwood dragged him between the containers and slid the knife into his heart.

Two down, two to go.

He looked toward the SUV. Brake lights shot on as it stopped. *One driver, one security guy, Tankian, and Clutch. Worst case, three to one. Likely case, two to one. The odds would never be better.*

Harwood waited. Saw the hulking security man step out of the passenger side and open the door for Tankian, who stepped out of the right rear of the vehicle. They came around and lifted the hatch of the SUV. With the two large men blocking his view inside the vehicle, Harwood couldn't see in, but he imagined that Clutch was lying there, probably on a backboard.

Harwood stepped from his protected position and

sprinted down the ramp holding his pistol in one hand and knife in the other. He still couldn't shoot, because a miss or pass-through could hit Clutch. The driver stepped from the vehicle and raised a rifle, aimed at him, and fired.

Harwood did a forward roll when he saw the rifle coming up. He popped up and fired two rounds at the driver, who was not in the line of sight with Clutch. Missed. The driver ducked and popped back up, fired again.

Harwood rolled again, like a wrestling move from the standing position. The driver moved away from the vehicle, which was a mistake for him. Harwood snapped off two rounds, connected with at least one.

By now, Tankian and his bodyguard had turned. The bodyguard was pulling a pistol from his holster, but it was caught on his loose shirt. Harwood gained an angle that took Clutch out of play and fired. Hit. Turned toward Tankian, who was rushing toward him. Ten feet, five feet, and on him. No chance to get a shot off.

"You!" Tankian shouted as he raised his fist.

Harwood was quick, but Tankian was surprisingly fast for a big man. The catcher's mitt of a hand pummeled his forearm and jarred the pistol loose, sending it skittering on the pavement. His left hand came up with the knife and nicked Tankian's arm, causing him to reel backward. They squared off like two wrestlers, circling. Sirens blared in the distance, but all Harwood could focus on was Tankian's flat, murderous eyes. He'd come to the end of the road. One man left. That was all that stood between him and Clutch . . . and a bit of redemption. He could never bring Samuelson or LaBeouf back to life, but he could save Clutch. There was no greater calling to him than this moment right now.

Tankian circled left, leading with his left hand. A southpaw. Blue lights spun in the background. Sirens continued to wail.

"Asshole," Tankian spat. He took a swipe at Harwood and missed. Harwood's knife also missed on his return effort. Harwood spotted his pistol as they circled. It had landed near the right rear tire of the SUV, just below the exhaust plume coughing out of the tailpipe. In his periphery, Clutch's inert body lay in the back of the SUV, presumably alive. Why else would they bring him back? All he needed to do was dispatch this brute and drive away. He could figure out the rest from there.

With the sirens getting closer, Harwood considered his options again, some of which weren't in his control, even though Command Sergeant Major Murdoch had taught him never to allow himself to be in a situation that he didn't control.

The look in Tankian's eyes and the lack of aggressive action on his part told Harwood all he needed to know. Tankian was stalling for the cops to arrive. He knew that a stowaway like him would have no standing in whatever country they were in. What Tankian had no way of knowing was that his two men inside the aircraft were dead. It was just Harwood and Tankian.

Harwood began edging toward the vehicle once he had circled to the driver's side. The door was maybe ten meters away. The police cars were close, maybe one hundred meters away. He charged Tankian, a risky move, the knife swishing in the air as if he were a Japanese chef. Tankian instinctively took a step back and held his arms high to block the attack.

Harwood spun and slammed the rear cargo door shut and then raced to the open driver's door, leaped into the bucket seat, and slammed the gearshift into Drive. The wheels boiled and shot the SUV toward the gate about a quarter mile away. The police cars were coming from the same gate directly at him. Harwood was relying on the chaos to help him escape, cutting across the grain.

His momentum carried him through the gate before security personnel had an opportunity to close it. He took a turn too fast and felt the alternating wobble of the SUV from one side to the opposite. The high center of gravity almost tipped them over, but it settled, and Harwood gunned the gas again.

Sheer cliffs greeted him on the right and steep dropoffs on the left. The GPS navigation aid showed he was hurtling to the south into a winding road that led to the coast. He spun to his right when the road bottomed out near the water.

The GPS showed the city of Thessaloníki as their location.

Greece. They had landed in Greece when they noticed Clutch needed medical attention. Harwood had never been to Greece and knew very little about it other than the names of a few cities. He had briefly passed through Skopje, Macedonia, one of the former

Yugoslav republics that many claimed was still a part of Greece. There was a U.S. logistics base in Macedonia.

Too far, he thought.

His best option was to get to ground and contact someone. Maybe Stoddard. Maybe Murdoch. Maybe Sassi.

Traffic was light at this time in the middle of the night. He entered the outskirts of the city, following the blue *H* signs, wanting to be near a hospital in case Clutch required attention. A few random cars came at him from the opposite direction, their bright headlights causing a dagger of alarm until the moment he determined they weren't police.

He steered the vehicle to a parking lot behind the hospital and parked in the far corner. He felt naked without his rucksack, but he'd had no time to go back for it. Taking inventory on his person, he found his knife, his phone, and his TacSleeve on his arm. In the well of the passenger's seat was a kit bag with two HKP30 pistols, ammo, and several burner phones. He walked from the driver's seat to the hatch and popped it.

As the rear door rose, Clutch rolled over and said, "Damn, Reaper. Where'd you learn how to drive?"

Harwood smiled and nodded. Clutch hadn't lost his sense of humor. Harwood did a rapid triage on his spotter. Flashlight in the eyes. Pupils about the right size. Face looked okay save a few nicks. Someone had replaced the bandage on his shoulder. Legs and arms were functional.

"Can you stand?"

"Yeah, I think so." Clutch's voice was raspy. He

needed water. Harwood held out his hydration system hose, which Clutch drained.

Harwood helped him around to the driver's side.

"I assume you can still pull a trigger," Harwood said.

"That and more. I'm okay. He was going to sell me to a politician in America. I overheard him talking."

"Sell you to an American politician?"

"Yeah, but that's not all of it. He's going to attack somewhere in Chicago or nearby. Those containers—"

"Have drones in them. And ammo."

"That's right . . . and chem."

The canisters.

Harwood nodded. "When is this going down?"

"Sounded like within twenty-four hours."

Clutch looked him in the eyes and said, "You were right."

"I usually am, but about what?" Harwood asked.

"You can do both. You can save the soldier and accomplish the mission."

Harwood nodded. "I guess that's right. Now, let's go finish this mission."

CHAPTER 26

Jasar Tankian

Tankian shouted at the pilots, "Take off!"

With the police chasing them down the Thessa-loníki runway, they scratched into the sky, banked, and headed northwest over Germany and France, following the route to the United States.

Using his satellite phone, he called Wolff.

"Update, please."

"The sniper got Nolte," Tankian told him. He could have hidden the fact that Nolte had been sprung from his captivity, but Tankian had found that it was always best to give bad news early and deal with the conse-quences.

Wolff sucked in a deep breath, similar to what he had done when Tankian first told him he had secured Nolte.

"Easy come, easy go, right?" Wolff said. He chuckled, but his voice had a sinister pitch to it.

"Nothing easy about this. But I'm telling you directly."

When Wolff finished laughing, he sucked in another deep breath and exhaled into the phone speaker before saying, "That you are. Details, please."

"Nolte was unconscious with a weak pulse. We had no medical personnel on board. No IVs. Nothing. If I'd had even the most basic medical supplies, I probably wouldn't have landed. Your instructions to me were to keep him alive at all costs. A one-hour diversion to a hospital to get him treatment was, I thought, a wise move. We just took off from Thessaloníki and are back on schedule for Chicago with the containers but no Nolte."

Wolff was silent for so long that Tankian almost hung up.

"Nothing changes," Wolff finally said. "You will go to Chicago and deliver the containers and meet with the woman I tell you. You will tell her that you still have Nolte. I doubt the Americans will be quick to announce that he was captive or that he has been secured. I have men in Thessaloníki, and I'll send them to capture both of them. I can get his location from the GPS of the SUV. I'll send my plane down to pick them up, and they'll meet you in America. If I change the airport. I'll let you know once I have the new location confirmed."

"Understand," Tankian said.

"And, Tankian?" Wolff hesitated.

"Yes?"

"It appears I wasted my money," Wolff snapped.

"I can still execute," Tankian said.

Wolff paused. "Okay, but if you don't execute this part correctly, there will be no further payment."

Tankian ignored Wolff's comment and focused on the man he had just fought, the man who had all in twenty-four hours destroyed his home, his entire workforce, and possibly even his future.

"Is Nolte's partner this Reaper you mentioned?" Tankian asked.

"Going for revenge?"

"Maybe. Not something I normally do, but I can make an exception."

"He has rather dismantled your entire operation."

"Has he?"

"Yes. As I texted you before, he is a notorious Army Ranger sniper they call the Reaper. Victor Harwood. He lives in Columbus, Georgia. Has an adoptive daughter named Monisha, who stays with the parents of his command sergeant major. When you are done with this delivery, I'll provide you the details, should you . . . need them."

"If you capture him, I want him. He cut me," Tankian said.

"We'll discuss once we get to that point. Right now, get those containers to the new airfield and execute. I may have my own plans for the Reaper if you don't handle him."

Wolff hung up. Tankian stared at the containers. Two Sobirat drones and ammunition all masked by two automobiles. Wolff told him that the ammunition was for the Hunter drones he had shipped a month ago. Last week, at Wolff's instructions, his men had backhauled a load of ammunition from Syria. He wasn't clued in to Wolff's plan other than he was originally supposed to deliver the captive soldier to a woman. The woman was going to ensure customs clearance of the two containers, and they were going to be loaded onto trucks and taken to a ship. The same ship, he presumed, that had departed from Tripoli a month ago.

What he didn't understand was the need for these two containers. The Hunter drones he had transferred from Latakia to Tripoli included a container full of ammunition and other supplies.

As the plane etched a white line in the black sky, hurtling toward whatever destination Wolff finally decided upon, he thought about the man who attacked his compound and destroyed everything he had built. And now, so soon after seeing potential recovery by delivering Nolte to the woman, this man took even that away from him.

He lamented the loss of his fortune and hated that the only path to reclamation of what he had built was through this man, Wolff, one of the wealthiest men in the world. His maxim had always been to steer clear of alliances that made him beholden to anyone. Little by little, he'd built Tankian Logistics Group. It was the one aspect of his life that gave him meaning.

Now he would take away everything from the Reaper that he cared about.

After Wolff disconnected from the call, he dialed Andrea Comstock, who answered on the first ring.

"I never purchased a burner cell phone before," she said. "It's surprisingly easy."

"I have our precious cargo inbound now to Sawyer International Airport on your home state's Upper Peninsula."

"Yes, I'm familiar with it, but why did you move it? Sawyer is in the middle of nowhere and hard to get to," she said.

"You have an airplane. Nothing is hard to get to," he said.

She sighed. "When can I go public with this? I've spoken with Senator Nolte, and it's only a matter of time before word leaks out. I made him swear on his son's life that he wouldn't say anything, but Congress is the worst."

"The airplane is set to land in ten hours at Sawyer. I need you to get clearance for this plane. And do it secretly, or everyone will know."

"What do you mean *clearance*?"

"This is not a normal flight. Do you think I can just put a prisoner of war on an airplane and get him there on American Airlines? I need your help. The plane is in the air. Call your contacts. If you want the credit, earn it. I've handed this to you on a platter," Wolff said.

Comstock didn't speak for a long moment, then said, "Give me the details. I'll see what I can do."

"Of course. There are two containers on board the airplane. They are part of the normal delivery run and will be off-loaded first so as not to raise suspicion. Once the containers are off, you will have Corporal Nolte."

"A lot of moving parts. What's in the containers?"

"What do you think?"

"Mercedes-Benz, of course," Comstock said.

"What I recommend is that you talk to the airport crew in advance and let them know that General Motors is accepting these two new prototypes, and then young Corporal Nolte will appear. Use your clout," Wolff said.

"I'm trusting you here, Max."

"And I'm trusting you. Once you are at Sawyer, you will have my request."

"Your request?"

"Yes. A simple favor. Focus on your chores first. Get set and then we will talk."

"You're scaring me, Max."

"You don't get scared, Andrea. It's really a small ask."

After a pause, she said, "I'll do my best."

"And what if I said I would do my best to deliver Corporal Nolte to you? Would that be good enough?"

"It's going to have to be," she said. "This was your idea."

"Of course," Wolff said after a pause. "Get to Sawyer, get the plane cleared, and be there when it arrives. You will be glad you did. Then we will talk."

"I'll be there," she said.

Wolff disconnected his call and looked at the American cable news channel playing on his television screen. He sent a text to a contact in New York City. Ten minutes later, the chyron started scrolling with a breaking news alert that Corporal Ian "Clutch" Nolte Jr. was kidnapped and in the hands of ISIS terrorists in Syria. A male news anchor in a crisp suit and tie appeared on the television and said, "The details are sketchy, but we have a first report that Corporal Ian Nolte, the son of Senator Ian Nolte from Indiana, has been kidnapped by ISIS rebels somewhere in Syria. The Defense Department has not responded to our questions, and it seems that they are learning about this development almost on pace with our reporting."

He switched off the screen. *That should get it rolling,* he thought. Looking into the darkness, he could see the white-tipped Alps etching an outline against the black night. *Contrasts,* he thought. What was real? Did it matter whether Nolte was on the plane or not? He was just a prop to get Comstock to do what he wanted. As long as she believed he was on the plane, that was good enough. While it wasn't necessary to have the two containers on the ship, it was the optimal method. To have the drones in range for all that needed to be done, they would need to be mobile. The ship was mobile.

Then he thought about what could hamper his plans. Everything was falling into place but could easily fall apart. Maintaining order required personal energy. Tankian had gotten lazy and let one person overwhelm his compound and destroy his business.

Wolff would not let that happen to him. He was a fighter to the end.

He sent a text to a contact that he had pre-positioned in Columbus, Georgia, telling him to stand by.

The best soldiers had no one with whom they were close. They would go off to war unconcerned about whether they lived or died. The Reaper, though, had Monisha, who might be useful in the future.

His phone buzzed with a text from Hans Becker, his man in Thessaloníki.

Package located.

Excellent, he thought.

Inform when package secure, he texted.

With that bit of good news, Wolff used his MasterEye platform and flipped to the screen of the *Sieg,* which was still anchored in Lake Michigan. He typed a message to the sentry, who then told Sam Kinnett to pull up the anchors and turn toward Port Inland, Michigan.

"Why Port Inland?" Kinnett asked.

Port Inland was a private terminal for bulk and break-bulk shipment of gravel, limestone, calcium, and other aggregates. From his experience shipping cars all over the world, Wolff knew port capabilities well enough to understand that Port Inland had limited ability to move containers. Kinnett would be skeptical.

"The arrival destination of our new cargo changed."

The guard's black eyes remained fixed on Kinnett, unblinking.

Kinnett nodded.

"Okay."

There was something in the way Kinnett nodded and

spoke that concerned Wolff. Part confusion and part defiance?

Port Inland would put Kinnett in proximity to law enforcement. Wolff had done his homework. Mackinaw County had a police force, though it was small and had a large, remote county to cover. Still, Kinnett could tap out a distress signal to the police on the LTE network. Wolff thought through all the possibilities.

On the monitor, Kinnett's hands fluttered around the control panel. He pressed the button to raise the anchors and set a new course for Port Inland, which would have them turning around and steaming south of Summer Island and north of Washington Island with its sheer granite bluffs and stately beauty.

The ship was en route. Wolff calculated about ten hours to the destination. He just needed this one last piece to fall into place to put Comstock on the horns of her own dilemma.

Revenge was close at hand.

CHAPTER 27

Vick Harwood

Harwood listened to Clutch outline a plan that seemed unbelievable but devastating beyond belief. Another 9/11, maybe worse.

"You okay to execute?"

"They don't call me *Clutch* for nothing, brother."

Harwood retrieved his phone and saw a text: *Reaper it's Sassi.*

Suspicious, he called the number. Sassi answered on the second ring.

"You never told me they call you *the Reaper,* Vick," Sassi said.

"You never asked. And by the way, where did you hear that? How did you get my number?"

"I remember now. When you came into my cell, you said, 'Reaper coming in.'"

"That was so Clutch would know it was me."

The phone changed hands amid some scraping noises.

"Sergeant Harwood, this is General Cartwright. I gave Ms. Cavezza your contact information. Where are you?"

General Cartwright? He was the man behind all this?

"Sir, I've got precious cargo, and we need to meet ASAP. Can you go secure?"

"Not on this phone, but I'll call you in a minute."

They hung up, and Harwood's secure satellite phone buzzed shortly after.

"Yes, sir."

"Tell me what you've got," Cartwright said.

"I secured Corporal Nolte, my spotter. We were on assignment in the Middle East."

"I know where you were. I was commanding and controlling that operation. I need to pull Sergeant Stoddard in, and we all need to link up. Patalino and Ruben didn't make it. They were killed in al-Ghouta on a recon mission. Something is going down in the United States. Where are you?"

He thought of Patalino and Ruben, two Ranger teammates. Something scratched at the back of his mind, but he couldn't place it yet.

"Roger that. I'm in Thessaloníki. Once you land, let me know and we will meet you at the airport."

"Roger. Stay alive. Bad people out there want you dead."

Cartwright hung up, and as if to emphasize that point, Harwood caught a movement out of the periphery of his left eye.

"Bogey, nine o'clock," Clutch said. He raised the pistol Harwood had given him and fired twice. The glass shattered outward as Harwood slammed the vehicle into gear and raced from the hospital parking lot.

He found the road, noticed a black Mercedes-Benz racing toward them, played chicken until the oncoming car veered away with the driver trying to shoot and maneuver at the same time. Harwood followed the road leading from the hospital and made a series of turns that wound around the edge of the city and into the highlands above the airport.

"See anything?" Harwood asked.

Clutch was leaning between the two bucket seats looking for any sign of pursuit.

"No, but they got a pretty good make on the car," Clutch said.

"That doesn't matter. They know precisely where we are because of the GPS," Harwood said. He pulled onto a small dirt road, followed it as it cut back and forth through a series of switchbacks and parked. "We need to un-ass the vehicle and set up an ambush," he said.

"Reading my mind," Clutch echoed.

They left the SUV in a small gravel turnout and climbed a series of rock ledges. With no long rifle— that, too, was back on the airplane—they were close, maybe twenty meters at the most. The air smelled of eucalyptus trees and salt water. A light breeze rolled over their backs as they lay on the ground next to each other.

Clutch said, "Thanks, man. I always knew you'd come get me."

"Bad breath and all," Harwood said.

They lay atop the rocky outcropping without their ghillie suits, rucksacks, or long rifles. Still, they were lethal with their pistols, knives, and most important, their minds. The night air was cool with a breeze coming off the Mediterranean Sea.

"So, what happened to make the airplane land?"

"I heard them talking about the compound being raided, and then when he dragged me out and threw me in the truck, I was still awake. He and his guy Khoury were bitching about what you did to their business. Like, it's totally gone. You killed a bunch of their employees. From what I heard, it sounds like a mix between a logistics operation and a private military contractor. They do a little bit of everything."

"Yeah, but why did they land?"

"Because I stopped breathing. I thumped on the wall of that stupid cooler and acted like I was going into a seizure. Assholes hadn't given me any food for two days and just a little bit of water. It was possible that I could have, you know?" Clutch smiled and shrugged. "My old man was a doctor before he became a politician. He taught me how to hold my breath for a few minutes without blacking out. We used to go diving in the Caribbean and that was a useful skill if the equipment went bad. We even did some free diving. And, you know, I figured you were coming for me. When I heard the attack at the compound, well, I just knew that was you. And I kept thinking back to a couple of days ago when I said you'd lost your two other spotters, like it was your fault." Clutch choked on his words. "I was wrong to say what I did," he said.

Harwood stopped him. "No. Never apologize, Clutch. Like I said, you could be playing pro ball, getting the big payday, and here you are with me scratching out a hiding place in the dirt, being chased by bad guys."

"I get it, Reaper, but still. This life is all about chances and choices. I had the chance to be an Army Ranger, and that's what I chose. You did the same thing. I know our backgrounds are different, but at the end of the day, we're both lying right here waiting for some tool to ping on the GPS."

Just then, Harwood's phone buzzed in his pocket.

"Cartwright wants us to move to the airfield in ten minutes. He's inbound. General aviation."

"Can't see anything coming our way. This was a narrow road, so probably an ambush," Clutch said.

"Probably right," Harwood replied. "There's a trail that goes out the back way over the ridge."

"Let's give it a shot."

They moved back toward the vehicle and entered. Harwood brushed some broken glass from the seat. Clutch buzzed his window down and leaned out the window, scanning. Harwood drove onto a minor trail just big enough for the SUV, forcing Clutch to retreat inside the vehicle as branches and leaves slapped at his face.

After a couple of ditches and washboard ruts that had the SUV swaying from side to side, they popped onto the main road that led to the airport with no sign of the pursuers in either direction. Harwood found the general aviation gate and buzzed in about the time headlights appeared in the rearview mirror.

"Bogey, six o'clock," Harwood said.

"I'm calling Cartwright," Clutch said.

The gate began rolling open slowly as Clutch got Cartwright on the phone.

"Send it," Cartwright said.

"Bogey trailing us in. Need overwatch."

"Roger."

Harwood wound through the parking lot and past the terminal building as he waited for another gate to open, providing them access to the runway. As they stopped, a man exited from the passenger door of the pursuing car. He was large, dressed in black, and carrying a pistol. Harwood watched through the rearview mirror.

"Coming up your side," Harwood said.

The general's G3 airplane was no more than fifty meters from the gate. Cartwright stood in the door with his arm level and his hand pressing against the frame of the jet doorway. Clutch was holding the pistol in his left hand, which was supported by his right forearm, with the muzzle aimed directly at the door.

"They want me alive," Clutch said.

"Then don't die," Harwood whispered, eyes fixed on the rearview.

A zipping noise creased the air not once but twice. The second was followed by glass shattering in the vehicle behind them. The big man was no longer in the rearview mirror. As they pulled through the gate and raced toward the G3, Sassi was lowering an SR-25 with silencer on the bore.

They exited the SUV and entered the G3, which began taxiing quickly. At the far end of the runway, police lights continued to bounce into the sky.

"Your doing?" Cartwright asked, pointing at the dozen or so cop cars and ambulances.

"Perhaps, sir," Harwood said.

"Good job getting Ranger Nolte back, son. The mission continues, though. We got word of a major terrorist attack going down in Chicago. That airplane you were on? Headed to Chicago with chem."

"I saw it with my own eyes. Made to look like just SUVs, but there was command and control, UAVs, ammo, and canisters that looked like they could hold chem."

"That's it, then. Jasar Tankian, the logistician of the Beqaa Valley, has supplied the means to attack the United States. The only question is, what are his targets?"

CHAPTER 28

As the G3 hurtled toward Chicago, cutting across Western Europe and the North Atlantic, General Cartwright explained his mission as it related to Harwood and Clutch.

"About a month before we sent you in to observe supply chains, we had a tip that ISIS was working with who we now know to be Tankian in the Beqaa Valley to perfect drone strikes. We hadn't seen much in the way of this happening but thought a low-footprint mission with some of our best operators would give us the intel we needed. A lot of our countermeasures rely on cutting the radio signals, and what Tankian has developed is a command and control platform that allows for drones to fly to GPS waypoints without any kind of radio signal."

"Limits our countermeasures," Harwood said.

"Exactly, Ranger," Cartwright said.

Harwood sat across from Sassi, who was next to Cartwright. Clutch was facing Cartwright in the two-by-two facing-seat configuration in the aft of the aircraft.

"I sent Patalino and Ruben in with Ms. Cavezza here, who I'm still not convinced isn't Italian OSIE or even our CIA, but we'll leave that aside for now. Your two teammates were killed by ISIS fighters planning this attack. Al-Ghouta is their version of Tarnak Farms, where Bin Laden planned the 9/11 attacks. What's happening here is something similar but perhaps on a grander scale. It could involve nukes. Everything is pointing at Chicago or that region. Information is sketchy because our ability to penetrate the tribes and governments of Lebanon, Syria, and Iran are almost nonexistent."

Valerie, Harwood thought. She was in Milwaukee, which was close enough to Chicago.

"Patalino and Ruben were good men," Harwood said. "I hope we're taking care of their families."

"As best we can. They'll get closure when we find them or their bodies."

Harwood nodded. Combat losses were always a gut punch. Nonetheless, the fallen would prefer that you continue with the mission, no question. It would be what he wanted whenever his time came. The last thing any Ranger wanted was to impede the accomplishment of the mission.

Then it hit him.

"Any clues?"

"No, why?" Cartwright asked.

"There was one, maybe two, bodies rolled in a tarp in one of those containers. The one with the ammunition."

Cartwright stared at him for a moment. "Okay. That's important. Might be them. We need to recover our fallen. We *always* recover our fallen."

"Tankian's people captured Sassi where Patalino and Ruben were. It makes sense that everyone was hauled back to the same compound."

Harwood nodded, knowing he had it right.

"Bottom line is that we know there are two containers on a big Ukrainian-built airplane headed to Chicago, and one of those containers has Patalino and Ruben in it," Harwood said.

"Not exactly," Cartwright said.

"I'm assuming that we've contacted all the right authorities and are tracking the plane?"

"The plane turned off its transponder somewhere over the Atlantic. It might be fish bait, or more likely it is in the final throes of executing its plan. There's no way it can land in Chicago. We've got U.S. Air Force patrolling the skies along the northern tier of the United States. We've called Canada and asked for their cooperation. They're thinking about it. We've got JSOC marshaling at Fort Bragg, which means your Ranger buddies, Delta, and some SEALs. The intelligence is lean. We know that Sassi here saw a rehearsal map, which she described as flowing from Syria to Tripoli in Lebanon to Cyprus to somewhere in the Midwest, most likely Chicago. There are other big cities that would make high-value targets—like Detroit, Milwaukee, and Minneapolis—if we go with the idea that they're striking in that region. We have to be careful. This is comparted. DHS is getting briefed right now. I've spoken to the president and SecDef."

"I have a contact in Milwaukee if that helps," Harwood said.

Cartwright nodded, urging him to continue.

"An FBI special agent there to protect the political convention."

"We've considered the convention as a target. We should make contact and share what little intel we've got."

"That airplane still has to land somewhere," Clutch said. "Assuming those two containers are part of the plan."

"We've got every airport in the northern tier of the United States on alert for any aircraft coming in without transponder. The F-15s and F-35s providing CAP will be able to respond based upon the grid where the plane enters U.S. airspace," Cartwright said.

"A lot of terrain out there. Like finding a small boat in the ocean if it's not pinging," Harwood said.

"True, but our radars can pick it up if we're scanning in the right directions. We've got all the Great Lakes covered," Cartwright said.

After a pause in the conversation, Sassi spoke up. "One thing that has bothered me about this entire conversation since I connected with you, General Cartwright, is that I saw very few 'terrorists' in the town of al-Ghouta after about a month of being there. Two months ago, creepy men with beards and shaved heads and beady eyes were all over the place. One month ago, there were fewer. And two days ago, even fewer. The basement where I saw the map was vacant. Only a few terrorists were there either day. There weren't enough people to train."

"Unless they had already finished training and had shitty OPSEC," Harwood said.

"OPSEC?" Sassi inquired.

Harwood explained, "Operational security. Any well-trained unit would have sanitized their rehearsal location. For some reason, they didn't. Might have been several rehearsal locations. Might have been they weren't done. Doubt we'll ever know. The fact remains, it seems like a major piece of the puzzle. When I was in a hide site waiting on nightfall to go in and get Clutch here, I heard drones buzzing up and down the valley all day. Trucks were moving in and out of the compound also. It's a major logistics operation. It's not out of the realm of possibility that this thing has been building up piece by piece over the last year or two. ISIS and the others who oppose us in the Middle East think in terms of years, if not decades, while we are focused on weeks or days or hours. If we have to wait more than ten seconds for a website to download, we get impatient and go somewhere else. So, to think in terms of contemporary clues might work against us."

"What he said," Clutch echoed.

A small television monitor was playing one of the cable news channels with a breaking news item.

ARMY RANGER AND SON OF SENATOR IAN NOLTE MISSING IN ACTION IN UNAUTHORIZED SYRIA MISSION

"I'm right here," Clutch said.

"But we're not telling anyone," Cartwright replied.

"I'm fine with that, but why?" Clutch asked.

"Might be related and it might be totally separate, but we've got traffic from the Daimler CEO, Max Wolff, going direct to GM CEO Andrea Comstock, who also happens to be a presidential candidate."

"That sounds too convenient for it not to be related," Harwood said.

"No law against two car manufacturers talking," Cartwright said.

"Then why are you listening to them? There's more to it than you're telling us," Harwood said.

Cartwright pointed at Clutch and said, "Comstock has apparently negotiated your safe release and will receive you at a location to be determined. She'll be praised for her negotiating skills and receive the appropriate bump in the polls."

"Sweet. Glad to be of assistance," Clutch said.

Harwood smiled. "You're trying to smoke her out."

Cartwright nodded. "I'm even willing to offer Mr. Basketball here to her if she'll tell me her location."

"Because she was supposed to meet the airplane with Clutch on it," Harwood said.

Cartwright's loaded thumb and forefinger fired an imaginary shot at Harwood. "You win the prize for the day."

The plane was losing altitude as it approached Gander, Newfoundland, for refuel. They landed, taxied, refueled, and took off within thirty minutes.

Once airborne again, Harwood called Valerie Hinojosa from the G3 communications suite, explaining to her everything that had happened.

"Where are you now?" he asked her.

"Milwaukee. Prepping for the convention. We've had buzz of some kind of attack but nothing to differentiate it from the million other crazies out there. Jihadis, white supremacists, Antifa, ISIS, and so on. Everyone trying to lay claim to wanting to disrupt the convention and cause damage."

"What we've determined is that two containers are inbound to Chicago, but they might change up airports on us. With the transponder off, it might be difficult to find this thing. We've got an idea we're working on. How mobile are you?"

"We've got a helicopter, some boats, and a King Air at the airport."

"Okay, stay ready. This thing is moving fast," Harwood said.

"Always does with you around, Reaper." Then she said, "Shit."

"That doesn't sound good."

"Fucking Andrea Comstock is in the air traffic control tower of Sawyer International Airport with the FBI, ordering TSA to clear an airplane to land."

"The presidential candidate car exec? What the hell?" Harwood said.

"I'm calling SecDef now," Cartwright said.

"I'm heading up there," Hinojosa said, and jumped off the call.

"If it lands, box it in," Harwood said. "Don't let anyone off the airplane."

Cartwright alerted the National Command Authority, who reacted to the new information.

Tankian's airplane landed smoothly at Sawyer International Airport on the remote Upper Peninsula of Michigan.

The pilots had navigated a path through Europe, over Greenland and Canada, and then poked across the border into the United States as they flew less than five hundred feet above ground level across Lake Superior. The plane taxied to the cargo hangar and pulled inside. It was 3:00 a.m. local time.

As expected, the woman, Andrea Comstock, was waiting for him in a black SUV. She was wearing a charcoal business suit with a white blouse underneath the blazer. The skirt was clipped at knee length, and she stood atop four-inch heels. Her hair swept back in an impressive flowing mane that would look good on television, provided she had something to talk about. Another car was parked behind the SUV. Probably a chase car. She was holding a phone to her ear, most likely talking to Wolff. Two men stood outside the car and SUV, definitely security. One of the men was stocky and built like a wrestler with bowlegs and long, muscled arms. The other was tall and wiry, all muscle and sinew packed tightly in a sleek body.

A cargo handler drove to the back of the airplane as the ramp lowered. The tractor pulled one container from the back of the airplane, drove it to a waiting Mack truck with flatbed, and deposited it on the back. It repeated the process with the second container. The trucks idled, waiting for him.

He walked to the woman and said, "I will leave what you came for in the container yard."

"He's supposed to be here now," she snapped. "I put my ass on the line. I had my team coordinate for your trailers and your cargo. I broke rules, maybe even laws to make this happen. Now, make good on your promise to deliver my . . . guest to me. I've already promised his return to his family."

Tankian towered over the woman. Didn't really know what to say. Wolff's instructions to him were to greet the lady, stall for a moment, deliver what he had, and then join the trucks.

He shrugged. "Take it up with the man."

"What man?"

"Whoever told you to do all of this," he said. He swept his hand across the hangar.

"You can't be serious. There are television reporters waiting on my word." Her voice carried an air of desperation. "Right out there." She pointed over her shoulder.

"I only know my part of the operation. I was instructed to tell you that your guest would be available in the container yard. Thanks for the help with all the logistics."

With that, Tankian turned and walked away.

"Hey!" she shouted.

He stopped and turned again. Her two security personnel were jogging toward him. He had a pistol in one pocket, a knife in the other. He wished he had the sniper's long gun, but that would have been too obvious. Especially now that he understood the plan. While he never intended to go operational in combat on American soil, was never fueled by enough hate, he did believe that if he persisted with this mission, he would draw the Reaper into his orbit.

And he would kill the Reaper, the man who had destroyed his livelihood. If there were ever a reason for vengeance, it would be this. If he were not to defend what he had built, then what would he defend? Nothing. There was also the practical matter that Wolff had promised him €2 million upon delivery of the containers and execution of the mission. As a logistician, he had the delivery part down cold.

The operational part might challenge him, but he had executed many complex tasks in the past. It was no easy task to conduct a fifty-mile logistics resupply from the Beqaa Valley into Syria. Especially when he was backhauling two or three ISIS terrorists at a time. They would rendezvous at his compound and then infiltrate to Tripoli, where, a month ago, they boarded the *Sieg* and loaded the Hunter unmanned aerial vehicles onto the ship.

He imagined that was where he was headed. Standing on American soil for the first time in his life with nothing but his future to believe in, he faced the two security men head-on.

"Ms. Comstock wasn't done talking to you," the wiry greyhound said.

"I'm done with her. I followed my instructions."

"You don't leave until we get the soldier," he said.

Tankian drew his pistol quickly and fired at the man who had mistakenly believed he was in a shouting match, not a pistol duel.

Comstock shrieked, "What are you doing?"

Tankian fired at the wrestler, because he knew it was only a matter of time before he gathered himself and seized the initiative. With both men on the concrete floor of the hangar, Comstock began pleading. She held her hands in the air, as if pushing against something, perhaps willing him out of the hangar. He had no desire to kill her. The way he figured it, Wolff had engineered this to kill her career. He aimed the pistol at her, saw liquid running down her legs, and turned around once more.

He walked through the door of the hangar and stepped into the nearest truck on the tarmac.

"Whattawe got back there in them containers?" the driver asked.

Tankian stared at the man and shrugged. "Vehicles. Drive to the gate, then stop."

His look must have been intimidating, because the man went pale, shifted the rig into gear, and stepped on the gas. Looking in the rearview mirror, he saw one other truck following his vehicle, while another two headed in the opposite direction.

They stopped. Tankian exited briefly. Opened the container. Took about five minutes. Closed the container. Reentered the passenger side.

"Now, go."

Then he called Wolff to tell him everything was back on schedule.

"Max Wolff, please!" Andrea Comstock shouted into the phone.

A moment later, Wolff answered the phone.

"Did everything go as planned?" he asked, knowing full well she was most likely on major nuclear meltdown.

"No! I'm standing here in bumfuck Michigan with about a hundred media people clawing at the fence like zombies!"

"What happened?"

"Don't play coy with me. You totally fucked me, you asshole."

"I should be so lucky."

Wolff could hear the click of heels moving at a fast pace.

"You sound distraught," he said.

"This beast just killed two of my best security men, you asshole."

"Surely not your best if they're dead," Wolff said. He picked some lint off his suit and looked at the Alps. It was 9 a.m. in Germany, and the morning sun glistened off the snow. "Now, listen to me. You've authorized an airplane to land on U.S. soil that is carrying weapons of mass destruction. You are complicit in a terrorist plot to attack your homeland. The attack might be on your home state of Michigan. Maybe Wisconsin. Maybe Illinois. Maybe all three. Who knows? Do you understand your role here? Your greed to become the most powerful person in the world has perhaps cost you that opportunity. The irony."

Her breathing was shallow and rapid.

"No . . ."

"Andrea?"

"Wha . . ."

Wolff grinned.

"Six months ago when you fucked me on the truck deal—a billion dollars!—I decided to find a way to bend you over a barrel and let you know how it feels."

"Max—"

"Don't you dare 'Max' me, you conniving bitch! You will do exactly as I tell you or your name will leak to the press as the one who planned this terrorist attack."

"It's too late . . ."

Comstock couldn't pull together any complete sentences. She ran a hand through her perfectly coiffed hair, knelt, and covered her face with her hands. *Ohmygodohmygodohmygod.*

"What . . . what do you need, Max?"

"Got your attention?"

She stood, did her best to shake it off and compose herself. "Definitely."

"You'll tell Senator Nolte that GM can't meet the manufacturing timelines and that you want it to go to Daimler. You make that call. You make that happen. And I'll make sure this doesn't stick to you. You back off, try to weasel me, you'll see the biggest attack you've ever imagined right in your backyard and your name will be released as the mastermind, like the kid who sets his girlfriend's house on fire so he can save it. Understand?"

"I-I . . ."

"You should be responding with a quick 'Yes, sir, I'll get right on it,'" Wolff admonished. "Instead, you're trying to figure out how you beat this. There is no beating it. Checkmate, bitch."

"Okay. Okay. I'll make that call."

"You'll close the deal. And you'll do it right fucking now."

Wolff hung up.

Comstock stood in the deathly silent hangar. Her two security guards were dead on the floor. The press was pushing against the gates of the secured cargo portion of the airport. The two containers she had secured passage for were on their way to God knew where. And she had to make a call to Senator Nolte without his son in her presence.

As if things couldn't get any worse, she stepped outside, stared at the tarmac and then the fence, and walked toward two lumps on the apron.

"What the—"

Two dead, stiff bodies were lying askew at her feet. She ran into the hangar and, self-survival always the first order of the day, called Senator Nolte. He answered on the first ring.

"Have him?"

"Not yet, Senator. It seems there's an additional demand."

"There always is, Andrea. Where's my son?"

"He's safe," she said. "We just need to do this one thing. In my assessment, I was overzealous in my estimation of GM's capabilities to fulfill the defense contract for the new truck fleet. It needs to go to Daimler."

"You're kidding me. You're being blackmailed over a defense deal to get my son back."

"It's just my best estimate of our capabilities," she said.

His sigh was audible over the phone speaker.

"I have legislation drafted to undo that deal and open the door for GM. It's practically a done deal."

"*Practically* is the operative word. We need this to happen. *You* need this to happen."

"You'll sacrifice a billion to your top line to get my son back? I'm not sure I believe that's really what's at play here."

"Trust me. It's the only way he comes back alive."

"Bullshit."

"Do I have your word, Senator? This is all happening right now." Comstock was shaking. She tried her best to hold her voice steady but couldn't.

"Are you being held at gunpoint somewhere? You sound scared."

"I'm scared. Not at gunpoint." At least not literally at gunpoint. Figuratively, yes.

She heard him call for his chief of staff. They argued for a minute, but Nolte got his point across.

"Okay. My chief is pulling the bill. The Germans get the deal. Where's my son?"

"Thank you. I'll communicate this message and then call you back."

She hung up, dialed Wolff, relayed the message, and asked where Nolte Jr. might be.

"When I see that the bill has been pulled and get a new letter of commitment, I'll release him to you," Wolff said.

"You can't keep moving the goalposts on me, Max."

"Letter of commitment. Now. Then I'll give him to you."

"Okay. Quickly. The senator is impatient."

Wolff hung up.

Comstock turned, her mind spinning. Called Nolte, but no answer. Called again. No answer. Left a message.

"My contact wants a letter of commitment first."

She hung up and dropped to her knees. What had she done?

CHAPTER 29

Vick Harwood

"I'm okay, Dad, but we can't tell anyone," Clutch said to his father over speakerphone.

"I've got Comstock calling into my phone. Answer me this to verify it's you, son. How many seconds were on the clock when you made that clutch shot for Notre Dame?"

Clutch smiled. "Trick question. Point zero eight. Less than one second."

"Okay. My God, you had me worried."

"Senator, this is Vick Harwood, Clutch's Ranger buddy. You've got a lot to be proud of with your son. We're in a situation now, though, and I'm curious how you left it with Comstock. She's in communications with a terrorist organization."

"Thanks for that, Vick. She's asking me to undo

some legislation that was going to ensure General Motors won a billion-dollar truck deal."

"She's giving away a billion-dollar deal?" Harwood asked for clarification.

"Exactly my thought."

"Being blackmailed," Harwood said, looking at Cartwright. "Wolff, the Mercedes guy."

"Exactly," said the senator and general in unison.

"What happens if you don't give her what she wants?"

"No idea. She just said, 'This is happening now.'"

"Can we ask that you don't call her back for a bit?" Harwood said.

"I'm not calling her back until I hear from you guys, but should we alert the National Command Authority?"

"I've got that covered, Senator," General Cartwright said.

"Okay, I'll stand by, then."

"Roger that, Dad. We're getting another call. Got to run," Clutch said.

Harwood punched the phone and switched calls.

"Vick. It's Valerie. Two of presidential candidate Andrea Comstock's security personnel have been shot dead. Comstock is in the hangar. She was supposed to meet someone to facilitate the return of Corporal Nolte," Valerie Hinojosa told Harwood.

He kept her on speakerphone so that Clutch, Cartwright, and Sassi could hear her report.

"Sawyer?" Harwood asked.

"Yes. I'm on the way up there. We never really

looked at it. It's way north on the Upper Peninsula. It's a stopover for a lot of logistics and cargo and services the city of Marquette. Comstock convinced TSA that she was cleared to land this thing. Corporal Nolte was supposed to be on the plane."

"That's a politician," Clutch said. "She got owned."

"Did they off-load two containers from an airplane?" Harwood asked.

"How did you know? The airport director said the plane took off directly after they off-loaded."

"I just know. That's the plane Clutch and I were on. Where are those containers? Still in customs?"

"With the circular reporting, this all happened about ninety minutes ago. And no. Comstock's people worked with customs to allow the containers to move unimpeded into the cargo yard. They're gone now."

Comstock was a minor tool in this cog, but an important one nonetheless.

"There's something else, isn't there?" Harwood asked. He knew Hinojosa had a penchant for delivering the best or worst news last.

"Right. You know me well, Vick. Comstock said she had secured the release of two captured Rangers but that the terrorists had killed them."

"Patalino and Ruben," Harwood said.

"Politicians," Clutch said, shaking his head.

Harwood eyed him, thinking about Clutch's father, as Valerie continued, "Locals are on the ground with a field agent who was checking the airport up there. He's on the scene, and it's all a bit sketchy."

"How long until you're there?"

"I'm in the King Air. Maybe fifteen minutes."

"Okay, we're maybe an hour out from Sawyer, if that."

"Want me to tell her that the senator's son is alive and well?"

"No. Hold that. We need to smoke out who's controlling this thing."

"Wilco," she said, then hung up.

Harwood turned to Cartwright.

"They landed in Marquette. Probably caught wind that we were mobbed up over Chicago and everywhere else. Sawyer airport is small. Never heard of it. Patalino and Ruben are home, which is a huge deal."

"Okay, that's good," Cartwright said. "Now we can execute with violence and not concern ourselves with finding our brothers in the aftermath."

"Roger that. The question is, where are they taking those containers?" Harwood said.

Sassi spoke up. "I don't know why I didn't think of this before, but on that rehearsal map, as you guys are calling it, was a picture of a slave ship, it seemed."

"Slave ship?"

"The oval hull of a boat with stick figures lying on that bottom like you've seen in the drawings of how slaves were transported overseas. They were chained down to the bottom of the lower hold of the boat, head to toe and toe to head."

"How's that relevant?" Cartwright asked.

"I know how," Harwood said. "He's got to load those containers on a ship. The ship is going to serve as a mobile launchpad for the UAVs. This has always been

about the drones. My man Clutch here was a target o
opportunity. Using him as a cover probably helped ge
the airplane cleared and the cargo passed through customs. Why not get one of the most powerful people
in the country to pull a few strings and land a couple
of harmless containers? Tankian probably had a plan
already, but why not have some insurance? What she
actually has done is facilitate a terrorist attack on the
United States."

The plane bored through the night. It banked slightly
with the new instructions. The only questions Harwood
had were: Which ship? Which port?

"Nearest port?" he asked.

"I've got a map up here, Vick," Sassi said, holding the general's iPad. "The nearest container port is
Green Bay. There are some other smaller things, but
that's our best shot. It's maybe a three-hour drive. So,
we've got about ninety minutes, if that's the case."

"I know Valerie is headed to Sawyer, where she
needs to be, but do we land at Sawyer or Green Bay?"
Harwood asked, looking at Cartwright. These were the
types of decisions generals got paid the big bucks to
make. Cartwright didn't hesitate.

"Give me the pros and cons of each," the general directed in his most general-like way.

Before Harwood could do that, Valerie called him
again. He put it on speaker. "We just had an anomaly
pop up on our system. Might be something. Might be
nothing," she said.

"Send it."

"We track any last-minute changes in rental cars,

airplanes, trains, buses, and, if it's coastal, ships or boats."

"Wisconsin is coastal," Harwood said.

"Right. More shoreline here than just about anywhere else in the world. My point is that a ship called the *Sieg* had berth time scheduled in the Port of Chicago for tonight, but it canceled, which put the transaction, or lack thereof, on our radar. When I check the papers on it, I can't really tell where it came from or where it's going. Only that it supposedly has over a hundred containers of balsa wood. Maybe from Africa?"

"Balsa wood? Okay. No other ports alerted to inbound traffic?" Harwood asked.

"None so far. If this is like the airplane thing, the ship may be calling an audible midstride. Hard to move an airplane and a ship, but they're doing it. Ask General Cartwright if he knows what's on those containers. How concerned do we need to be?"

"This is Cartwright," the general said over the open speaker of the phone sitting between them on the table. "We're on an unsecure line, and none of you are cleared for this compartmented information."

"I'm sure that will look good during the congressional testimony, General. I can see the headlines now: 'General Preserves Key Information: Allows Major Terrorist Attack to Occur,'" Valerie said. Harwood smirked. She was never one to hold back.

"I hope you feel better getting that off your chest. We have no idea who's listening in on this unsecure line. I'll discuss with the team on board, and then we can talk face-to-face. Suffice it to say that our intel indicates that it is the highest national emergency to find these containers and detain them, but not to fire on them with any munitions. And there will be no testimony, because we're going to stop it from happening."

"Noted," Valerie said. "We're about to land at Sawyer."

The line went dead. Harwood looked at Cartwright, whose face was lined with worry. His eyes were somewhere else, lost in thought. Maybe he was visualizing the packed hearing room Valerie referenced, or perhaps he was considering how best to stop the attack that seemed to be materializing.

Harwood snapped him out of his reverie.

"Pros and cons, General. We have to make a decision now. And whatever we do, we can turn Valerie around or split our efforts to maximize coverage. If Green Bay is the destination, we could beat them there and set up an ambush, plus find whatever they're delivering it to." Something hung in the back of Harwood's mind, but he couldn't grab it, so he continued, "If it's not the destination, then we're pissing up a rope, wasting time."

"What's your recommendation?" More general talk from the general.

"I recommend we take five minutes and do a quick analysis of the roads out of Sawyer and if there are any ports closer in."

Cartwright nodded. Harwood turned to Clutch and said, "Use that iPad to pull up all the ports within three hours of Sawyer. Sassi mentioned Green Bay. I'm sure there are others." He turned to Sassi and said, "Can you look at ships leaving Beirut and Tripoli? I'd focus on Tripoli. Have Sergeant Flanigan help you find the right databases. Might have to cut some corners."

"I can do that," Flanigan said from the communications console.

Sassi said, "You're thinking a different ship left the Med a long time ago and is just now here?"

"It's a possibility. Your slave ship thing. I'm thinking what you saw wasn't new. This could be the second shipment. Or third. Or fourth. We have no way of telling when we came into the cycle." It was more than a possibility, Harwood thought. It was a probability.

"I can tell you that my mission—your mission—was predicated on intelligence chatter we were picking up about a potential drone strike of some type. Nothing was adding up, just a few random logistics calls referencing Hunter and Sobirat drones operating as teams. Most of the intel was coming from the Beqaa Valley. Then Syria and Hezbollah attacked the Golan, and we lost focus," Cartwright said.

"Intentionally so," Harwood said. "What Clutch and I were seeing was almost a deliberate attempt by the Syrian Army to impale themselves on the wire in the Golan. Like a fixing effort. A feint, but with significant contact."

"To convince us the Hunter drones were part of that effort. Meanwhile, they were shipping drones to the United States, literally. But to attack what?"

"The political convention," Harwood said. "That starts tomorrow and lasts several days."

There it was. The aircraft fell silent, the only sound that of the metal-on-wind whistle and the whine of the Rolls-Royce jet engines forging a path through the sky.

"Damn," Clutch said. "But if they're burned, they'll want to act now. How far can those drones fly?"

"The Hunter is a Russian fighter drone with specialized swept wings. They can fly over 500 miles. So, make it 250 out and 250 back."

"And the recon drones we saw? They were armed also," Harwood said.

"Smaller, less payload, but still lethal. They call them the *Sobirat,* Russian for 'gather.' Hunter-gather."

"Only it works the other way around. They gather intel, then they hunt. Okay, take five minutes and let's do some research. We have some decisions to make," Cartwright said.

After five minutes, Clutch had a list of ports, which included Marquette, Marinette, Escanaba, Port Inland—which was a private terminal—Dolomite, and a few others.

"Marquette is the most convenient, being thirty minutes away by truck, but they'd have to get the boat back through the channel between Lake Superior and Lake Michigan if they wanted to be mobile into Lake Michigan. That's a major choke point. Green Bay is right at three hours but has the best facilities for containers. Escanaba is an hour and has decent equipment. This Port Inland thing is maybe an hour and a half. It's small and private, and I'm not sure they would have the equipment to move containers. They do mostly bulk and break-bulk. Dolomite is the same, only farther," Clutch said.

"Maybe they don't need the ship at all," Cartwright said. "Maybe Tankian will ground-launch."

"Good thought, General. There was a command and control platform in one of the containers, but wouldn't Tankian want to be with the main force?" Harwood said.

"Not if he's the supporting effort."

Sassi looked up from the screen that Sergeant Flanigan continued to pinch and expand using his thumb and forefinger.

"Going back exactly thirty days shows hundreds of ships departed Tripoli, obviously, but I added a filter for destination in Cyprus. I figure that is a good place to switch manifests, bills of lading, and to change the proverbial license plate of the ship—help it get lost in the paperwork. I read somewhere that there are hundreds of ships every year that never get to the port they were scheduled to visit."

The plan came into partial view for Harwood. A ship serving as sort of an aircraft carrier floating in one of the Great Lakes able to strike Chicago, Detroit, Milwaukee, or any of the smaller towns within range. The drones he and Clutch had seen a few nights ago from their recon perch on the Lebanon-Syria border were heavily armed reconnaissance platforms. He began to get a general sketch of the concept. A ship with weaponized drones, a poor man's aircraft carrier, patrolling the Great Lakes, attacking the major industrial cities of the Midwest. Planners were always looking at New York City, Los Angeles, and Washington, D.C., because of the easy reach and population centers, but this plot seemed to turn those conventions on their heads. Harwood didn't know much about the waterway from the Saint Lawrence River to Lakes Michigan and Superior, but he knew enough to understand that big ships transited those waters.

"We're looking for an aircraft carrier," Harwood said.

"A what?" Cartwright replied.

"I get it," Clutch chimed in. "A ship. The drones. Mobile platform."

"That's right."

"Now tell us what's in those cylinders I saw," Harwood demanded.

Cartwright ran a hand across his face.

"Most of Assad's chemical stockpiles. Sarin gas, mostly. We tracked it from al-Ghouta after we intercepted some Russian communications about two months ago. The stuff was being moved from Damascus to Latakia when ISIS raided the convoy and stole it. Or so the story goes."

"The convoy was passing through al-Ghouta," Harwood said.

"Close enough. We tracked communications to al-Ghouta and lost the bubble. Your entire mission," Cartwright said, pointing at Harwood and Clutch, "was to find the logistics convoys and watch for transfers to artillery units. These are artillery shells and rockets. The Hunter drone can drop these things or fire them from pods."

"We know. At least we know they can fire from conventional drones."

"Since you're waffling, General, I say we have a C-130 with parachutes meet us at Sawyer. We get the coast guard working out of the bases along Lake Michigan, and we get a sub-hunter plane in the sky."

"You're going to jump into Lake Michigan?" Cartwright asked.

"Love it," Clutch said.

"You're the general. Get the resources for the trigger pullers. Isn't that what you guys are always talking about?" Harwood said.

"I know my job," Cartwright said.

"Then do it. You want Patalino and Ruben hanging around your neck forever? Let's stop whatever's happening."

Cartwright stood, walked to the cockpit, and leaned in. The plane tilted and began to lose altitude. Flanigan sat down at the communications console as Cartwright began to lay out the shopping list Harwood had described.

"You can't do this alone," Clutch whispered to Harwood.

"I'm not. If you're healthy, you're coming with me."

"I'm well enough . . . and I'm in," Clutch said.

CHAPTER 30

The Port Inland crane operator wasn't too thrilled to be dragged from his bed to conduct a precarious loading of two containers using a swing crane designed for smaller bulk loads as opposed to heavy containers.

When the second container was loaded, the operator stepped down from the cab and said to Tankian, "That's five thousand dollars."

Tankian waved the two truck drivers over and acted as if he were reaching for his wallet. Instead, he pulled his pistol from his waistband and shot the operator first, then one of the truck drivers who was too stunned to run, and then finally winged the other truck driver, who managed to slide under the empty bed of his truck.

Not having the time to pursue the man, Tankian walked past the large limestone domes and conveyors to the berth where the *Sieg* was docked. The gangplank barely reached the pier. As Tankian scaled the steep incline, the platform bounced beneath his weight. He climbed the ladder to the bridge and stepped inside beyond the two guards who had their weapons aimed at a white man, most likely the captain.

"Jasar Tankian," he said. "We need to get moving. Why are these men aiming their weapons at you?"

The man didn't speak for a minute, his eyes darting from Tankian to the two guards. Finally, he nodded and shook Tankian's hand. "Sam Kinnett. I'm the river pilot. It has been this way since I boarded in Québec. All of this is highly irregular."

"I know it must seem that way, but all we need to do is head toward Milwaukee and you'll be fine."

"I just watched you shoot those three men. It's four in the morning. We loaded undesignated contraband on the ship. There's nothing *fine* about this," Kinnett said.

"Seeing how you're the only one who can drive the boat, we're going to need you to get moving. If you choose not to assist, we can deposit your body out by the others. Or you can do this job and be handsomely rewarded."

Kinnett swallowed hard, a golf ball rolling down his throat.

"Now, let's get moving," Tankian directed.

Kinnett pushed some buttons and turned some dials, and the ship began to nose away from the pier. A single streetlight shone on the pier, the two dead men awkwardly displayed like theater actors in the last scene of a tragedy. Tankian wondered about the man who'd escaped. Should he have taken an extra five minutes to make sure there were no survivors? Operations were always a crapshoot. Do you sacrifice speed and momentum for perfection, or do you capitalize on momentum and move beyond the imperfection?

Once the ship was cruising in the middle of Lake Michigan—more like the Michigan Sea—Tankian walked belowdecks with one of the guards. The man was a fit, military-age male with a shaved head, muscular frame, and AK-47 slung across his black cargo pants and shirt.

"I am Kareem from the al-Ghouta cell. I am the commander of this operation," the guard said.

"My name is Tankian. Now you are second-in-command."

"I know who you are. Your men moved us from al-Ghouta to Tripoli so we could board this ship. You can command as long as we accomplish the mission," Kareem said.

Tankian nodded. "We will."

When he opened the door to the main hold, Tankian was impressed. Wolff had described to him the extent to which this ship had been retrofitted in the Iranian port of Hormuz. Less than a year to retrofit, Wolff had said.

Tankian understood his mission and had to admit that the series of events that landed him here on this ship had been unique enough to make him consider that, perhaps, this was where he was meant to be.

Spread before him was a cavern nearly three soccer fields long and almost half a field wide. About ten men who appeared almost identical to the guard next to him were arming S-70 Hunter drones on what was nothing other than a flight line. They were parked nose to tail, five on each side, and were every bit exactly like F-35s or F-14s parked on an aircraft carrier. Another five cargo drones were parked along the far outer wall. They were tilt-rotor technology and could carry four combat-equipped men nearly one thousand miles.

On the outside, the vessel had appeared as though it were stacked with containers ten high. On the inside, it was obvious that the façade was a mere ruse, a shell exterior to make way for the aircraft. The bow of the ship began to lower, metal shrieking against metal. The entire front of the vessel opened like a nutcracker jaw until it was level with the deck of the flight line.

An ingenious design. Tankian smiled. He appreciated innovation, and the entrepreneur in him silently applauded this creation.

"They are testing the launch," Kareem said.

Tankian nodded. He missed Khoury, his trusted assistant. Khoury would be able to calculate the battle plan. If the original plan was to attack the political convention, he was eager to see what he was supposed to execute.

Four men walked across the floor below their perch, and after considerable hammering and drilling, they had opened the sides of the two containers Tankian had delivered by airplane. They rolled the Mercedes cars out of the way and pushed the Sobirat Gather drones onto the runway, carefully handling the boxes of ammunition. They moved the command and control pod to the far end near the bridge, opposite the bow. In short order, the crew had the platform set up just as Khoury had designed it back in the compound.

Each of the drones had rails beneath its wings that could carry missiles and bombs. Tankian was duly impressed. The first Sobirat drone was ready for takeoff. The operator revved its engine, released its brakes, and launched it through the gaping mouth. Brief applause rippled through the deckhands.

Tankian walked to the bridge and then stepped outside, all under the watchful eye of the guard, who handed him a cell phone. He watched the drone angle and dart like a dove fleeing the hunt.

"For you," Kareem said.

Tankian took the satellite phone and said, "Yes?"

"Jasar, everything seems to be on schedule. Excellent work. I need to give you the final plan."

Wolff.

"I'm not sure where we are going or what the mission is," Tankian said, concealing his fascination with the handiwork of this aircraft carrier.

"We are on a secure line. On my command, you will attack the political convention in Milwaukee. If I get confirmation that my demands from the Americans have been met, you will turn the ship around and let Mr. Kinnett steer it out to sea so we can save it for another day. If we choose to attack, our element of surprise is quickly fading, so we must act now. You have a concept of operations in a tablet that Kareem should be holding for you. I'll let you choose when to strike based upon the conditions you see. You're a smart logistician, which makes you an even smarter operator. Between the conventional and unconventional weapons, I want you to cause as much destruction as possible. Comstock is supposed to be in the arena today. It would be good to kill her. If you miss, she might be seen as a martyr, so . . . don't miss. She is now connected to this, and I want her entire country to know she invited this chaos upon her United States. Use the reconnaissance drones first, then the attack drones to soften the landing targets, followed by the personnel drones that will deliver the fighters, who have been training for this mission. They've rehearsed Milwaukee, so there is some wisdom in letting them attack the targets they have there. The arena will be packed with political people all week."

"I understand."

"Plan for Milwaukee—nine a.m. local. My team on board knows their targets. You are their commander. Don't let me down. Your future depends on success here. Execute on my command."

Tankian considered his options.

He could run from his past. Defecting to the United States might be a little difficult after he'd already killed four people and become a wanted man. Or he could assist Wolff in executing his nefarious plan and bet that Wolff would make good on the second half of the payment. He had the initial €1 million in the bank, but that was not enough to restart his business or go into exile. It was chump change. With Khoury dead, though, Tankian wouldn't be splitting anything. So, that was something.

Wolff was reading his mind. "And before you ask, Jasar, I'm prepared to deposit the second million in your account if you are successful. You'll have enough to re-build your business, if you want, when you're done in the next day or two."

"My business was my life," Tankian said. "And this Reaper took it from me."

"An eye for an eye is a reasonable outcome," Wolff said.

"The only outcome. I've come this far," Tankian said.

"Then go all the way. But accomplish my mission as well. Kareem was the commander. If you want it, it's yours. He'll make a good second-in-command."

"That is my plan."

Tankian disconnected the call and stared at the black firmament above. Diesel fumes wafted past him, mixed with the fresh smell of lake water. The night was cool but comfortable. The sky was a black sheath dotted with millions of yellow pinpricks.

The Sobirat drone banked in a tight circle, raced well ahead of the ship, and then aimed directly at the bow. It closed the gap quickly and disappeared in the hull, landing, ready for use again.

He closed his eyes and for perhaps the first time in his life felt the thrum of excitement that stemmed from the desire for revenge. Visualizing the Reaper, who had placed him on this ship, he vowed to show the soldier no mercy should they meet again . . . and he was certain they would.

He returned to the bridge, where the man who called himself Sam Kinnett was staring at the communications console.

A voice was blaring from the speaker, "This is a U.S. Coast Guard vessel. Please identify yourself. I repeat, this is a U.S. Coast Guard vessel. Please identify yourself."

Tankian turned to Kareem. "Give me four men. Two on the top container with long rifles and two mobile, ready to attack."

"Yes, Commander."

The coast guard ship edged closer, its white-and-red paint recognizable in the night.

"This is the United States Coast Guard. We intend to board this ship."

"Kareem, have Mr. Kinnett tell them it is okay to board. That we have balsa wood going to Chicago. If he says anything else, kill him."

Kareem smiled slightly and left his side.

The coast guard ship edged even closer. A rope ladder shot out from a cannon and landed near him. Two of the men Kareem had gathered secured it and looked at him. He nodded, and they fastened it to the gunwale. Tankian's two fighters moved silently to the bow as he stood near the rope ladder. A four-man Coast Guard team was crawling up the ladder below him while two of the Coast Guard crew on the vessel trained long guns on him.

Once the four men were either fully or partially on the rope ladder, one of Tankian's snipers fired two rounds at the men with long guns on the coast guard ship. Both dropped. The men on the ladder swung wildly as Tankian retrieved his knife and severed the ropes, dumping the men into the lake. As they attempted to climb back onto their ship, the snipers sent them hurtling into the water with deadly accurate fire.

Kareem reappeared by his side, breathing heavily from running and doing the coordination.

"We have rockets, right? Destroy that ship," Tankian said.

Briefly, a .50-caliber machine gun from the stern of the coast guard ship spun and began spitting lead at them, but Tankian's snipers quelled that action quickly. Within a minute of Tankian's giving the order to destroy the coast guard vessel, his snipers had traded their rifles for rocket launchers, and they pummeled the vessel with high-explosive grenades, causing secondary explosions and creating an inferno on the lake.

Tankian watched the ship burn and thought, *This will get the Reaper here.*

CHAPTER 31

Harwood and Clutch stood outside the Casa 312, its propellers spinning and blowing hot jet fuel vapors against their faces. They were rigged in sport parachutes they'd "borrowed" at 4:00 a.m. from the parachute club at the Air National Guard base in this northeasternmost part of Michigan, where they had landed.

General Cartwright and Sassi stood in a circle with the rigged paratroopers. The airplane's running lights lit the night as one of the pilots walked down the cargo ramp and shouted, "Gotta go!"

Cartwright put his hand on Harwood's shoulder. "A coast guard C-130 electronic warfare aircraft has located twelve ships transiting in Lake Michigan and has been able to contact seven of those, all of which have responded in the affirmative that they're legit.

That leaves five. We'll get you in the air and vector you to the right one."

"Sounds like a plan," Harwood said.

"You sure you're up for this, Corporal Nolte?" Cartwright asked.

"Yes, sir."

Cartwright lifted his phone to his ear. "Yes, sir," the general said.

Harwood looked at Clutch, who shrugged.

A three-star general only called a few people "sir." Four-star generals, the president, and, maybe, members of Congress.

Senator Nolte, Harwood thought. Clutch must have seen the look on his face, because he shook his head and pointed at the airplane and then swirled his index finger in the universal "let's get going" symbol.

"Sir, this is an unsecure line, and I cannot discuss this matter at the moment. We have an active situation that requires our full atten— Yes, sir, I know you're the chair of the Intelligence Committee. I've testified before your committee— Yes, sir, I understand what you're asking, but you of all people should know that I can't give out that information— Yes, sir, I know what kind of control you have over my career prospects, but frankly, sir, I saw you as being above that kind of veiled threat."

Cartwright snatched the phone away from his ear and spun around, muttered some expletives, regained his composure, and faced Harwood and Clutch.

"Your old man is a piece of work," Cartwright said.

"Nah, he's a pussycat. Just worried about me. Good to know," Clutch said.

For all his determination, Clutch was a good-natured man. Harwood saw in him an easygoing, relaxed vibe even in the face of imminent threat and danger. He was the perfect spotter or sniper. Ice water in his veins and always ready to go.

"Let's get on this thing and go find this boat," Harwood said.

"Ms. Cavezza and I will be in the command and control Black Hawk, acting as a relay for you guys. It's inbound right now. The coast guard is pushing everything they've got into the water from Michigan, Illinois, and Wisconsin. All the metropolitan areas are on notice that the threat level has increased significantly, and we've got rush-hour traffic in about two hours," Cartwright said.

Harwood nodded and led the way up the ramp with Clutch following. The ramp closed quickly behind them, and the plane began taxiing directly into a short runway takeoff, lifting, banking, and leveling across the northern tip of Michigan.

As they ascended into the sky, Harwood glanced at Clutch. His face was stoic as he held his left arm gingerly across his chest. Sometimes the need to heal the psyche outweighed the need to heal physical wounds. The gunshot to the shoulder was stabilized, but Harwood knew that Clutch needed to be here with him just as much as he needed Clutch. Completing the mission was important to both of them.

One of the pilots removed his seat belt and stumbled into the cargo hold.

"We've got a coast guard ship on fire about forty miles south of us," he said.

"Has to be them," Harwood said. "Go there. Get us over the target and drop the ramp."

He held out his hand, grasped Clutch by the forearm as Clutch did the same to him, and they bumped shoulders.

"Let's get some," Harwood said.

"Roger that."

Sassi stepped onto the Black Hawk helicopter with General Cartwright and donned the headset as she chose a rear-facing seat across from the general.

"Breaking all sorts of rules having you out here, but you saw the picture and you pegged the slave ship thing, which has given us an opportunity to prepare the population for potential air strikes, especially something involving chemical weapons, maybe even nukes."

"I've always just wanted to make a difference, General. Your Reaper saved my life. Now I want to help him and you."

The helicopter rattled, lifted off, and nosed over.

"Coastie Six One, this is Nosebreaker Six," Cartwright said.

"Send it, Nosebreaker," the voice came back through the headset. It was scratchy and distant, but distinguishable.

"Reaper element inbound to target area. Confirm when you have positive lock on target vessel."

"Aye. No confirmation as of yet. Have eight of now thirteen ships confirmed as valid vessels on the Great Lakes Waterway." He paused. "Make that ten of thirteen. Narrowing it down."

"Are the three remaining in one area?" Cartwright asked.

"Couldn't be more spread apart," the coast guard watch office said. "North, central, and south near Chicago. We're working it as fast as we can. Have ships closing in on the one in Chicago area. Have a C-130 pinging the one near Milwaukee. Have another C-130 chasing the one that's just south of Green Bay."

"Roger. Has to be one of the two northern ones. Keep me advised."

"Wilco."

Sassi waited for the conversation to end before saying, "Is it possible they don't have one of the ships? It seems the one in the north is too far north and the one in the center is too far south from what we know about the times and distances."

"Anything's possible, but remember, we don't know where the trucks met the ship, if there's a ship."

"There's a ship," Sassi said. "I saw the picture. It all makes sense now. The way that town was vacant of even ISIS fighters. The hollowed core from the chemical attacks and cleanup. Everything points to that place being vacated a month or so before save that small leave-behind force."

"Could be they just went somewhere else," Cartwright said.

"No. I can feel this," Sassi said. "I may not be a

soldier, but I know as much about terrorists as anyone on the planet."

"Why do I believe that?" Cartwright said.

"Because it's true."

"Okay, then where should we go to help out?"

"I say north. It's either the northern ship or one that they haven't located yet. I've had no luck on the logs, but the coast guard should know something. It's not like these ships can just pass through these locks and narrows without being registered and noticed. But what will we do there when we arrive?"

As she spoke, her voice rattled with the vibration of the rotor blades whipping overhead.

"We're making this up as we go. We've got two of the best warriors in the army in an airplane ten minutes ahead of us. They're rigged to jump into the night, possibly the cold lake. Might be we have to assist them. Might be they'll get on the ship and need someone to talk to. Might be we have to land on the ship."

"A lot of 'might bes.'"

"Roll with it."

General Cartwright gave the instructions to the pilot to fly toward the last known location of the ship the coast guard was monitoring.

The night was giving the first hint of morning, a gray edge pushing far off in the east, nudging against the blackness, trying to make its presence known. They were flying at 150 knots and were well over Lake Michigan monitoring the coast guard UHF radio net and satellites communications.

"Mayday! Mayday! We are being attacked! We are—"

The voice went silent as if the radio had been cut off. Cartwright imagined the worst. A terrorist on board slitting the throat of the radio operator. That image was all he needed.

"Find that ship and go there," he ordered.

CHAPTER 32

Jasar Tankian

Tankian did Khoury's job and calculated the distance to Milwaukee—thirty-five miles. All the drones had plenty of distance to reach the targets. He stared at the horizon, believing he could see buildings etched against the sky, but it was most likely a mirage.

There was a shift in him that he had a hard time understanding. Everything for Tankian had always been about the transaction. No emotion. Get the deal done. Now, though, the transaction was devoid of currency and more appropriately focused on the Reaper, the man who had destroyed his business, perhaps his life. Defeating the Reaper became the transaction. He thought about Milwaukee and what a soldier does. He protects his country. Inflicting damage on Milwaukee, or any place in the United States, would be tantamount to wounding Vick Harwood.

He nodded, his mission clear, and walked belowdecks to the cavern holding the aircraft and ordered all his men to gather around him, which they did.

"This morning, we go into battle. Our mission is to attack Milwaukee by air and land. Move through the city swiftly and execute the plans you have rehearsed. Because we are going earlier than we'd anticipated, we are going with option number two. Do not focus on the arena but your other targets."

The men nodded. They had rehearsed. They looked confident, and so was he. Their quick defeat of the U.S. Coast Guard buoyed him.

Tankian turned to Kareem and said, "Execute option two exactly as you rehearsed it. I'll be in the lead aircraft."

Kareem said, *"Inshallah,"* and dashed to the control room. Tankian walked along the centerline of the runway as the bow began opening again. The first yellow hues of morning licked against the horizon. His men were maneuvering the drones into the center of the runway.

First to fly were the Sobirat reconnaissance drones. They catapulted from the ship and banked to the west, toward Milwaukee. Next were the Hunter S-70 Russian attack drones laden with Russian R-60 air-to-air and air-to-ground missiles. They were programmed to hit offset targets from where the personnel were landing.

Last were the personnel drones, one of which carried the canisters of chemical weapons Wolff's terrorists had secured from Assad by way of al-Ghouta. Tankian boarded the control aircraft that carried the chemical weapons canisters.

He hunched over and moved to the nose of the aircraft, squeezing between silver chemical bombs that he would push out of the drone over the designated targets. The canisters were secured to the skin of the aircraft with bungee cords. He turned and studied the control panel. Even though Kareem would control all the drones from the ship's command and control platform inside the flight operations area, there was a manual override that Tankian would use if he had to.

Two security men boarded with him. Given his weight and that of the chemical canisters, he imagined they decided to only allow three, not four, personnel on this drone.

The four tilt-rotors hummed with precision as the commandos pushed his aircraft into the centerline. The engines revved to a high pitch, ready for takeoff. Tankian waited for that moment of the brakes releasing and waited . . . and waited.

Gunfire echoed in the chamber. The two commandos in his aircraft stared at him for direction. There was an emergency release to open the ramp above his head on the starboard side. The release could open the rear ramp or the nose cone. Because the engines were on the wings, the fuselage was almost entirely cargo space, allowing for frontal- and rear-loading platforms.

Tankian was confused, though. Why weren't they moving? Were the snipers killing the rest of the coast guard in the water? But that wasn't possible, because the snipers had collapsed from the top and boarded their own drone.

His stomach boiled with uncertainty. Was this the Reaper?

Tankian shouted into his radio, "Launch! Launch!"

Harwood and Clutch tucked into delta dives after they'd exited the Casa. The wind buffeted Harwood's face, pushing his skin into all kinds of deformed shapes, peeling his lips back from his teeth, making him feel like a baying animal lunging for the kill.

He cued on the fire still raging on the water and then picked up the container ship sliding south quickly. More than twenty knots and less than thirty. Without any real reference points, it was difficult to judge the speed. They would gain canopy about one thousand feet above sea level.

The relief of the ship became clearer by the second. An anomaly jumped out at Harwood immediately. The ship's bow had a platform extending forward. Suddenly one, then two, then three aircraft shot from the ship like bats from a cave. They banked hard right, to the west, and then leveled into steady flight.

More aircraft—drones, he presumed—took flight from the ship. They had been correct. This was an aircraft carrier steaming into the American heartland to launch a blindside terrorist attack.

Harwood motioned to Clutch. They pulled rip cords and gained canopy. Harwood toggled so that he was coming in low over the ship's stern and tumbled onto the top row of containers that were stacked high above the deck. Clutch followed suit. He engaged his canopy release to prevent the wind from dragging him and then unhooked his harness as he retrieved the M4 he had snatched from the Air National Guard armory. Being that the weapons were used only for guard duty, ammunition was limited, giving them each only four twenty-round magazines. Pathetic, but better than nothing. Just barely.

He felt naked without his customary rucksack but appreciated the lightness with which he could move. The buzzing sound was deafening—like a thousand hornets in a hive ready to bust loose.

"Follow me," he said to Clutch.

They ran to the bow and watched two more large drones fly through the gap and lift into the sky, banking and joining the others flying to the west—an aerial armada headed west.

Harwood climbed down the containers and swung onto the runway, hanging from a chain and landing on the balls of his feet, his rifle at eye level. Clutch performed a similar maneuver from the opposite direction.

Four large cargo drones just like the Sabrewing aircraft that had crashed with Clutch on board, where this had all started, were lined up, ready for takeoff, tiltrotor blades spinning and buzzing.

Two men were at the far end of the runway, maybe three hundred meters away. Easy shot with his SR-25. Fifty-fifty with this M4. He fired, causing the men to duck and maybe hitting one of the two. Clutch fired s well. The backfire was quick, forcing them to find carce cover. Harwood ran toward the lead Sabrewing-ike aircraft and used its fuselage as protection, though was a risky move with the drone at full rpm, ready or flight.

Clutch shouted something that Harwood couldn't lear. The drone inched forward, pushing against the rakes, when the nose cone lifted up and Tankian bar-eled out at him, tackling him and swatting his rifle way.

The shock and surprise quickly ebbed as Harwood rabbed his knife. Bullets washed past his head, and le didn't know if Clutch was shooting at Tankian or if Tankian's troops were firing at them.

Tankian charged him, ignoring the knife, and lifted Harwood in an acrobatic wrestling move that belied he man's bulk. Harwood slashed and punched, but the ig man was too strong. His muscles were like coiled teel cables controlled by hydraulics, squeezing and queezing until Harwood could barely breathe.

They were moving to the lip of the vessel when Harwood landed a knife slash in Tankian's shoulder, ausing him to release just enough pressure, where Harwood landed three punches with his left hand while Tankian controlled his knife hand.

In his periphery, Clutch was fending off multiple ter-rorists with his pistol and M4. They were in the mid-dle of the hornet's nest, complete with buzzing sound effects.

He and Tankian traded blows on the edge of the ship. Harwood connected with a leg sweep, tripping

Tankian, who landed with a thud on the metal deck. He moved in for the kill when something slapped at his shoulder. He immediately knew he'd been shot but failed to realize how close he was to the lip of the platform. He rolled, felt himself falling, and hung tenuously on to the edge of the metal jaw.

As Harwood pulled himself up, he saw Tankian standing above him with a pistol aimed at his face. A shot rang out. Harwood fell into the water.

And everything went black.

CHAPTER 33

Tankian turned around after he had shot the Reaper and saw the Reaper's partner and his former captive, Corporal Ian Nolte Jr., fending off his commandos. The man had considerable fighting skill but would be overwhelmed in short order.

He spoke into his radio. "Kareem, do not kill the American. Take him prisoner."

"*Inshallah.*"

Four of his commandos surrounded the man, who now was pulling a trigger with no ammunition in the magazine. Tankian walked up and punched him directly in the wounded shoulder.

"I had that tended for you in Greece. This is the respect you show?"

Nolte stared at Tankian, looked skyward, cocked his head, and said, "I think you misjudge your position, Tankian."

Rotor blades chopped in the air. A helicopter banked and then began spitting machine-gun ammunition at them. Tankian dove to the ground as everyone scrambled. Smoke grenades skittered across the deck, billowing thick gray clouds of noxious gas. Tankian scrambled to the first drone, reentered, and shouted into his radio, "Launch!"

Nothing happened after a minute, which was a lifetime in this environment. He found the manual override panel and began the process of setting the GPS waypoints as smoke boiled through the open nose of the aircraft. He cursed and crawled forward to close the front end.

Harwood bobbed to the surface of the water, thrashing, freezing. The chill was bone deep.

He'd let go just before Tankian pulled the trigger, but that didn't stop the bullet from grazing him as he'd released. He felt his shoulder and found he was missing a chunk of flesh. A hit that could have been much worse.

The container ship loomed gigantic in front of him. He swam as best he could toward the ship, found the maintenance ladder, and began climbing the side of the massive hull. With each pull, his shoulder screamed with pain.

Finally reaching the top, he flipped over the gunwale and took a few deep breaths, steadying himself. The helicopter roared above. Cartwright? Coast guard? He couldn't tell. The sun was peeking above the horizon, ut the shadows were long and the light still dim. Smoke billowed over the lip of the ship.

He crouched and ran low toward the smoke, climbing down to the deck level where he'd just fallen a few minutes before. The front end was completely covered in smoke, a gray cloud like a San Diego marine layer inverting and hanging low. He walked into the smoke, following the sound of the whining rotors.

The nose was still up on the lead cargo drone. He continued toward the opening with no weapon other than his determination. As he approached, a dark shadow appeared to be crawling forward. This time, Harwood didn't hesitate.

He leaped forward and tackled Tankian, who was reaching up to close the nose cone. Harwood's forward momentum pulled Tankian into the aircraft while the big man managed to close the front end by sheer physics, his grip, weight, and strength snapping the nose cone shut. His massive hand was grasping the handle. Harwood's unstoppable force propelled him backward.

They rolled into the cargo hold as the aircraft leaped forward, bumped along the runway, and lifted into the air. Four silver containers were strapped on either side of the aircraft. Oxygen tanks?

Tankian crouched low and began swinging wildly. He was a brawler, hoping to land one in ten punches that might crush a skull.

Harwood was a technical fighter. He used leverage and quickness. About a half foot shorter than the giant, Harwood parried the roundhouses from Tankian.

Each of them had to balance as the aircraft was shifted its altitude and azimuth. The drone didn't fly smoothly Rather, its corrections were sharp and quick, like a nervous driver on the brakes.

With his lower center of gravity, Harwood waited for the next shift and struck as Tankian stepped backward to regain his balance and placed a hand on the ceiling of the aircraft. With Tankian's midsection exposed Harwood pummeled away with his right fist, his left rendered 50 percent effective from the gunshot.

Tankian doubled over, clasping his gut, which provided Harwood with an opportunity to bring an MMA-style knee to Tankian's face. The man's nose cracked, and blood splayed everywhere inside the mostly white interior. Still, Tankian barreled forward and tackled Harwood, using his fist to strike near his left shoulder. The blood in his eyes made his punches less accurate, giving Harwood an opening to land three elbows to the man's temple.

Tankian rolled back, his hand slapping the lever that opened the back ramp. The wind whistled in as Tankian charged Harwood, who leaped to his right. Tankian's wingspan stretched across the cubic dimensions of the interior. A massive claw snatched his ankle as he kicked at Tankian's face.

From his prone position, Harwood could see the shoreline where Lake Michigan met Wisconsin, most likely. Tankian kept his iron grip on Harwood's ankle despite Harwood's repetitive kicks. Harwood reached up and grabbed the bungee cord securing the silver tanks. It snapped loose in his hand, the containers tum-

ing onto the floor, banging and clanging together.
etal on metal. Something in Tankian's eyes told Har-
ood these were no oxygen containers.

The containers rolled off the ramp, dropping into the
ke like bombs from a World War II D-day bomber.
arwood whipped Tankian's face with the hook of the
ingee cord. Tankian wasn't fazed. Slowly, inch by
ch, Tankian regained strength. He wiped the blood
om his eyes and leered at Harwood, whose ankle
lt as if it were shackled in a manacle. Whatever con-
rned him about the loose containers had evaporated.
ankian took another glance over his shoulder at the
ort side of the aircraft. More containers. Something
gistered in his eyes. The leering smile reappeared.

The aircraft jerked right and then leveled, causing
em to shift and hang on. The wind whipped across the
en ramp.

Tankian spat. Blood framed his teeth like a bad
ampire costume on Halloween. Tankian's other hand
ached for Harwood, who kicked Tankian in the face
ultiple times. The man howled with pain but kept
oming. Tankian's movements had slowly brought them
oth to the edge of the ramp. They were both flapping
the breeze. One wrong move and they would fall a
alf mile to the lake.

Tankian lifted Harwood, who was holding on to the
ydraulic rod of the ramp. The grease and hydraulic
uid didn't help him. His hand slipped, and if Tankian
adn't been holding him, he might have fallen, but he
ould see in Tankian's eyes that the big man wanted one
st moment with him.

Harwood twisted and wrenched his ankle free. H
fell from the ramp, his only purchase that of the sli
pery hydraulic rod. He was a gymnast doing a pe
pendicular body hold as the aircraft followed its GF
waypoints.

Tankian smiled, eyed Harwood's two hands th
were losing traction by the millisecond. Harwoc
swung his left leg up to the ramp and dug his heel in
the nonskid pad. Tankian towered above him, standin
on the ramp, hair blowing in the breeze like a surf
riding a wave.

He raised his foot and aimed at Harwood's hands

Sassi watched General Cartwright throw the smol
grenades on the deck when they had seen Harwoc
falling into the ocean and Corporal Nolte fending o
terrorists like Mike Durant in Mogadishu. Dead bo
ies were piled around him like cordwood.

As they banked to avoid enemy fire and circle
back around, the cargo drone escaped from the bo
of the ship. He ordered the pilot to land on the dec
in the smoke, a dangerous task, and pick up Corpor
Nolte, which they did.

Now they sped after the drone that was traveling
solid fifty knots. The Black Hawk had far more powe
but as they closed with the drone, he saw Harwood an
Tankian battling on the lip of the ramp.

"Nolte. Get a fresh mag and do your thing," Car
wright said. "Chief, get some rope and secure it like w
were rappelling."

The crew chief handed Nolte some 5.56 mm ammu

ition, nodded, grabbed a coiled rope beneath him, nd said, "Roger."

Nolte zipped a monkey harness around his torso and napped into the anchor ring on the floor as he leveled ie rifle onto Tankian.

The crew chief tied a bowline into the anchor ring nd knelt next to Nolte, holding the rope. They were naybe fifty yards from the drone. Close enough for the hot, but too far to help Harwood, who slipped and fell rom the ramp. He held on to the hydraulic rod that ontrolled the angle of the ramp. He wouldn't last ten econds like that.

Tankian rose above Harwood for the coup de râce. The big man towered over Harwood's powerful ody, holding on by the thinnest of threads, maybe two ngers on each hand gripping the metal bar like a rock limber on El Capitan, knowing those fingers were all nat stood between him and an unceremonious fall to ne base.

Sassi had worked with soldiers in many combat ones. She watched Cartwright, Harwood, Nolte, and he crew chief all focus on a single task. She'd never een anything like it during her time abroad. The gritty etermination and sheer willpower. Bodies hanging out f a helicopter to save their buddy on the cargo ramp f a drone. Harwood dueling with a giant of a man and arely hanging on. She wanted desperately do something, but sometimes it was best to stay out of the way, et the team work their magic on the field. This was one f those moments.

The Milwaukee skyline was closing in on them fast.

The Northwestern Mutual building loomed large, an
they were rapidly gaining on it. Beneath that was th
Milwaukee Art Museum with its fish-spine spires po
ing high into the sky. In a few seconds, they'd eith
bore through the glass high-rise or impale themselve
on the white spikes reflecting in the morning sun.

Nolte fired, stopping the big man for a momen
but Tankian kept going. Nolte fired again. And agai
Finally, Tankian stood on the deck, unmoving, an
looked at the helicopter as if he'd figured it out. He trie
to move, but evidently didn't have control. He began t
fall toward Harwood, which would be fatal for the
both. Nolte emptied the mag into Tankian, who stun
bled once, twice, and then fell inside the cargo bay.

Harwood's hands were slipping. The crew chief wa
frozen, indecisive.

Sassi snatched the rope from him, tied a bowlin
knot around her waist, and shouted at the crew chie
"Closer!"

The Black Hawk inched to within ten meters an
slightly above. The white fish bones of the art museur
were approaching fast. Sassi ran from the starboard t
the port sides of the helicopter and leaped, cycling he
arms and legs through the air as she scrambled to ge
enough altitude and distance to land on the ramp.

She made it, rolled lightly, and popped up as sh
reached over and grabbed Harwood by his outer tacti
cal vest, the only thing she could reach.

Harwood slipped and let go of the hydraulic rod
Sassi's strength being the only force preventing hin
from falling. The drone banked as it approached lan

and began to lose altitude and airspeed about a quarter mile away from the skyline. Sassi's grip failed briefly, but she managed to get her other hand on the vest.

She was prone on the cargo ramp, holding Harwood, whose arms were pinwheeling in the air until one hand managed to find the ramp. Slowly, Sassi pulled him in and up onto the ramp as if she were retrieving a man overboard.

The tilt-rotors made another adjustment at a moment when neither of them was holding on to anything structural. They stumbled but managed. A dark shadow emerged from the cargo hold.

Tankian. Somehow the beast was still alive. He took a wobbly step forward. His eyes were blank, soulless, blacked-out headlights.

Harwood turned and tackled Tankian, slitting his throat with his Blackhawk knife, severing the neck all the way to his spine.

The Milwaukee skyline was closing in fast. Sassi retied the rope around both their waists. The drone corrected again. It was headed directly toward the tallest building in downtown Milwaukee. The helicopter wasn't going to be able to maintain its parallel separation with the drone. The rope between the helicopter and Sassi and Harwood was going to pull them all into the face of the building if they didn't make that leap of faith.

Sassi hugged Harwood and started to leap, but Harwood stopped her.

"Chemicals!" he shouted. "Where's your knife?"

Sassi didn't hesitate and produced her knife, cut

the rope, and followed Harwood inside. The drone was aimed directly at one of the most populated office buildings in Milwaukee. It picked up speed to achieve maximum ramming force and explosive property.

Harwood dove into the cargo hold over Tankian and found the controls. He couldn't see through the nose cone but knew it was only a matter of seconds before impact. If the drone collided with the building, there would be a chemical catastrophe not unlike the attacks Assad had delivered on his people.

On the GPS display, the buildings and streets were in three-dimensional relief. He pushed the manual override button and felt the drone drop like a rock until he worked the cockpit handle just like a video game. He banked hard to the right, watched the GPS, stayed centerline over the road, waited for an opening, and turned east over the lake.

He slowed the drone, its engines whining as he tilted them from forward propulsion to vertical landing. They were maybe two hundred meters over the lake when bullets began to stitch across the side of the fuselage. One of the chemical tanks was pierced and began hissing.

Harwood grabbed Sassi and leaped off the back ramp, dropping over one hundred feet into Lake Michigan.

CHAPTER 34

Harwood held on to Sassi as the Black Hawk came in low. The crew chief tossed them a rope. They tied a quick knot, and the Black Hawk lifted off with Harwood and Sassi dangling below. As they ascended, Harwood was shouting at the crew chief, whose feet were hanging over the lip of the helicopter. Harwood was certain the man couldn't hear him over the whine of the engines and chop of the rotors.

"Drones!" Harwood shouted. "Attack drones!"

Two Hunter S-70 attack drones were lined up in formation and coming directly at them. The lead one fired two missiles, which spun into the sky like wild pitches from a pitcher tossing hundred-mile-per-hour fastballs.

The missiles whooshed past them, leaving white contrails. The drones banked high, exposing their broadside much as they had done only days before in Syria as they prepared for another gun run. The Black Hawk banked, trying to avoid the missiles and machine-gun fire from the Russian drones.

The rope slid along the sharp edge of the cargo bay sliding and grating against the frame. Harwood knew this rope. It was the basic rappelling rope the military used, seven-sixteenths thickness and 120 feet long. Less than a half an inch was securing his and Sassi's weight. The helicopter banked around a circular rotunda poking into the water and then dove for the water.

The rope was fraying fast. There was nothing he could do other than hold on to Sassi tightly as they once again tumbled toward Lake Michigan.

Valerie Hinojosa stood on the observation deck of Milwaukee's Discovery World, which was a three-story white science museum that poked into Lake Michigan just south of Veterans Park where she had finished her run yesterday morning. The art museum's spiky finial poked harshly into the sky just beyond Veterans Park. Deke Bronson stood beside her, dressed in his standard Zegna blue suit, white Boss English spread collar shirt, pink Hermès tie with tiny balloons floating upward, and burgundy Louboutin leather shoes. Conversely, Valerie was dressed in practical khaki cargo pants, brown hiking boots, Carhartt plaid shirt, an outer tactical vest with ammunition in the pouches. Her pistol hung on her right hip and a set of binos were draped around her neck.

They had traveled to Sawyer International Airport, secured the remains of the two dead soldiers, and placed

Andrea Comstock in "protective custody," which to Valerie was a prelude to arresting her. Comstock was being watched by FBI agents in her hotel room on the top floor of the Pfister Hotel, Milwaukee's swankiest digs.

"Has to be the Reaper at the center of all of this," Bronson said.

"Have everyone evacuate every high-rise! Look at that."

He pointed at two types of drones swarming high in the sky. The smaller drones seemed to be finding targets while the larger drones swooped in and attacked.

"Evacuate everything. Tell people to go where they would go for a fire drill," Bronson directed. It was a close call. Stay inside and risk a building collapsing 9/11-style or go outside and risk being strafed by the drones.

"I've got a call in to the air force. They should have jets on station in a few minutes, if not sooner."

"Few minutes is too long," Bronson said.

Two drones chased the helicopter, and the others formed up over Lake Michigan and began flying directly at them, rockets and machine-gun rounds peppering the traffic on I-794 along the Lower East Side. Traffic had been at a standstill. Now people were running from their cars and finding cover.

Valerie worked her radios and cell phones, coordinating with local and state law enforcement. They watched the action unfold as Harwood dangled below the drone. A woman leaped from the Black Hawk and saved him from the duel with the giant on the ramp.

The drone smashed into the Northwestern Mutual building about midsection. Fire erupted and burned, smoke pouring from the gash in the façade. The Black Hawk disappeared to the north side of the skyline.

"Oh my God," Valerie said. "Vick."

"One hundred percent shit show," Bronson said.

For a few minutes, they waited and stared at the horizon, willing the helicopter to come back into view, willing Harwood to be alive.

"Vick taught me to ask, what should I be doing that I'm not? From my vantage, we've got the air force on the way. We've got Comstock on house arrest. We've got law enforcement, hospitals, and first responders focused on the destruction and casualties. What are we missing?"

"Why the additional containers? They obviously had a lot already on that ship."

Valerie thought for a moment. Indeed, why?

"WMD," she whispered. "Oh my God. It's got to be WMD."

On the horizon to the east, the formation of drones looked like an air show coming in slow and low.

Max Wolff was neither happy nor unhappy with the developments. His goal had been to politically destroy Andrea Comstock and make the United States pay for what it had cost him with its withdrawal from the Iran deal.

Five billion euros.

He watched through the MasterEye software his company had developed. He could see any drone's full-motion video or have multiple feeds up on his screen all at once. He'd purposely told Tankian to have the two chemical weapons drones loiter and then come in on the second attack wave to catch people who would have fled outside.

The Hunter S-70 in the trail of the formation was providing him the view. He could see the entire Milwaukee skyline, and while he had anticipated this attack occurring at dusk, when the convention center would be full, no plan ever went exactly as rehearsed. The martyrs that had been training in al-Ghouta had done well enough. He'd exacted his revenge and was now just leaning back in his Garmisch conference room, where he'd browbeat Andrea Comstock into submission. The ninety-inch HD display showed everything he needed to see.

Including Andrea Comstock standing on the roof of a hotel.

He moved the joystick that controlled the camera and zoomed in.

She looked disheveled. Her hair was tossed from the wind. Black streaks painted mascara lines down her face, no doubt remnants of the heavy makeup she had applied for her big TV moment. She held her heels in her hand. Her gray blazer was unbuttoned. Her head turned and looked at two men, who were holding pistols aimed at her.

FBI, Wolff thought. How appropriate. "Please die," he whispered. With Tankian apparently having bit the bullet, Comstock was the only real link between him and everything that was occurring.

She held up her hands and mouthed something in apparent surrender.

Wolff flipped the override switch so that he could control the weapons platform of the Hunter.

As he prepared to press the button, everything went blank.

He furiously jammed his thumb on the red Fire switch, but the screen remained blank.

In his rage, he switched back to the onboard view. The camera showed Sam Kinnett standing in the bridge with no guard. Smoke boiled and then died down from the front of the ship. Kinnett retrieved the emergency kit, extracted the flare gun, and carefully opened the door that led to the ladder. Wolff switched cameras, following Kinnett as he climbed down into the flight deck area. Kinnett stopped and had a puzzled look on his face.

He had to be surprised that there were no containers, that it was like the inside of an aircraft carrier. To Kennett's left was Kareem, standing in the middle of a command and control platform not unlike where he had just been at the helm. Monitors showed different sections of the Milwaukee skyline. Kareem was focused on two monitors to his left and talking into a headset at the same time.

Wolff knew that Kinnett had watched the drones fly from the ship, had seen the weapons firing, had smelled the spent gunpowder. He reached out and tried to stop Kinnett's next action, which was to lift the flare gun and fire it into Kareem's body. The terrorist spazzed as if he were being electrocuted with the hot phosphorous burning inside his body.

Kinnett watched him for a minute, scanned the deck of the ship for others, and then walked over to the command center, where he pushed a master override lever up, causing all the monitors to go blank.

Harwood and Sassi splashed into Lake Michigan, about a quarter mile from the shore. A coast guard boat raced toward them and slowed as it approached. Four men in life preservers and tactical gear were aiming M4 carbines at them.

Harwood gasped for air and searched frantically for Sassi. Saw her about ten meters away and swam in her direction. She was floating facedown in the water.

"Sassi!" he yelled. The musty lake water filled his nostrils and mouth. The bullet wound bit at his shoulder. Someone jumped in behind him. Another splash. Two divers secured him and Sassi, who was unconscious.

On board, they began resuscitating her.

"Sassi, wake up!"

Then he saw the bullet wound in her chest.

"We need casevac at the pier!" one of the coast guardsmen shouted. The boat raced. Sirens wailed. Everything faded away. Sassi opened her eyes and blinked, licked her lips.

"I made a difference," she said.

"No. Don't go, Sassi," Harwood said. "Stay right here. Hold my hand."

"It's okay," she whispered.

"No, it's not. You're not leaving. You don't get off this easy."

She licked her lips and closed her eyes, then smiled.

EPILOGUE

Two weeks later, Harwood and Clutch were back in a hide site a half mile from Garmisch, Germany.

Their spot was muddy from the thawing snow, but that was fine. Helped with the camouflage.

"Your old man okay?" Harwood asked.

"He was pissed at me for a few minutes, but he got over it. I should have told him I was okay, but we couldn't risk it."

"Turns out, he gave us some good intel. That he did. What happened with that truck contract thing? A billion bucks? WTF, bro," Harwood said.

"Well, it's going to an American company, that's for sure. Jobs, man."

"No reason we can't start making trucks for a billion bucks," Harwood said.

"Ha! Yeah, I wish." Clutch chuckled. "Target standing on the balcony."

"He needs to come around that pylon. He's just standing there. I can only get half his shoulder."

"Patience, grasshopper."

Harwood smirked. Indeed. Sassi was recovering in Walter Reed, where he had convinced Bronson to take her. The bullet had punched a hole in her right lung. The coast guard had delivered her in time to a trauma team that was already set up for a mass-casualty event. The drone with Jasar Tankian was found at the bottom of Lake Michigan, along with four containers of sarin gas that could have killed tens of thousands of people. Add in the four that rolled out the back into the lake, and there was the potential to slaughter nearly one hundred thousand people in Milwaukee and surrounding areas.

Andrea Comstock was still in the presidential race, having fully admitted her role in trying to secure the release of Corporal Nolte. Voters were split on lionizing her or condemning her. That was probably the norm going forward in American politics, Harwood figured. Comstock had delivered Max Wolff's name as the mastermind, confirming the intercept of the call between Tankian and Wolff a few days ago.

And so here they were, on an authorized mission that wasn't on the books or sanctioned in any official capacity. Both he and Clutch were winged but had recovered well enough to be the ones to execute this task.

Harwood's cell phone was leaning against a rock to his left. He glanced at the device when it lit up in silent mode: *CSM Murdoch.*

"No hiding from the sergeant major," Clutch said.

"Ranger One," Harwood answered. His voice was firm, but his heart was falling through his stomach. There was only one reason that Murdoch would be calling him right now.

Monisha.

"I know you're executing, but I've got to warn you. Monisha has been missing from Mini and Pops's house for about two days. I found my parents unconscious on the floor when I showed up. Took us a while to uncover all the back-and-forth about who was spending the night with whom, but it turns out there are three girls missing and there is some evidence they are overseas."

"What evidence?"

"Interpol has photos of three teenagers being hurried into a van at the executive terminal in Munich."

Munich. Close to Garmisch.

"Here he comes," Clutch said.

Harwood simulated pulling the trigger.

Deke Bronson and Valerie Hinojosa came into view, racing around the deck corners from opposite directions, mouths moving, probably yelling, "FBI!"

Wolff held up his hands but was smiling.

"What's in his left hand?" Harwood asked Clutch, who was looking through his spotter's scope.

"It's closed around something, not sure."

"Do not shoot," Harwood said into his microphone. "Suspect has something in his left hand. Could be a detonator."

"Roger," Hinojosa said.

Hinojosa's hair swirled behind her as she raced toward Wolff, who had quickly reached into his coat pocket and retrieved a pistol. The barrel was now against his head, and he was shouting.

Both Bronson and Hinojosa were in shooter's stances, pistols up and aimed at Wolff. If they didn't kill him, he might kill himself.

He was saying something to Hinojosa, whose face dropped. She looked through the sliding glass door. Harwood moved his scope. Monisha was bound and gagged along with two of her friends. They were all secured by duct tape with suicide vests slung over their shoulders. Monisha's eyes were wide, wet with tears.

Harwood growled.

"Easy, Vick. I see them. We've got this."

"He's saying if we don't let him go, he will kill everyone. Monisha's here," Bronson said.

"I know," Harwood said. "Let him go. We can follow."

"Vick—"

"Just do it, Deke. That's my daughter," Harwood said.

For a full minute, the standoff continued. Then Wolff began backing into the house. He reappeared on the east side, a speck in the distance, carrying something heavy against his chest. A helicopter alighted on a helipad and picked him up.

Harwood and Clutch were up and sprinting down the ridgeline. They had five hundred meters to cover.

Bronson and Hinojosa disappeared inside the house.

"Vick! Vick!" Hinojosa was yelling, but the radio communications were spotty when they were angling down the ravine toward the mountain retreat.

They scrambled up the back deck of the house and found Bronson and Hinojosa tossing the suicide vests over the balcony into a swale.

He saw two teenage girls huddled in the home against a sofa.

"Where's Monisha?" he barked.

Bronson squared up with him and said, "Vick, Wolff took her."

Harwood bolted out the front door as the helicopter spun into the distance.

ACKNOWLEDGMENTS

Big thanks to Nick Irving for his leadership and friendship. He's a great role model—exceptionally creative and fun to work with. I'm certainly privileged to be partnered with Vick Harwood on the Reaper books. Likewise, thank you to our editor, Marc Resnick, and assistant editor, Hannah O'Grady, of St. Martin's Press/Macmillan Publishing. Their input is invaluable in helping keep Vick Harwood razor sharp. Thanks also to the fabulous editors and marketing team who worked hard to make *Reaper: Drone Strike* an exciting read. This project is possible because of the vision of our collective agent, Scott Miller at Trident Media Group. Nick and I are grateful that Scott continues to be a great mentor and to build author careers. Lastly, thanks to you, our readers, and your investment in Vick Harwood and his adventures. You make it all worthwhile.